OUTLANDER

DARK. BIZARRE. DANGEROUS AS HELL. WELCOME TO NECROMUNDA!

IN THE FUTURISTIC hive city of Necromunda, from the top of the hive spire to the very depths of the underhive, there is only one rule: survival of the fittest. Brutal gangs prowl the darkness, hideous mutants and unspeakable monsters lurk in the forgotten and lonely places. For the enterprising mercenary, a respectable living can be made. But be warned: allies become enemies all too quickly when the ultimate prize is survival itself…

When a stranger arrives in the settlement of Fall Sands, he soon attracts the attention of the ruling gang. Sensing that the stranger is more than just a drifter, gang leader Lakatos soon learns that the man has some very useful forgery skills. But the stranger has a hidden agenda and the only thing on his mind is revenge!

More storming action from Necromunda

SALVATION
C S Goto

SURVIVAL INSTINCT
Andy Chambers

JUNKTION
Matthew Farrer

BACK FROM THE DEAD
Nick Kyme

FLESHWORKS
Lucien Soulban

KAL JERICO: BLOOD ROYAL
KAL JERICO: CARDINAL CRIMSON
Will McDermott

NECROMUNDA

OUTLANDER

MATT KEEFE

Thanks, too.

A BLACK LIBRARY PUBLICATION

First published in Great Britain in 2006 by
BL Publishing,
Games Workshop Ltd.,
Willow Road, Nottingham,
NG7 2WS, UK.

10 9 8 7 6 5 4 3 2 1

Cover illustration by Clint Langley.

A CIP record for this book is available from the British Library.

ISBN 13: 978 1 84416 411 0
ISBN 10: 1 84416 411 X

Distributed in the US by Simon & Schuster
1230 Avenue of the Americas, New York, NY 10020, US.

See the Black Library on the Internet at
www.blacklibrary.com

Find out more about Games Workshop
www.games-workshop.com

In order to even begin to understand the blasted world of Necromunda you must first understand the hive cities. These man-made mountains of plasteel, ceramite and rockrete have accreted over centuries to protect their inhabitants from a hostile environment, so very much like the termite mounds they resemble. The Necromundan hive cities have populations in the billions and are intensely industrialised, each one commanding the manufacturing potential of an entire planet or colony system compacted into a few hundred square kilometres.

The internal stratification of the hive cities is also illuminating to observe. The entire hive structure replicates the social status of its inhabitants in a vertical plane. At the top are the nobility, below them are the workers, and below the workers are the dregs of society, the outcasts. Hive Primus, seat of the planetary governor Lord Helmawr of Necromunda, illustrates this in the starkest terms. The nobles — Houses Helmawr, Catallus, Ty, Ulanti, Greim, Ran Lo and Ko'Iron — live in the 'Spire' and seldom set foot below the 'Wall' that exists between themselves and the great forges and hab zones of the hive city proper.

Below the hive city is the 'Underhive', foundation layers of habitation domes, industrial zones and tunnels, which have been abandoned in prior generations, only to be reoccupied by those with nowhere else to go.

But... humans are not insects. They do not hive together well. Necessity may force it, but the hive cities of Necromunda remain internally divided to the point of brutalisation, outright violence being an everyday fact of life. The Underhive, meanwhile, is a thoroughly lawless place, beset by gangs and renegades, where only the strongest or the most cunning survive. The Goliaths, who believe firmly that might is right; the matriarchal, man-hating Escher; the industrial Orlocks;

the technologically-minded Van Saar; the Delaque whose very existence depends on their espionage network; the fiery zealots of the Cawdor. All strive for the advantage that will elevate them, no matter how briefly, above the other houses and gangs of the Underhive.

Most fascinating of all is when individuals attempt to cross the monumental physical and social divides of the hive to start new lives. Given social conditions, ascension through the hive is nigh on impossible, but descent is an altogether easier, albeit less appealing, possibility.

> excerpted from Xonariarius the Younger's
> *Nobilite Pax Imperator – the Triumph
> of Aristocracy over Democracy.*

PROLOGUE

NOT ALL UNDERHIVERS are native-born children of the warm dark domain beneath Hive City. The teeming Underhive takes all to its bosom: the dispossessed, the hopeful and the desperate, all are equally welcome in the great dark depths.

Nor are all these souls simply condemned to it – there are those who choose the life of the Underhiver. It seems unimaginable that those who are rich and powerful might want to share the miserable equality of the downtrodden, yet there are such people: men with strange accents and unfamiliar names, or no names at all, men without a past, with an agenda of their own: hiding. searching. questioning. tasting the sweet fruits of danger denied to those who live in quiet splendour above the Wall.

Who can really say what drives the outlander who quietly sips his Wildsnake in a dark corner, away from the traffic and the cares of the world? None could say, because none would ask, or at least that's how it should be.

But this was Ash Season, when the raging storms out in the wastes beyond the hive build to such intensity that they sweep through the hive's lower reaches, turning the already filthy air into nothing more than an impenetrable grey haze in which no man should be abroad. Yet this stranger was, oblivious to it all, and that alone was reason enough to ask.

CHAPTER: ONE

'WHAT BUSINESS?' SAID Erket, slamming his tankard on to the bar as a sign of his growing impatience. Secretly, Erket had little stomach for the filthy slop it contained, least of all at the height of Ash Season, and hoped that a little might spill out over the sides and spare him the hurt of drinking it, or the indignity of leaving it unfinished. And slop out it did, though no one would have noticed amongst the puddles of filth that already covered the slime-encrusted, buckled old stanchion that served as a bar.

The stranger showed no such impatience or lack of stomach, calmly knocking back his Wildsnake, taking one last puff on his toxstick and raising his hat just enough to scratch the scalp beneath before turning to the impertinent juve.

'*My* business,' the stranger answered at last. He was as calm as Erket was impetuous.

Erket's rage flared instantly. His blood boiled and his face turned a furious red. If Erket had yet proven himself worthy to wear the full mask of a Cawdor, he might have hidden his face, and with it his growing rage. As it was, his skin painted an angry red halo around the black leather mask that covered his face around the eyes, and it was clear to all, not least this implacable stranger, that Erket was losing his temper.

It had been barely an hour since the stranger had arrived in Fall Sands, strolling out of the ash storms as though it was a clear day in the Spire. Already the entire town was abuzz with talk of the stranger, as mad or as brave as he must have been to risk the storms, alone and unaided.

Whilst others gossiped in doorways, Erket resolved to take a rather more direct route. So it was that he had found the stranger holed up in the Pipe Under Mile, Fall Sand's only watering hole and, as Erket saw it, a place this stranger had no right to be.

'And what business is that, outlander?' said Erket, calmer than before. It cut at his pride to stay cool in the face of this arrogant outlander but he was slowly beginning to realise that his failing temper just might be exactly what the stranger wanted. Still, he was livid inside. Here was Erket, and here was this nameless nobody who thought he could defy him. *Him*. Erket. Erket of the Union. The Union ruled this town, and in Erket's mind, that meant *he* ruled the town, and he wasn't about to let some wandering fool challenge that.

The stranger said nothing. His toxstick had gone out since he last drew on it, and he concentrated on relighting it. As he raised the small, sparking slate towards its tip, Erket snapped and smacked the stranger's hand down, knocking the thumb-sized slate to the floor where it burned up in a phosphor green flash.

That was enough. The stranger was on his feet and in Erket's face in the blink of an eye. His right hand clutched the collar of Erket's robe, pulling it so tight around his throat that Erket could utter only an undignified gag where he had aimed for a furious curse. The stranger's left hand flashed up to Erket's face and wrenched the little mask off in an instant, meeting the frightened juve's gaze with his own.

'Now see here, little man,' said the stranger. 'My business is my business, and till I go asking you about yours, I reckon things are gonna stay that way. You got me?' Everything the stranger said was measured, calm, and impossibly menacing. Erket writhed, but the stranger's gnarled hand just tightened its grip, choking Erket and leaving him with no choice but to nod weakly and raise his hands in submission.

The stranger released him at once, sending the cowardly Erket plunging down on to one knee before he regained his balance, narrowly avoiding an embarrassing fall onto his backside. The leather mask fell from the stranger's hand and landed at Erket's feet, forcing yet another undignified stoop, then another as the nervous little juve first fumbled his mask before finally snatching it up in his terrified white fingertips.

The stranger just settled back down onto his stool, drawing deeply on the toxstick pressed between his lips. It was lit again somehow, though Erket could swear the slate had never touched it.

Erket staggered backwards, pulling the mask back on to restore his anonymity, if not his dignity. Behind him, the others were already on their feet, closing in on the scuffle, and Erket stopped with a jolt as he backed into the tall, muscular Lakatos.

'What's going on?' said Lakatos.

Erket cowered and wriggled out of the way, perching himself behind Lakatos's shoulder, without the nerve to answer the question. His leader could deal with the stranger.

The crowd that gathered around the outlander was vast. The watering hole was full, and it seemed almost everyone knew Erket while no one knew the stranger. The Pipe Under Mile was quite literally that, a section of collapsed pipe with a raft of fallen debris as a roof, so that it had no walls but rather a single circular exterior formed by the pipe itself. With the huge crowd surrounding the stranger, the little circular building took on the appearance of an arena more than a simple watering hole.

The Union was here to a man – a dozen of Erket's Cawdor brothers and all the pistols, shivs and garrottes they could hide about their persons. Erket sneered viciously from his hiding place behind Lakatos. Now that damned outlander was going to get it.

'What's going on?' Lakatos said again as he cast his glance directly at Erket. Erket had yet to master his cowardice and eventually it was the stranger who answered.

'Seems your friend has a problem with a man enjoying a little Wildsnake in a storm,' said the stranger, not even bothering to rise from his stool or turn and face Lakatos.

Silence reigned for a few moments before Lakatos sat himself down on the stool recently vacated by Erket and gestured for two more Wildsnakes. By rights, even for the Cawdor to be there was a sin, but with the claustrophobic terror of the ash storms playing on their minds, well, sin was virtually medicinal. The bartender clutched both bottles in one hand as he skimmed the lids from them with the edge of his knife before planting them down firmly in front of the burly Cawdor leader. Lakatos passed one of the Wildsnakes to the stranger and Erket's heart sank, torn by a mixture of disappointment and anger while his face betrayed his utter bemusement. Why wasn't the stranger getting what he deserved?

'I just asked him his business,' protested the confused Erket. Lakatos ignored him entirely.

'Well, never mind my friend,' said Lakatos, keeping his gaze fixed on the stranger. 'We don't have a problem with you getting your Wildsnake, Emperor judge us all,' he said, covering his own sins with the hasty admonition.

'What we got a problem with, is your face. We ain't seen it round here before,' he continued, raising the glass bottle to his lips while awaiting a reply.

There was still no sign of emotion on the outlander's face as he turned to face Lakatos.

'Well there's a thing, 'cos I ain't seen your face at all,' he said, drawing attention to the black leather mask that covered every inch of Lakatos's face. Combined with his dark robes, heavy breeches and worn leather gloves, Lakatos was a creature upon whom not an inch of flesh was visible. He was perfect, thought Erket.

In another bar, such quick wit would have brought raucous applause, but here it brought the most expectant of silences. The Union's gangers pressed nearer while the bar's other patrons flitted nervous glances towards the stranger and then towards the door, hurriedly averting their gaze if they caught his eye, or those of the assembled Cawdor.

The silence prevailed just long enough for Lakatos to finish his Wildsnake and return the bottle to the bar with a delicate clinking noise that ushered in the briefest of commotions.

The circular crowd broke into chaos as two of the Cawdor gangers, Durn and Rubik, dashed forwards and grabbed the stranger by the shoulders. He rose instantly from his stool to meet them, his fists in their stomachs as if about to fling off their grasps. Before he could do any such thing, a dagger was pressed to his throat, brandished by a third onrushing ganger, Antal, while two more pointed their rather decrepit looking autopistols at his head from where they stood at the edge of the crowd.

Erket grinned. Now this was what he wanted to see.

But this outlander was no fool. Against such overwhelming odds he simply slumped back down onto his stool, his shoulders still in the vicelike grip of the two Cawdor heavies, the dagger still held firmly against his throat and the pistols still trained right on him. He put up no fight as the two gangers wrenched the long, tattered coat from his shoulders and clamped his arms behind his back.

Erket was delirious with glee. That stranger had cost him in front of his betters in the Union, and now he was going to get payback. Cocky as only a juve could be, Erket stepped out from behind Lakatos and strolled right up to the stranger, knocking his hat from his head with a single swipe of his hand. Erket laughed and pressed his face close to the stranger's, sneering viciously.

It was only now that he got a good look at him. With his broad-brimmed hat and long, dark coat, the stranger was almost as well covered as a Cawdor. Erket had mistaken him for thin, lanky. He was indeed tall, but the long sweep of his coat had hidden broad shoulders and a powerful frame. Three identical tubes emerged from his flesh just below the jawbone before disappearing into ugly, scabrous bionic ports in his chest, and his left eye was bionic too. The enhancements were certainly the worse for wear, but they were clearly well made, not some makeshift, Underhive bodge jobs.

The dark ochre of the stranger's skin coupled with his gnarled, stubbly features did much to hide the grime that covered his flesh, giving him a ruddy rather than dirty appearance, something with which all these mysterious outlanders seemed blessed – the ability to wear the inescapable dirt and grime of the Underhive like a carefully crafted badge of office. His lips and nostrils were covered in a fine layer of the toxic grey ash from the storms raging outside, though Erket presumed from the tubes emanating from the stranger's throat that a mouthful of the stuff would do him little harm.

Most obvious of all was the stranger's lack of any visible weapon, a sure sign of a hidden device on him somewhere. Erket stepped forwards and, while Durn and Rubik held him firmly, began to search the stranger. Sure enough, the small of his back hid a pistol, held in place by one of the half dozen fibrous chords that bound what appeared to be a once-resplendent breastplate on to his torso.

The armour was badly worn, and the right side was missing entirely while in many other places individual patches hung at odd angles, evidence of hasty, makeshift repairs. Nonetheless, the armour was clearly of a calibre higher than Erket had ever seen before. Behind him Lakatos squinted, viewing the stranger with the same curiosity as Erket.

Erket pulled the pistol from its hiding place. A bolt pistol: a heavy, shell-firing device, again a rarity, though nothing Erket hadn't seen before. He glanced back at his leader to see Lakatos's own bolt pistols displayed proudly in the holsters at his hips.

Erket dropped the clip and inspected the weapon. It seemed in perfect condition. It took much of the Union's wealth and resources for Lakatos to maintain his brace of pistols, so for the outlander to keep just a single bolt pistol in working order was no mean feat. Erket thought for a second about taking this example for himself, though Lakatos's stern glare made him think better of it. He passed the bolt pistol to Lakatos before rifling through the assortment of pockets that covered the stranger's trousers.

Erket could find little of interest in the pockets (not even the spare sparkslate he was sure would explain that damned burning toxstick) but as he patted his hands against the stranger's boot, he narrowly avoided a concealed dagger sheathed in the leather. Erket pulled his hand away on instinct, just as the handle and three inches of exposed blade popped from their sheath with a telltale *hiss*. Pleased with himself and his find, Erket took the blade by the handle and whipped it out of its hiding place, waving it menacingly in the stranger's face before breaking into a deep belly laugh. Lakatos could keep the fancy pistol, thought Erket. This dagger would do just fine as a memento of the soon to be dead out-lander who had dared cross him. Erket pushed the knife down inside the top of his own boot, stood, and returned to his vantage point behind Lakatos.

'This isn't all he's carrying,' said Lakatos. 'A bionic eye like that is trained to a sight, and this pistol doesn't have one. He's hiding something.' Lakatos gestured at the stranger's bionic eye with the butt of the gun Erket had earlier taken from the outlander. Lakatos weighed the pistol in his hand for a moment longer before stuff-ing it under his own belt and stepping forward to where the stranger sat. Reaching him, Lakatos ripped the stranger's coat sleeves clean off his arms with a sin-gle mighty yank.

Sure enough, an elaborate harness on the inside of the man's forearm housed a second pistol, a mere stub gun, yet this one did indeed sport a laser sight, no doubt the one Lakatos was sure must be relayed directly to the bionic eye. Erket could feel the triumph of his find slipping away from him, and cursed himself for not searching the stranger more thoroughly, though he was too much of a fool to be angry at his own neg-ligence and cursed the stranger instead.

Another ganger, Berzel, stepped forward from the crowd and plucked the pistol from its harness before inexpertly attempting to remove the harness from the stranger's arm, a task he quickly abandoned, leaving the harness hanging by a tangled mess of cord, half-disassembled with latches, bolts and springs falling from it as evidence of Berzel's ineptitude. The patter of their fall was the only noise in the otherwise deathly silent Pipe.

Lakatos, meanwhile, was meticulous. He had the stranger's coat spread out on the bar and searched it with a thoroughness that only made Erket even angrier with the damned outlander who had made such a spectacle of him, and in front of his gang no less.

Lakatos's search yielded a handful of parchments, though none of them seemed to grab his attention and he tossed them casually into a pile beside him on the bar.

'Just kill him,' yelled Erket. He was the only one stupid enough to shout such a thing, but it was clear that most of the assembled Cawdor were thinking pretty much the same thing.

'No,' said Lakatos, coolly stopping and turning to face Erket. 'A man needs a pretty good reason, or a real big problem, to venture out in Ash Season, and I want to know what it is.' Lakatos glared at the stranger who dipped his head and aimed his gaze at the floor, remaining staunchly silent.

That much was true, thought Erket. It was a good three days walk through the storms from the nearest settlement; a week's walk from the nearest settlement that wasn't under Cawdor control. How the outlander had survived so long out there alone was something Erket couldn't fathom, though in truth he didn't much care.

Lakatos carried on searching the coat, drawing a dagger and ripping the garment's seams open just in case its lining hid anything of interest.

Then he stopped.

Lakatos stared at the pile of discarded parchments for a moment, dropped the jacket and reached over and brushed the top three or four parchments out of the way. He snatched up the particular sheet that had caught his eye. In flinging it to the bar, Lakatos had accidentally dropped the parchment into a foul smelling puddle of liquid, probably the same filth Erket had cunningly spilled from his tankard earlier. The right-hand side of the parchment was soaking, and where the liquid ran it revealed something most surprising.

The surface of the parchment looked like nothing more than a plain old grant of passage, a simple docket the stranger had used some time in the past to cross, in this case, Orlock territory without difficulty. But the slop revealed another layer, hidden beneath the writing on the surface, and this was what caught Lakatos's eye. He dragged the parchment through the puddle of spilled liquor, dousing the rest of the parchment to reveal the entire inscription.

It was a chart of some sort, a ledger with what appeared to be designation codes scribbled in the left-hand column, with a series of ticks, crosses and numerals filling the columns that ran out across the rest of the page.

Lakatos snatched up Erket's half-full tankard from where it stood on the bar, and the juve breathed a sigh of relief as Lakatos poured its contents unceremoniously over the entire pile of parchments. His leader had disposed of the filthy stuff and spared Erket from drinking it without him having to suffer the indignity of refusing it.

Lakatos flicked through the pile, tearing many of the sodden parchments in his imprecise, leathery grip. He tossed many of them aside, but two more parchments revealed the same hidden layer as the first. One of these was another ledger while the second took the form of an intricate diagram Erket couldn't make out from his poor vantage point. Lakatos snatched up the magic parchments in his fist and turned to face the stranger.

The stranger looked up, his good eye blinking a little faster than normal, but his bionic eye remained still and he showed no other signs of nervousness, even now that Lakatos had apparently chanced upon his hidden cargo.

'What are these?' asked Lakatos, striding up close to the stranger.

'I don't know,' he said. 'I'm just the courier.'

Lakatos allowed himself a faint chuckle. Erket marched forward and parked himself right behind his leader, peering over his shoulder. This time, his voice was just a whisper.

'Let's kill him. We don't need him. I bet we can sell these things for a fortune. Come on, let me finish him, boss.'

'I don't think so,' said Lakatos. 'He's got a fancy bolt pistol, but a busted up little stubber with a laser sight on it. That's quite a thing to do, to put a sight on a battered weapon' said Lakatos, beginning to pace in circles round and round the still restrained stranger.

'Even if you were just the courier, someone like you doesn't come cheap. These must be real important, don't you think?' Lakatos waved the parchments beside the stranger's face, trying to frighten him with the sudden noise from behind.

'Maybe they are.' The stranger still held his nerve. He didn't let his eyes wander, and even as Lakatos paced behind him, he kept his gaze fixed dead ahead. 'I wouldn't know. I just carry 'em.'

'But real important to who? Where were you going?' asked Lakatos. 'That's what bothers me. This place isn't on the way to anywhere, and you don't seem like somebody who got lost in the storm. There's more to you, outlander, isn't there?' Lakatos's intimidating black mask came within an inch of the stranger's cold, hard stare. 'Much more, I think.'

Lakatos raised himself to his full height, and with a casual flick of his gloved fingers he gestured to Durn and Rubik, their hands still clamped down on the stranger's shoulders like ripper jacks to a kill. For a second, Erket was sure his leader had just given the signal to kill the stranger, and he snarled in delight, though he was disappointed that he couldn't do it himself. Then, once more, the juve's tumultuous temper raced skyward as he realised Lakatos's real intention.

Durn and Rubik released their grip on the stranger and stepped back. The stranger took a moment to roll his shoulders in their sockets, working off the stiffness of the past few minutes' detention. Then he rose from his stool and stood to face Lakatos.

'You know what amazes me the most?' said Lakatos rhetorically. 'Just because a man has reason enough, is desperate enough, to try his luck out in the ash storms, doesn't mean he's going to make it.'

The stranger seemed to be paying little attention to Lakatos. Instead his foot slid across to where his hat lay on the floor. He slid his toe under the rim and kicked it hard upwards. Several of the Cawdor gave a start. Pistols were raised back to aim on the stranger's head and daggers came forth from their sheaths while many of the bar's other patrons dived for cover.

Not so Lakatos and the stranger. Both remained implacable. The stranger's hand flashed out to his side, catching his hat by the brim and flicking it back onto his head with a single motion. Lakatos raised his hand and signalled to his gangers to lower their weapons. The stranger's gamble had done little to shake Lakatos but, as Erket gazed around the room, it was clear that fear was the only thing holding back many of the other gangers' trigger fingers.

'What amazes me,' said Lakatos confidently, 'is that you came here at all, that you made it here, especially when, well… when…' Lakatos's voice trailed off. He was playing with his audience, confident he had solved this stranger's riddle. At last he continued.

'These stormy days are unpleasant,' said Lakatos, a wry smile forming on his face. The other members of the Union gazed at each other half in shock, half in fear.

'Yes,' said the stranger, emotionless, but with a hint of a question in his voice. 'For strangers to travel…'

Erket cursed and without realising it stamped his foot to the ground in rage. He could hardly remember the password at the best of times – something Lakatos reminded him of frequently – and here was this damned outlander. How could he know the password? He wasn't one of them, he couldn't be. Erket was sure he couldn't be.

Lakatos obviously thought otherwise. Erket grimaced as Lakatos broke into a broad grin and slapped the stranger firmly on the back, clutching his arm warmly with his other hand and leading him out of the watering hole like a friend who had not passed this way in years. Berzel, Morden and the others rushed up to the stranger, thrusting his pistol and the tattered pile of parchments back into his hands, eager to appease him. Many patted him on the back, just like Lakatos had done, welcoming him warmly where minutes ago they would have thought nothing of slitting his throat.

Erket turned and spat on the floor as he watched the boisterous crowd leave the watering hole, the stranger in their midst. Damn that stranger, he thought. Damn that outlander.

CHAPTER: TWO

'YES, FOR STRANGERS to travel,' said the stranger, repeating the same ancient code that had just hours ago proved his allegiance and earned him entry to this hallowed place.

The other members of the Union clapped and hollered at the sound of this confirmation, delighted that a brother had arrived in their midst. Except, that is, for Erket, who just scowled in the corner. Lakatos caught sight of him and made a mental note to give the thankless urchin something truly unpleasant to do later.

'Brothers,' said Lakatos, rising from his seat at the end of the long plascrete slab that served as a meeting table in the poorly lit, poorly ventilated, claustrophobic little room that the Union called home.

'Brothers, I give you Brother Jurgen,' he said, reaching his hand out to the man to his left who had already risen from his seat.

Every one of the Cawdor gangers from the Pipe Under Mile was there, each seated around the table, barring Erket and the two other juves who were forced to lurk in the hall's dimly lit alcoves. Besides these men there were half a dozen others; long-standing members of the Union whose age and physical condition excluded them from the life of a ganger, though their place in the Union remained as assured as ever.

For all the relief he must have felt at finding a place amongst friends, Jurgen allowed none of his mystery to slip. He was not Cawdor – Lakatos knew that for certain, having questioned the stranger at length before bringing him to the Union's hideout-cum-shrine. No, this Jurgen was what one might call a convert to the cause. Lakatos could decipher little more of his past than that. He was determined to find out what he could, in time, though for the time being he had little wish to push the subject so far as to alienate the newcomer. That could wait, thought Lakatos. This Jurgen was clearly a very useful man, and Lakatos had no wish to waste any time in bringing him before the Union and putting his considerable talents to work.

'Brothers,' said Lakatos, returning to his seat, 'I give you a marvel of Jurgen's making.' He flung the parchments down the long table, their hidden ledgers and diagrams still visible on the damp paper. The other members of the Union leant forwards across the table, clustering round the parchments in small groups and scrutinising them zealously.

'Go on, Jurgen,' said Lakatos. 'We are all of one mind here. Tell our brothers exactly what you told me.'

Jurgen leaned forwards over the table, his hands held wide as he began his explanation in his customary cool manner.

'The charts, they're dockets… invoices. The guilders use them to make sure their employees aren't stealing anything. You can send out a caravan and an invoice with it, but whoever you send with it might just steal some of the merchandise and then alter the invoice to make it look like the stuff was never there.

'The guilders give these to their employees instead,' said Jurgen, pointing at the ledgers Lakatos had found hidden in the parchment. 'The employees think they're just plain grants of passage, so they hand them over, no question, when they get to their destination. The buyer at the other end, see, he knows about the hidden invoice. He checks it against the invoice in the shipment, and if they don't match, well, then they know someone's trying to rip the guilders off. Those invoices mean you can't cover your tracks.'

'And this?' asked one of the older Cawdor, Hengar, waving the third parchment imbued with an indecipherable diagram, quite unlike the ledgers Jurgen had just described. 'What is this?'

'That's for the real valuable stuff,' replied Jurgen. 'goods so precious that the guilders send them in locked boxes. You need a code to open the lock, so they send it hidden like that,' said Jurgen. 'That way, even if someone steals the shipment, they can't get into the boxes. I mean you can't even krak these things open. They need the code and they wouldn't know where to look for it. The diagram is a picture of the lock and the ciphers show you how to set the dial so it opens.'

Hengar leaned back in his chair and nodded, clearly impressed. Many of the other Cawdor continued to study the parchments, but it was clear all were similarly taken with the newcomer's peculiar knowhow.

Jurgen turned to Lakatos and nodded, a gesture that he was finished. Lakatos stared at him for a moment and then erupted into laughter.

'Oh, that is not quite all, is it, friend Jurgen?' said Lakatos. 'I think you missed out the most exciting part of the tale.'

Jurgen gave an uneasy sigh. He was clamming up again. They'd left him no choice but to explain the parchments, but he still didn't seem any more willing to explain himself.

'Come on,' said Lakatos, 'tell us all how you came to be throwing yourself upon our mercy.'

Jurgen wriggled uneasily in his seat. He hunched his shoulders and leaned forwards, his voice dropping to little more than a whisper as he continued reluctantly.

'Every man has a past,' he said. 'It's the Emperor's mercy that he can leave it behind when he... finds a cause, you could say, so I don't see as it helps any of you to know my past, just my situation. Fair?' Jurgen looked up, casting his gaze around the table, looking in turn for each man's response.

Most nodded, others shrugged, though none argued with his request. Whatever the stranger wanted to tell them would suffice for now.

'Have you ever heard the tale of Alderman Greim?' asked Jurgen, not waiting for an answer. 'Greim worked metal and stone like a courtesan works the flesh. He was a genius, he could fashion anything. He fashioned this entire place.'

Several of the Cawdor gazed around the room, confused by the reference.

'The hive, I mean. Alderman Greim built Hive Primus, or at least a hundred thousand proles built it just like he told them to. A lot of the hive was here before Alderman, of course, but in his life he rebuilt so much that what we have now is his work and no one else's. Greim left his mark. He built the Spire, just as it is now, higher and more slender than they said was possible. No man has ever built anything more astonishing,' concluded Jurgen. Several gasps of genuine astonishment rang out from around the room. Beneath his mask, Lakatos smiled, delighted that his new charge's story so gripped the others.

'And when it was finished,' continued Jurgen, 'Helmawr – Sadacah Helmawr as it was then – agreed that this was indeed the most astonishing work of man and that nothing would ever surpass it. Or, at least, Helmawr decided that nothing ever *should* surpass it,' said Jurgen.

'Nothing ever would, surely?' came the baffled interjection from another of the gangers, Lirbus.

'No, it's not likely that it could,' said Jurgen. 'Unless, of course, Alderman Greim was somehow to surpass it himself. Suppose Greim had in mind to build something even finer, not for Helmawr, but for his own noble family. Suppose the House of Greim should surpass that of Helmawr in its splendour. Suppose there should be a second spire, even taller and more magnificent than the first. And suppose, Alderman Greim should be the one to sit atop it.'

Another astonished gasp followed. Jurgen continued, as relaxed in his delivery as Lakatos was smug in his discovery.

'This was what Helmawr feared more than anything and so, with Alderman Greim's greatest work finished, Sadacah imprisoned him within it; within the Spire he himself had built,' said Jurgen. 'Within its very walls. Not so much imprisoned, as *entombed*.

'You see, Alderman Greim had fashioned something that Helmawr could never allow to be surpassed, or even repeated, and so Alderman Greim had to be disposed of.

'So you see, in these cunning devices,' said Jurgen, pointing at the parchments on the table, 'I have achieved much the same: fashioned something that the guilders never wish to see understood by any but themselves, and so, they have decided that I must be disposed of.'

Lakatos leaned back in his seat, beaming with pride. The astonishment amongst the other members of the Union was palpable. They had accepted Jurgen as a brother, a fellow in the cause, and they had taken him for a man with knowledge or one who trafficked in such things. They had taken him for a very cunning thief, perhaps, but not for a moment had they thought he might be the architect of such astonishing things as the guild ledgers he brought with him.

'*You* made these?' asked Hengar, not quite believing it.

'Yes,' said Jurgen confidently, 'and I can again.'

Lakatos erupted into laughter from beneath his mask. A few moments later, the room was a riotous cacophony of laughter and applause. Cawdor men hammered their palms against the table and those that had them in reach snatched up the ledgers and waved them triumphantly in the air. All assembled realised the worth of this stranger – this Jurgen – and the secrets he brought with him, and all assembled well understood the power that his arrival promised them.

The din died down at last as Lakatos once more took to his feet. Two solid claps of his gloved hands silenced the crowd and Lakatos turned once more to Jurgen.

'So then, Brother Jurgen, you say you *can* produce such marvels again. Will you?' he asked. The room stood still for an agonising pause, smothered in silent expectation. After what seemed an eternity, Jurgen spoke.

'Yes, of course,' he said. 'On one condition.'

'Anything,' said Lakatos.

LAKATOS'S MEASURED STRIDE raised a terrible noise on the rusted metal beam beneath him, the haphazard collection of metal studs and shards of glass, which Lakatos customarily hammered into the soles of his boots, grating against the surface as he went. Lakatos thought it fitting; a chorus to announce his arrival, and sure enough two cloaked figures emerged from the shadows up ahead. Each brandished a torch in one hand and were bedecked alike in flowing, blood-red robes. Their faces were covered, hidden beneath tall conical hoods, which added much to their apparent height, and their menace. They were deacons, Redemptionists.

One clutched a chainsword in his free hand, its teeth grumbling and jolting a little as the weapon came to life, quickly forming a terrible, snarling blur as its bladed links raced away clockwise down the handle. The other clutched a pistol in his hand, its shape mostly obscured by the long folds of sleeve that hung down from his outstretched arm. Only the flickering blue pilot light at its tip gave the weapon away as a flamer. Even as he halted midway across the beam, Lakatos knew he was well within the flamer's reach.

'These stormy days are unpleasant,' he called out, nonchalantly pulling the glove from his left hand as he did so. No reply came.

Lakatos hurled his glove down onto the beam, the heavy leather gauntlet kicking up a puff of ash and grime as it landed at his feet. Lakatos held out his bare hand, palm up, and gazed expectantly at the two cloaked figures ahead of him. Still no reply came.

When at last it did, it came first with a low grumble as the chainsword's whirring teeth drew to a halt. Much flapping of blood-red robes followed, kicking up yet more of the fine ash that covered everything at this time of year, as the deacon on the right returned the weapon to a hanging clip on his belt. With his chainsword holstered, his hand plunged once more into the ungainly robes. A few more seconds' fumbling and the hand emerged clutching a long, blackened iron rod, the outline of a three-pointed crown forming a brand at its tip.

The deacon reached out, holding the brand across the beam where his brethren bathed it in flame with the most delicate of touches on his flamer's trigger. Even so, the burst raced towards Lakatos's face and he felt his eyes become painfully dry in the searing air. Just when Lakatos feared he might have to blink, the flame died away. The deacon reached forward, holding out the brand, and Lakatos duly took it by its handle. Upending the thing, he plunged it straight into the palm of his bare left hand.

Once he might have winced, but now Lakatos just repeated the words as the brand seared the same old pattern into his already scorched flesh.

'These stormy days are unpleasant...' he said. Handing the rapidly cooling brand back to one of the hooded figures, Lakatos at last got the reply he had been waiting for.

'Yes, for strangers to travel,' said the deacon on the left, at the same time stepping aside and beckoning Lakatos to advance. The other deacon stooped quickly, half-bowing as he scooped up Lakatos's glove from where it lay on the floor, handing it back to him in a gesture of deference before he, too, stepped aside and allowed Lakatos to pass.

Lakatos strode forwards confidently. His flesh was still searing hot, and he felt a little of the glove's lining melt to his skin as he pulled it back on, though he showed no pain. He stepped from the end of the beam onto the narrow 'crete platform on which the robed figures stood.

Lakatos brushed past them, marching along the platform. The walls quickly closed in around him, so that after half a dozen steps it was more like walking through a tunnel than across the high platform he had reached by such a precarious route. Another few feet and the platform broadened, the ceiling above him shooting rapidly upwards to form the vertical wall of the next, higher dome into which Lakatos emerged.

Perhaps a dozen or so figures, robed like those at the entrance, crossed the steps at the centre of the dome, performing various rites and duties Lakatos had seen a hundred times. All were male. Nothing so unclean as a woman would be allowed within this hallowed place, for this shadowy arena was the latest territory taken by the Helm of the Emperor; a Redemptionist cult, and masters of Lakatos's every deed.

None of them questioned him – the deacons at the entrance were more than trusted to allow none to pass that shouldn't – and so Lakatos was unhindered as he ascended the steps. At the top, a row of torches ringed the steps, each mounted on a stake stabbed into the floor, forming skewers through piles of the malformed skulls of mutants, heretics and deviants.

Lakatos had never visited this place before. The cult's constant proselytising invariably drew the attention of what little authority existed this deep in the Underhive, and so the poor, honest men of the Helm of the Emperor were forced to continually move from territory to territory, taking each as a temporary hideout before scrutiny of their activities once again forced them to move on. Still, this unending exodus did nothing to shake the faith of the cult's members. It was just another hardship they must endure to prove their loyalty to the Emperor, while their constant persecution was another mortal sin for which the unbelievers would have to be punished.

Everywhere the cult went it formed this makeshift temple in precisely the same manner. Lakatos, like many of the cult's associates throughout the hive, recognised its layout immediately, even though he had last seen it a great distance from here, in a different dome entirely. He followed the outermost ring of torches and soon reached the top of the dome where a dozen or more slabs of rubble, sheets of scrap and

collapsed sections of walkway had been dragged
against the wall, piled together to form an unstable-
looking shack.

Lakatos stooped as he stepped through the shack's
low doorway. He felt the whole thing wobble as his
broad shoulders brushed against the two plasteel
sheets that acted as jambs, and reached out a gloved
hand to steady them lest the whole thing come tumbling down. He took two more steps – never looking
up, never looking ahead – carefully measuring his
advance by a series of marks scrawled on the floor
before falling to the ground in genuflection.

'Rise, Lakatos. You are welcome here.' The words
came the second Lakatos's knee struck the cold stone
floor; clearly his master had no desire to make Lakatos
stand on ceremony. This was a good sign.

As he rose, Lakatos cast his gaze across the marks on
the floor: a single line scratched in the ground directly
in front of him, and at either end a scrawl of arcane
symbols. 'Leader, Leader of the Cawdor', they read.
Beyond him three more sets of arcane symbols, each
representing the spot where men more worthy than he
might approach and kneel before their master. Master,
bodymaster, grand master; ranks to which, Lakatos told
himself, he would one day surely rise.

Lakatos stood to his full height and, with his master's
welcome, stepped beyond these ritual stations.

'Grand Master Catafengi,' he said. 'Praise the
Emperor that I go on in his service. Praise the Emperor
that I go on in *your* service.' Lakatos bowed his head a
little as he concluded his well-practiced greeting.

The old man sat atop a throne that rose a little off the
ground. Lakatos stopped himself. He had always taken
Catafengi for old, though in truth he had no way of
knowing whether or not he was indeed an old man. It
was a question that troubled Lakatos greatly. How old

did one have to be to attain grand mastery? Lakatos himself was no longer a young man, certainly not by Underhive standards, and had long thought his time must have come. Perhaps Catafengi's arrival hailed just such an event.

'You serve him well,' said Catafengi in equally ritualised reply. 'Tell me, loyal Lakatos, how is our latest acquisition?'

'Well. Very well,' said Lakatos. 'Fall Sands is ours entirely, grand master. They pay what we demand and they keep their silence. It has been a most profitable acquisition.'

'Very good, Lakatos, very good indeed,' said Catafengi. 'Would that all our brothers were as accomplished as you in their endeavours.'

'Then all is not well elsewhere, grand master?' asked Lakatos, hesitantly.

'No,' said Catafengi, 'all is not well.'

Lakatos offered a quizzical sigh in response.

'Handomel is dead.'

Lakatos was momentarily stunned into silence. 'Handomel?' Lakatos finally asked, more words rushing from his lips quicker than he intended, such was his surprise. 'Dead? Who?'

Catafengi sighed and sank in his seat a little as if defeated by the question.

'An enemy with whom I had not reckoned,' said Catafengi in reply, long though it was in coming. 'A man I do not know. A man named Lago.'

'Why has he killed Handomel?' asked Lakatos. 'What does he want with us?'

'This,' said Catafengi, 'I wish I knew. Handomel was never less than discreet. I cannot imagine he would have been careless enough to come to the attention of the watch, or the guilders. Handomel has ruled his territory with an iron hand for a decade; he has no natural enemy there. This Lago, I can only imagine, is either a new enemy, or a very old one.'

'One of the other Houses?' ventured Lakatos.

'Perhaps, though I think rather it is a case of no House at all. Seems he came only to murder Handomel, and then disappeared without trace. He took nothing and made no claim to territory,' said Catafengi. 'His reasons for killing Handomel were clearly his own, and this troubles me greatly.'

Lakatos well understood the implication, and the reason for Catafengi's concern. Catafengi and his cult wielded great influence. All the Cawdor gangs from a great distance in any direction served him, just as Lakatos and the Union did. While those who openly followed the cult might draw unwanted attention and find themselves perpetually hounded by the authorities, their agents across the Underhive acted on their behalf in dozens of settlements without drawing such unwelcome scrutiny. These gangs, like the Union, ruled over what territory they could, harvesting its profits not only to sustain their own hold on power, but also to fund the broader cult's activities.

Subject to his master's wishes, Lakatos ruled over Fall Sands, the settlement he and the Union had in recent months completely subdued, leaving its tremulous inhabitants entirely at their command. It paid well.

Handomel was Cawdor also, as was the neighbouring gangleader Addec, and each ruled over territory elsewhere within the cult's domain. Addec's territory – the greater part of the Ash Bluff and the Fulcrum Spike – bordered Fall Sands, with Handomel's beyond that.

The Union and its counterparts were simple gangs, just like any other, but with virtually every Cawdor gang in the area similarly sworn to the cult's service, they invariably fared far better than the disparate and quarrelsome gangs of the other Houses. With their mutual borders well defended, the other Houses presented little threat to the well-organised Cawdor. Little by little this small corner of the Underhive was becoming nothing less than a single domain ruled over by the cult and its master, Catafengi. Any threat to one of these constituent parts threatened the cult in its entirety, and Lakatos well understood that Handomel's murder heralded trouble for them all, not least his own territory of Fall Sands.

'You wish for me to deal with this Lago, master?' asked Lakatos expectantly.

'Perhaps,' said Catafengi. 'First I would rather be certain of things in Fall Sands, Lakatos. You tell me things go well, but what have you to show me?'

Beneath his mask, Lakatos smiled. He reached down to his waist and drew forth a heavy, leather pouch. He passed it to Catafengi, watching the old man's wrist sink with the full weight of the fifteen hundred credits the pouch contained: a fortune. Catafengi weighed the bag in his hand, clearly impressed.

'Well,' he said, 'things have clearly progressed *very* well. Perhaps you are wasted in Fall Sands, good Lakatos.'

Lakatos's gaze rose at once. This, more than anything was what he had waited to hear all these long years.

'Master, you wish me to serve you elsewhere?' asked Lakatos, showing his eagerness, convinced that his time had come, that at last he would leave the shabby dealings of gang life behind and join the cult proper as a Master of the Redemption. His foot shuffled around nervously below him, running back and forth over the second of those scrawled worship lines, the line for which he now clamoured.

'I would,' said Catafengi, purposely cool, 'but I cannot leave Fall Sands without a leader. It is too valuable, and I would do nothing to weaken Addec further with Handomel already dead.'

'Grand Master Catafengi,' said Lakatos, his formality showing his desperate need. 'I will attend to both matters at once, and then join you wherever you require.'

'*Both* matters?' said Catafengi.

'Yes, master, both. And I will not delay,' said Lakatos. 'I will find Handomel's killer and find a worthy successor for the Union forthwith; someone who will ensure that Fall Sands is well guarded, and someone who will be well allied with Addec.'

'Very well,' said Catafengi. 'Do so, and return to me here when they are done, *Master* Lakatos.' He laboured the phrase in a manner that sent Lakatos into rapture.

Master. Master of the Redemption. One simple task lay between him and such a grand title. Just one, thought Lakatos, for in the matter of his successor he was quite certain that fate had that very same day gifted him the perfect candidate.

LAKATOS'S STEP WAS uncharacteristically light as he drove on, head down, through the raging ash storm that confronted him as he completed his descent into the submerged dome of Fall Sands. The domes above were in little better repair but at least their height lifted them clear of these accursed storms.

Crossing the haphazard ruins and exposed foundations of walls long ago lost to decay, Lakatos drew nearer to the settlement, where the maze of crumbling architecture at least offered some shelter from the howling gale.

Turning against the wind, he brought himself at last to what passed for the main street of Fall Sands and headed swiftly for the Pipe Under Mile. He did not reach it, instead stopping some distance short as he was confronted by a most curious sight in the street up ahead. The Union was there and a crowd had gathered. Lakatos smiled to himself as he caught sight of the figure at its centre.

Jurgen, it seemed, was causing quite a stir.

CHAPTER: THREE

'THIS ONE?' ASKED Berzel, completely disbelieving.

'Yes, this one,' Jurgen said for the third time. 'Clear them all out.'

Berzel shook his head, still disbelieving, but did as he was told. He turned to the girl nearest to him, placing his large gloved hands on her delicate shoulders as if to drag her away. The situation seemed to leave Berzel clueless, and his inept attempt at moving the irate girl accomplished nothing more than earning him a slap in the face. The girl broke free of his grip and slunk back a few paces to where the other girls lurked against the wall.

Berzel stepped forward as if to grab her again, signalling for the other reluctant gangers to follow suit. As he did so the girl stooped, snatched up a chunk of rubble and hurled it squarely at Berzel. A moment later and all four of the ragged-looking women did likewise, pelting the confused gangers with a hail of rubble.

Into the midst of this chaos strode Lakatos, and Berzel winced at the sight of his leader's return. Jurgen all the while stood calmly back, just in front of the crowd of bemused onlookers that had gathered on the other side of the street.

'What's going on?' asked Lakatos.

'Jurgen's crazy. He wants us to clear out this place,' said Berzel, jabbing a finger in the direction of the building behind him.

'Need a place to work,' said Jurgen, anticipating Lakatos's next question, 'and you did say anything,' he said, reminding Lakatos of his earlier promise.

Lakatos paused for a moment before turning back to Berzel. 'He's right, give him what he wants,' he said. 'Give him anything he wants.'

Berzel threw back his head in astonishment. This was simply the most ridiculous thing he had ever been asked to do. 'But... but... a *brothel*?' he stammered incredulously.

Lakatos shrugged and walked off down the street, leaving his baffled gangers to evict the building's irate tenants and give Jurgen his own peculiar choice of den.

Berzel grew tired of the ruckus and grabbed the girl again, more forcefully than before. This time she didn't even let go of the rock and instead smashed it hard into the side of Berzel's head with her fist. He flinched, angry more than hurt, since even the substantial weight of the rock added little to the girl's feeble blow. Yet the embarrassment was enough to finally make Berzel lose his temper. He dragged the girl to the floor, wrenching her arms behind her back and carted her bodily across the road where he flung her slight form into the midst of the crowd of onlookers.

Berzel's example finally convinced the other gangers that this wasn't just some odd hoax and the whole lot of them crossed the dusty street to where the remaining women stood in the building's doorway. These four were not quite as irate as the younger girl who raged at Berzel from the centre of the crowd, but they put up a fight nonetheless.

Having evicted the first girl single-handedly, Berzel thought that he was entitled to do little more than supervise the continuing scuffle. He could barely suppress a laugh as he watched Lirbus, Deveres and Morden all struggle to get sufficient leverage on the fattest of the whores and nearly split his sides as the ungainly scrum toppled over, trapping Lirbus in what might have been considered a position of mortal sin.

As the other gangers at last dragged the unwilling molls away from the building, Berzel drew Jurgen near, leading him past the scuffle and into the newly vacated building.

'PERFECT,' SAID JURGEN as the pair entered the three-storey building's highest useable chamber. There was another floor above, but it was roofless and uninhabitable. Several floors, perhaps dozens, also lay beneath them, but at those levels centuries of ash from the raging storms formed drifts so deep that the area was effectively lost, drowned in ash. Indeed the 'streets' of Fall Sands were nothing more than the uppermost level of this ashen silt, compacted by the comings and goings of those unfortunate enough to dwell in such a place. With each passing year, those 'streets' rose as the storms hurled more of their sooty cargo over the settlement and in time, though perhaps not for some centuries, even the room in which Berzel and Jurgen stood would eventually be smothered and filled by this same choking ash. This was just how things were. The hive, the old saying went, rose upwards, ever upwards, while it's people only ever fell down. The mounting rafts of ash around them were no exception, however gradual their ascent might be.

Berzel cast his eyes around the room. It was bare, the other members of the Union having already hurled what few furnishings there had been out onto the street in the hope that their owners might follow without resistance. They hadn't, and at the thought of it, Berzel was sure he could still hear the pandemonium out on the street below.

'You could have picked an easier place to hide out,' said Berzel, still annoyed at the newcomer's choice.

'Had to be this one,' said Jurgen. 'It's the right shape and it faces the right way. See these?' he said, pointing at a row of motionless, fan-bladed vents embedded in the wall. 'These are just what I need. Gotta have the right atmosphere, the right ventilation, if the parchments are gonna come out right, y'see.'

Berzel was far from convinced but saw little point in arguing now the deed was done. Lakatos seemed taken with Jurgen, and Berzel was certainly impressed with what he had seen of his carefully crafted parchments. He was willing to give the stranger a chance, for now, even if that meant embarking on what had been undoubtedly the most humiliating episode of his time in the Union.

'Let's bring the supplies in, and then I can get to it,' said Jurgen, and Berzel's mind was at once back on the matter at hand.

'HE WANTED US out,' said Berzel. 'Said he was gonna work in the dark, and I didn't see much point in sitting there like a blind fungus.'

In actual fact, it had been hours since Berzel had left Jurgen, at Jurgen's request, to allow the outlander to begin work on his masterpieces. Still, Berzel decided it was best not to mention how long ago that was, especially since he had spent most of the intervening time in the Pipe Under Mile with Deveres. Anyway, Lakatos had only asked him why he had left Jurgen, not how long ago.

'Fair enough,' said Lakatos, providing Berzel with an unexpectedly prosaic response. 'There's plenty more for you to be doing anyway, and for the rest of you.'

Berzel gazed around the room. The others seemed just as disappointed that there was yet more work to be done, just as reluctant as he was. Lirbus, in fact, still seemed to be suffering considerable back pain and Berzel wondered just how long he had ended up pinned to the street.

BERZEL FOLLOWED HIS route automatically. It was a task he had been assigned a hundred times before: visit Goddlesby and collect the taxes. But there was definitely something else going on.

Berzel put such thoughts out of his mind as he hauled himself up through the narrow access shaft that offered the quickest route to Mayor Goddlesby's shack. He hauled himself onto the narrow ledge and pushed open the airtight, circular, steel door that shut Goddlesby off from the outside world. Berzel had long ago given up knocking when it came to Goddlesby, and the little creep knew better than to ever lock his door to the Union.

Upon entering, Berzel was not surprised to find that one of the women from the brothel – the particularly ample one who had nearly crushed Lirbus, in fact – had apparently taken up residence in Goddlesby's 'chambers', as he termed the dingy little hole. Berzel was convinced that it was an old septic tank.

'I hope you're not paying for that out of our money,' said Berzel, making a rather noisy entrance. Berzel's sudden entrance clearly surprised Goddlesby and he nearly toppled from his chair. Still, thought Berzel, he couldn't have been well balanced on it to start with, not with him being so small and having something so peculiarly large on his knee.

Goddlesby leapt to his feet while the woman offered no more of a response than a highly professional frown.

'N-no, sir. No, Mr Berzel... Not your money, no.'
Goddlesby was instantly all a fluster. He was terrified of
Berzel, terrified of the Union, and he made no attempt
whatsoever to hide it.

He instantly dashed across the room to the hole in
the wall where he hid all the 'taxes' the Union obliged
him to collect on their behalf. Goddlesby snatched up
the sack of credits, and then was forced to stop, scrabbling on all fours as he gathered up all the credits that
his nervous bumbling had scattered across the floor.
Hardly composed, Goddlesby at least found sufficient
equilibrium to drag himself to his feet and hurriedly
presented the bulging pouch to Berzel.

Goddlesby's eyes blinked at a furious pace as he
waited for Berzel to relieve him of the sack and its contents. He was almost willing the Cawdor to take the
credits and leave, but Berzel made him sweat. He took
his own sweet time in taking the sack from Goddlesby's
outstretched hand and took even longer as he paced
around the room, choosing a spot to count the loot. At
length he chose Goddlesby's desk, though two or three
other flat surfaces were both nearer and more conve-
nient to him. Berzel brushed past the ample woman,
though he had no real need to do so other than to
cause Goddlesby maximum anxiety, and sat himself
down in the mayor's rickety old chair.

With one great swipe of his gauntleted right hand he
swept a whole clutter of documents from Goddlesby's
untidy desk, sending all the little man's affairs crashing
to the floor. Another brush of his gloved palm cleared
the dust from the surface and Berzel at last dumped the
sack's contents out on to the desk.

Berzel took a well-timed eternity counting out the
credits, first putting them into piles of five, then counting the piles, and then starting all over again when the
tally he hastily scratched into the desk's surface seemed

to disagree with the currency before him. All the while Goddlesby sweated, and all the while his cheap consort frowned.

At last, Berzel looked up from the stacked credits.

'It's short,' he said.

Goddlesby's face flashed to white in an instant and a terrified gulp was the only noise he could muster. He dropped to his knees and scampered across the floor. Berzel thought at first he was fleeing, until the little man reached the hole in the wall where he stashed the credits and began frantically scrabbling through the rubble that surrounded it. Sure enough, wedged in a crack in the floor, was a single credit. Goddlesby whisked it out of its hiding place and leapt to his feet, breathing a sigh of relief.

'Must have missed it,' he said, handing the filthy metal token to Berzel.

'I mean *really* short,' said Berzel.

Goddlesby gulped again.

Berzel calmly scooped all the credits back into the sack. Last of all he fatefully dropped in the lone escapee Goddlesby had just scavenged up from the floor, allowing the menacing clink of its fall to ring out before stepping out from behind the desk and pacing across the room to where Goddlesby trembled in fear. Berzel drew his knife and held it to the mayor's quivering cheek.

'It's short, but I reckon your eyes will just about cover it,' said Berzel.

Goddlesby let loose an agitated squeak and flinched away before Berzel's hand closed round his throat.

'It... it... wasn't me...' sputtered Goddlesby, at last mustering the courage to speak. Berzel said nothing but slowly released his grip on the man's neck and turned away chuckling.

'Who was it then? Huh? Who was it, her?' Berzel jabbed his dagger in the direction of the large lady in the corner who was still frowning for all she was worth. Goddlesby flinched terribly as Berzel moved the dagger, fearing his time had come, though he finally found the courage to reply.

'I… I…' Goddlesby just stammered. The woman gave him a moment, though it was obvious that Goddlesby clearly wasn't the kind of man to defend a woman's honour and so she erupted in a fit of rage.

'You little toad,' she bellowed, storming across the room. 'I haven't touched a damn credit and you know it.'

Goddlesby wriggled in Berzel's grip, unsure who was the most threatening: the stocky Cawdor ganger or the outraged dame rushing towards him.

'Oh lord, oh lord,' said Goddlesby, mumbling before breaking into a desperate wail. 'I don't know what happened! I just don't know. It can't be short, it just can't be!'

'I know little man, I know. Same time next month,' Berzel said, releasing the little man from his grasp. They both knew full well every credit was there, and yet the little urchin couldn't bring himself to swear it once Berzel got nasty. Berzel could not stop chuckling to himself as he clambered back out of the mayor's grubby little hole and headed back towards the Union's ganghouse. He lived for moments like this, making weaklings like Goddlesby fear for their lives, good reason or no. Besides, Berzel's treatment was nothing compared to what Goddlesby could expect from the woman he had just as good as accused of ripping him off. Berzel chuckled again as he thought of Goddlesby taking a beating, having the life thrashed out of him by that hussy of all people.

* * *

'EVERY CRED,' SAID Berzel. 'What did you expect? That little maggot Goddlesby was so terrified, he was virtually begging me to take it off him. It's all there, every single cred, just like every time, Lakatos. You know you can trust me.' Berzel smirked as he slammed the bulging bag of credits down onto the table.

Lakatos said nothing. He gave the bag one long look before knocking it over with a sweep of his gloved hand, sending credits shooting across the table to where the fidgety Erket sat playing with his weapon.

'Count it out,' Lakatos said to Erket. 'Half a share for each man and the rest divided two-thirds, one-third, okay?' Erket gave a resentful sneer as he snatched up a handful of the metal tokens and started to pile them in front of him. Berzel wasn't sure whether Lakatos meant to count the stash to check it was all there, or simply to apportion it. He knew every single credit was there – he had counted it himself – but he still grew more than a little nervous every time he returned to Lakatos with the haul.

As he followed Lakatos away from the table, Berzel made sure to push over the first half a dozen piles Erket had counted out in front of him. Erket sneered and looked ready to leap to his feet and strike Berzel. Lakatos's eyes were instantly pinned on him, though, and the juve clearly thought better of it and instead simply returned to counting the credits, cursing Berzel under his breath.

Lakatos dropped to his haunches beside a fire that burned in the corner of the room and Berzel followed suit. The blaze was held within the remnants of what must have once been a pipe that ran up the height of the building. Now it was broken off just a metre or so above the floor and formed the ideal site for an ad hoc stove of sorts. Lined with whatever flammable scav the gangers could find, it provided the only fire in the building, though the effluvium that drifted down the south-west corner for the same three hours every day provided some additional heat and the mould lining the ceiling gave off additional light in the form of its eerie, green phosphor glow.

Berzel watched Lakatos snatch a giant rat out from the flames, skewered on a rusty metal spike and burned to a crisp. He ran his knife precisely down its belly. A second and third cut and he had severed the rat clean in two, throwing half to Berzel who picked fussily at it as they spoke.

'Your friend Jurgen has a very odd choice of hideout, Lakatos,' said Berzel, still put out by the morning's events. He had every intention, though, of fathoming his leader's intentions, and began with this circumspect broaching of the issue.

'Yes,' said Lakatos, 'he does, but he has some rather unusual talents, which I'm not willing to waste. Give him what he wants, Berzel, whatever he wants.'

'Very well,' said Berzel, increasingly unconvinced by the outlander, and of Lakatos's faith in him.

'Besides,' said Lakatos 'it certainly doesn't pain *me* any to see that little den of sin purged.'

Berzel squirmed uncomfortably, trying to find a reply that would seem neither defensive nor too much of a protest. As it was, his awkwardness was easily avoided, thanks to the arrival of Morden.

'Morden,' said Lakatos, seeing him enter by the door closest to Erket, 'come.'

Morden predictably swiped at Erket's neatly counted piles as well, and Berzel breathed a sigh of relief. The chances of the stash actually being counted were diminishing rapidly as Erket's rage flared and his concentration vanished. It was the same every time. Berzel counted the stash when he collected it, but never quite trusted himself enough to be sure he hadn't made some mistake, and mistakes, he well knew, were something Lakatos simply did not tolerate. Still, no matter. Now it would be Erket's mistake.

Morden strode over to the two older gangers and similarly fell to his haunches in front of the fire. Berzel picked one last choice morsel from the rat's carcass with the tip of his knife before tossing the rest – a good half of what he himself had been given – to Morden. He had been in the Union far too long to wait to be told to share with his brothers. Lakatos might be a strict master, but he was a fair one, and greed was not tolerated.

'You sent for me, Lakatos?' said Morden.

'Yes,' replied Lakatos. 'There is work to be done, and plenty of it.' Lakatos raised his head, gazing past the other two gangers. 'Erket,' he yelled, 'have you counted those shares out yet?'

Erket muttered something under his breath before replying. 'Yes, master. All here.'

Berzel chortled to himself. Erket was as predictable as he was cowardly. He was more scared of making Lakatos wait than he was of miscounting the stash and had simply lumped the credits into piles without counting them.

'And the rest?' asked Lakatos.

'Two-thirds, one-third, right here,' said Erket.

'Bring it to me,' said Lakatos, holding out his hand and gesturing as though he expected Erket to have already anticipated his demand. Erket would learn, thought Berzel, but probably the hard way.

Erket dashed across the room to Lakatos, both hands clenched out in front of him. Erket's left hand comfortably held the one-third while with his right he struggled to prevent any of the rather more cumbersome two-thirds share from slipping from his grasp. Sure enough, at least two – and quite probably four or five – credits fell from his grasp as he ran.

Beneath his mask, it was clear Lakatos was frowning. He held out his hand impatiently, snatching the one-third chunk of credits from Erket and dropping them deftly into a pouch taken from his pocket, and returning the pouch to his pocket just as quickly.

Erket looked around desperately for somewhere to offload the increasingly hard to grasp two-thirds. Lakatos frowned and jabbed a thumb at Morden, and Morden reached out both his own palms to take the credits from the struggling Erket. Morden pulled them close to his body, pressing them against his stomach before pouring them carefully into his lap. From there he transferred them safely to a purse drawn from the belt around his waist.

'Take them to Addec, clear?' said Lakatos. Berzel thought he saw a look of disappointment creep across Morden, his shoulders sagging and his head dipping.

'In the storms, Lakatos?' asked Morden, disbelieving.

'Yes, in the storms,' said Lakatos angrily. 'It must be done.'

Morden sighed and Berzel felt a hint of pity for the man. No one ever ventured out in the storms; what Lakatos was asking was terrible. Still, better him than me, thought Berzel, and he considered this further proof of big things happening, though he needed little convincing. Of that much he was already convinced. Sending him out to collect what the townsfolk owed might be nothing new, thought Berzel, but for Lakatos to send Morden out of town – and in the middle of Ash Season no less – meant something was definitely going on: something big. Berzel puzzled his leader's motives and listened intently in hope of them being revealed.

'Take Addec the credits and ask him what he knows of a man named Lago, understand?' Morden just nodded. 'Good,' said Lakatos. He stared at Morden for a moment before Morden realised that he was meant to leave that very moment. His shoulders seemed to sag further before he picked himself up and headed for the door, clearly not relishing the trip ahead of him.

'Lago?' asked Berzel.

'No matter,' said Lakatos. 'At least it shouldn't be.'

At that, Lakatos looked up. Berzel followed his gaze. Jurgen had joined them, though he hadn't made enough noise to give himself away. Berzel was a little spooked but hushed the gasp that formed on his lips beneath the heavy leather of his mask.

'Jurgen,' said Lakatos. 'Good. Do you have them?'

'Yes,' said Jurgen, reaching into his pocket and pulling out several vials of inky black fluid. Lakatos gestured towards Morden with his knife, who was about to head out the door, and Jurgen passed the vials to him. Morden seemed uncertain what to do with them.

'Jurgen will explain all to you, Morden, don't worry,' said Lakatos before turning to Berzel. 'Go now, Berzel. Your work is done for the day.'

Berzel nodded and left the room, stopping only to snatch up his humble share of credits from the table as he passed. He was curious about the vials and no mistake, but he certainly wasn't foolish enough to ask, certainly not when Lakatos had told him to leave. He'd already pushed his luck by asking at mention of the name Lago, and Lakatos certainly didn't seem keen to answer that question. He figured he would find out the answers soon enough.

CHAPTER: FOUR

MORDEN FLUNG BACK his head, dipping slightly as he stepped under the broad walkway and at last entered the cleaner air. To Morden, after three days of arduous trekking through the storms, the relief was ecstasy.

Addec's territory lay well below the level of Fall Sands but, by a fortunate quirk of fate, was not nearly so wracked by the seasonal ash storms. Its outer reaches were annually besieged much the same, but the derelict industrial domes at its heart suffered little.

The area had once formed the lungs of the hive, housing thousands of recycling and decontamination units. Their vast chimneys rose up the outside of the hive like arteries, returning the best of the air to the best of places above. These systems had long ceased to function, and even the zones they once purified were now derelict or else consumed by the hive city sprawl, but the architecture of the place still afforded its inhabitants some benefits.

Disused siphons, vents and convection chambers rose up for hundreds of metres above the dome, creating a more powerful current of air than could be found elsewhere in the Underhive. At the dome's base, ancient tunnels led deep into the rock below, creating a cyclical movement of gas and air throughout the dome, which, for the most part, created sufficient atmosphere to repel the raging ash storms beyond.

The walkway under which Morden walked had once been a bridge of the type commonly found over liquid channels in the heavily industrial areas of Hive City. Indeed, the bridge's abandonment had clearly been swift and the walkway remained partly raised at one end, so that anyone traversing it would find themselves faced with a leap at the end. There was no need to go over it anymore, though, since its channel long ago dried up and Morden simply strolled down the plascrete trench and from there went into the narrow gas separation ducts that the channel had once fed.

Beyond these ducts there was no ash, and Morden breathed deeply; a welcome luxury after three days spent crossing domes so riddled by the storms as to be virtually ash bound. Such a journey was unheard of, and Morden still had precious little idea why it was so urgent that he was sent. He could have died and his pride demanded there be a damned good reason for such a sacrifice.

Then again, thought Morden, the outlander had braved the storms just days earlier. Perhaps Lakatos knew that they weren't quite so ferocious as to be lethal at the moment. Or perhaps he didn't care.

The outlander, Jurgen. Morden reached his hand into his pocket and fingered the vials Jurgen had given him. He had virtually forgotten that he still carried them and breathed a sigh of relief as he found they were undamaged. They hardly seemed a worthwhile reason for such a dangerous trek, but reason they were, and their value was deceptive.

Morden emerged from the ducts and found himself in a square – the exposed floor of a building no longer blessed with walls – where peddlers and street hawkers assailed the passing crowds. It was a good time to be selling. The ash storms cut the settlement off from the outside world; even the guilders wouldn't be passing through in this weather and those with something to sell, no matter how illicit or how scandalously overpriced, invariably found a buyer at this time of year.

No matter the wondrous commodities to be had, every pair of eyes fell instantly on Morden as he emerged into the crowded courtyard. He was Cawdor, and in a town like this that alone gifted him a certain air of dread, but he was mystifying also. The black leather of his gloves and mask, and the deep blue cloth of his robes were similar, but not quite like those worn by Addec and his men, and this most subtle of differences made Morden's appearance more disconcerting than a genuine stranger's would be.

Morden cast his gaze across the crowds as he passed, playing on their fears and letting them worry themselves stupid just a little more than was strictly necessary. At length he crossed the square and disappeared from view behind the ruined walls that surrounded it.

Morden had not been in the Fulcrum Spike for fully four years and he remembered little of it. He had been certain that he at least knew the way to Addec's residence, but as he meandered through the ruins beyond the square he became less certain.

A gang tattoo, scrawled on the wall up ahead of him, was instantly recognisable, though. The flaming skull logo was Addec's, with the crown atop its brow a nod to Catafengi and the broader cult. Yet when Morden had seen it last, this logo had marked Addec's own hideout. Now Morden saw it again, he found it marking nothing other than a crumbling stone wall, a chasmal pit beyond it, and two more crumbling walls to either side.

Nonetheless, Morden was convinced that this was the place. A rudimentary dig through the rubble at the crater's edge revealed little more than a handful of spent bullet casings, and Morden was satisfied that whatever had destroyed the building was an accident or the passing of time and nothing more sinister. Decay was the way of things in the Underhive.

Morden could only presume that Addec had left the place long ago, and hid elsewhere within his territory, yet where that might be he had little idea. Given that he had just swaggered past the town's inhabitants like a vengeful daemon from the pit, Morden decided against going back to ask directions and was determined to wait it out.

He leant against the wall and allowed himself a short rest after the arduous slog through the storms. If his entrance had accomplished one thing, it had created enough of a stir to ensure that somebody would be looking for him, and he simply decided it best to wait until they found him.

'BROTHER,' CAME THE voice. 'Brother,' it came again, this time accompanied by a vigorous shaking of his shoulder.

Morden slowly opened his eyes, coughing a little as he did so, thanks to the ash that had clearly settled in his lungs since he escaped the storms. He looked up groggily, straight into the face of a brother Cawdor.

'These stormy days are unpleasant,' said the other Cawdor.

'Yes,' said Morden, slowly rising to his feet with the aid of an outstretched hand, 'for strangers to travel.' He was greeted with a sturdy pat on the back as the other Cawdor pulled him upright.

'Fitting, don't you think?' said Morden, though his wry sense of humour seemed to pass the other man by entirely. He was dressed in long black robes, only the hood showing any colour, and that a brown so dark as to be almost black. His gloves and mask were lighter, though, of a rich tan leather. He was one of Addec's men.

'What brings you here, brother...?' asked the Cawdor.

'Morden,' replied Morden. He wasn't sure whether the man was questioning his motive or his identity, and so voluntarily answered both. 'I must speak with Addec. I bring news from Lakatos.'

'Very well,' said the other Cawdor. 'Come with me.'

EVEN SEATED, ADDEC was a tall man, though rather more slender than the bulky guards around him. He made much of his height with his choice of full robes, rather than wearing the cape and breeches for which most Cawdor opted. Instead, his hooded cowl lay atop long robes with three layers falling in tiers towards the ground. The uppermost garments were blue and open at the front, while beneath heavy black robes covered Addec entirely and hung so low as to drag on the floor when he moved. His sleeves, likewise, possessed a great deal more hang than was really needed and it all conspired to produce a rather sinister appearance. Had Morden not once served Addec, he might very well have been overwhelmed upon arriving in his dimly lit room.

As it was, Addec was pleased to see the old man again. Morden had served him loyally and had never truly wished to leave, though he understood the need for it. The Helm of the Emperor had ambitions, and those ambitions had placed the fate of Fall Sands in the hands of an ambitious, but still inexperienced leader named Lakatos. Back then, it was decided that the young man would benefit from a seasoned lieutenant like Morden in a way the experienced Addec simply would not.

It all made perfect sense and Morden had gone willingly to assist the young Lakatos as was Catafengi's wish. In his heart, though, Morden had always been uneasy about changing gang allegiance in such a way. They might all serve the same master, but loyalty was loyalty, and deep down Morden still considered himself one of Addec's men. He only hoped that Addec thought of him likewise.

'Greetings, old friend,' he said, his hands upraised as he approached Addec where he sat in the corner.

Addec simply nodded in reply, but the cold sombreness of it did not unnerve Morden. Addec had always been a man of great reserve, and he had aged greatly since Morden last saw him. His calm detachment was to be expected.

'What tidings do you bring, Brother Morden?' asked Addec. Morden unstrung the pouch from where it had hung on his belt for the past three days and passed it to Addec.

'By Lakatos's request, Addec. He thinks you may well be in need of it,' said Morden.

'Perhaps,' said Addec. 'Perhaps.'

'I also bring a question, Brother Addec,' said Morden.

'A question of Lago?'

'The very one,' said Morden. 'Tell me, what do you know?'

'That he killed Handomel, that much I know, though I suspect Lakatos knows as much already and that is why he has asked.'

Morden said nothing. He had no idea Handomel was dead though thought better than to evince his ignorance to Addec. He hoped his silence would prompt Addec into further admissions, but none were forthcoming.

'Where can I find this Lago?' asked Morden.

Addec just shrugged. 'I do not even know who he is, let alone where he could be found,' said Addec, clearly sensing that Morden knew little of matters thus far.

'Who does?' asked Morden. 'Who saw the killing? Handomel's men? Some of your own, perhaps?'

'None. No one saw it,' said Addec. 'No one saw *him*.'

'What?' said Morden, his ignorance of the matter suddenly surfacing amidst his consternation.

'Handomel was a fool. He did not take enough care and he paid the price for it. There were none there to help him, or even to see his end,' said Addec.

Morden was sure that Addec wasn't being deliberately cryptic, but he spoke in a manner typical of one of his age, and his meaning was often obscured to more youthful ears.

'How do you know this Lago did it?' asked Morden, an obvious next question but one Addec seemed unlikely to answer without prompting.

'His name was written in Handomel's ashes,' said Addec.

Ashes? The impulse to ask Addec what had happened to Handomel was almost irresistible, but Morden suppressed it. He was certain that he would regret asking if he did find out just how Handomel had met such a grizzly end in any case.

'Lakatos will want more,' said Morden, trying to avoid direct questioning.

'Then perhaps,' said Addec, 'he will have to find it out for himself. I do not know who this Lago is, nor do I know what he wanted with Handomel, but I know that Handomel was not the wisest among us. I'm sure his demise was his own doing. I am not so sure we need to trouble ourselves with this Lago now that he has taken his scalp.'

'But perhaps…' said Morden, uncertain. 'I mean, another gang…?'

'Yes,' said Addec, 'I think that might be the greater danger. With Handomel gone, our enemies may well fancy their chances, but we have always fought the other gangs, and we will continue to do so. We will do so all the more effectively if we do not distract ourselves with this Lago.'

'I am sure you are right, wise Addec,' said Morden.

'These credits,' he said, shaking the pouch Morden had given him, 'will do much to make sure Handomel's gang survives these difficult times. I will arm them myself and ensure they find a suitable successor. Be vigilant, Brother Morden, but do not be worried. This is Cawdor territory. Is this all, Morden?' he asked.

'Not quite,' said Morden, reaching into his pocket. He drew nearer to Addec, only pulling the vials from his pocket once he was so close to the old man that he alone would see them. The stuff had an odd look to it. The light came through the vials in strange ways and the liquid's colour seemed to shift and deepen closer to the edges where it should have been lightest. Addec peered at the vials from arm's length though his eyes were clearly not all they had once been and so Morden passed him one for closer inspection.

Morden's voice fell to a whisper.

'These are crucial times, Addec, and Lakatos wishes that we take no risks in our business,' said Morden, doing little more than repeating what Lakatos had told him before sending him on his way. 'We are to use a new system for messages, Addec, a secret one: one only Lakatos, myself and you are to know about.' Morden felt little need to mention Jurgen, though the system was his and the vials Morden clutched were fruits of Jurgen's labours.

He passed the vials to Addec. 'Write in this ink and only this ink,' he said, 'and write on scrap, something any man might be found carrying. Once you've written a message, wait an hour and it will have vanished. Don't worry, just have your men bring us the message and we'll uncover it. If you receive such odd-looking sheets from us, here's what you must do.'

Morden reached into his pocket again and pulled out a folded parchment, one of Jurgen's earlier works, given to him by way of example. Addec massaged the paper between his thumb and fingers, as if expecting it to peel away or crack wide open and reveal its secrets. It didn't. It simply creased, tore and hung limply from his hands.

'It's just parchment,' said Addec.

Morden pulled a canteen from beneath his robes and sprinkled a few drops of water on the parchment, smearing it over the surface with his gloved hand until the whole thing had a sheen of water across it. He passed it to Addec who at once saw the message hidden cunningly within.

'Impressive,' said Addec. 'I understand. This will remain a closely guarded secret. Go now.'

Morden nodded, dipping a little as he did so, so that his knee brushed the floor for the briefest of moments before he turned and left the room. He had never said goodbye to Addec, not even when he left his ranks, and he had no intention of doing so now. The old man was wise, and Morden was sure he would see him again.

THERE WAS NO time to waste in returning his news to Lakatos, yet Morden thought it simple madness to venture into the ash storms again so soon. Night was as good as day in the Underhive and a few hours recuperation would do little to delay Morden. So he found himself seated in the Chapel, as the younger members of Addec's gang termed their hideout.

Morden knew almost none of them. Most were too young to remember him. Those few gangers who survived from Morden's day had mostly risen to the point where they attended Addec in his chambers across the dome. The separate hideouts were a peculiar quirk of Addec's that Morden had almost forgotten. Still, he was glad to be able to rest in safety without burdening the old man further.

One of the juves drew near to Morden, holding out a bowl of fungus soup. Morden took it in both hands and placed it on his lap. He took the rusty spoon out of the bowl and discarded it. The trick with fungus soup was to drink it quickly before the foaming chemical reactions in the broth made it too hot to drink. To do this, Morden cupped the bowl in both hands and swiftly chugged it down. He placed the empty bowl on the ground in front of him and looked across the room to see two rather less savvy gangers wincing in pain as the poisons released by the fungi reacted with one another and burned their tongues.

A figure appeared in the doorway, though the heavy shadows there hid his features from Morden. At the sight of him, the juve raced over, offering a bowl of the same potent broth, but with a brush of his hand the figure declined. Perhaps it was another youngster, perturbed by the sight of his inept friends burning themselves.

Except, as the figure drew near, Morden could see he wore the fuller mask of a more experienced ganger and what he could see of his face was well-worn. A scar on his chin, already well healed, spoke of years living the life of a ganger.

A scar on his chin… Deeran, realised Morden with a start. It was Deeran, come to see him. Morden leapt to his feet and grabbed him by the hand.

'Hello, old friend,' said Deeran as Morden greeted him. 'I missed you at the old man's place.'

'I wasn't there long,' said Morden. 'There seemed to be little he could tell me.'

Deeran frowned and gestured for Morden to return to his seat atop the worn stone steps at the rear of the Chapel. Deeran swept his cloak aside and perched himself beside Morden.

'Perhaps,' he said with a definite air of concern in his voice, 'but I fear there is a growing gap between what the old man knows and what he wants to admit to himself.'

'What?' said Morden.

'He dismisses talk of danger too lightly, simply because he is too tired to deal with it,' said Deeran, needing little prompting. 'Lago's threat is real enough, but Addec is blind to it.'

'Who is this Lago?' asked Morden.

'No one really knows, that much is accurate,' said Deeran. 'A bounty hunter, almost certainly. He seemed to act alone, and only sought Handomel's blood. I can't imagine another gang would be so discriminating.'

'Then Handomel made his own trouble and paid for it?' asked Morden.

'Perhaps, but if he had brought a bounty upon himself, how come this Lago never claimed it?'

'How do you know he didn't?'

'Claim the bounty? On a pile of ashes? The guilders normally ask for a little more proof than that,' said Deeran. He was right.

'I suppose he could have taken the head, or the hands,' he continued, 'but I really don't think it was a simple bounty.'

Morden swallowed hard as Deeran spoke. He didn't like what he was hearing, and he liked less the fact that Addec hadn't told it to him. Reporting this to Lakatos would not be easy.

'Somebody wanted Handomel dead and they hired this Lago to do it,' said Deeran.

'Then it's still the same,' said Morden, slightly relieved. 'Handomel made trouble and paid for it. So it wasn't the guilders, it wasn't a bounty exactly, but somebody wanted him dead and now he is. Lago's gone, job done, surely?'

'If it was just a bounty, I could believe that, but who wanted Handomel dead, and why?' said Deeran. 'Without that, who's to say what happens next? Who's to say Lago's gone?'

'You're spooking me, Deeran. Why do you think Handomel was killed? What are you saying?' asked Morden.

'I'm not sure, old friend, really I'm not,' Deeran replied, 'but I was with Handomel's men two days ago, and things are not well there. He has no clear successor and Vilhame and Coyne are already at one another's throats.'

'Catafengi won't stand for a leadership contest,' said Morden.

'I don't see how he can stop it,' said Deeran. 'To pick one of them would alienate those loyal to the other. What then? Kill them? And divide our number further? No, no, this is all very bad. We are faced with strife, Morden, and I can't help but wonder if this wasn't exactly what this Lago wanted.'

'I don't understand,' said Morden.

'Well, suppose he's working for another gang.'

'There's hardly another gang left within five domes of here,' said Morden. He was right. The allegiance of Cawdor gangs had all but eradicated the competition.

'That's true,' said Deeran, stroking the scar on his chin as he spoke, 'but there are plenty who remember what we did to them, plenty who escaped and set up elsewhere. Who's to say one of those gangs hasn't come back, and Lago with them?'

'They'd have attacked us as a gang. They would have raided Handomel's territory,' said Morden.

'Yes, yes, perhaps you're right,' said Deeran, rising from the steps, 'but I'm still worried that we are turning a blind eye to a grave threat.'

'If you're so worried, how come Addec isn't?' asked Morden.

'Addec is old,' said Deeran, his tone almost one of anger. 'Were he anywhere else, he would have left this life long ago. It is not for one of his years to be leading a gang in this stinking hole,' he said, clearly upset. Addec was, after all, his father.

'But we are more than simple gangs, are we not? And the pacts we have struck allow no return to the city,' he continued. 'He has spent his life in the service of Catafengi. The House will not take him back now. They cannot take him back now. Too many eyes up in Hive City look upon us. We must not allow them to see our grand old House consorting with the Redemption.'

Morden stared at Deeran in disbelief. His anger sounded dangerously close to something Morden didn't even want to contemplate.

'I'm as loyal as you, old friend, don't mistake me,' said Deeran, 'but the places above fear the Redemption and they will not deal with it, or its agents. That we Cawdor serve the Redemption might be an open secret, but it is a secret nonetheless, and it must remain that way. It would destroy our House for it to be otherwise.

'As it is, my father must see out his days down here. We will all have to, in time. Perhaps it is a curse that he has lived so long at all; it tires him now. He chooses to turn a blind eye to danger because he no longer has the strength to fight it and this I fear is why he talks so lightly of Lago and Handomel.

'Heed my father's words, Morden, as you wish, but do not assume that that is all there is to it. Promise me that much?'

Morden nodded meekly and Deeran departed. Suddenly the ash storms seemed like a more inviting prospect.

* * *

THE STORMS WERE not as fierce as Morden had feared. Here and there he could even see the remnants of his own tracks. In harsher weather, they would have vanished in mere hours. He had made good time and just two days travel had brought him close to Fall Sands, though he dreaded reaching it.

Deeran was his oldest friend, but time had clearly changed him and Morden was uncertain what to make of his prophecies of doom. Likewise, he trusted Addec's judgement completely, and was greatly reassured by his apparent calmness, but deciding exactly how much of this tale to relate to Lakatos gave Morden great cause for concern.

He shut such thoughts out of his mind and concentrated instead on the matter at hand: navigating the ash storms without becoming lost entirely.

The gusting winds had moved many of the deepest drifts eastwards and where on the way out Morden had been forced to traipse endlessly over high dunes, he found his return journey a flatter one, along something of a temporary valley between the great walls of ash.

The one drawback of this easier lie to the land was that it badly obscured his vision in almost all directions. Elsewhere, this had proved less of a problem, since the low roof of the dome had been visible and Morden had followed its slowly rising curve out towards the centre. Now that he approached Fall Sands – itself in the middle of the dome – the roof was entirely obscured by the raging, ash-laden winds above, and he could not be entirely certain of his direction.

Morden periodically scrambled up the dunes to either side, scanning for landmarks over the short distance he could actually see. Two or three such ascents had proven fruitless, and a fourth was looking similarly disappointing. Morden followed the crest of the dune along for a distance, though it was terribly hard work since such bluffs were made of only the softest, least compacted ash, and Morden sank knee deep with each step.

Still no landmark presented itself, but there was something. At the base of the dune, down the opposite side to which Morden had ascended, there ran a second broad, flat valley, like the one he had been trudging down. Elsewhere, the ground to either side simply drifted off into a sea of dunes and Morden hoped that the occurrence of a second such valley might mean he was nearing home. He shimmied down the dune's side, deciding to take this second valley as his new course and he plodded on down it.

Perhaps an hour or two passed before Morden found tracks, leading away from him down this temporary channel. They were not his own, as he had first thought, for the print of the boots didn't match his. The only other person he could imagine that had been out in the storms was Jurgen. Perhaps this was the route by which Jurgen had first entered Fall Sands.

Morden's step quickened, heartened that even if he wasn't close to Fall Sands yet, he was at least on the right track. He followed the footprints closely and was glad to see they continued unbroken for some considerable distance. The wind, too, in this trench seemed far less biting, as if it were being held back by the abnormally high dunes, which formed to either side, and Morden found the going a good deal easier.

Following them for several hundred metres more, the tracks shortened, the feet falling closer and closer together as if their maker were tiring rapidly. Soon, they were virtually overlapping; prints made by a man doing little more than staggering forwards. Morden then realised in utter disappointment that the tracks vanished entirely.

He stopped dead on the spot, gazing around. Morden had continued to periodically ascend the dunes and look for landmarks. Perhaps Jurgen had done the same, breaking his tracks. Morden took a few careful steps forwards, but the trail did not restart. He turned and started clambering up the dune to his right. Any tracks here would have faded away rapidly, but at least if this was the spot where Jurgen left the track, Morden might be able to glimpse Fall Sands.

The dune was high and his feet sank with each step. He was barely halfway up when his lead foot failed him and Morden fell onto his side, slipping some metres back down the dune's side. He cursed but wasn't hurt, and quickly regained his feet. He gazed up the dune and as he did so, something terrible greeted his gaze.

Where Morden had fallen, the ash had slipped away, falling down the dune beneath him and leaving a great empty furrow in its side. Within that furrow, Morden saw a body: a dead, lifeless body. His boot must have struck it as he climbed, and that was what had caused him to slip.

He scrambled up to the body and hauled it out of the thin covering of ash that remained on top of it. The fine flakes of ash, blowing this way and that in the howling winds, had eaten away at the body, eroding its very flesh, and the skin in most places was nothing but a mass of tiny lacerations, leaving the body a horribly flayed, bloody mess. Some places were worse than others, presumably since those parts buried the deepest had been least affected, but the face was in tatters and only the body's substantial frame gave it away as male.

Pulling open the thick black jacket in which the body was clothed, Morden was quite surprised to find it armoured. Competently made – if unspectacular – flak armour covered the chest and the arms as far as the elbows. Patting the legs, Morden was certain the same

armour extended over the thighs as well: a pretty useful
suit.

Morden began to search the body for clues as to its
identity. The man was well equipped, and his pockets
were filled with ammo as well as several other pieces of
equipment such as grapnels, binoculars and a tox-
detector, none of which had done their owner any
good, of course.

Fumbling around inside the jacket, Morden pulled
out a wad of papers. The high winds rushing over the
steep sided dune whipped the uppermost sheets from
his hands before he could read them and Morden
wisely turned his back to the wind, holding the papers
in the shielded area between himself and the body. He
could find nothing to identify the man, but as he
unfolded the largest of the parchments he gawped in
amazement.

It was a wanted poster, of the kind issued only by
guilders, and staring back at Morden from its centre
was the face of one Jurgen Ducott, the outlander Jurgen
to whom he had been introduced just days before.
Morden already knew Jurgen was a wanted man but he
was stunned nonetheless, firstly to find that bounty
hunters were so close on Jurgen's trail and secondly to
find that, according to this poster, Jurgen was not
wanted for fleeing the guilders, but rather for forgery.
Something was not quite right.

THE ROPE BIT into Morden's flesh as his shirt again
came loose and rose up over his stomach. He clumsily stuffed the cloth back inside his belt, trying to
keep the taut, rough rope away from his skin. It was
hardly a dignified end to his journey, but Morden
was damned if he was going to carry a stinking body
all the way in to town. As it was, the soft ash offered
little resistance, and the body glided along behind

Morden, sled-like on the end of the rope tied round his waist.

Two great crowned pillars – in fact a crumbling building with cornice in tact – rose up ahead of Morden and, passing beneath it, he found himself once more in Fall Sands. He had clearly not been following Jurgen's route after all, but the dead man was at least on the right track, if too late, and Morden had found the settlement with little difficulty by continuing in the same direction.

He was greatly reassured to be back and concerns over how much to reveal to Lakatos had vanished from his mind. Having found the body of a man who died in the storms, Morden unsurprisingly found it easy to concentrate on his own well being. Only now did he start to concern himself again with what news to report. In any case, he had much more to discuss than just Handomel.

He had gone no great distance into the settlement before Erket and Lirbus emerged up ahead. Morden blocked sight of the body, but the unusually large puffs of ash kicked up in his wake and his own peculiar gait clearly caught their attention and they both hurried down the street towards him.

'You've brought us back a present,' said Lirbus mockingly.

'Yes,' said Morden, 'and you can carry it the rest of the fragging way.'

With that, he cut the rope loose from around his waist and marched off ahead. Lirbus and Erket gazed at the body, and then at Morden, and then at each other.

ERKET ROLLED THE body off his shoulder and slammed it down on the table, Lirbus having opted to 'get the doors' on the short trek back to the ganghouse. Lakatos, Morden and the others were already assembled around the table, though Jurgen was absent, still consumed by his curious ciphers. A fact for which Morden was immensely thankful.

Lakatos looked down at the body, one gloved fist pressed to his face, index finger across his mouth. He said nothing, prompting Morden to explain with a simple nod of his head instead.

'He was out in the wastes, dead already, but I have no idea how long. He could have been there weeks, or the ash could have done this to him in hours. His tracks were still fresh, though, so I guess not long,' said Morden.

'Who is he?' asked Lakatos.

'Nothin' on him to say,' said Morden, 'except...'

He flung the wanted poster down on top of the dead man's chest. Lakatos and most of the others leaned closer. There was silence for the second it took them to make out the face before an astonished gasp rang out from the assembled Cawdor. Lakatos raised his head, staring at the ceiling in contemplation and stepped away from the table. He began to pace around but said nothing.

'He's a liar,' yelped Erket. 'Damned outlander's a fraud.' He seemed ready to go on with his vitriol, but a swift slap across the back of the head silenced the irksome little juve. Morden wasn't sure who had slapped him but certainly thought it a wise decision. He manoeuvred himself closer to Erket, in case further chastisement was needed. Morden needed to keep a tight rein on this discussion and he wasn't going to let the chip on Erket's shoulder derail that.

Deveres stepped away from the table, shuffling over towards the door where Lakatos paced. The others followed, forming a loose crowd at the end of the table where the body's feet lay.

'What do you make of it, boss?' asked Deveres.

Lakatos frowned as he looked up. 'I'm not sure...' he said. His voice trailed off as he began to pace again. 'This can wait. Morden, tell me about Lago.'

Morden coughed. 'I asked Addec and...'

His voice trailed off as his and every pair of eyes in the room turned and focused on the figure that had just appeared in the doorway. It was Jurgen.

'Lago?' he asked, before noticing the unusually attentive crowd around him. 'Did you say "Lago"? What's going on?'

Morden placed his hand firmly on Erket's shoulder, almost holding him by the neck, just in case the juve had any rash ideas about making this his moment. The room remained utterly silent as Lakatos turned to Jurgen.

'Lago?' asked Lakatos. 'Who is Lago? What do you know about him?'

'He...' Jurgen seemed, for the first time, a little nervous. 'He's the bounty hunter the guilders sent after me. They tried to kill me in Fortune Caves, but I escaped so they sent him after me. He nearly caught up with me in Dead Man's Hole a month ago. That's when I fled and ended up here.'

'They sent Lago after *you*?' asked Lakatos, his emphasis clear to Morden but meaning little to Jurgen or the others.

'Yes,' said Jurgen, more nervous than before, 'and he won't stop till he gets me. He's a psychopath. He doesn't do it for the bounty. He thinks he's some kinda saint, out to get all the sinners. He won't stop till he's killed me. What's going on? Why are you talking about Lago?'

Lakatos raised his gloved left hand and snapped his fingers. A moment of scuffling followed before Morden pushed his way through the crowd, wanted poster in hand, and passed it to Lakatos. Erket was the least of his worries and Morden strolled over to stand between Jurgen and the door, just in case.

Lakatos remained as calm as ever as he passed the poster to Jurgen. Jurgen paused for a moment, staring at the poster. His lips didn't move as he read it, making him an accomplished reader by Underhive standards, thought Morden.

'Well I'll be damned,' he said at last. 'Where did you get this?'

'Is it true?' asked Lakatos.

'Is it true that I'm wanted?' said Jurgen. 'You know it is. That's why I came here, to get away from the guilders.'

'Is it true,' said Lakatos, 'that you are a forger?'

'See here,' said Jurgen, still rattled, 'the guilders can't go saying "Wanted: Jurgen Ducott for writing us an unbreakable code" now can they? Soon as they do that, they give themselves away, and everyone knows about the code. They might not know where it's hidden or how it works, but they'd know it exists.

'Now where did you get this? And what's this talk about Lago? Did he give you this?' he finished.

Lakatos stepped back. He held his arm to his side, pointing towards the table and instantly the crowd of Cawdor gangers parted, revealing the body. Jurgen squinted in amazement before strolling up to the table and running his hands over the body.

'We found the poster on him, Jurgen. That dead guy was carrying it,' said Morden.

'Oh no,' said Jurgen, peering into the dead man's eyes. 'This man works for Lago.'

CHAPTER: FIVE

'THIS IS ONE of them?' asked Catafengi as he stooped over the body dumped unceremoniously on the stone floor. 'You are quite sure?'

'Quite sure,' said Lakatos. 'He had Handomel's name and likeness in his pocket when we found him. He died out in the storms, between Handomel's territory and mine.'

'Hmm,' said Catafengi. 'It was my understanding that this Lago had acted alone in killing Handomel.' Catafengi returned to his throne and sat himself down in it, all the more puzzled.

'Lago alone killed Handomel, yes,' said Lakatos, 'but it seems he does not always work alone.'

Catafengi bowed his head a little. 'What does he want with us, Lakatos? What does he want with us?'

Lakatos shook his head. 'I do not know, master, but I will find out soon enough and I will remove this thorn from our side. Do not worry.'

'Very well, Lakatos,' said Catafengi. 'Do not fail me.' Catafengi nodded, as if dismissing Lakatos, but he remained.

'There is one more thing, the other matter, master,' said Lakatos.

'The *other* matter?'

'Yes, master. The matter of my succession.'

'Hmm,' said Catafengi, surprised by Lakatos's boldness. 'I fear this is a little premature while we have an enemy upon us Lakatos.' The pair remained silent, eyeing one another for a moment before Catafengi relented.

'Go on,' he said. 'Is it Morden?'

'No, master,' said Lakatos. 'I thought that had you wanted him to succeed me, you would have named him.'

'Very wise,' said Catafengi. 'You have read my intentions well, but then who have you chosen? I am not so sure there are any who are ready for it, Lakatos.'

'There is one,' said Lakatos. 'I am quite certain. He is a new recruit, master, and a most promising one at that. He has served me well this past time. I have brought him here to meet you. More than that, I think he may well hold the key to dealing with our other predicament.'

'Oh?' said Catafengi, raising his head, his curiosity piqued.

Lakatos bowed and turned back towards the door. He stood in the doorway, motioning to someone outside. As he returned, a second man followed; a strangely garbed man that Catafengi had not seen before.

'Grand Master Catafengi,' said Lakatos, 'I give you Brother Jurgen.'

The second man halted some distance away and dropped to his knee, bowing his head and remaining motionless on the cold stone floor. Catafengi shuffled over to where Jurgen knelt and scrutinised him closely. He had none of the garb of either a Cawdor or a Redemptionist and his appearance troubled Catafengi greatly.

'A convert?' he asked.

'Yes, mas–' began Lakatos, before Catafengi's upraised finger silenced him.

'I ask the newcomer,' he said.

'Yes, master,' said Jurgen, never lifting his gaze from the floor. 'I have journeyed far and I have often been made unwelcome. I have gone amongst others who didn't know my allegience, master. Forgive me.'

Catafengi paused for a moment's thought. This Jurgen seemed honest enough and he was certainly not the first of the cult's members to go plainly into the wider Underhive.

'Very well, Brother Jurgen, you are welcome here,' Catafengi said at last. Jurgen gave one last nod of his head in appreciation and rose from his kneeling position, daring at last to look upon Catafengi.

'Tell me, Brother Lakatos,' said Catafengi in a tone of voice designed to test Lakatos's patience, 'what has our new recruit done to impress you so?'

'Jurgen...' said Lakatos.

Jurgen stepped forwards, drawing a wad of parchments from his pockets. He unfolded them and removed the top two sheets. He held them out in his hand, offering them to Lakatos who waved him off. Jurgen instead passed the sheets to Catafengi directly.

Catafengi inspected the sheets. One was a wanted poster of the sort typically posted by guilders. The other was a simple grant of passage and Catafengi remained unimpressed.

Jurgen drew near, taking the sheets back from Catafengi, though holding them at arm's length the whole time, like the reluctant grasp of a conjuror who presented his offerings from a distance so as to allow no hint of trickery. Jurgen even spun the sheets on their corners, showing them front and back to Catafengi as he backed away. Catafengi nodded and waved his hand for Jurgen to continue. The spectacle was amusing if nothing else.

Jurgen pulled a canteen from his coat and, finding it difficult to both open the stiff canteen and hold the parchments, he passed the sheets to Lakatos who held them by their corners in the same ginger manner. Catafengi was intrigued as to why the pair of them seemed so suspiciously proud of these simple parchments.

Jurgen tugged at the canteen's stopper. It came away with a high-pitched *plop* and he raised the canteen over the parchments and emptied the contents over them, dousing them so that both sheets quickly became heavy. The sheets folded in on themselves and hung from Lakatos's grasp like heavy rags.

Jurgen took one sheet from Lakatos, pulling it taut by its sides, and walked back towards Catafengi. Lakatos did likewise, straightening out the sheet he held in his own hands as he went.

Jurgen passed his sheet to Catafengi, who was increasingly baffled by the display. He frowned as he took the sheet, less than thrilled to have the paper dripping all over his robes. He held the paper out in front of him and was instantly aghast.

A verse, copied word for word from the ancient ideologum that Catafengi had furnished Lakatos with long ago, was hidden beneath the wanted poster's surface, apparently embedded in its very fibres in an ink that had remained invisible until wetted.

'Astonishing,' said Catafengi as Lakatos passed him the second sheet. It similarly bore hidden text revealed by the dousing.

'They are quite undetectable and they will allow us to communicate freely with our friends all over the hive. Even our friends in the highest of places, master,' said Lakatos. 'There is simply no danger of their contents being uncovered. They are of Jurgen's making, master,' he continued. 'We have a ready supply of suitable documents, master. They merely need impregnating with Jurgen's magic.'

'Impressive,' said Catafengi, his mind boggling at the possibilities offered by this new recruit's peculiar talents.

'There is more,' said Lakatos. He nodded again to Jurgen and the newcomer drew another sheet of parchment from his pocket. He unfolded it once more and, this time without waiting for a prompt, handed it directly to Catafengi in his throne.

Catafengi took the sheet from Jurgen, pulling it close to his face so that his old eyes could make out the dark print on the grubby parchment. He gawped in astonishment, which quickly turned to anger.

'What is the meaning of this?' he barked. 'Lakatos, what have you done?'

In his hands, Catafengi clutched a wanted poster, just like the rather more anonymous example with which Jurgen had demonstrated his hidden writing. This one, however, was instantly familiar, bearing as it did, Lakatos's masked countenance on its sepia background.

Lakatos chuckled as he approached the old man. 'I thought it a rather good likeness,' said Lakatos. 'Don't you? He's as much an artist as a forger, our Jurgen,' he said.

Catafengi raised his head and, through his tall, conical hood, glared at Lakatos with one eye. 'Then this is a fake?' he asked at last, only slowly starting to understand.

'Quite,' said Lakatos. 'Though I wouldn't call myself innocent of everything it says.' He gave a deep belly laugh as he finished, far too proud of his own foolery for Catafengi's liking. This Jurgen, Catafengi thought to himself, was proving rather interesting.

'I didn't have it in mind to make it known to the others,' said Jurgen, 'since you never know who you might need to fool, but I thought it only right and proper that I avail myself to Lakatos.'

'And I, you,' Lakatos said to Catafengi in turn.

'Good, good, good,' said Catafengi. 'You are right, and I am glad none know about your forgery. Indeed, you never know how much more smoothly things might pass the fewer people know about them. We will keep this our secret,' he said. 'Understand?'

'Yes, master,' said Lakatos.

'Yes... master,' said Jurgen. It took a swift dig in the ribs from Lakatos to elicit the address but Catafengi cared little. He only really enjoyed the formality when it came from arrogant fools like Lakatos.

'You see,' said Catafengi, 'we must be careful in all things not to reveal ourselves. We have many enemies, many troublemakers who need to be removed, but to act against them openly invites scrutiny. We must wait until an opportunity gifts itself to us. Until now, that is...'

'Master?' asked Jurgen.

'If our enemies also happened to be wanted by the guilders, it would be rather easier for us to deal with them, would it not?' said Catafengi.

'Of course, master,' said Lakatos. 'We could strike them down with total impunity, if only they were wanted by the guilders.'

Catafengi detected the same smug tone in Lakatos's voice as in his own, and the pair both turned quizzically to Jurgen. He took a moment before nodding in reply, a wicked smile forming on his lips. Clearly, he understood the plan.

'Then I will go at once, master,' said Jurgen, 'and make wanted men of our enemies.'

'Patience Jurgen,' said Catafengi, turning to Lakatos. 'And the other matter? What does Jurgen know of it?' asked Catafengi.

Lakatos stepped forward with a start. He had clearly forgotten it.

'Ah, ah yes,' he blurted. 'This Lago is not unknown to you Jurgen, is he?'

'No, not at all,' said Jurgen. Catafengi leaned forward, listening closely as Jurgen began his tale of Alderman Greim followed by his own. He continued with the tale of Lago on his tail and a half dozen daring escapes from his clutches. Catafengi remained silent as the tale concluded, careful to give away nothing of his own feelings.

'If I were a rash man, Jurgen,' he said at last, 'I might jump to the conclusion that it is you who has brought Lago to our little corner of the hive and brought this trouble upon us.'

Lakatos gulped. His arrogance had led him to overlook this rather obvious conclusion and Catafengi enjoyed watching him squirm. In the end, it was Jurgen who answered the accusation.

'Perhaps, master,' he said, 'but I do not think you are a rash man.'

Catafengi was impressed. Jurgen clearly hid a wisdom easily the equal of any possessed by his other servants. Still, Catafengi was not yet sure of his motives.

'Lago may well be looking for me,' said Jurgen, 'but I didn't bring him here. I have never heard of this Handomel, and I don't know what Lago wants with him. Seems to me we're in this together.'

This much at least made sense to Catafengi, and he was satisfied that Jurgen was not more trouble than he was worth, though the mystery of Handomel's demise still troubled him greatly. Even if Jurgen didn't know the answers, Catafengi felt sure he was the man best placed to discover them.

'How, then, do you suppose Lago's bounty hunter found you here?' asked Catafengi.

'Well,' said Jurgen, 'I can't be sure he did. Could just be blind luck. The fool got lost out in the storms and just happened to be carrying my poster on him when he did.'

Catafengi nodded. It was certainly possible.

'Or it could be the guilders know more than I reckoned,' said Jurgen. 'I swore myself to the Redemption long ago, but I did my best to keep it from them.'

It was a familiar story to Catafengi's ears. The Redemption had adherents throughout the hive, from the very highest families of the Spire to the very lowliest dregs of the sump. Only two things united this disparate congregation: their unrelenting devotion to the Emperor's good works, and the hateful persecution that their beliefs invited from the rest of the hive's population. To those who did not believe, the Redemption was a dangerous, destabilising cult. They loathed its influence and feared its unseen agents, and hence punished all those who made their devotion known. Catafengi bitterly hated this ill treatment of his brothers, but he understood their need for secrecy and thought no less of Jurgen for his secret loyalty all these years.

'I could be wrong,' said Jurgen. 'Perhaps they always knew I was secretly faithful. If they did, then Lago's just going through the list, I guess, and checking out every Redemptionist refuge he can find. He might not even know I'm here yet. Maybe that's how Handomel ended up crossing him.'

Catafengi paused. This was compelling speculation. 'Very well,' he said at length. 'Jurgen, take one of Lakatos's men to meet what remains of Handomel's gang. Find out from them what you can, and then decide how to proceed. Once the matter of Lago is in hand, we can progress.'

'Progress?' asked Jurgen. From his post behind Jurgen's shoulder, Lakatos nodded deferentially, but

Jurgen was as yet unaware of the greater scheme unfolding around him. Catafengi had no desire to waste his time explaining and was mercifully relieved when Lakatos hurriedly stepped forwards in interjection.

'Yes, ah, Jurgen, there is *much* we must tell you.'

THE THREE OF them strolled over the cracked steps at the base of the dome. Most people averted their gaze as Catafengi passed. He seldom left his shack these days, and even those that travelled with him would be more accustomed to seeing his rarefied litter than the man himself. The red-hooded men that scurried around, trying to look busy in the presence of their prophet, would take Lakatos and Jurgen for great and powerful figures to have drawn Catafengi from his chambers, and it was an impression Catafengi certainly wished to cultivate.

When the time for crusade came, it was men like Lakatos and Jurgen to whom he would have to entrust much of his plan, and any faith in them he could inspire now would be priceless. As much as he sought to introduce Jurgen to the ways of the cult, it was just as vital to introduce the cult to him. He foresaw greatness for this Jurgen... Great and fiery things indeed.

'These are our brothers, Jurgen,' Catafengi said. 'These are our brothers who bear the mantle openly, and they suffer greatly for it,' he said.

Jurgen looked away in thought.

'It is the reason, no doubt, that you are before me dressed as you are,' said Catafengi. 'I think you know well how our faith suffers at the hands of unbelievers?

'The unbelievers hound us, in the name of the dark things in their hearts and in the name of that bastard Helmawr. They fear us because our faith in the Emperor is so great that we resist their lies and do not blindly serve them when it is not what the Emperor asks. Helmawr acts for himself, and all who work for him do likewise. They are infidels, cowards and traitors. They do not serve the Emperor as we do, they enact nothing of his will but that which will make them fat and bloated, or sate their perverted appetites and fulfil their wicked desires. And yet they hound us.'

At this, Lakatos raised his gloved palm, firmly patting a passing Redemptionist on the shoulder as if in a sign of solidarity. It will take braver actions than that, thought Catafengi, though he refrained from pointing it out. Lakatos was arrogant and prone to gesture, but he was faithful and his well-aimed zeal served Catafengi well.

'We are not alone, of course. Our enemies prove their own cowardice in that they dare not fight us when we come in the guise of that brave House, Cawdor. That is why you are so important to us, you and your kind,' Catafengi said.

'You see, Jurgen,' he continued, 'it is not solely Lakatos who has pledged himself to our cause, but there are many like him all about this place. The time is coming when, all together, we will act.'

'Master?' asked Jurgen.

'That we can hide ourselves away here is thanks to the hard work of Lakatos and his Union, and Addec and the others like them. It allows for time away from prying eyes, for the time to plan and to prepare for what is coming. Do you know what is coming, Jurgen?'

'Redemption is coming. Redemption comes for us all,' said Jurgen, his voice strong and certain in his words.

'Very good,' said Catafengi, 'but it does not come quickly or easily. Nor does it come quietly when not called for. It comes by blood and sweat, and sacrifice. It comes by crusade, Jurgen, it comes only by crusade. That is what is coming: the crusade for redemption.'

Catafengi watched for the newcomer's reaction, but it was muted and hard to place. Indeed, Lakatos, who had heard such words many times before, seemed the more startled. Perhaps he detected in Catafengi's voice the imminence with which he saw events unfolding.

'I do not think we need wait long before our crusade begins, brothers,' he said at last, as much to confirm Lakatos's suspicion as to inform Jurgen. Jurgen, he was sure, understood already, no matter how recent his arrival. Great things. Great and fiery things.

'You see,' Catafengi continued, the three of them still strolling slowly across the rubble at the foot of what once must have been a considerable causeway. 'You see, there have been many crusades, many brave and devout martyrs, Jurgen. They came as raging tides of fire and they swept away much that was unclean, but like all tides, they were driven back. It will not be this way for us, Jurgen.'

'Emperor wills it,' said Jurgen.

'Indeed he does. That is why he has gifted us such territory as we now hold: Fall Sands, the Fulcrum Spike, the Ash Bluff, the Seven Domes of Fire. We bear all these things in his name, though to our enemies they appear divided and spread amongst many gangs. All the Redemption holds, they take from us, the unbelievers, but all Cawdor holds, they fear to touch, the cowards.

'That is why they do not drive us out as they have our brothers. They do not realise what they face. They do not realise that we are so many, and when the time comes, they will be too few to stop us, I am quite sure.'

'I am sure there is no one who could stand against us, master. We are well prepared,' said Lakatos, his arrogance and craving of attention forcing him to butt in when he had little to say.

'Indeed we are, though there are yet a few preparations to be made,' said Catafengi, 'and that is your job, Jurgen, to complete our preparations so that our crusade may begin.'

'Me?' asked Jurgen, his voice hinting at a modicum of surprise.

'Yes,' said Catafengi. 'I have decided that when our crusade begins, Lakatos will be at my side. The Union will have its part to play, however, and it is you who must direct it. Are you ready for this responsibility?'

'Yes,' said Jurgen, 'as the Emperor wills it, so it is done.'

'Very good, Jurgen. Very good. There was a man named Handomel, what do you know of him?'

'I've heard a thing or two from some of the others,' said Jurgen. Lakatos hissed his annoyance. Still, thought Catafengi, if nothing else it proved Lakatos had at least chosen the most tight-lipped of his apprentices for a successor. This would prove a wise choice, he was sure.

'Handomel is dead,' began Catafengi, 'and I am not sure that any of those he has left behind is yet ready to complete his work: our work. I will not have one hand with a missing finger before we begin, Jurgen. Just as Lakatos has made sure of the Union's strength, we must be sure that Handomel's men are still strong without him.'

'You wish me to replace Handomel, master?' asked Jurgen.

'No, Jurgen, no. I simply wish to know that Handomel has been replaced by one of his own; someone with whom you can deal.

'Unity has always been our strength, Jurgen. Communication is vital to that, and your secret messages will do much to bolster it. It is the Emperor who dictates this crusade, but it shall be I who interprets, and as I do so, word must be spread. It will be up to you, Jurgen, to see that all our brothers know their roles without our enemies discovering them.

'You must make contact with whoever is fit to succeed Handomel – at once, or you may wait until Lago is dealt with, I leave it to you – but then you must share your secrets with them so that we will have a network. Then you must spread word across it, exactly as I tell you, when I tell you. Do you understand?'

'Yes, master,' said Jurgen. 'I understand everything.'

'We have already made such preparations with Addec, master,' said Lakatos, quick to interject.

'Good. Soon we shall begin, but quietly at first. You will produce wanted posters for the most dangerous of our enemies, and we shall eliminate them without suspicion and leave their gangs leaderless. Then we shall begin in earnest. Are you ready to begin?'

'Yes, master,' said Jurgen. 'I am ready for all of this.'

'Very well,' said Catafengi. 'Go now, and do as I have said. Our crusade begins soon.'

'Yes, master.' Jurgen dropped to his knee in a hasty bow. He rose quickly, instantly turned on his heel and was gone, hurrying across the steps.

Lakatos tarried a moment longer, stopping on the steps as if awaiting Catafengi's approval. Catafengi was well pleased with Lakatos and his actions but had little desire to bolster the man's ego further and granted him no more than a single nod. This was enough, and Lakatos was gone. Their destiny awaited them all and all knew it was within touching distance.

Catafengi breathed deeply of the smoke-laden air around him. Exhaling, he felt more powerful than he had in decades. His time was at hand, a time for great things. Great and fiery things.

CHAPTER: SIX

'DEVERES!' LAKATOS SHOUTED the name even before he reached the entrance to the ganghouse. Deveres didn't think it especially wise to let him shout it again and quickly scrambled down the ladder from his perch on the roof.

'Go with Jurgen,' he said.

'Okay,' said Deveres. 'Where?'

'The Ore Chasm. Jurgen is going to see Handomel's gang.'

Deveres's heart sank. All around him he heard titters of laughter. Only Morden offered a sympathetic half-smile.

'In the storms?' asked Deveres, though having seen Morden sent out just days ago he knew any protest was pointless.

'Yes,' said Lakatos, 'and take this stinking thing with you.' Lakatos kicked the bounty hunter's mutilated body where it lay on the exposed iron skeleton of the building's plascrete floor. 'Get rid of it.'

'NO, WE'VE GOT to get right away from the track,' said Jurgen. They had trudged through the ash for the entirety of the previous day and Deveres was sure there was no way anybody would find the body out here anyway. He had little stomach for a journey right out into the dunes.

'There'll be hell to pay if anyone finds out one of Lago's men is dead. For a start, there'll be a hundred damned bounty hunting idiots looking to cash in on all his unfulfilled contracts. Those contracts include me, and the rest of you I shouldn't wonder, so let's make sure we leave him where no one will ever find him.'

Deveres wasn't sure the rotting corpse they hauled behind them deserved quite such an effort, but Jurgen was stubborn on the matter, to the point of seeming almost fearful, and Deveres saw little point in going against him.

'Who the heck is he, anyway?' asked Deveres.

'I don't know his name, but I've seen him before. He works for Lago.'

'Lago?' asked Deveres. 'I mean, I know he's a bounty hunter, but what makes him so special?'

The pair trudged over the shallow bluff to their left, heading away from the more easily traversed route, which followed so far.

'Lago is something else,' said Jurgen. 'He was the guilders' first choice of hired gun for the most part. Back in Glory Hole, they used to say the only guilders not using Lago were the crooked ones; the ones Lago was probably already after.'

The ash began to drag at Deveres's feet and with each step he seemed to be sinking deeper into the stuff, but Jurgen marched on, trying to get further and further from the track. At least with Deveres's lagging, his section of the rope was going slack and Jurgen was doing most of the pulling. Deveres reluctantly followed him, jogging along so as to stay close enough behind for him to be able to make out what Jurgen was saying.

'They trusted him, too, in a way you just can't trust a hired gun. When I was still working for the guilders,

Lago was the man they chose every time someone ripped them off. If one of the shipments came in not matching the inventory in the cipher, then Lago was the one they put on it.'

They crossed another spine of dunes, Deveres almost tumbling down the opposite side as he incautiously ran over its crest. Ahead of them, there was nothing but an endless, shifting sea of ash and Deveres was sure this would be far enough, but Jurgen slogged on.

'He was quiet, see, no fuss. Never left a clue as to why he'd come or gone. The guilders wanted it that way. You make too much mess knocking off the kind of people that he was knocking off, and someone's gonna join the dots, gonna realise that the guilders are onto whoever's ripping them off. If that happens, well, it's only a short step until someone realises *how* the guilders got onto them, and that was a secret worth protecting, like I told you.'

'Is that why they set him after you?' asked Deveres. They'd stopped walking – or rather Jurgen had stopped walking and Deveres had followed suit – and both men gazed around them. The dunes rose up in every direction, one after another, in waves. The winds were stronger here too, causing the dunes to grow and melt away right before their very eyes. There was no danger of navigable tracts here.

Jurgen pulled a shovel free from the kit roped to his back and dug its blade down into the ash, leaving the tool standing firmly upright as he delved into his pocket and pulled out a curious looking metal triangle. He fiddled with the metal object before dropping it to the ground at his feet as he answered Deveres's question.

'I reckon so. See, the guilders kill me, and people are going to wonder why. What did I do? What did I *have*?' he said. 'Bounty hunters are scum for the most part, in for what they can get. If they had the faintest idea that the guilders were after me for something I took, they'd find it. They'd have found those parchments, I could have bought my life by sharing the secret with whoever caught me and where would the guilders be then?'

Deveres and Jurgen both churned shovel after shovel of ash, but it was hard going. The high winds drove ash across the shallow hole and seemed to fill it almost as quickly as Deveres could dig. Jurgen was having better luck, though. Deveres looked across at him. He seemed to be almost digging across the ground, creating a shallow angle so that the winds worked with him, blowing the ash clear of what was already dug. Deveres did likewise and saw the hole deepen quickly, though it took him a minute more to realise he should really be piling the ash downwind of the hole.

'Not Lago, though. They trust him,' said Jurgen, still shovelling away vigorously. 'I bet they sent him after me to make sure I was done for, and to get the parchments back. You know, apart from me, I bet he was the only non-guilder who knew about those things,' he said, patting his pocket in a brief break from the backbreaking digging. Deveres dug on, though he was making nowhere near the headway that Jurgen was.

'Except for all of us, now,' said Deveres, his speech slightly rushed as he struggled for breath, exhausted by the heavy going with the shovel.

'Yeah,' said Jurgen, laughing, 'except for all of you, and that's just fine by me,' he said.

The hole was still remarkably shallow, but Jurgen seemed satisfied. He said nothing, but laid down his shovel and moved over to the body, stooping by its feet. Deveres followed suit, bending down and grabbing the dead man's shoulders. He spoke as they shuffled towards the freshly dug shallow grave.

'Where in the hell did this Lago come from?' asked Deveres. 'I've met plenty of bounty hunters, and they weren't anything like you describe.'

They stopped at the hole's edge. The body was heavy and neither man waited more than a moment before unceremoniously dumping it into its ad-hoc resting place.

'No, perhaps not,' said Jurgen, picking up his shovel and pushing the first shovelful of ash back on top of the body. 'Truth is, I don't really know where Lago came from. I doubt anyone does. I heard a few things though.'

Deveres grabbed his own shovel, turning ash into the hole, but for the most part he found kicking over the great heaps with his feet to be more effective. Jurgen fell silent. Deveres looked up from his shovelling and Jurgen at last continued his story.

'Well,' he said, 'I heard one time that he was from the Spire, a bodyguard of sorts, but that his master was betrayed and killed, and all his men with him.'

'Except Lago?' asked Deveres.

'Except Lago,' said Jurgen. 'He escaped and made it down here, and ever since he's been loyal to whoever it was he served, or loyal to something they asked of him maybe, or loyal to a cause, an ideal. Kinda like he thinks he serves the dead or some crazy bull like that. Except he picked the wrong cause,' said Jurgen, laughing.

'Amen to that, *brother*,' said Deveres, before returning to the body in the hole before them. 'Loyalty like that is a pretty rare thing down here, so I guess it stands to reason that he'd have to be from up there.'

'You think it's any different up there?' said Jurgen, and Deveres paused for thought. It was a rhetorical question, though, and Jurgen carried on.

'Then again,' Jurgen said, 'another time I heard he wasn't even real, and that every time the guilders wanted to put the frighteners on someone, they said

Lago was after them. Anybody the guilders hired, they got to be Lago until the job was done. Then again, others say he's real, but not really human. They say the guilders kinda just grew him in a vat to do their work for them, so who's to say?'

'Maybe he's already dead. Maybe he died out in the storms just like this guy,' said Deveres, dropping his tool to the ground as the last shovelful of ash filled the hole. The howling winds had already transformed the landscape around them and bare seconds after the implement hit the ground it was covered in ash. The hole – or rather the shallow grave of this unfortunate bounty hunter – likewise was instantly indistinguishable from the ground around it and Deveres was quite certain it was a job well done. He looked up from the ground to congratulate Jurgen, but he was nowhere to be seen.

'Jurgen!' he yelled out. 'Jurgen!' But there was no reply. Deveres turned around but there was still no sign of Jurgen. Damn these storms, he thought to himself as the wind bit at his face and the ash clogged his eyes. The wind had picked up dangerously and Deveres could hardly stand. Where the hell was he? Where the hell was Jurgen?

Deveres almost leapt out of his skin as he felt a firm hand on his shoulder. He realised that, when he had turned away from the grave, he had completely lost his bearings, and even turning back on the spot he couldn't be sure he faced the same direction in which he had begun. He gave a silent prayer that Jurgen had him in his sights all along.

'Come on,' he said, 'let's get back to the track.' Jurgen dropped to his haunches, almost kneeling in the ash. By his feet was the curious, triangular metal object which Deveres had seen him drop when they first reached the spot.

Jurgen held another curious metal implement in his hand: a skeleton-like rack of metal rods. Jurgen pulled at it with his gloved hands, unfolding the contraption and when he had finished Deveres saw that it was a triangular frame, a little larger than the other triangular object, with the rods forming odd little legs of different lengths.

Jurgen placed it over the first triangular object and pushed it down into the ash until the triangular frame at the top clicked with the object's edges. With that, Jurgen tapped it, and pulled the block and frame away, curiously leaving the rods in the ash. Deveres stared in amazement.

Jurgen pulled out one particular rod, taking great care to pinch it at the point at which it left the ash. He held it up to his face and by the awkward way in which Jurgen seemed to be moving his fingers up the rod, Deveres presumed he was measuring something. Jurgen froze for a moment, rubbing his chin before he at last rose to his feet. As he did so, he swiped the triangular object over the rods and they all leapt out, clinging to it. It seemed as though the object was a magnet of some sort. With that Jurgen was off, pacing across the dunes. Deveres dashed to keep up.

'What was that?' he asked.

'An old ratskin trick I picked up,' he said. 'We can't just go back the way we came, 'cos we can't really be sure which way that is. Besides, winds this strong will be pushing at us all the way we walk, pushing us off course, maybe pointing us the wrong way, you know?'

Deveres well understood what he meant.

'That little trick catches the ash up against its edge, so I can see where it's come from, and how much of it's piled up. Gives me the direction of the wind, its speed and the amount of ash it's shifting. It's enough for us to correct our course as we walk. You got me?'

Deveres nodded enthusiastically, though in truth he had barely heard half of what Jurgen had said, let alone followed it. He couldn't care less what he was on about, he was just relieved to be following someone with such a grasp of the treacherous conditions that surrounded them.

'I'll show you sometime,' he said. 'It might come in handy.'

JURGEN'S ROUTE HAD been quick enough, but it had brought them to what appeared to be a different track entirely, not at all where Deveres had expected. They had saved a great deal of time, according to Jurgen, but the drawback was that this next stretch would be all the more perilous for it, through the worst of the storms across a dome so ancient and so long abandoned that it no longer even had a name. Indeed, it wasn't even really a dome anymore. Places like this were normally called deeps, for they surely didn't deserve even the semblance of order that the word 'dome' conjured up.

They were the most decrepit edges of the Underhive, their architecture so utterly blasted, so totally collapsed to nothing, that they had become shapeless wildernesses with nothing to distinguish one region from another. They were uncharted and unchartable, and what form they originally took could only be guessed at from the intact domes further inhive. They were not nearly as deep as the sump or the lower regions, but at least there a constant trail of effluvium and by-products from the city above created areas of sufficient interest to attract settlements and, once in a while, even provided sufficient resources for people to survive.

Not so here. These forgotten edges of the hive's broad base benefited from no such run-off and were dry, blasted wastelands that Deveres could only imagine were every bit the equal of the terrible ash wastes that lay beyond the wall of the hive. He didn't know for sure since he had never left the hive, but he couldn't imagine the outside being any worse.

Indeed, right now, he wasn't very far from it. This western edge was where the ash actually entered the hive. A sheer wall covered with colossal turbine downshafts that in an earlier age inhaled clean air from the atmosphere outside now did nothing but leak the ruined atmosphere's foul detritus into the hive itself. That was why places like this had been abandoned, when the terrible smog of centuries in the world outside had built to such a level that it kicked back into the ventilation system. That was when the great and the good abandoned such places. They rose above them; building over the regions they could not repair and the people they had no desire to save. No matter the poison outside, the Spire always rose above it while those beneath it drowned. That was how Deveres felt now, drowned.

Jurgen seemed unperturbed, and Deveres was grateful that the ropes they had used to drag the bounty hunter's body out into the dunes were still tied around their waists. More than once he'd fallen to his knees and had been dragged over by Jurgen as he ploughed on ahead. Right now it was the only thing allowing Deveres to keep up with Jurgen.

The next stretch lasted less than an hour, but Deveres was a wreck by the end of it. Jurgen had led them right to the very wall itself, reasoning that being under the vast downpipes was probably the safest place to be. He was right, since their immense size meant they launched their ashy shot some hundreds of metres into the air, creating a kind of sheltered area directly beneath them where the air was still, though still choking thick with dust.

Now that they were at the foot of the wall, all Deveres wanted to do was sleep. There was little chance of that, though, as Jurgen kept up his frantic pace. It was too much for Deveres and he soon fell to his knees again. This time he didn't stand but instead gathered what remained of his strength to pull back hard on the rope, halting Jurgen's furious march and drawing him back towards him.

'What's up?' asked Jurgen as he returned to the kneeling Deveres.

'Rest,' said Deveres, barely able to muster that one word.

'Fine,' said Jurgen, replying in a terse tone.

'COME ON,' SAID Jurgen. 'Let's go.'

'Huh?' said Deveres, only slowly waking up as Jurgen shook him by the shoulder. He rubbed his eyes and stretched his sore shoulders, finding the strength to stand. 'That's it?' he asked. It felt like bare minutes since they had stopped to rest.

'That's it,' said Jurgen. 'Let's go.' And with that, they did.

THE WINDS SEEMED a little less severe as they continued their trek, or perhaps Deveres was better rested than he thought. He was grateful that they had avoided the worst of the storms, but following this southerly route along the wall had left them with a rather longer journey to the Ore Chasm than Deveres would have wanted. Still, he knew from taking the route in kinder seasons that the most direct route lay through half a dozen high-roofed, open and exposed deeps, and he couldn't imagine how much worse the storms would be there. Three days in and Deveres was close to exhaustion. He was sure he wouldn't have lasted three days by any other route.

Jurgen, though, seemed as strong as ever and his pace never slackened. Deveres struggled increasingly to keep up and soon found himself forced to jog to match Jurgen's walking speed. More than once Jurgen had offered to slow down, but Deveres wasn't about to admit weakness and, despite his exhaustion, he knew full well that if he didn't keep up the pace they could be out here for days, and he dreaded that more than anything.

After another hour or two the landscape changed. A change in the direction of the wind, as often happened towards the end of the Ash Season, had driven the dunes up against the hive wall itself, as though the escaping winds had sucked the dunes up against it. Furrows close to the wall which had previously allowed safe passage were quickly vanishing before their eyes as the pair were forced to cross the treacherous drifts, further draining Deveres's failing strength.

The dunes seemed to grow in size as they ploughed on, some of them so sheer that the men were forced to run in order to climb up them. One, two, three dunes in a row presented mounds so high that they could not be crossed at all and so the men's route became increasingly circuitous.

Another dune hove into view, smaller but all the steeper for it. Jurgen raced up, skidding a little but moving with sufficient momentum to carry him over it. Deveres followed, racing up the side, but his legs gave out. He crashed to the ground right atop the dune. He flung his arms forwards and rolled his bodyweight over the crest so that he wouldn't just slide back down to the ground and managed to haul himself down the other side. Clumsy as it might be, he had at least crossed the dune.

He pulled himself to his feet and gazed ahead. Jurgen was nowhere to be seen. He reached down to his waist, but the rope was gone. He cursed himself. He had untied it before drifting off to sleep earlier on. The rope's bulky knot had been uncomfortable, pressing into him as he lay, and in a moment of folly he had untied it.

'Jurgen!' he yelled out. 'Jurgen!' But there was no reply.

Deveres turned around but there was still no sign of Jurgen. Damn these storms, he thought to himself as the wind bit at his face and the ash clogged his eyes. The wind had picked up dangerously and Deveres could hardly stand. Where the hell was he? Where the hell was Jurgen?

CHAPTER: SEVEN

COYNE RAN HIS fingers uneasily over the clip, turning it right round three hundred and sixty degrees, and pushing it back in until he heard the satisfying click before pulling back down on it and beginning the manic pattern all over again.

The gun had barely left his hand since Handomel died. Since Handomel was *killed*, that is. He'd reached for it the second he found the body – or at least what was left of it – and his finger had clutched the trigger every panicked step of the way back to the hideout. There had been no reports of Lago since then, but that didn't reassure Coyne any, and for the first few days he had cradled the gun day and night because of it. Now he cradled it for another reason. He cradled it because Vilhame cradled his pistol just the same, and the pair hadn't taken their eyes off each other for hours.

'This is my time, Coyne,' said Vilhame, his own manic fondling of his pistol betraying his attempts to present a menacing calm. 'You know Handomel would have picked me, if he'd lived. You know he would have. Don't make this any harder.'

'Handomel's not here to pick you, you dumb frik,' said Coyne, nerves showing through his genuine anger, 'and it doesn't seem like anybody else is picking you either.' Coyne didn't dare take his eyes off Vilhame, but he felt the support of the half dozen gangers shuffling around behind him.

'I'm picking,' said Frork from his position behind Vilhame's shoulder.

'And me,' said Chem next to him.

That was how this had all begun, with an honest attempt to stop the strife. Handomel's death left a terrible vacuum, and tempers threatened to fill it. Coyne had been successful enough in getting the others to agree to a vote, but he hadn't been so successful in making it stick. It was six to two in his favour, but the two backing Vilhame were Frork and Chem: the former carrying a heavy bolter, the latter a heavy stubber. Those two weren't the smartest, so perhaps they thought their vote should count for more than the others. Either way, they figured Vilhame was the winner, and now the rules had changed. This was not going to be decided by a vote.

That had always been the difference between Vilhame and Coyne. They had always acted as Handomel's left and right hands, but they were totally unalike. Both possessed unrivalled leadership qualities, but Coyne practiced the smart-savvy kind of leadership where Vilhame acted as a fighting general, a follow me and no going back kind of leader. In Handomel's day, they had complemented each other perfectly. Coyne's cunning, his shrewd reasoning and quick wits used to get them out of trouble, Vilhame's fearlessness came into its own when the trouble had to be dealt with head on, while Handomel ruled over the whole bunch with his legendary oratory.

Handomel was more a preacher than a leader, and Coyne had always seen him going that way towards the end. He certainly hadn't seen him going so soon.

They weren't playing by Vilhame's rules yet. A few minutes of pointed pistols had quietened them down and left the entire gang stuck in the current standoff round the table. But they weren't playing by Coyne's rules anymore either, and the longer this went on, the more chance Vilhame would just finish it his way – swiftly and violently. It was impossible to tell who would be the winner in the midst of this chaos, and Vilhame was smart enough to know that, and so for now at least Coyne could still try to win this battle with his wits alone.

'It's not as simple as that, is it Vilhame?' said Coyne. 'This isn't just about who replaces Handomel. This is about who serves Catafengi, and you know it as much as I do.'

The others round the table shuffled nervously at the mention of his name. Some knew nothing and cast questioning glances to one another; others knew the name, but feared to hear it mentioned so openly; and some still doubted the wisdom of doing so. That the gang – like all of House Cawdor – served the Redemption was no secret. That they served Catafengi and his cult in particular was not, however, common knowledge.

Coyne and Vilhame were well acquainted with Catafengi, having been Handomel's deputies and also his intermediaries, and they had dealt frequently with the master. The others, however, were either ignorant or scared of him and so Coyne used his name like a weapon.

Sure enough, Frork and Chem became immediately uneasy at the mention of Catafengi. They were more than happy to use their brute force to pick their own leader, but to pick Catafengi's disciple? Perhaps even pick the wrong one... The oafish, muscular pair suddenly seemed far less certain of themselves as the realisation dawned on them that this was exactly what they were doing.

'Frag it!' yelled Vilhame as he rose from his seat. He spun his pistol in his palm, brought it instantly to a trigger grip and pointed its charred barrel directly at Coyne's head. In an instant the cluster of gangers behind Coyne raised their own weapons, every one of them trained on Vilhame. Coyne remained seated, resisting the urge to raise his own weapon. He knew full well this rash display was Vilhame's old battle savvy coming to the fore.

Vilhame had gambled and Coyne knew it. He'd aimed his weapon, but gambled that the others wouldn't shoot him instantly, and so he had created the standoff. All Vilhame needed was for Frork and Chem to let their tempers get the better of them, and Coyne and his supporters would be riddled with holes before they could get a single shot off.

But Coyne had already made his own play. He'd made his point. Frork and Chem knew they could triumph with brute force and heavy weapons right there and then. They would live, and Vilhame would be leader. And after that? How could they be sure that they were supporting the right man? Coyne could read the uncertainty in their eyes – kill him and what would Catafengi say? It was a question they clearly didn't want answered.

Vilhame could still shoot his own pistol, of course, but he'd only get a single shot off before Coyne's men gunned him down, and then what would Frork and Chem gain by opening fire? Coyne, it seemed, had won the battle. Brains over brawn. Vilhame could still unleash his own customary havoc, but it would be suicidal. Coyne was ready to lay down the final challenge.

'Seems to me,' said Coyne, 'we could resolve all this with another vote. Bullets aren't going to sort this, are they boys?' He cast a stern glance at Frork and then to Chem. Their body language conceded defeat and even

Vilhame seemed to realise he was undone. He holstered his pistol and returned to his seat.

Boom.

It was as though Coyne could hear nothing but that single word whispered inside his own head. Blinding light flared around him, but the world seemed silent as he fell to the floor, a searing heat racing over his flesh. There was something before the *boom*, though, the last sound he could remember: breaking glass.

The window. A frag grenade had crashed through the window just as calm had returned, and now the chamber was engulfed in chaos once again. Vilhame, Frork and Chem were nowhere to be seen. The latter's heavy weapons lay burnt and twisted on the floor as the only evidence of their recent, explosive demise. The table at which they had been sitting pinned Coyne to the wall. One splintered corner was buried in his thigh, pinning it to the floor, while the table's top lay flat against his chest, face and left arm. Only his right arm remained clear of it, and he wriggled it up and down desperately to prove to himself that he was still alive. Coyne's head was pinned facing to the left, however, leaving his right arm out of sight, and his frantic grabbing at the air was not visible to him.

After a moment or two the panic subsided and Coyne drew his right arm closer to his body, wriggling it into the gap between the table and the wall. Coyne exhaled and arched his back against the wall as he began to push with his right arm and the table tilted forwards. It moved enough to release his head from the painful pressure, but at that upright angle it suddenly seemed as if it might come crashing back down on him all the harder. He had no time to waste, and Coyne roared in pain as he used his impaled leg to give him the extra push he needed to tip the table up and away from him, sending it crashing back to its original place in the middle of the floor, albeit upside down. He slumped back against the wall and breathed deeply, not yet daring to gaze down at his mangled leg.

The smoke had begun to clear and ahead of him he saw a pair of figures moving quickly out of the door, lasguns in hand. Scarr and Track had been caught in the blast too, but mercifully were flung clear, and without any rubble to trap them they quickly returned to their feet and dashed out in the direction of the unknown attacker. Whether it was by vote or default, Coyne was the leader now, and he realised that he couldn't leave the survivors to deal with it alone.

He reached his arms up behind him, his fingers finding their way into the mass of holes and cracks that covered the wall's plascrete surface, giving his battered arms precious leverage with which to draw himself up onto his feet.

His right leg was a terrible mess, a gaping wound filled with scorched wooden splinters, and its tattered ligaments screamed with pain as he brought his weight onto it. His left leg remained as strong as ever, proving the value of the bionic one Doc Vesty had fitted for him a decade ago. The pain made it almost impossible to walk, and Coyne quickly found himself resorting to a hastily improvised gait, leaning the knee of his wounded right leg against the sturdy adamantium of the left. This provided a kind of moving crutch and allowed Coyne to stagger forwards in something of a cross-legged hobble.

His steps were pained and hurried and interspersed with desperate lunges for the wall, and the doorway. Coyne took every opportunity to grasp any solid structure he could see to take some of the pain off his horribly wounded leg. In this fashion he lurched out of the door and gazed out across the tangled mass of metallic walkways that ran for hundreds of metres in front of him. Track was kneeling down by the doorway, his gun pointed purposefully out into the dome, providing cover for Scarr who was already far up ahead, picking his way over the gantries in pursuit of some half-glimpsed enemy.

'Where are the sentries?' asked Coyne, his voice an agonised rasp, rising uncontrollably in pitch and tone as intermittent shivers of pain tore through him. Track just frowned in reply and Coyne realised his error.

The juves had always feared Vilhame. He was a terrifying bully and the careers of more than one of the gang's own juves had ended at his hands. Coyne had relied upon such terrified youngsters for support and it had been his idea to call them in from their sentry posts so that they could participate in the vote for leadership. Now they had all paid the price for such a lack of vigilance.

The pain in his leg grew again, and Coyne rested his hand on Track's shoulder as he rose and started to shuffle forwards carefully, taking up a new vantage point from which to better cover Scarr's advance. A heavy V-shaped tunic hung across Track's shoulders and over his robes. Coyne tugged on it. Track understood his meaning and quickly cast the thing off, passing it to his wounded leader.

Coyne drew his knife from his belt and slashed through the tunic's cloth, cutting a metre-long strip from it with which he bandaged his leg as best he could. The pain was still agonising, but at least it seemed constant, and he could hobble forwards without collapsing in pain. He followed Track as he moved out onto the slender gantry that connected the gang's den to the wider dome beyond.

Track made a quick hand gesture and disappeared up a ladder at the gantry's edge, quickly rising out of sight. Up ahead, Scarr lurked behind a broad, circular pillar

at the centre of a hexagonal platform that formed a hub
in the dome's centre from which six walkways radiated
at every level. Scarr waved his hand in a downward
motion and it was clear to Coyne that their attackers
were lurking somewhere on the level below (the den
being located on the fifth of six largely intact levels).
Coyne shuffled as far across the gantry as he could
without exposing himself completely, just far enough
to draw a line of sight down onto the platform below
Scarr. He chanced a quick glance upwards and saw
Track on the level above, two gantries away so that their
combined lines of sight covered virtually the whole
lower level. Both men nodded and Scarr nervously
stepped out from behind the pillar, beginning the perilous descent down the ladder mounted on its side.

Instantly, a harsh report sounded and the noise of
bullets ricocheting off the ladder rang throughout the
dome. Scarr lost his grip, swinging sideways so that
only one hand and one foot remained on the ladder.
He hung perilously between floors, but at least he was
able to press his body close to the pillar, escaping from
sight.

Track unleashed two rounds of his own lasgun, and
Scarr wasted no time in shimmying the rest of the way
down the ladder under such cover as it provided. Scarr
disappeared from sight as he dismounted onto the
lower platform and Coyne hurried forward as best he
could to take up a new position on one of the crossing
gantries that turned the already confusing web of walkways into a veritable maze.

Coyne shuddered as a heavy clanking noise streaked
over his head, then sighed in relief to see it was only
Track, likewise taking up a better position as the trio
nervously stalked their prey. That they had this chance
at all seemed like a miracle to Coyne. Surely in the confusion of the blast, their enemies could have gunned

them down to a man. Unless, he thought, barely
believing it, they weren't *enemies* at all.

He was quickly given reason to discount the theory as
a shot thundered into the walkway beneath him, dent-
ing the mesh panel that hung down at the gantry's
edge. The shot had come from the far right hand side
of the dome, the complete opposite direction from
which the last shot had come, and Coyne was suddenly
afraid they were surrounded.

The same thought must have struck Track and Scarr,
for both gazed nervously at Coyne, their confidence
gone now that their careful advance seemed to have
come undone. They were too few to avoid being surrounded, thought Coyne, but he could at least reassure
the other two and give them a fighting chance.

He took a frag grenade from his belt and hurled it
high into the air, watching it arc towards the source of
the last shot. It must have detonated in the air, the
noise of its crimson blast ringing out before any tinkling of a grenade hitting the floor could be heard. The
edges of those distant gantries were briefly illuminated,
but no living thing showed itself in the blast and Coyne
couldn't be sure there was still anyone down there.

It would have to do, thought Coyne. It would have to
do.

Coyne shuffled forwards again, nearing the platform
directly above Scarr. This has to be a trap, thought
Coyne as he advanced, but why? Surely they were sitting ducks in the moments of panic following the blast.
This made no sense, no sense at all.

Two more shots rang out from ahead of them, aimed
at Scarr, and there was only a moment's pause before
another round rang out, followed by a dull groan.
Coyne leaned over the platform's edge to see Scarr
fallen to the ground beneath him, clutching his leg. He
had been hit.

Damn it, thought Coyne, and without wasting another second he raced down the ladder, his hands and feet skimming down its smooth edges. He simply had no time to climb down it properly. Coyne was nearly sick with pain as the soles of his boots struck the platform below, his wounded right leg crumpling with the force.

He didn't bother getting back to his feet and just hauled himself along the tightly spaced steel bars that formed the platform until he reached the prone Scarr. A bullet wound punctured his thigh. The wound was burnt black at the edges, though not nearly neatly enough to be a las-blast. Scarr had been hit by a solid shell; nothing fancy. That at least gave Coyne hope that they might have a chance.

It was a short-lived hope. As he stared at Scarr's wound, a terrible shriek rang out above him and he looked up to see Track teetering on the gantry's edge, his arms upraised, his lasgun falling from his grasp. It seemed to hover in midair for a moment before plummeting downwards, its heavy bulk giving off a deep tolling sound as it bounced off gantry after gantry. The weapon rushed past Coyne and Scarr where they crouched on the platform.

Track followed a second later, plunging to the ground from his perch on the highest level. He looked lifeless as he fell, and Coyne prayed that he was indeed already dead, for he had seen men survive a fall even as great as this one and that would be the cruellest fate of all.

Scarr looked up terrified, his tear-stained eyes begging Coyne to help him. Coyne was certain that there were two groups. One up ahead and to the far side of the platform that had earlier shot at Scarr when he went beyond the pillar; and a second group almost directly beneath the building whose upper storey housed the gang's den. It had been this second group that had gunned down Track as he approached too close to the gantry's edge.

There were three ways out of the dome: one to the rear-right gantry, one to the front-left one, and one straight ahead. Either of the diagonal exits would, by Coyne's reckoning, bring them into the sight of both groups. The exit up ahead, although presumably occupied by their enemies, was at least shielded from view by the base of the six-tiered platform on whose fourth tier Scarr and Coyne sheltered. They would have to go that way.

Coyne crawled on his belly, rounding the pillar and approached the platform's far edge. Scarr scrabbled along behind him. Nothing. No shots. He breathed a sigh of relief. The enemy was still clearly beneath them, and staying low had kept Coyne out of sight.

Scarr crawled on past Coyne, laying his body over the top of the ladder going down. He nodded, and Coyne hurled another frag grenade, this time in the direction of the entrance. At the sound of its blast, Scarr rolled his weight over the ladder and plummeted down to the next level in a necessarily haphazard scramble. He landed, rolled onto his knee and unleashed a volley of las-blasts, just enough to buy Coyne the time he needed to follow him down the ladder.

There were no covering positions from here on in. Coyne just rose up, hauling Scarr up by his hood to follow, and ran down the gantry as fast as he could, his laspistol unleashing shots into the darkness ahead. Scarr followed and Coyne hoped that this weight of fire would be enough to open up the way ahead.

Fifty metres of agonising stagger and he reached the elevated doorway that led out of the dome. He grasped its black metal edge and pushed his gun barrel quickly around to the other side: no one. Whoever was here had been driven off. That at least would give him and Scarr time to escape.

Breathless but relieved, he turned back to tell Scarr they were safe.

Scarr was dead. His body lay outstretched on the metal walkway, just metres from Coyne. He lay face down, his hood covering his face, but torn wide open at the back where a fist-sized hole pierced cloth, flesh and skull alike. Dum-dums: nothing else could have left a hole in his head like that, not without a blast.

'Shit,' yelled Coyne as he dragged himself round the door. How had they hit Scarr from there? It made no sense.

As he pondered it, his hand ran over a series of indentations in the metal of the broad buttress beside the door. They were fresh marks; the only part of the whole thing that glinted silver. Taking his glove off, Coyne could even feel a little heat coming off them. Ricochet marks.

They fell with an unnatural regularity, all centred around the same spot, none of them more than a hands-width apart. A horrible realisation came to Coyne at last.

The burn marks around the wound on Scarr's leg was from a solid shot. The noise of pistol fire directly beneath him while bullets came from up ahead… Scarr killed from behind as they fled… There weren't two groups at all, just one. Not even a group, just one person.

A handful of masterfully aimed shots had ricocheted off the bulkhead, filling the air around Scarr where he stood earlier on the platform and creating the impression of two separate shooters while all the while their enemy closed in from behind. Only solid shot could do it since las-blasts would never ricochet like that. That was a professional's trick.

Coyne started to run, dropping his glove to the floor such was his panic, but it was too late. A vice-like grip wrenched his arm backwards while a sharp, stabbing kick cleaved into his wounded leg. He fell to his knees and dropped his laspistol all at the same moment, landing painfully and rolling on to his side. One word ran through Coyne's mind as he rolled onto his back and tried desperately to scramble his way backwards. One word ran through his mind as a hefty boot slammed down into his chest, pinning him to the walkway where he lay. One word ran through his mind as he gazed up into the face of the terrifying figure that stood over him, stub gun aimed at Coyne's head. One word ran through his mind as the final shot rang out: Lago.

CHAPTER: EIGHT

'DONE?' SAID LAKATOS. The sudden raising of his voice caught Durn's attention. He looked up to see Berzel and Lirbus enter the hideout.

'No problem,' said Berzel, dropping his heavy sack on the table. Durn had little interest in the stash of credits Berzel had collected; he'd learned to wait for his own meagre share to surface. It saved disappointment. He nodded a brief greeting to Lirbus and then carried on sharpening the stash of shivs on the table next to him, until mention of a familiar name caught his attention.

'I told Goddlesby, just like you said, next week's money better include Bok's share, or the pair of them are gonna pay for it,' said Berzel.

Bok, thought Durn. What were they doing taxing Bok? Durn had been around long enough to remember when the Union first took over Fall Sands. He had a bionic left arm to remind him of how well Bok took the news when they first demanded money for his 'protection'.

'Good,' said Lakatos, reclining on his stone chair, 'and what did the little rat have to say to that?'

'Well, he kicked up a hell of a stink,' said Lirbus. 'Said Bok will never pay; says he can't make him, says it's not his fault, all of that.'

'It'll be fine,' said Berzel. 'Goddlesby has never dared once step out of line.'

'Not quite true, Berzel,' said Lakatos. 'He's managed a good few mistakes in his time, and I'm sure more than a few of them have been wilful.'

That was more than true, thought Durn to himself, putting down a shiv and walking slowly to the middle of the room where he could hear more easily. He rubbed the metal of his left hand with the rough skin of his right. He had Bok on his mind.

'Perhaps we can help poor little Goddlesby out,' Lakatos said, 'just this once.'

'What?' asked Berzel.

'Well, maybe we ought to explain to Bok how all of this works. Besides, way I see it, he owes us plenty enough in back-taxes to justify a visit,' said Lakatos. 'See to it.'

With that, both Lirbus and Berzel left the room.

Durn grinned from ear to ear to think of Bok getting his comeuppance at last and, as he returned to his table and picked up the next shiv, he ground it against the stone all the more vigorously, picturing Bok and thinking of how the Union owned him. It would be just a matter of time before he stepped out of line, and Durn hoped he would be the one to set Bok straight.

'You too, Durn,' said Lakatos from behind him. Durn dropped the shiv in an instant.

'With them?' he asked. 'To Bok's?'

'No, I mean there's work for you, too,' said Lakatos, reaching into his pocket. He produced three sheets of parchment, offering them out at arms length. Durn paced towards his leader, taking the sheets from him and flicking through them. They were wanted posters from the guilders.

'It seems,' said Lakatos, 'that some of these here good townsfolk have been doing things they shouldn't have, and it seems like some of those things are going to catch up with them.'

'You want me to bring them in, claim the bounty?' asked Durn.

'No, no,' said Lakatos. 'No need for that. In fact, we're going to do all these good folks a favour. Tell them they're safe, that the guilders won't be coming for them. We're going to protect them, but they're going to be paying a little more from now on, understand?'

Durn laughed a deep and wicked laugh, the only sign Lakatos needed that he understood. He stuffed the wanted posters under his belt and headed out of the door.

OLBERT DIRK. HMM, he always had been a shifty little so and so. Morten? Durn found it hard to believe old Morten had gotten himself into trouble with the guilders, but there it all was in writing on the wanted poster. It also struck him as odd that three such men should find themselves wanted all at once.

True, Ash Season often had the effect of leaving Fall Sands woefully behind the times, and the season's lifting would often be accompanied by a rash of news flooding into the town, but the storms hadn't yet lifted, and the sudden emergence of these wanted posters struck Durn as rather odd. No matter. Durn didn't give a damn what these people had done, he was going to bleed them dry for fear of the guilders and he was going to enjoy every moment of it.

HE FLICKED TO the last poster as he strolled through town. Lam; now there was a natural born victim. He would begin with Lam.

Durn crossed over the broad street and turned left into the maze of metal gantries that extended outwards like a cliff-face colony at the very edge of Fall Sands.

These gantries were in fact the remnants of disused cranes, deployed in an ultimately fruitless attempt to save the failing dome, and the machines themselves were abandoned just as quickly as the dome they had been intended to rebuild.

Centuries had passed since then, and where the standing cranes had once been a bare-bones skeleton, they had since been filled with a mass of rusted insulation and blackened, scrap metal skin. Their own beams were crisscrossed with dozens of others; girders flung down to create walkways between the pinnacles. Makeshift habs had sprung up all over the structures, occupying engine rooms, control boxes and maintenance baskets. Still other habs had been fabricated from scratch: sheet metal bolted to the hollow steel frames to provide four untidy walls and a shaky roof for their desperate occupants.

Generations of such down-and-out ingenuity had made the gantries home to a teeming mass of humanity, clinging on precariously, high up this most distant edge of the dome. It was a desperate place looking for all the world like it should fall at any second. It never had, but it was named such nonetheless: the Falls. The ageless drifts that butted up against it in turn eventually caused the place to be called Fall Sands.

Durn loved this place. He had been born in Hive City, in a high-hab. When he first entered the Underhive, he had lurked for a long time with a gang at Wind's Edge, a dome surviving on the site of an abandoned space dock, where the wind howled ceaselessly across the forest of docking pylons. Being high up was where Durn felt safest, where he felt the thrill most keenly, and the Falls were as high as it got for him these days.

He strolled out onto the nearest gantry, instantly feeling the elevation. From here he could look out over half a dozen domes unfortunate enough to lie further down than Fall Sands itself. Some were abandoned, but some thrived, at least by Underhive standards, and it was an open secret that soon enough these domes were destined to become part of the Union's territory, too.

There was no rush, though. The sheer height of the Falls made attack from below impossible, and having made the curious plateau of Fall Sands their own, this was a building time for the Union. The din of battle and the nervy rush of forays out into another gang's territory, that would all come again, but not yet. Grand plans were being laid, and Durn was content to wait and see them unfold at the will of his betters.

He dreamed of such things as he swung down from the gantry, onto the crisscrossing support girders beneath, which functioned as a makeshift ladder. He swung himself down by his hands, descending twenty metres in mere seconds. From here he swung inside the structure, descending now by an enclosed ladder until he reached Jop Lam's little hab.

A row of tiny turbines, each no bigger than a man's hand, lined the deck at floor level, turning in the wind. As they spun, ash and muck caked onto the blades. As the blades turned, they ran through a row of stiff brushes mounted behind them, shaking the detritus into a grubby trough full of liquid below. Lam was a sifter, and the filth collected in this trough would be painstakingly drained, strained and sifted to harvest whatever miniscule specs of precious ores and minerals the ash storms carried in its grey haze.

As Durn stepped out onto the deck, Lam's arm snaked out from the window cut into the shack's iron front wall. He held a shallow, mesh-bottomed pan in his hand with which he scooped a load of the stuff out of the trough. As he drew the pan back inside, he caught sight of Durn and dropped the pan in sheer fright, giving voice to a girlish shriek as he did so.

'Now that's no way to greet an old friend, is it Lam?'

'Get away from me!' yelled Lam, slamming the shutter across his window. In his panic he seemed not to have noticed that the door remained open, and Durn stepped inside to see the little man cowering by the portal. He leapt in fright as Durn approached.

'Unh! What do you want?' he asked, fear etched into his grubby, whiskered face. Lam had always been terrified of Durn. Back in the early days, when the Union had first come to this place, there were plenty who thought they could put up a fight, thought they could resist the Union's rule, and these were people that, one by one, had been made to disappear.

The Falls had been one of Durn's favourite places for making people disappear. It was three hundred metres down to the next dome, and the fall never left enough of a man for anyone down there to notice the slit throat or shiv in the guts that had really killed them. Accidents, on the other hand, were commonplace in the Underhive, and the victims of such unfortunate tumbles never aroused any suspicion or unwanted attention.

That was when Durn had first met Lam. He remembered seeing the scrawny man's terrified eyes gazing out of that same little window as Durn clambered down on to the deck and unceremoniously hoofed a troublesome settler's warm corpse off the edge. He'd hurled it from high above, but Durn had been new to the business back then and a dull thud had told him the body had landed on something only halfway down – leaving it there was a risk Durn couldn't take. He'd clambered down by the exact same route he had just taken and found the body slumped on Lam's deck, its shattered legs hanging unnaturally off the edge. His second push had been decisive and from there he'd watched the thing tumble out of view, dusting off his hands and congratulating himself on his good work, he remembered. It was then that he'd turned to see Lam quivering on the other side of the window. A swift threat of the same treatment had left the old sifter terrified of Durn ever since.

'What are you doing here?' asked Lam, unnerved by Durn's long pause.

'Oh, you know why I come down here,' said Durn. 'I need to give my throwing arm some practice.'

Lam squealed in fright. He knew well enough what that meant. Having seen the effect on Lam the first time, Durn had ever afterwards made a point of dragging new members of 'the ole disappearing gang' as he called them down to this particular deck. No matter the extra effort. To Durn it was more than worth it every time he saw the terror in Lam's eyes when he was forced to watch another bye-bye dive.

Durn had always told Lam it was his turn next, told him he was getting old and that when he couldn't lift the big ones anymore, he'd be lifting a little one like Lam instead. He toyed with Lam, grabbing him by the collar, hauling him off his feet and instantly bringing to mind that well-aged threat.

He hauled Lam towards the door, the old sifter's feet kicking frantically in the air. He stopped in the doorway, reached into his pocket with his free hand and thrust the wanted poster into the terrified man's face.

'Now,' he said, 'any idea what this is about?'

Lam nervously opened his eyes, having shut them tight in fear of his imminent plunge. He squinted and Durn could read his lips as he struggled over the words on the poster in front of him. He squeaked as he reached the end and saw his own picture. Durn dropped him to the floor of the shack.

'I… I… It's not me, it's not me. I don't know what this is,' said Lam.

Durn just laughed. 'Well let me tell you,' said Durn. 'It says here, you are wanted for the "unauthorised peddling of uncertified ore, the trafficking of which has resulted in the contamination of guild supplies." Now that sounds pretty serious to me, Lam, and, oh look, yes,' Durn continued. 'They are offering a reward for you… dead *or* alive. Now I'm thinking that makes you a pretty big catch.'

'It's not me, it's not me,' Lam said. 'I haven't done anything!'

'No?' said Durn. 'Well it's your picture. Look at it, right there.'

Lam began to sob.

'Well, look here, Lam,' said Durn. 'Seeing as we're such old friends, I'm going to help you out. I don't think you did these things it says, so I'm gonna look after you. Me and all the Union boys, we're going to look after you. Who could get you with us looking out for you, Lam? Eh? Who? No one, that's who, not with us protecting you…

'I mean, think of it Lam. Think of all the terrible things you've seen happen round these parts and yet you've always been safe, haven't you, Lam?' The fact that almost all of those 'terrible things' were acts in which Durn himself had a hand was something he chose to omit, but Lam seemed to get the point regardless.

'I didn't do it,' said Lam, still sobbing.

'And I believe you, Lam, I told you,' said Durn. 'And I'm going to help you. But you've got to do something for us in return.'

'What?' asked Lam, leaping to his feet.

'Pay up.' Durn's voice lost every pretence of civility. It was a snarling, menace-laden demand, a growl bringing instantly to mind every terrible thing Durn could possibly do to Lam, if he didn't pay up.

Lam sank to his knees. He was skin and bones, his poverty was obvious, but he clearly realised he had no choice. He dragged himself over to the metal counter that ran along the wall and provided the room's only furniture, and pulled open one of the ill-fitting tin drawers wedged into its side. Durn saw him scoop his hand along the bottom of the drawer and instantly held out his own hand. Lam winced and dropped three credits into the bigger man's gloved palm. Three measly credits. It was nothing to the Union, but it was doubt-less all Lam was worth. The fact that he had paid up at all was enough to show Durn's mission had been a success.

'I won't be coming back,' said Durn, letting false hope well up in the sorry spectacle before him, 'but you'll be paying Goddlesby the same three credits extra each time he comes calling. He'll see it gets to us.'

Lam fell against the wall, sobbing, and Durn was on his way, smirking as he had seldom smirked before.

DURN'S EVIL SMIRK remained as he bowled through town, pushing his way through the crowds like the petulant bully he was. Lam had been easy, and Morten had protested little more and tried even harder to keep hold of his credits, while Dirk had given him the kind of murderous look to rival Durn's own, but it had been three easy scams in the end, just as Durn knew it would be. Nothing could dampen his wicked spirits. Nothing, that is, until he saw her.

Her. Scoosme, standing in the street, raging and stamping her feet at the bartender who blocked the door back into the Pipe Under Mile. She wasn't just try-ing to get in. It was all too obvious from her drunken slurring as she yelled that she had been there for some time already, and it didn't look like it had been her choice to leave. Oleg, the younger of the two bartenders that worked in the Pipe, held the doors barred firmly shut behind him as the stroppy girl flung herself against his chest, pounding his shoulders with her fists and trying desperately to squeeze past.

Durn wasn't close enough to make out every word of what she was saying, but the little he could pick out, coupled with the accusatory stabs of her finger made her meaning all too clear. Scoosme was one of the girls from the brothel, though Durn hadn't seen her there during the eviction. Drunk and bitter, she stood in the street railing at those amongst the settlement's inhabitants who had long made use of her services, only to turn their backs and feign ignorance as she was cast out. Durn shuddered and a terrible fear rose up inside him. Guilt, and then anger, replaced it soon enough.

Scoosme had a point. She was only in Fall Sands because the business was good and would have left long ago if so many of the locals hadn't been willing to indulge, as Durn knew all too well. But Ash Season was as lonely as it was long, and girls like Scoosme were an affordable comfort. It was little surprise the town offered such rich pickings.

As Durn drew nearer, her words became more audible, though no clearer, thanks to the drunken garble of her furious tirade. The bartender held her at arms length while Scoosme lunged forwards, yelling over his shoulder at the patrons inside.

'You've let them do this, you fraggin' idiots! They'll take every credit you've got,' she cried, pointing at the approaching Durn in his distinctive Cawdor robes. 'At least I gave you something in return, you bastards!' she yelled.

With that, the bartender had clearly had enough and pushed her away harder. Scoosme's drunken legs failed her as she tried to walk backwards and she stumbled, falling to the ground and rolling backwards, feet over head. She lay sprawled on the ground, much the worse for wear, as Durn passed.

He didn't notice her get to her feet. At least, not until she was right behind him, pounding her tiny little fists against his back. He turned and snatched at her wrists, pinning her arms together in front of her body. Durn was all set to fling her to the ground and carry on his way, until he looked into her eyes. She gazed back and he realised a terrible truth.

She recognised him.

How could she possibly recognise him, thought Durn? He had only ever gone there barefaced, so that no one would know who he was. Now, in the middle of the street, robed from head to toe with just his stubbled chin on show, how in the name of the Emperor could she have picked him out as one of the dozens of men who passed through her establishment every week? Every week for years, if Durn was honest, though he shuddered to think of how it was all catching up with him.

'You...' she hissed, and there was no escaping the fact that she recognised him, plain and simple. He prayed for a second that he had mistaken the look in her eyes, but there was no doubting it. She knew him instantly, and the name 'Caldus' – which he had always used as his alias when he was with her – formed on her lips. She broke one hand free of his grasp and struck at his face with her grubby hand, desperately trying to get hold of his mask.

'You, you're the worst of them, you fragging hypocrite,' she yelled.

He forced her hand away but didn't loosen his grip on her. He couldn't let her carry on in this state, not now that she knew who he was, and not now that she knew one of her clients was also one of the gang who had turfed her out of her premises that very morning!

Durn wrestled the girl down to the ground and dragged her to the narrow shaft opposite the Pipe Under Mile, an easy feat given her diminutive size and drunkenness. Rusted girders lined the shaft and Scoosme squealed as the sharp metal cut her bare feet. Durn let go his grip on her, letting her fall to the floor. He stood at the shaft's entrance, making quite sure she couldn't burst back out onto the street and continue her tirade.

'You bastard!' she yelled. 'You're one of them, and after all the times you've…'

Durn hurriedly shushed her, pushing his hand over her mouth, and she slumped drunkenly back against the wall of the shaft, clearly exhausted by her outburst.

'You won't get away with this,' she said, more calmly as Durn slowly removed his hand. 'I'm going to tell every single one of them just what you do, just how you like it and just what you–'

Durn dropped to his knees and thrust his gloved hand over the girl's mouth once more. She mumbled through it, but the sound was indistinct.

'Shut up,' said Durn, whispering in her ear. 'Emperor damn your lies. I'll kill you if you say such things again.' Some of the struggle seemed to go out of the little waif and Durn chanced to remove his hand from her mouth.

'What's the bigger sin, you coward? Killing a girl or paying her to–' she said with a crazy look in her eye before Durn's gloved palm once more silenced her.

'Once more, and I'll kill you right now,' he said. He felt her laugh a crazy drunken laugh as once more he dared to remove his glove.

'You won't,' she said, her voice barely a whisper, as if playing along with Durn's desperate plea for secrecy. 'You can't kill me with all these people watching.'

Durn turned his head slowly to peer over his shoulder. Damn the girl, she was right. Her earlier outburst hadn't gone unnoticed and a crowd now milled around outside the Pipe. They certainly wouldn't try to stop him, he was too feared for that, but Durn didn't exactly relish explaining to Lakatos why he was *seen* killing the little tramp or, rather, explaining why he had killed her at all.

'Go away,' he said, spitting the words as loud as he could without the crowd overhearing. 'Leave here.'

'Make me,' she said, laughing. 'Make me go away.'

Durn ground his teeth together, but he knew there was no other way. He thrust his hand into his pocket and pulled out the credits he had scammed from Lam, Dirk and Morten. He looked down at the tokens in his hand, knowing he would regret it, but thrust them at Scoosme all the same. He had no choice.

'Now leave,' he said, 'and if you ever come back, I will kill you.'

With that, he pushed past her and walked further down the shaft, deciding it best he return to the gang-house by another route entirely.

DURN TOOK AN age making his way back. He dallied at every opportunity, wracked his brains endlessly for a way to make the credits back and present them to Lakatos so that no one would ever know he'd bought off that little hussy to ensure her silence. He thought about shaking down some of the other townsfolk, extorting yet more credits from them to cover his earlier indiscretion, but he didn't really have dirt on any of the others to guarantee their compliance. He wasn't afraid of them fighting back, but one of them might just have enough spine to speak out against the excessive taxes, and he was in no mood to explain to Lakatos exactly why he was re-taxing the townsfolk.

He was so lost in his troubled thoughts that he hardly noticed when he had reached the Union's hide-out and, his heart pounding with fear, he stepped inside. Lakatos was in his 'throne' – the worn stone trough in the corner – and Durn unleashed a deep sigh as he stepped in.

'Done?' asked Lakatos.

'Done,' said Durn.

'No problems?' asked Lakatos.

'No problems,' said Durn. 'They'll be paying God-dlesby the extra every week, just like you said.' Durn toyed with the idea of telling Lakatos that he hadn't collected any 'back-taxes', that he didn't realise that was what Lakatos meant, but in the end he decided acting stupid probably wasn't the best bet.

At that instant, a voice rang out from the doorway behind him, the voice of a saint.

'You better listen up, Lakatos,' said Jurgen, striding into the room full of purpose with a rather bedraggled looking Lirbus in tow. 'It's all gone down,' said Jurgen, 'and it's not good, not good at all.'

Lakatos leapt to his feet and paced across the room, stopping face to face with Jurgen. Durn couldn't believe his luck. Lakatos was engrossed, and Durn's mission and the expected profits were all but forgotten. Both Lakatos and Durn listened intently as Jurgen began one of the most horrifying tales Durn had ever heard.

'ALL OF THEM?' asked Lakatos, clearly disbelieving Jurgen's frantic account.

'All of them,' said Jurgen, sternly. 'You're lucky I heard the ruckus, or you could add Lirbus here to that tally.'

He was right. Lirbus's tale had been no less harrowing either, thought Durn.

Durn had never heard anything like it: how Deveres got lost in the storms, how Jurgen found Handomel's

gang, the Scarlet Skulls, dead to a man and fled as fast
as he could, only to run right into the gunfight at Bok's.
Durn had spent most of the week in the hideout and he
hadn't seen hide nor hair of Deveres since he set out.
He wasn't back yet and, though no one dared say it, it
was plain he wasn't coming back. There was no point
looking for him, either.

'Damn it, damn it, damn it,' said Lakatos, his voice rising as his anger grew. He slammed his fist into the wall
next to him and paced back and forth.

Durn was sure Lakatos was going to explode when Jurgen suggested that some of the Scarlet Skulls might have
killed each other in a leadership challenge. This certainly
angered Lakatos, but he seemed to find the suggestion
sadly predictable.

Durn had listened to Jurgen and Lirbus's earnest
accounts, all the while expecting Lakatos to smash them
down at any second, to blame them for the catastrophe,
but he seemed more ready to criticise the dead men for
their idiocy. This surprised Durn greatly. Perhaps his own
indiscretion would receive the same leniency, if ever
uncovered. Slim hope, he told himself.

Lakatos continued to pace back and forth. No one
dared speak, not even the outlander, while their leader
racked his brains for what to do next.

'Addec needs to know,' he said. 'If the Skulls are gone, he
needs to take their territory and quickly, else he's unprotected. Someone has to tell Addec,' said Lakatos. 'Durn, go
to Addec; tell him what happened. Tell him he has to capture Handomel's territory, *now*.'

Durn wasted no time in following his leader's orders,
ducking out of the door and making good his departure,
or rather his escape. If the matter of the newly raised taxes
hadn't been forgotten already, it surely was now, and with
Addec's place three days travel away, there was no way it
would ever be remembered by the time Durn returned.

He had gotten away with it, he thought to himself as he dashed away from the hideout. He had gotten away with everything.

HE'D HAD just about enough for one day. The taxes were an unexpected chore and the meeting with Scoosme was an unexpected problem. Durn had gotten away without his philandering or his pilfering being uncovered but he was thoroughly exhausted by the whole thing.

He couldn't get out of the ganghouse quickly enough with the guilty memory of Scoosme and those missing credits racing through his mind. Despite that, he could do without the effort, and obvious danger, of venturing out in the storms.

Durn, though, was no native of this cesspit, the Underhive's most miserable depth. He was Hive City born and venturing this far down required the use of a dozen ancient routes with their myriad turns and doublings.

For creatures pitiful enough to be born in this lowly pit, crossing the derelict domes, which bore the worst of the storm's fury, must have seemed like the only way, but Durn was not convinced. He was sure that he could find another route, crossing the hive at a higher level in domes that were free of the Ash Season's tyranny before descending into Addec's territory by means of the high vents, of which Fulcrum Spike formed the base.

He ascended the ladder at the rear of the ganghouse, first reaching its roofless second storey, which he was forced to ascend by means of its protruding window frames. Then he trod his way carefully along the crumbling wall's top edge, bringing himself to the neighbouring building where a solid ladder allowed him to ascend in safety once more.

Three more storeys and he left the ladder to cross a broad, if not entirely stable walkway, which crossed the

settlement's main 'street'. In fact, this street was nothing
more than an agglomeration of ash, dirt and rubble
piled so deep that it had buried the floor of the dome
and its lower storeys entirely, creating a flat, even surface where in fact it should be the same irregular,
haphazard mix of walkways, beams and ladders as were
found at greater heights. Solid ground was something
Underhivers rightly feared – being found naturally only
out in the deadly ash wastes – and Fall Sands's pretence
of it did much to add to its reputation as a place to
avoid.

From this height, the falseness of the 'floor' was
apparent, and Durn could clearly see that the apparent
first storey of buildings, like Jurgen's hideout and the
ganghouse, were in actuality the seventh or eighth
storeys of this lost generation of buildings for which
the dome was constructed.

The thought of it caused Durn to cast his mind back
to Jurgen and his peculiar choice of hideout. Jurgen
had picked the building for its location, saying his
work required certain conditions like the right ventilation. Durn wondered whether these 'conditions'
included underground rooms where complete darkness could be found. It seemed a reasonable enough
idea and Durn well knew that the brothel was one of
the few buildings in Fall Sands that still possessed an
accessible lower, now subterranean, floor. The likes of
the ganghouse had become flooded at lower levels with
the same tide of detritus that gave the dome its dusty
streets, but a handful of buildings had been in sufficiently good repair to resist the filth's incursion and so
came to possess labyrinths leading down to what was
once ground level. Perhaps this was why Jurgen so
prized that particular building. The Emperor knew its
basement had once been Durn's favourite part of the
building, too.

Without thinking, Durn cast his gaze down towards the street in general and the brothel in particular. His heart froze in terror.

Scoosme crossed the street, a heavy iron bar in her hand, heading straight for her former place of employment.

The crazy bitch just wasn't going to let it lie and Durn had no choice. Fortunately, getting down was much quicker than getting up. He dashed to the walkway's edge where a small, but nonetheless dangerous leap brought him to a platform pinned against the uppermost reaches of the same pipe that, at the dome's floor, contained the Pipe Under Mile. Here, a tangle of other pipes and conduits, mostly no thicker than a man's arm, ran down the outside of the much larger 'Pipe'. Durn wrapped his legs around the nearest one, crossed them at the ankles and grabbed the pipe with both hands as he began his perilous descent.

His gloves allowed him to slow his slide before he let go his grip and dropped the last couple of metres onto the corrugated iron sheet. It butted out from the side of the pipe, forming a roof for one of the many ramshackle, temporary outhouses that constituted the Pipe Under Mile's guest quarters.

A few astonished gasps from below did nothing to slow Durn as he plunged from the roof and dashed down the street, staying out of sight thanks to the tangled maze of structures that extended outwards from the base of the pipe.

It took Durn a moment to spot Scoosme, but he found her easily enough. She marched up the tiny alley alongside the former brothel, iron bar still in hand. Durn slunk through the shadows behind her and edged to the alley's entrance, peering round cautiously.

Ahead of him, Scoosme wedged the iron bar into the rusted up wheel in the centre of the building's back door. The wheel clearly hadn't been turned in years, but with the bar for leverage, the girl's tiny form had just enough force to budge it. A few minutes more strenuous heaving at it, and the back door was open. Scoosme pulled the iron bar clear of the wheel and strode in, looking just as angry as she had been when Durn first saw her, perhaps an hour earlier.

He waited a moment after she disappeared inside and then slipped out from his hiding place. Half-crouching as he ran down the alley, Durn slipped inside the wide open door. He'd always known that he would have to deal with Scoosme sooner or later, and it looked like she had just made it an awful lot easier for him.

CHAPTER: NINE

'WHAT THE...?' SCOOSME pushed at the door but it didn't budge. She stepped back and gazed up the wall above, though she couldn't make out anything untoward. One more push and, with no further luck, she banged her palm hard against the door several times, yelling out in between thuds.

'Lenka! Lenka!' No reply came. 'Banya! Gully... Morla?' Scoosme's voice faded from a powerful yell to a confused, hopeless mutter as she called out the names of the other girls. No reply.

She looked around for some clue as to what had happened to them, but there was nothing. She followed the wall to the corner and turned down the narrow alley that ran alongside the building, though she knew full well that the door on that side had been locked for years.

'Step away,' came a voice from behind her. She turned to see two cloaked and hooded figures standing at the street's edge: Cawdor.

'Step away,' the taller of the two repeated. 'This is our territory now,' he said.

'What?' asked Scoosme. 'What do you mean?'

'We already turfed your friends out and we made quite a mess of them, too,' said the shorter one, walking slowly towards her as he spoke. He was far smaller than the other Cawdor – shorter than Scoosme herself in fact – but he had a vicious, sinister sneer that suggested a soulless, hateful wickedness deep inside him. Scoosme was afraid of him in a way she wasn't normally afraid of any man.

'Don't make us do the same to you,' said the wicked little man.

Scoosme gave a moment's thought to making a dash for the door and seeing if she could get inside. The second Cawdor, further back on the street, drew his pistol and gave her good reason to drop the idea. Still far from sure what had happened in the days she had been absent, Scoosme shuffled back towards the street, feeling a hint of revulsion as she wriggled past the sinister little man who sneered and leched at her all the way. She stepped out into the street and slowly ambled off, turning and looking back every few steps, uncertain and desperately scared for her friends.

FOR THE LIFE of her, Scoosme couldn't fathom why the Cawdor had ordered her and the girls out of their modest little place. As she knocked back her fourth Wildsnake in quick succession, she wasn't getting any closer to working it out, either. It had been like this all day since dragging herself into the Pipe Under Mile after those two robed thugs had turned her away from her former home-cum-workplace.

Sure the Cawdor despised fornication in all its forms, but they were smarter than to openly attack its purveyors. Half the dens in the Underhive were operated by guilders anyway, and those that weren't were obliged to provide the guilders with any hospitality they desired free of charge, just like everything else in the Underhive. With the guilders involved, everyone just turned a blind eye to such things. Sin was, after all, simply too profitable to be prevented.

Everyone knew House Cawdor was in thrall to the Redemption, but its members were careful never to make such an allegiance obvious. Cawdor was a respectable House, a bastion of Hive City, but the Redemption was banned and its members outlawed, and there was but a fine line dividing the two. No Cawdor wanted to cross it. Attacking a brothel so blatantly would probably serve to do just that.

Besides, if the Union was on some kind of moral crusade, Scoosme was sure they would have made much more of a point of it. As it was, she had simply been thrown out into the street with not so much as a judgement passed on her profession.

All the Cawdor seemed to be after was the building, but as Scoosme knocked back her sixth Wildsnake, even that didn't make sense. They couldn't want the building for their hideout; it was right in the middle of town and would be useless for that. Everyone knew the Union was holed up on the edge of town, right atop the only reliable route into and out of the dome, exactly where they needed to be to keep their iron grip on Fall Sands.

There were other ways in, but not without knowing the intricacies of the derelict tunnels and vents that lined the dome. Scoosme had found her way through these very tunnels when she first came to Fall Sands, by accident as much as anything, and she doubted greatly that any rival gang would manage to traverse them. No, the Union was best off where it was, guarding their only flank, and besides, when she found the brothel it had been all but deserted. The gangers would have been all over the place if they'd taken it for a hideout.

The seventh and eighth Wildsnakes offered few answers and, as Scoosme sat in the Pipe Under Mile

growing increasingly bitter and angry, she was left
with only more questions. After the ninth, tenth and
eleventh Wildsnakes, Scoosme thought that it might
be a good idea to ask her questions out loud.

'Do you know who I am?' she yelled at the wrinkled woman behind the bar.

'Excuse me?' the woman replied.

'Do you know who I am?' Scoosme repeated. 'He
does,' she said, jabbing a half empty Wildsnake bottle in the direction of the bartender. The woman –
his wife – snorted and turned to face her husband,
one eyebrow raised quizzically.

'Ask him,' said Scoosme, not willing to let it lie.
'Ask him who I am and ask him what I do,' she continued. 'He knows. They all do. Bastards.' She swept
her arm in a wide arc, casting an accusatory hand at
virtually everyone in the watering hole, and then
promptly fell off her stool. They hardly even looked
up anymore. Virtually everyone in the place had
heard Scoosme engage in this exact same rant many
times before. This was always how it started, and
pretty much how it ended, too.

'That's enough,' yelled the bartender, dashing out
from behind the bar to silence Scoosme before she
could reveal any more of his little indiscretions to
his wife. He scooped her up from under the arms
and dragged her to the door. Scoosme was not
unconscious and regained her feet somewhat as he
dragged her. As they reached the door, she had
enough of her senses about her to fling her arms out
wide, holding on to the doorframe, refusing to leave,
making it almost impossible for the bartender to
make her.

'You know,' she slurred as she struggled to keep her
grip on the doorframe. 'You all know. You do, Jeb,
you know,' she yelled, pointing an accusatory finger

at one of the bar's older patrons, and that was her undoing.

'*You* know, Deak.'

With her hand raised to point at another hapless passer-by, she relinquished her grip on the doorframe and the irate bartender at last succeeded in barrelling her out onto the street.

She landed in a crumpled pile on her knees, but she was full of the unnatural energy of one drunk on Wildsnake. She leapt to her feet and dashed back towards the Pipe's still swinging door.

Inside, the bartender glanced over his shoulder and saw her coming. Before she could reach the door he was back outside, his stanchion-like arms pinned across the doorway. She crashed into him as she ran and he grabbed at her, pushing her away as she desperately tried to wriggle past and get back into the Pipe.

Scoosme knew how drunk she was. She yelled curses from deep within her subconscious and even her own brain registered little of what she said. She was lost in a haze of anger and hate. She bawled through the Pipe's door. As nonsensical as her drunken wails might have been, the accusatory stabs of her finger made her meaning all too clear. Drunk, bitter and angry she stood in the street railing at those amongst the settlement's inhabitants who had long made use of her services, only to turn their backs and feign ignorance as she was cast out. She could see the guilt and fear on all their faces as she railed on.

They all owed Scoosme, she decided, and she wasn't going to let them forget it. She was only in Fall Sands because the business was so good. She would have left long ago if so many of the locals hadn't been willing to indulge, as those sorry fools feigning ignorance in the Pipe knew all too well.

And yet, when she had needed something, they had all turned their backs. They had left their sins at home, while her home was taken from her. She railed at their indifference, their abandonment, and their betrayal. That's what they had done, she thought. They had all betrayed her, and she was going to tell them so.

'You've let them do this, you fraggin' idiots! They'll take every credit you've got,' she cried.

The stupid bartender, Oleg, held her at arms length while she lunged forwards, yelling over his shoulder at the patrons inside. He flung her back a little, and the jolt turned her head. She gazed down the street. Up ahead, a figure approached, garbed from head to foot in his distinctive Cawdor robes. She pointed yet another jabbing digit at the approaching ganger and continued her ranting.

'At least I gave you something in return, you bastards!' she yelled.

With that, the bartender had clearly had enough and pushed her away harder. Scoosme's drunken legs failed her as she tried to walk backwards and she stumbled, falling to the ground and rolling backwards, feet over head. She lay sprawled on the ground, feeling much the worse for wear, as a long shadow fell over her.

The Cawdor, she thought, and suddenly her strength returned. Righteous anger wasn't the sole preserve of the Redemption and she had plenty.

The Cawdor ignored her and the shadow he cast moved quickly away as she scrambled to her feet. He didn't notice her, or pretended not to, until she was right behind him, pounding her tiny little fists against his back. Now she had his attention.

He turned and snatched at her wrists, pinning her arms together in front of her body. She suddenly realised how much larger and stronger he was than her, and realised, too, that she had absolutely no idea what to do next. She struggled in his grip and stared him right in the eyes, her lips getting ready to spit in the bastard's face.

She stopped suddenly. She stared him straight in the eyes and she realised something extraordinary.

She recognised him.

His face was covered by one of those ridiculous masks the Cawdor always wore, but it was him nonetheless. He was robed from head to toe with just his stubbled chin on show, but she couldn't fail to pick him out as one of the dozens of men who passed through her establishment every week. Every week for years, come to think of it. This was one of her most regular visitors, and she simply couldn't fail to recognise him.

'You...' she hissed, struggling to bring a name from her mind. She thought for a second that perhaps she had been mistaken, but as his eyes opened wide in terror, there was no doubting it. She knew him instantly, and now the name came to her.

'Caldus,' she said, though in truth the word had barely formed on her lips before her speech descended into another bout of drunken shrieking. She screamed madly as she renewed her ineffectual assault on him.

She broke one hand free of his grasp and struck at his face with her grubby hand, desperately trying to get hold of his mask.

'You, you're the worst of them, you fragging hypocrite,' she yelled.

Caldus forced her hand away but didn't loosen his grip on her. She couldn't break free of his powerful hold, but she wasn't going to give up. She wasn't going to let him get away with it; not now that she knew one of her clients was also one of the gang who had turfed her out of her premises!

Scoosme kicked and screamed as Caldus wrestled her to the ground and dragged her to the narrow shaft opposite the Pipe Under Mile. She could do little to fight back given her diminutive size and drunkenness. Rusted girders lined the shaft and Scoosme squealed as the sharp metal cut her bare feet. Caldus let go his grip on her, letting her fall to the floor. Scoosme leapt at once to her feet, dashing back towards the street, but Caldus stood at the shaft's entrance, making quite sure that she had no way out.

'You bastard,' she yelled. 'You're one of them, and after all the times you've...'

The Cawdor hurriedly shushed her, pushing his hand over her mouth, and she slumped drunkenly back against the wall of the shaft, exhausted by her outburst. She hardly cared what happened now.

'You won't get away with this,' Scoosme said, more calmly as the man slowly removed his hand. 'I'm going to tell every single one of them just what you do, just how you like it and just what you–'

At this, the Cawdor dropped to his knees and thrust his gloved hand over Scoosme's mouth once more. She mumbled through it, but doubted anyone could hear her.

'Shut up,' Caldus said, whispering in her ear. She could smell his breath as he did so and she was more convinced than ever that it really was Caldus, or whatever his real name might be. 'Emperor damn your lies. I'll kill you if you say such things again.'

The struggle went out of Scoosme and she relaxed her tense, aching muscles. She remained still and quiet for a moment and sure enough the man removed his hand from her mouth, but Scoosme wasn't done yet.

'What's the bigger sin, you coward? Killing a girl or paying her to–' she said with a crazy look in her eye. Almost instantly, his gloved palm muffled her voice again.

'Once more, and I'll kill you right now,' he said.

Scoosme unleashed a crazy drunken laugh. That didn't scare her, not anymore. She continued to laugh and Caldus once more dared to remove his glove.

'You won't,' she said, her voice barely a whisper, playing along with his desperate plea for secrecy. 'You can't kill me with all these people watching.'

The man turned his head slowly and peered over his shoulder. Scoosme giggled as he at last saw what she had been looking at the whole time. Her earlier outburst hadn't gone unnoticed and a crowd now milled around outside the Pipe, staring straight at the burly Cawdor and scrawny girl scrapping in the shadows.

She knew the crowd wouldn't try to stop him, they were all too terrified of the Union for that, but she gambled that he couldn't be seen killing her. That would leave too much explaining for him to do, not least to his own saintly masters, she thought. They might not care a jot for her life, but they would have precious little mercy for one of their own using one sin to cover another. She giggled as the man cursed and thumped his fist against the wall of the alley. He had clearly come to the same realisation.

'Go away,' he said, spitting the words as loud as he could without the crowd overhearing. 'Leave here.'

'Make me,' she said, laughing. 'Make me go away.'

With that, 'Caldus' thrust his hand in his pocket and pulled out a handful of credits. He hurled them at Scoosme.

'Now leave,' he said, 'and if you ever come back, I will kill you.'

With that, he pushed past her and walked further down the shaft, clearly thinking it best to avoid the gathering

crowd. Scoosme just lay back on the girder beneath her
and laughed her crazy, drunken laugh.

DERGEN RECK RAN the kind of trading post that every
dreary, hopeless little settlement this deep in the
Underhive seemed afflicted with. It was a ramshackle
little heap. The kind of place apparently stocked with
everything except what you wanted. Its sole selling
point was that it catered to those unable to afford
Bok's rather more varied and reliable wares sold from
his shack on the edge of town.

Reck's wares could hardly be described as new, but
they could hardly be described as old either. Useless,
busted or trashed would be more fitting descriptions
for the vast majority of Reck's stock. An array of pistols was on the table nearest the door, each had the
wrong kind of bullets helpfully laid out next to it, in
a vain attempt to disguise the fact that Dergen's collection of pistols seldom complemented his supply of
bullets. The sharpened shards of scrap metal that pop-
ulated Dergen's prize 'knife rack' – which was what he
called the slab of resin into which they were all
stabbed – and the free homemade sheaths with which
each came, were all so shabbily made as to virtually
guarantee injury to the user should he be fool enough
to actually try and wear one.

Least promising of all was the collection of 'Rare
Items and Specialities' that littered the counter: the
much vaunted bionic eye with its ominous offer of
'free installation'; the 'reconditioned' grapnel with its
snapped cable hastily tied into a cumbersome knot
halfway down; and the 'master-crafted', one-of-a-kind,
archeotech hand-flamer. Its fuel canister bore an
uncanny similarity to the seltzer bottle that had mysteriously gone missing from the Pipe Under Mile some
weeks earlier.

Scoosme wondered how a hopeless little shack like this kept its roof on, let alone stayed in business. In truth, she knew full well that Reck survived by selling weapons to hopeless wretches like herself.

Scoosme perused the pistols on the table, if perused meant picking up and looking at items which one had no idea how to use. The first one she picked up was heavy to the point that she almost dropped it. The second one, well, she could hardly tell which end was which and thought it best to return it quickly to the table, nervously lying it on its side to make sure *both* ends were pointing away from her. The next was more promising: a little stub gun. She'd seen one like it before. Lenka used to carry one, and it was the only kind of gun she had ever held in her own hands. This one was similarly dainty, though not nearly so clean and shiny as Lenka's cherished 'special' had been.

Nonetheless, she found its similarity reassuring – that, and the fact that stub guns could fire virtually any bullet you could cram into the chamber, making Dergen's idiosyncratic stock-keeping less of a problem. Besides, she only needed one bullet. Well, maybe six just to make sure she wasn't squeezing on the wrong chamber. She picked up the stubber and spun it open.

Beside its resting place on the table was a pile of bullets: a particularly ill-matched mix of shapes and sizes. She went through the pile, one bullet at a time, checking their fit into the gun's chambers and, when she had a bullet safely nestled in each of the six, she strolled out of the shop, loaded stub gun precariously in hand.

DERGEN WAS NOT foolish to sit behind the counter, or indeed in his own shop. Most weeks, at least one passing imbecile would request a test firing, invariably inside the shop's four shaky walls. As a result, Dergen was always to be found perched on an ammo crate outside, taking payment from those who left the shop alive.

Scoosme strolled up to him, waving the pistol with ill-advised nonchalance.

'How will you be paying for it?' asked the toothless old trader, a seedy twinkle flashing across his foggy, cataract-grey eyes.

A disappointed sulk spread across his face as Scoosme dumped a handful of credits onto the chest beside him. She gave a disgusted *humph*, turned on her heel and marched off down the street. As she reached the corner, she whipped her skirt up to the thigh and jabbed the little pistol into her suspenders. It was hardly necessary to hide the weapon, but she had left the old man two credits short, after all.

Scoosme crossed the street and walked calmly past the Pipe Under Mile. As she passed the grate on the door, the bartender caught sight of her and dashed forwards to intercept her. She didn't enter, though, she just blew the man a kiss and passed on by.

Fools, the lot of them, thought Scoosme.

The Pipe's collection of ramshackle outbuildings – at least half of them had collapsed – provided fine pickings for any scavenger and so Scoosme stopped to rummage through the nearest heap of rubble, quickly finding a twisted old iron shank that would be just perfect for the job at hand.

She scurried down the alley, right up to the rusted metal door at its end. It was part of the same building as the brothel, though exactly which room was behind it, Scoosme couldn't be sure. No one had used this particular entrance in living memory.

The door itself was large, very large. It had no handle but was instead operated by means of a wheel in its centre. Pistons and bolted arms ran over its rusted, grey metal surface, connecting to the wheel at the door's centre so that by turning it pressure might be relieved and the door unlocked.

Scoosme already knew she had no hope of opening the door by hand, and so instead thrust the iron bar down behind the rail that ran around the wheel's outer edge. She jammed it sideways so that the bar rested against one of the many winding handles running round the wheel's circumference. In this way, the bar formed a solid lever at right angles to the wheel itself.

She pushed hard against the bar but it didn't budge an inch. Another good push and the winding handle tore clean off the door, sending the metal bar tumbling to the floor and Scoosme with it. She shrieked as she stumbled but was not perturbed. Dusting herself off, Scoosme again thrust the bar into the wheel, butting it against the next winding handle down. By chance this second choice actually seemed to be a better angle and Scoosme was able to put all her weight over the bar, pushing right down on it.

Fortunately, this second winding handle was not riddled with the rust that had torn the first from its bearings and, with the bar pressed down hard on it, the handle drove the wheel ever so slowly clockwise, away from the frantically straining Scoosme. Flakes of rust fell away from the wheel as it ground slowly round and it seemed for a moment as though the whole thing might simply canker and fall away like so much crushed rubble.

She managed a full half turn before trying to push the door itself. Nothing. She persevered with the metal bar, though having turned the wheel almost two-thirds of a rotation caused the angle to be awkward. Scoosme was forced to position herself behind the wheel, on the opposite side to the iron bar and, with her feet and back wedged squarely in the door's frame, she continued to pull, rather than pushing on the metal bar, using every ounce of her little weight to drag the iron bar agonisingly past the upright position.

At last it came and the iron bar fell away, coming loose as the wheel reached a full turn. It was sufficiently loose that Scoosme could turn it herself, using the winding handles at its edge. Dropping to the floor from her precarious perch between the jambs, she did just that, and in a moment the heavy girders, locking pistons and plated hinges that covered the door began to creak and grind to life.

A second later and Scoosme was forced to leap back out of the way. Quite to her surprise the door did not open outwards but upwards and, with the wheel loose enough for it to do so, the whole thing lifted up in an eerie levitation.

The building alongside – one of the Pipe's derelict outbuildings – had clearly been built in the long years since this wheeled door last opened. The door rose up when opened, but its edge jammed hard against the neighbouring building before it could even become horizontal. Having slumbered so long, the heavy mechanisms of its lock were in little mood to give up now, and the force drove the adamantium door right into the masonry of the outbuilding next to it, carving a rut almost a metre long out of the building's wall. At last, though, the outbuilding's structure proved too much and the door froze, less than fully open, stuck in place against the wall. With its uppermost edge buried in the plascrete of the outbuilding, the door was as firmly jammed open as it had been jammed shut minutes earlier.

Scoosme cursed, not because the door was only partly open – its vast size meant that even half-open it formed a perfectly adequate entrance – but because she had intended to close it behind her. Scoosme could do without drawing attention to her little reclamation attempt, and leaving the door open would do that. She cursed again but could do nothing more about it and cautiously hopped over the door's raised lip and into her former residence.

The room she entered was not really a room at all. Its walls were entirely metal, seamless and airtight, and barely three metres ahead there was a second metal door identical to the one she had just come through. This one, mercifully, was caved in, hanging awkwardly through the doorway itself, as if sucked through by some unbelievable pressure. In fact, it probably had been, for two airtight doors so close together could only mean an airlock for access to whatever volatile substances the building had once been used to cultivate, harvest, or process.

She'd seen something like it before, near the sump, where such chambers could occasionally be found to still contain their precious chemical treasures. Extracting them was tricky, though, and when Scoosme used to prowl the explorator's shacks along the sump's edge she more than once heard tell of foolhardy prospectors sucked to their doom by incautiously breaking the seal on such airtight containers. They would be stripped to the bone by a rushing torrent of chemical filth from within, released by the colossal pressures built up inside over centuries of ill-maintained containment.

She shuddered to think that such dangers could lurk even here in Fall Sands, though on reflection there was no reason why they shouldn't and she merely offered thanks for finding this particular container cracked, empty and entirely harmless.

Scoosme passed through the second, cracked door and found herself on a high gantry that ran along all four walls of a perfectly square, high-ceilinged room. Beneath the gantry, the room was full of ash. Clearly this had once been some store or silo, and the gantry was used for inspection and access. She had never been in this part of the place before. In the depths of the building, some bleed or run-off pipe must be cracked open, thought Scoosme, allowing the whole system to fill with ash and creating this curious dusty reservoir over which she now stood.

The ash rose up to just a metre or so below the gantry, presumably level with the street outside. Here, though, without the hundreds of feet pounding daily over it, the ash was not nearly so compacted and its fine flakes moved almost like liquid in a pool. Waves and ripples cavorted over the ash reservoir's surface, occasionally spitting puffs of ash up into the air as gas from the decrepit pipes below finally wriggled its way free at the surface. It was all rather disorienting, and Scoosme hurried down the gantry along the wall and out of the room at the other side.

As she entered the next room, Scoosme heard a heavy thud behind her. She halted and her hand shot down to her thigh where the stub gun nestled against her leg. She considered drawing it and then banished such thoughts. The door by which she had entered hadn't been opened in decades and, Scoosme told herself, the first few gusts of wind to pass this way in so long would surely cause a little noise. The door's locking and opening mechanism probably hadn't completely given up the fight either, and Scoosme reassured herself that the noise was almost certainly just some crank still clunking uneasily against the jammed door. The ash pool, likewise, had a curious life to it: foaming, spitting and frothing, and offered up a few eerie sounds of its own. With this in mind, Scoosme was quite sure that she was alone, and the noise was nothing more sinister than the cacophony of decay.

This new room was small and offered only two exits, neither of them doors. A ladder led upwards on the wall to the left, while opposite that a small ventilation shaft was set into the wall. The shaft was too dark to see down, but a waft of familiar scent made Scoosme certain of her bearings. She was behind the rooms proper: the rooms that she had known in her time in the building, and the shaft led directly to one of the living rooms off the corridor leading from the front door.

Scoosme wandered over to the shaft. The creepy noises still coming from the rooms behind her frayed her nerves, no matter how much she told herself that no one was there, and so she cast a quick glance over her shoulder before flinging her arms up and hauling herself into the ventilation shaft.

The shaft was surprisingly clean. The gentle breeze that perpetually drifted through it allowed less ash to settle here than elsewhere and Scoosme dragged herself along without difficulty. A few more minutes and she emerged into a familiar room at last.

The bar, or what passed for it in an establishment like this. Tall metal urns mounted on the wall had been used to ferment all manner of noxious house specials, though Scoosme now realised that they once must have acted as release vats for whatever chemical soup had lain in the reservoir before the ash came. Suddenly the taste of the house cocktails she drank day and night to numb the mind was a little less appealing.

The urns were bereft of liquor now, though they were not disused. What had once housed Scoosme's noxious cocktails now contained a concoction of an entirely different kind. The urn nearest the ventilation shaft contained an inky black mixture, much thicker than water and surprisingly cool to the touch. The next urn held a liquid of the same consistency, though it was bright red in colour. The other urns each held similar formulations, varying in colour and occasionally consistency.

Scoosme dipped her finger in the farthest urn as she glided through the room. It was the consistency of water and she thought for a time it might be drinkable, though placing her finger on her tongue she discovered the liquid was not nearly rank enough to pass for drinkable liquor. She spat on the floor and wiped the rest of the muck off on her dress. It dried as it touched the cloth and, although deep brown in the urn, the liquid's colour faded, lightening almost to the colour of her dress. Indeed, if it wasn't for the fact that the liquid made hard patches on the supple cloth, it would have been entirely invisible once dry.

She stole on through the room and out into the main corridor. At last her ears picked up on a definite sound above her and up the stairs. Scoosme pulled the pistol from its hiding place and sneaked slowly up the metal stairs towards what had been her and the other girls' boudoirs.

Nearing the top of the stairs she gazed straight ahead into the first room. She held the pistol out in front of her and inched through the door. It was empty except for a number of pieces of tattered parchment hanging from wires that were crisscrossing the ceiling. Most appeared blank, except the parchments on the foremost wire, all of them bearing lines of still-wet black ink on their surfaces. Scoosme couldn't read, however, and could make out nothing more than this.

She shuffled back out of the door, turning into the long corridor that ran right to the front of the building with care not to reveal herself too quickly. Rooms lined the right hand side of the corridor while the left simply continued on from the metal staircase by which she had come up.

She passed the doorway of the next room on the right. It was dark and empty and so she gracefully sidled down the corridor towards the sound of what was now the only noise she could hear – a faint, wispy scratching sound accompanied by movement. The next room down the corridor, Lenka's room, was also empty, and the sound grew louder as Scoosme continued on down the hall.

The fourth room yielded what Scoosme had been looking for: the outlander. She saw him as she nervously peered round the doorframe. He sat at a large table in the middle of the room, facing away from her. His shoulders were hunched over as he worked at something in front of him on the table. The scratching noise broke off as the outlander raised his left hand and brought it inadvertently into sight. In that hand he held a long stylus mounted on a metal arm attached to the desk. Miniscule cogs in the arm whirred as the outlander guided the stylus away from his body and dipped its tip into a pot of black liquid beside him: the same liquid Scoosme had seen in the urns downstairs.

The outlander returned the stylus to its place in front of him and the scratching noise resumed. Noise enough, thought Scoosme, for her to make her move.

She tiptoed into the room, her bare feet padding softly on the grimy floor, the pistol held out in front of her. She got to within a metre of the outlander when he seemed to sense something and raised his head. No matter. She was close enough.

'Bastard,' she yelled, aiming the gun straight at the back of his head.

He showed no panic. The outlander calmly rose from his seat and turned to face her, moving sufficiently slowly so as to show no threat, and seeming completely unfazed.

'What do you want?' he asked calmly. His voice had poise and measure of a sort seldom heard in the Underhive. Scoosme had heard voices like it before, though; she was sure of it.

'I want you out,' she said. 'This is my place: mine and the girls'. Get out.'

The outlander seemed to smirk a little and Scoosme's finger tightened round the trigger, suddenly afraid he had something up his sleeve.

'It won't do you any good,' he said. Whatever game he was playing, he was winning and Scoosme could feel her courage ebbing away.

'What do you mean?' she asked timidly.

'This place. Being here will do no good. It'll be better if you leave, I promise you that,' he said.

'You don't scare me,' she said, half-lying. 'Not you and not those Union thugs. Damn 'em all to hell, they don't scare me!' She waved the pistol threateningly but the outlander didn't flinch.

'So shoot me,' he said, and at last she could place it; his voice, his peculiar accent. There was only one other she knew like it, and that was Morla's. She'd never known where Morla was from, or why she spoke the way she did, but her speech had always had a power to it. It was like a well-crafted weapon in its way, and there was only one place in the hive where the tongue was a weapon. That certainly wasn't Fall Sands and yet the outlander spoke in that same measured tone that sounded at once both wise and cruel.

'Go on, shoot me. That'll show them you're not afraid,' he said. Scoosme stared into his eyes – both real and bionic – but his gaze was almost too vexing to bear. Then she realised with horror that he wasn't looking at her at all, but right past her shoulder. He was staring past her shoulder at something, or *someone*…

Oh frag, she thought, as a gloved hand clamped down over her mouth and she felt the cold steel of a dagger pressed to her throat.

CHAPTER: TEN

LIRBUS HATED SENTRY duty, especially sentry duty on the front door. No one would ever be stupid enough to attack the front door, so what was the point of posting sentries there? At least on the other sentry posts you had something to do. It had been months since anyone seriously threatened the Union, but before that, sentry duty had at least offered a few good shootouts. Even now, sentry duty on the more distant posts at least offered the opportunity to loose pot shots down into the crowds of townsfolk to keep them on their toes. Not so on the front frikking door.

Worse still was the fact that Lirbus was assigned sentry duty on the front door with Erket. Juves were bad enough; Erket was the worst. Lirbus had met humble juves – the kind so eager to please you quickly wished they weren't – and he'd also met cowardly juves. He could live with either of them since both did as he told them.

Erket was a gobby little runt, owner of an ego inversely proportioned to its owner. He never let his gun down once the whole time he was on sentry duty, his scowl always just a little too serious, his grip on the pistol just a little too tight, his posture keeping it just a little too close to his crotch. All of this gave Lirbus ample reason to dislike Erket. Everything else Erket did gave Lirbus reason to distrust him, as well as dislike him.

It wasn't long before Erket seemed to have another urge to show off his weapons. He continued to cradle his pistol in one hand, but now drew his knife and held it upright, clenching it in his left hand. He sat rigidly upright, every muscle in his body straining as he dutifully grasped his pistol and knife. Exactly what he sought to achieve by doing so was beyond Lirbus, but it seemed to please Erket. With his knife held upright like that, Lirbus wondered whether he could slap Erket hard enough on the back of the head to make him stab himself. He slipped the magazine of his autopistol down into the palm of his glove in anticipation of the attempt.

He wouldn't get the chance. Lakatos and Morden strolled into view up ahead and Lirbus thought it best not to brain one of the juves in front of their leader and his most trusted ganger. At least, Morden always used to be Lakatos's most trusted ally. These days Lirbus was starting to wonder whether the outlander might have usurped Morden's position.

As they drew nearer, Lirbus could see Berzel scurrying along behind them, the shorter man hidden behind the imposing Lakatos and Morden.

'Take one of these two with you,' said Lakatos as he passed. Lirbus knew instantly what that meant. There was work to be done, and he could either go with Berzel or be left here with Lakatos. As a leader, Lirbus thought the world of Lakatos. As company, he left much to be desired. Lirbus leapt to his feet before Erket could even loosen his grip on his pistol and heartily slapped Berzel across the back of the shoulders.

'Come on,' he said, 'what needs doing?'

'Taxes,' was Berzel's smarmy reply. Behind him, Lakatos slumped onto the rusted metal steps beside

Erket. He was, at least, fair in his sharing of duties, and Lakatos was never one to shirk the sentry's post.

'Put that knife away, you idiot,' Lakatos said to Erket and Lirbus couldn't help but chuckle out loud as he turned to follow Berzel down the ladder to street level.

'Wait,' said Lakatos, and a wave of fear passed through Lirbus; fear that his smirking had been taken as disobedience. Berzel hauled himself back up the ladder and the pair stood patiently in front of their seated leader. As ever, he seemed in no rush, but eventually pulled out a folded-up parchment from where it was tucked under a cord around his arm.

'You can tell Goddlesby he's got a new donor,' said Lakatos. Berzel took the parchment and unfolded it as Lirbus peered over his shoulder. 'And tell him to be sure he collects.'

Lirbus squinted. His reading wasn't the best, especially not with the fancy language the guilders used, but he nonetheless recognised the document as a wanted poster, and he immediately recognised the face as that of the trader Gern Bok, a longtime thorn in the Union's side.

'I will,' said Berzel. He tapped Lirbus firmly on the shoulder, folding the parchment back up before Lirbus had managed to make out what Bok was accused of. Berzel scampered down the ladder towards the dusty streets below and Lirbus wasted no time in following suit.

'Put that knife *down*,' was all Lirbus could hear as he descended out of earshot, still tittering to himself.

IT WAS A journey Lirbus hadn't made often. Collecting 'taxes' from Goddlesby was Berzel's job, really, and he was no friend of Lirbus's. Today, though, faced with the choice between Berzel and Erket, Lirbus was glad to pick the former. For his part, Berzel seemed less objectionable than usual. Perhaps he was also counting

himself lucky not to be charged with the feckless little
juve as a companion.

Lirbus followed Berzel and hauled himself up
through the narrow access shaft that offered the quickest route to Mayor Goddlesby's shack. He rose from his
knees as he stepped onto the narrow ledge and pushed
open the airtight, circular steel door that shut Goddlesby off from the outside world. It seemed Berzel had
long ago given up knocking when it came to Goddlesby, and the little creep knew better than to ever lock
his door to the Union.

'Back so soon?' asked Goddlesby in a rare act of
courage. It faded quickly enough as the pair strode
across the room, and Goddlesby quickly shrank into
the corner behind his desk.

'We missed you,' said Berzel.

'Didn't you miss us?' Lirbus chipped in.

'No company today, Goddlesby?' said Berzel.

Lirbus hadn't the faintest idea what he was on about.
Lirbus was no fan of Berzel's irreverent style of menace,
but it seemed to do the trick with Goddlesby and he
decided to go with it.

'Not to worry, little man, we've got a new friend for
you,' said Lirbus, snapping his fingers and beckoning to
Berzel with his upturned palm. Berzel passed him the
folded-up poster and Lirbus clumsily opened it, tearing
it a little along the creases before flinging it down onto
Goddlesby's desk. Goddlesby took one look at it and
gulped in terror.

'Oh no,' he said, 'not Bok.'

THE PAIR STEPPED out into the open air.

'That little runt hasn't got the balls to shake down
Bok,' said Lirbus.

'Hmm, I don't know. Who's he more scared of?'
asked Berzel. 'Him or us?'

That gave Lirbus cause to think. True, Goddlesby was in the Union's pocket out of fear and nothing else, but Bok himself was a fearsome proposition. He was the one trader in town who didn't fear the Union and he had never paid them a cred in taxes. He sold what were without doubt the finest weapons in this part of the hive, and even the Union had to pay good money to get them. His shack was a virtual fortress and the man himself stood as tall as a scaly and almost as wide. The Union could have disappeared him long ago, like they did with other troublesome individuals, but Bok wasn't without friends, and it had never seemed worth the bother of crossing him. Now that he was a dirty man, clearly that had changed. A wanted sign made any man an easier target, even Bok.

'What did he do? To make himself wanted, I mean,' asked Lirbus. Passing the poster to Goddlesby had given him time to take another look, but his benighted mind didn't allow him to understand it any better. Berzel just laughed.

'What did he do? He crossed us, that's what,' said Berzel.

'What?' said Lirbus, his temper flaring as he started to suspect that Berzel was playing games with him.

'That's all that got his face on the wanted poster, nothing else,' said Berzel, 'and that means we can protect him just like we said. He pays up, nobody will ever catch up with him, no matter how "wanted" he is.' Berzel broke into another deep, cacophonous laugh.

'He must have done something,' said Lirbus, 'for the guilders to want him.'

'You see, Lirbus,' said Berzel, 'I don't think it's the guilders that want him at all.'

'What?'

'I saw Jurgen earlier – before he left town with Deveres – handing something over to Lakatos. I'm pretty sure it was that wanted poster,' said Berzel.

'Then where the hell did Jurgen find it?' asked Lirbus, not yet able to shake the feeling that he was being toyed with.

'Oh, I don't think Jurgen found it all,' said Berzel. 'I think he made it. All that stuff about him being a forger – the wanted poster they found on that bounty hunter's body – it's all true, I'm sure of it.'

'I don't get it,' said Lirbus. 'He had those guilder codes and the hidden messages. He had them and he knows how to make them. He's not a forger.'

'Maybe he wasn't at first,' said Berzel, 'but even if what he says is true, he hasn't worked for the guilders for a long time. Perhaps he's turned his hand to forgery since then. I think that's the skill he's been using to get by on the run and it's a skill he's using for us now, though I guess Lakatos doesn't want us to know.'

'No, I guess he doesn't,' said Lirbus, still uncertain. 'Let's not make him think we do.'

Berzel just nodded.

'NO PROBLEM,' SAID Berzel, dropping his heavy sack on the table. Durn was perched at the far end of the table, a clutch of shivs in his hand. He looked up and nodded a brief greeting to Lirbus but seemed uninterested and quickly returned to his work.

'I told Goddlesby, just like you said, next week's money better include Bok's share, or the pair of them are gonna pay for it,' said Berzel.

'Good,' said Lakatos, reclining on his stone chair, 'and what did the little rat have to say to that?'

'Well, he kicked up a hell of a stink,' said Lirbus, with an honesty he knew would irritate the showy Berzel. 'Said Bok will never pay, says he can't make him, says it's not his fault, all of that.'

'It'll be fine,' said Berzel. 'Goddlesby has never dared once step out of line.'

'Not quite true, Berzel,' said Lakatos. 'He's managed a good few mistakes in his time, and I'm sure more than a few of them have been wilful.'

Lirbus and Berzel remained silent. It was a silence that, after a thoughtful pause, Lakatos broke.

'Perhaps we can help poor little Goddlesby out,' he said, 'just this once.'

'What?' asked Berzel.

'Well, we ought to explain to Bok how all of this works. Besides, way I see it, he owes us plenty enough in back-taxes to justify a visit,' said Lakatos. 'See to it.' His stern tone and terse conclusion left Lirbus and Berzel little room for retort. Both thought better of it and left the room.

BOK'S SHACK WAS indeed a fortress. Lirbus had never paid it such close attention before, but then again he'd never really had to. He'd always been content to leave well enough alone, and now that he was here on a mission guaranteed to raise Bok's ire, he suddenly noticed what an imposing fixture the place was.

Bok's shack was, in fact, the fortified entrance to the dome above Fall Sands: Pilgrim's Spire. The story went that, in an age long gone, the dome had in fact constituted the highest pinnacle of the hive (just as, Lirbus reasoned, many domes must have done over time). Legend told that at that time Necromunda had been ruled over by a rather more devout ruling House, and the highest dome had also been the most revered place of worship in the hive, earning it the nickname of Pilgrim's Spire.

The story was often told within House Cawdor, and the vision of a hive topped by an unshakeable bastion of faith was a vision they struggled daily to recreate. To House Cawdor, the Spire should be the greatest and most worthy symbol of man's devotion to the Emperor, not merely a high loft of decadence from which decrepit, dilettante rulers looked down uncaring upon unbelieving subjects.

Still, that dream was not yet real, and the Pilgrim's Spire was little proof it had ever really existed. It was impressively well built, however. The wall of the dome, which must have once divided ancient Spire from ancient city, was still imposing and bore only a single entrance: a broad, armoured gate twenty metres high. Centuries of ash storms had long ago barred it shut, piling such a weight of detritus against it that it could never again open, but its imposing figure still marked the edge of Fall Sands.

Bok's shack was, in fact, one of the gatehouses that adjoined this ancient entrance. Other similar buildings provided the only routes through to Pilgrim's Spire now that the main gates were forever closed. The gate-houses were abandoned and, with the exception of Bok's own shack, the wall provided no real barrier for all its solidity. The gatehouses allowed a man on foot to pass through easily enough but there was certainly no way through for the colossal transports that once made use of the gate proper. It was because of this that places like Fall Sands had slowly become isolated and fallen into dereliction.

Bok's shack was a gleaming reminder of another time. The adamantium surface of the building was kept as polished as possible, where it wasn't already irre-deemably scarred by rust, and the pistons that raised and lowered the blast shutters that covered door and windows alike were all in full working order – the only such working pistons in this part of the hive, as the mechanically minded Lirbus well knew.

The blast shutters they mounted were all but impen-etrable, but today they were raised, revealing a heavy, metal door in the centre of the shack's front wall with two slim, tall windows to either side. Lascannons protruded from the windows, turning them more into murder holes than viewing portals. Lirbus had never seen the lascannons fire, though he was certain they would be in full working order. This, after all, was Bok's shack.

Lirbus himself was nervous, and Berzel seemed all the more so as they approached the sturdy door. Berzel gave a glance to Lirbus, but then seemed to decide it was better not to waste any time and pushed the door wide open. For all its sturdiness, the door was not kept locked. This was, after all, a trading post, at least by Underhive standards.

Bok was nowhere to be seen. This was instantly worrying. Racks of rifles – autopistols, lasguns and bolters – lined the walls. Trunks of ammunition covered the floor. Most ominously of all, bullet holes peppered the floor and ceiling.

The pair strode through the claustrophobic room, suddenly aware of just how little light penetrated the windows and just how much space was lost to the metre-thick adamantium walls. The 'counter' was in fact a broken down old console from which the gatehouse's former occupants would have received sensory information on everything going on outside their little bastion. Two screens were cracked and three remained in tact, though all, of course, were lifeless. Lirbus stopped to look over the console for a moment before silently and cautiously following Berzel into the anteroom beyond.

Nothing. This room was much more lavish. Indeed, it looked like it once must have been positively comfortable. It was rather more humble now, however, but still infinitely more welcoming than the dark little hole they had just left. Well, it would have seemed more welcoming, thought Lirbus, if it wasn't for Bok's eerie absence. Something was wrong, very wrong.

Lirbus only advanced three or four steps into the room. Stopping so soon might well have saved his life. Berzel up ahead of him already stood motionless in the middle of the room, and as Lirbus came to a halt a hush fell over them, which allowed him to hear just the faintest *tick-tock, tick-tock* from a stack of boxes in the corner.

Lirbus didn't wait for a second. He dived back through the door by which he had just entered, stumbling and falling as he did so. Berzel charged through behind him, almost landing on Lirbus. Berzel was first back on his feet, leaping onto the counter in a head-long dash for the door. The *tick-tock, tick-tock* went on and Lirbus wasn't sure they had time to make it out. Desperation made his mind quick, and in an instant he was gazing up at the doorway through which he had just come.

Sure enough the frame still housed a heavy, adamantium blast door. Like everything else in the shack, Bok had kept it in perfect working order and for all its weight, Lirbus had no difficulty in slamming the door shut. He grabbed a fly handle on the wheel in the centre of the door and sent it spinning with all his might. The door rattled as Lirbus's spin sent the locking mechanism racing and barred the door tight just as a dull, crumpling *oomph* emanated from the room beyond.

Lirbus fell to the floor in shock as the door buckled outwards, but breathed a sigh of relief as nothing more than a hissing gout of smoke streamed out from its edges. The door had held and the blast had been contained. He'd dodged the bullet, or more precisely, the bomb. Berzel, shaking in fear, nervously inched back away from the door, reaching out his gloved hand to help Lirbus up from the floor.

Their relief was premature. A grinding noise above them alerted Lirbus to a circular hatch in the ceiling. Damn it, he thought. It had never occurred to him this might be a two-storey building. He flung himself to his feet, grabbing at Berzel's arm as he did so, before barging past and sprinting for the door.

The hatch dropped open and Bok appeared. He stood over the opening with a heavy stubber pointed down through it, bandoliers of ammunition thrown over each of his hulking shoulders. He opened fire, sending a line of bullets chasing after Berzel and Lirbus that snapped at their heels as they fled. Mercifully, Bok's height, coupled with the narrow angle of fire through the hatch, saved them, and the volley fell away as they got within a couple of metres of the door. Not for a second did they stop running, though.

They charged on so hard that Lirbus almost lost his footing as he leapt from the door back out onto the ashy ground. Berzel burst through behind him, barging past and skidding quickly down the ashy slope that led down from the shack. Lirbus regained his footing and followed suit.

He made it only another metre before he stopped dead and recoiled back against the shack's wall. Up ahead of him, Berzel dissolved into a mass of smoke and flame. The lascannons mounted in the windows had grumbled into life, swung about and cut Berzel down at the junction of their scything beams. Lirbus squirmed up against the wall, too close to the cannon to be found by their ranging arcs.

He scurried to the left, ducking and scrabbling right under one of the throbbing barrels. He stayed close to the wall, sprinting as fast as he could for fear old Bok would abandon the lascannon and cut him down with that heavy stubber. If Bok came out of the shack now, Lirbus would be a sitting duck. Lirbus had to get to cover, and quickly.

He hardly dared pause to look around, but careering headfirst away from the shack was just as likely to get

him into trouble, and so he found the resolve to drop
to the ground and allow himself a second to look for
cover.

He spotted it instantly – another gatehouse. It was
the best Lirbus could hope for.

He clung close to the wall and dashed with all his
speed towards it. Clanking to his rear alerted him to Bok
leaving his shack and a raft of ammunition flew over his
head as he reached the gatehouse. He dived inside, slamming the door shut just in time for a volley of shots to
clatter into it, leaving a circle of indentations in the metal
like the probing fingers of some angry giant.

Lirbus was pretty sure the door would hold against a
heavy stubber but he had no idea what else the maniac
Bok might bring to bear. He looked around. The room
was identical to Bok's shack, though lacking in
weapons and ammunition. He really could do with
some right now, thought Lirbus to himself.

He made straight for the anteroom, hoping it would
afford him a route out into Pilgrim's Spire. He reached
the rear chamber just as a second volley of shots raked
the door. They hit with a furious noise far above that of
the first salvo and Lirbus was sure that Bok was closing
in.

Lirbus dashed to the door at the back of the room. Its
rusted handle tore off in his hand as he grabbed it and
as his shoulder slammed into the equally rusted surface, the door showed little sign of giving way. He flung
the handle to the floor and pulled his pistol out from
its holster, ducking back behind the doorway joining
the two rooms. He was trapped and his only hope lay
in a lucky ambush.

A thud rang out in the gatehouse, followed by a dull
metallic clang and a bright phosphor glow streaming in
through the doorway. Bok had melta-bombed the door
off its hinges and sure enough a raking volley of shots

screamed in just a moment later. Lirbus crouched beside the doorway in the anteroom.

Two, three, four more metallic clangs rang out as Bok plodded over the collapsed door and into the first room. Lirbus heard a dissatisfied grunt come from the wily old trader, followed by a rather ominous *plinkle-plinkle-plop*.

A grenade. Shit, thought Lirbus. A flat metal disc rolled out into the middle of the anteroom floor and Lirbus scrambled to his feet in panic. Even in this state of blind terror he knew that heading back through the door would be instant death and he somehow kept his wits about him enough to wriggle behind the anteroom door where it lay open against the wall behind him. He pushed the door forwards just a fraction, wriggling himself into an impossibly small gap between it and the wall.

Somehow it worked. The grenade unleashed its fury, and Lirbus was nearly crushed as the force of the blast pressed him flat against the wall. It felt like an eternity before he could breath again, every ounce of oxygen wrung from his lungs by the heavy, metal door pinning him to the wall, but at least he was alive. At last the door released its bear hug on him and he slumped to the floor. His ribs ached, every one of them broken no doubt, but he had no time to waste.

He wriggled out from behind the door and crouched, pistol held out towards the open doorway. He would only get one shot, so he'd better make it count, he thought to himself.

Another grunt, this time a pleased-sounding one, was uttered. Bok must think I'm already dead, Lirbus thought. He even dared to hope Bok might leave without looking for his body.

It was a vain hope as a second later the tip of the heavy stubber barrel snaked through the door, tracking left and right, and it took all of Lirbus's nerve not to fire instantly, but he had to wait until he could get one good clean shot at Bok. Inch by rusty inch, the barrel came forwards, and then Bok's hand came into view, his front leg, and his other hand. It was an agonising wait.

Suddenly a shot rang out. It wasn't the stubber – it remained motionless in the doorway in front of Lirbus – and Lirbus gasped, terrified that his frightened hands had fired without his nervous mind commanding it. He tipped his pistol up a little to look at the barrel, but no smoke meant no fire.

He turned his gaze back to the door in time to see the heavy stubber fall to the floor. Another moment passed before Bok keeled over behind it, dead. His huge frame slammed into the floor and on reflex Lirbus leapt up, planting one foot on his back and aiming his pistol at Bok's head. He was definitely dead, though, and as much as Lirbus wanted to shoot, it would be nothing more than a waste of a bullet.

'What the...?' he mumbled nervously to himself before realising a third man stood behind him. He turned, terrified... only to see Jurgen's grinning face with a toxstick wedged firmly between his teeth.

'You gonna tell me what happened or just stand there pretending *you* shot him?' asked Jurgen, winking as he returned his pistol to its hiding place in the small of his back.

'THAT'S THE MOST damned luck I've had in days,' said Jurgen. Lirbus jogged along beside him, still shaking with fear.

'It was a lot luckier for me,' Lirbus said.

'You think?' said Jurgen, his meaning not at all clear to Lirbus.

'What do you mean? What bad luck?' asked Lirbus, deciding to return to the earlier point.

'It's not good, Lirbus, it's not good,' he said. 'I lost Deveres on the way. Damned fool just wandered off. I only hope he made it back here by himself. As for the others, well, they didn't make it anywhere.'

'What?' said Lirbus, biting his lip. He'd been gone most of the day, but Deveres certainly wasn't back in Fall Sands by the time he'd left, and if he wasn't back by then, well, Lirbus was smart enough to know he probably wasn't coming back at all. 'What about the others?' he asked.

'Handomel's gang, Scarlet Skulls or whatever they called themselves,' said Jurgen. 'They're dead. All dead.'

Lirbus gulped in disbelief. 'How?' he asked.

'One big bloody mess, that's how,' said Jurgen.

'Emperor judge us all,' squealed Lirbus. 'Do you think Lago is back? Do you think he's still after them?'

'Well if he is, he got them,' said Jurgen.

'Then do you think he's after us?' asked Lirbus. Jurgen said nothing at first. He just seemed to be thinking it over in his head.

'Thing is,' he said a moment later, 'half of Handomel's men were dead in their hideout – I found the gang badge graffed on the wall – and a bunch more were dead all over the place.'

'So?'

'So, if Lago did this – and I'm not saying he didn't – I'm not sure he did all of it.'

'What?' said Lirbus. This was all too much: Deveres, Berzel, Handomel's men.

'I wonder if some of those Scarlet Skulls weren't a little too eager to replace Handomel, putting themselves before the cause, if you know what I mean, brother,' said Jurgen. 'Can't be sure they didn't go and shoot themselves up. Maybe Lago was there, who knows, but maybe they made themselves easy pickings for him.'

Lirbus frowned. He was confused and frightened and had little stomach left for the fight. He remained silent the rest of the way as he and Jurgen headed back to the hideout.

'ALL OF THEM?' asked Lakatos, clearly disbelieving.

'All of them,' said Jurgen, sternly. 'You're lucky I heard the ruckus, or you could add Lirbus here to that tally, too.'

'Damn it, damn it, damn it,' said Lakatos, his voice rising as his anger grew. He slammed his fist into the wall next to him and paced back and forth.

Lirbus was right; Deveres wasn't back yet. No one was saying it, but he hadn't made it. There was no point looking for him, either.

Lirbus had listened to the whole sorry tale again as Jurgen told it to Lakatos: how Deveres got lost in the storms, and how Jurgen found the Scarlet Skulls dead to a man and fled as fast as he could, only to run right into the gunfight at Bok's. Lirbus was glad of that last part, at least. He hadn't instantly taken to the out-lander, but he owed him his life now, and what's more, he trusted him implicitly.

Lirbus was sure Lakatos was going to explode when Jurgen suggested some of the Scarlet Skulls might have killed each other in a leadership challenge, and it cer-tainly angered him, but he seemed to find the suggestion sadly predictable. Deveres, too, and Berzel. Lirbus was sure their deaths would send Lakatos into a fit of rage, with him and Jurgen to take the blame, but Lakatos seemed more ready to criticise the dead men for their idiocy. Now he just paced back and forth. No one dared speak, not even the outlander, while their leader racked his brains for what to do next.

'Addec needs to know,' he said. 'If the Skulls are gone, he needs to take their territory and quickly, else he's

unprotected. Someone has to tell Addec,' said Lakatos.
'Durn, go to Addec; tell him what happened. Tell him
he has to capture Handomel's territory, *now*.'

Lakatos paced to the edge of the room as Durn
wasted no time in following his leader's orders,
ducking out of the door and making good his departure.

'Goddlesby,' said Lakatos, his voice barely more than
a whisper, muffled by the gloved fist he held over his
mouth.

'What?' asked Morden from his spot in the centre of
the room.

'Goddlesby, the little runt, he must have done this.'
'What?'

'The little bastard said he wouldn't collect Bok's taxes,
didn't he?' asked Lakatos. Lirbus just nodded in reply.
'I bet he decided to tip him off about it.'

It made sense. Goddlesby was a worthless little coward.

'Well then,' said Lakatos, 'let's give our town's fine
mayor one last chance to make his proper contribu-
tion.' Lakatos's anger turned to a cruel laugh.

'What do you want us to do?' asked Lirbus, realising
that the uncollected taxes were probably still his problem.

'Go and get Bok's body,' said Lakatos. 'Remember,
he's a wanted man.'

Jurgen looked up, offering a single nod to Lirbus.

Lirbus nodded three times in reply. It made perfect
sense.

'I WON'T DO it. I can't do it,' Goddlesby said. His already
filthy skin was washed clean in places by the endless
streams of sweat working their way down his bald head
and onto his wrinkled face. He was the very picture of
terror, and yet he was resolute nonetheless.

'That man is not wanted for anything, dead or alive, and I will not pay a single credit of bounty on him,' he said.

'I've got his wanted poster right here,' said Lirbus, taking the parchment from his pocket and thrusting it into Goddlesby's face. 'Or don't you remember?'

Jurgen stood silent in the corner with Bok's body at his feet. Lirbus followed Goddlesby's gaze as the little man stared at the corpse, frightened out of his wits.

'I don't know what's going on, but if Bok was wanted I would know about it. I'm not paying up. I can't pay up.'

'It's not even your money, Goddlesby,' said Lirbus. 'I know you've got that special stash the guilders leave with you, for paying out on their behalf. Now you be a good boy and pay out.'

'I won't do it,' said Goddlesby. 'You want the money, you take him to the guilders yourself.'

Lirbus turned to Jurgen and frowned. It seemed Goddlesby had left them with no alternative. He'd blown his last chance, and now he had to disappear.

'I'll take him with me,' said Lirbus, turning to Jurgen.

'No,' said Jurgen, 'I'll go. Seems I'm having more luck out there than most.'

LIRBUS PLODDED BACK to the hideout. He was dreading being there. They had lost two men in a day, after a year without so much as seeing a man go out of action, and all that on top of the news that some of their most important allies were dead, apparently having torn themselves to pieces.

Sure enough, the atmosphere was so tense as to be painful as Lirbus returned to the hideout, every pair of eyes rising up to see if he was the bearer of more bad news. He walked to the rising steps at the back of the room in silence and slumped in a corner. He wouldn't sleep a wink and he didn't dare say a word to any of the others. As exhausted as he was, Lirbus almost wished it was him and not Durn going out into the storms.

CHAPTER: ELEVEN

MAYOR ERB GODDLESBY gulped a gulp of deep and unshakeable nervousness.

'Oh no,' he said, 'not Bok.' This was bad news, very bad news, indeed. He took another look at the wanted poster lying face up on his desk. It was Bok sure enough. Erb couldn't believe it. Bok was a tough, ragged brute of a man, but one who had never so much as wriggled one little toe over onto the wrong side of the law.

Wanted, it read, for the theft of armaments sanctioned only for use by enforcers, watch and Hive City patrol agents. Surely this couldn't be true, could it? Erb gulped again.

'What are you going to do?' he asked. The two Cawdor took their time answering him. They loved making him squirm, and he'd never really been able to avoid doing so. The one on the right was Berzel. He knew him. He wasn't so sure of the other one's name. He wasn't sure he had seen him before, or rather wasn't so sure he could tell him apart from any of the other vicious thugs that plagued the town.

'Nothing,' said Berzel, 'nothing at all. You're going to do it for us.'

'What?' said Erb. 'What do you mean? I can't bring him in! Not Bok!' He still wasn't sure that the wanted poster was genuine, or that Bok had really done the things it said. Even if it the poster was genuine, and Bok had done the things it accused him of, Erb certainly wasn't going to be the one to bring Bok in. He wouldn't stand a chance against a man like that. Civic duty could go to hell when it came to colossal arms dealers with bad tempers. Civic duty wasn't for dealing with people like that, Erb told himself meekly.

'Don't worry little man,' said Berzel. 'We don't want you to bring him in. We're going to look after Bok;,protect him. Same as we protect all of you in this town. We've always looked after you, haven't we, Goddlesby?'

Goddlesby certainly didn't consider himself looked after, but he wasn't going to risk a beating by telling them so.

'Wh-what are you going to do?' he stuttered, his already short supply of nerve dwindling fast.

'Well, here's the deal,' said the other Cawdor, the one whose name Erb didn't know. 'We're going to protect Bok, and make sure nobody makes good on the "Wanted: Dead or Alive" part, but it's going to cost him.'

Erb gulped that familiar gulp. He could feel it coming every time he got nervous. He was nervous a lot of the time. He gulped a lot, especially when the Union was around. They weren't going to ask him to bring Bok in, but they were going to ask something just as perilous. They wanted him to *tax* Bok. Of all the townsfolk, Bok was the only one who had refused to bow down to the Union's extortion and gotten away with it. Others had tried and paid the price for it, or caved quickly when they saw others pay the price for it, but Bok had persevered and, as far as Erb knew, the Union hadn't troubled him for months. As far as he could tell, they had given up on squeezing so much as a single credit out of Bok. Until now, that was.

'I… I…' Goddlesby stuttered again, lacking the nerve to get straight to the point. 'Bok won't pay,' it came at last.

'Bok's going to have to pay,' said Berzel. 'He pays, or his hide pays for it. No other choice for him. It's us or the guilders, Goddlesby. You can tell him that when you go collect his taxes.'

'I… I… just can't. I can't get money from Bok. He'll laugh in my face, or punch me in it. I won't do this, I *can't* do this!' Erb's protest was passionate, but clearly making little headway with the hooded bullies in front of him. They were ignoring every word and already heading for the door.

'Same time next week, Goddlesby,' said Berzel as the pair departed. He had no choice. He would have to pay a visit to Bok.

BOK'S SHACK WAS an imposing fortress on the edge of town. It was a place Erb hated. He hated everything about it: how far it was from his own little hole, how big and nasty it looked. He hated the things inside it: all the guns, the bullets, the big vicious arms dealer himself. Erb hated guns, he always had. He used to own a little six-shooter as a token gesture but got rid of it after he accidentally blew two of his own fingers off when his braces snapped.

Erb stopped about ten metres short of the shack's entrance. He didn't want to knock on the door, let alone walk in unannounced, and instead stopped in clear view of the windows, took his hat off and waved it in the air as he shouted out.

'Bok! Bok!' he said. 'Bok, I have to speak to you.'

A single shot rang out and Erb's hat flew out of his hand and landed right at his feet with a smoking hole clean through the middle. He stooped down to pick it up. From the shack up ahead of him, he heard a heavy thud as the door swung open. Looking up, Erb saw Bok appear in the doorway, a lasgun wedged under his arm.

'Then what are you doing standing there and waving like a target?' asked Bok. Erb wasn't exactly sure what mood Bok was in, and why he had just shot at him, but he decided to take the man's advice and scurried quickly up the slope to the shack.

By the time he reached the door, Bok had retreated within. Erb pushed on the heavy door. It was an effort just to open it and, as he squeezed in through the tiny gap he had made between the door and jamb, the thing threatened to shut on him and crush him against the frame. It was hardly a dignified entrance. Then again, he was hardly in a dignified position.

'Bok,' he said, 'I've been getting trouble again. It's the Union, you see, they've been, erm... They're...' his speech trailed off into another haze of nervy doubt.

'Those sons of bitches, what's it got to do with me? They leave me well enough alone, and I don't give a damn what they get up to,' said Bok.

'You see,' said Erb, 'they showed me something today, um, they showed me, kind of, like a poster... A wanted poster.'

'What are they doing? Showing off? Somebody finally put their ugly mugs up where they belong?'

'No, Bok. I mean, they showed me a wanted poster... for you,' said Erb. He fumbled with the brim of his hat as he fell silent and in those few brief moments he realised he had absolutely no idea how Bok was going to react. He could have guessed, though.

'What the frag?' Bok roared as his fist smashed clean through a mercifully empty gun rack beside him, reducing it to splinters with a single blow. Erb gulped. It was time for a gulp. He'd felt it coming on for a while.

'They say you've been, um... The poster, it said...'

'Spit it out, Goddlesby!' Bok's temper didn't appear to be soothed any by the long time it was taking Erb to find his words.

'The poster says some of these guns are official weapons: weapons from the watch, the enforcers,' said Erb. 'The poster says you stole them, Bok.'

One of the broken pieces of the gun rack was further reduced to splinters as Bok picked it up and bashed it repeatedly into the floor, though this did little to dissipate his rage. He rose to his feet, roaring in anger: an animal cry from which Erb could make out no words. He half expected Bok to start beating his chest.

'This is a stitch-up,' he roared. 'I'm not standing for this.'

'Bok, Bok,' said Erb. 'It's okay. I don't think you did it. I'm not here to take you in.' Erb stopped, realising the stupidity of what he had just said, but Bok seemed to have found an ounce of calm inside his hulking frame and Erb continued quickly in an attempt to gloss over the faux pas.

'I don't think anything is going to come of this, Bok, but they say they want payment to keep quiet.'

'Uh-uh,' said Bok. 'I've never paid those crooks a cred, and I'm never going to.'

'Bok, it's only the same as everyone else has been paying all these years. It's not that much really, and if it keeps them off your back, then–'

'Keeps them off my back?' said Erb, butting in before Erb could finish. 'I'll keep them off my back *my* way, don't you worry, and it won't cost me a damned cred. You go tell them that; tell them they're getting nothing,' said Bok.

'I can't tell them that, Bok, please,' said Erb. 'You're making this hard for me. Just think, it's not much for a quiet life.' Erb pleaded but Bok was unmoved. He was already behind his counter, hauling out some truly monstrous metal boxes. Erb didn't dare ask what was inside.

'Bok, listen, if you don't pay up, I don't know what they're going to do. You remember what happened to the others?'

Undoubtedly Bok did. He'd been around long enough to remember the sorry ends of all those who had tried to resist the Union's demands when they first arrived in town, but Bok had escaped all that and had done okay ever since. It didn't seem as if reminding him of it was going to sway him any.

'Bok, please.' Erb tried one last time, but Bok was ignoring him completely, lost in his frantic assembly of a terrifying-looking weapon that he was putting together from pieces pulled from the metal boxes that now covered the counter. Erb sighed in resignation and turned to leave.

He walked lightly down the ashy slope outside. A moment or two later he was startled by the most terrible grinding noise coming from behind him and he turned back to see the shack's armoured frontage rising up in two spots on either side of the door. As Erb watched with amazement – not least because such ancient machinery still worked – the blast shield revealed two tall windows. Erb stared in awe that quickly turned to horror as that same monstrous barrel he had seen on the counter slid into place in the left hand window. The sight of that thing was enough, and Erb turned tail, scurrying away from the place as quickly as he could. He had no idea what the Union was going to do if Bok didn't pay up, but he realised that what Bok was planning to do to avoid paying up might be much worse.

This meant trouble for everyone, Erb thought to himself as he scurried back to the rotten little dump he called home.

'OH NO,' SAID Erb as he gazed down into the dead man's lifeless, yet still wide-open eyes. 'What have you done?'

Bok's huge frame lay on the floor of Erb's 'mayoral chambers' as he liked to refer to his little shack. A third eye – a blackened, bloody, brain-spattered mess of one – joined the mortified white ones to either side, erupting from the centre of his head like a sump-orchid in bloom.

It was a stupid question, really. What they had clearly done was kill Bok. Pretty swiftly by the looks of it: one shot clean through the back of his head.

'I won't do it. I can't do it,' Goddlesby said. His already filthy skin was washed clean in places by the endless streams of sweat working their way down his bald head and onto his wrinkled face. He was terrified, yet he was resolute.

He had been terrified of the Union since the day they walked into town. He had been terrified of Bok, too: terrified of going to his place, terrified of telling him he was wanted, terrified of telling him he had to pay up, but when it came down to it, he was just that little bit more terrified of the Union. So, he had gone along with it and, for all his fear of Bok, he had done what they had asked.

If there was one thing that terrified Erb more than the Union – and there was one thing – it was the guilders. No matter what the Union could do to him if he didn't pay the bounty, the guilders would do worse if he did. It had come to a point where Erb was damned either way and that gave him no reason to cower any longer. He was done for, and all he could do was go with a little pride by standing up for himself just once before the end.

'That man is not wanted for anything, dead or alive, and I will not pay a single credit of bounty on him,' he said.

'I've got his wanted poster right here,' said the Cawdor they apparently called Lirbus. He took the parchment from his pocket and thrust it into Goddlesby's face. 'Or don't you remember?'

He remembered it all, of course, but he didn't trust it at all. Erb wasn't exactly the most powerful man in town, but he was its mayor. As much as he might be a puppet of the Union, his position did hold certain responsibilities, and paying bounties in the absence of a guilder was one of them. The little stash left with him by the guilders for just such an occasion was the one and only thing over which Erb truly had control. Even the Union feared the guilders, or at least didn't see the point in crossing them, and for all the credits that stash contained, they had always left well alone.

They could have demanded that Erb hand it over at any time. He wouldn't have, but they could have killed him and taken it all the same. Now they seemed to have found a way around the problem – by demanding that he pay them bounties from it – and they weren't about to give up now that the stash was at last in their sights. Erb couldn't stop them from getting it, but he sure as anything wasn't going to be the one to give it to them.

'I don't know what's going on, but if Bok was wanted I would know about it. I'm not paying up. I can't pay up.'

The outlander stood silent in the corner with Bok's body at his feet. Erb had heard nothing but talk of this outlander since he arrived in town, but this was the first time he had ever laid eyes on him. Erb couldn't resist stealing quick glances, trying to get a good look at him, but always fearing to be caught in his steely gaze. He wondered if it was the outlander who had killed Bok – he was sure it must have been – and that made him all the more frightening to Erb's poor, terrified mind.

'It's not even your money, Goddlesby,' said Lirbus. 'I know you've got that special stash the guilders leave with you, for paying out on their behalf. Now you be a good boy and pay out.'

'I won't do it,' said Goddlesby. 'You want the money, you take him to the guilders yourself.'

Lirbus turned to the outlander and frowned. They were clearly unhappy but Erb wasn't going to budge, and they knew it. That was as much as he hoped to achieve: to be strong, confident, resolute, just this once. It was done, and he knew what was going to happen next. They were going to make him disappear.

'I'll take him with me,' said Lirbus, turning to the outlander.

'No,' said Jurgen, 'I'll go. Seems I'm having more luck out there than most.'

The outlander stepped over the fallen Bok and grabbed Erb by the collar, dragging him out of the room. Erb just gulped.

'WHAT'S YOUR NAME, mister?' asked Erb. For some reason he felt compelled to talk to the strange outlander as he marched him out over the dunes.

'You don't need to know my name,' said the outlander.

'I want to,' said Erb.

'Then my name is "mister", you guessed right,' came the reply.

Erb sighed. It was a shame the outlander was so uncommunicative. Erb had the distinct feeling that a little conversation might make the time between now and the end a little easier, though he was pleasantly surprised at how he was holding out. It was a wonder what standing up for yourself could do, thought Erb. Ironic, really.

He'd known this day was coming. He'd always known this was how it would end. He'd known ever since they made him mayor.

They had only picked him for being so cowardly. He still remembered that day long ago, scrabbling at the ash, and digging handfuls of the stuff out from under that huge stone slab in the middle of town. He'd panicked, dived to the floor and scrabbled desperately at the ash. Somehow, he had dug enough of it out of the way to dig a hole big enough to fit in; a hole he had hidden in as it all went down in the square in front of him.

He'd been no more than a passer-by, but one with bad timing. He was crossing the square, right outside Mayor Hawk's, just as the Union closed in on the place. Hawk had been a good man: strong, wise and brave. He had put up with nothing when the Union arrived in town. Half of them had done time in his cells when their violence first spilled over into the settlement and Hawk had never backed down, fighting against every one of their wicked little schemes.

He'd got away with it until Ash Season. That was when they came for him. No word could get out and it was old Mayor Hawk all alone against them.

And here we are now, thought Erb, another Ash Season, another dead mayor. Why did things like this always happen in Ash Season? He hated Ash Season. It didn't matter. This was surely his last.

The outlander stopped, reaching out and tugging the back of Erb's coat to bring him to a stop, too. Erb was vaguely relieved that this would be the end at last. He was sick of walking and wondering what it would be like. Best it just happened.

The stranger snapped open a box of toxsticks. With a deft flick of the tin's metal lid, the outlander flung one of the toxsticks up, catching it effortlessly between his lips. He held out the open box, offering its contents to Erb.

'No, no thank you,' said Erb. 'No point in starting now.'

'No harm in trying,' replied the outlander.

'No, perhaps not,' said Erb, reaching out to take the offered stick. He spun it round in his fingers, not really sure which end to put in his mouth. Not like it really mattered, he thought, and stuffed the thing between his lips. The stranger held out a sparkslate and the end of the stick flared into life in front of Erb's nose.

Erb sighed as he drew his first breath on the thing. No harm in trying, he thought.

CHAPTER: TWELVE

'ANTAL,' SAID LAKATOS. 'Mero, Rubik, Todor, Galamb: come to me.'

It came across as nothing more than a grainy crackle to Antal, perceiving everything, as he did these days, through the bionic implant in his ear. Nonetheless, Antal was slowly learning to interpret those grainy clicks, crackles and whines for their own sake, and followed his leader's order easily enough.

The five of them wandered over to where Lakatos stood in the doorway of the gang's hideout, some getting there more quickly than others. Rubik and Galamb seemed particularly reluctant to put down their tools and do as they were told.

The outlander, Jurgen, was behind Lakatos in the doorway. Antal had barely said a word to the man since he arrived and he hadn't seen him since he and Lirbus had been sent off to deal with Goddlesby. That sounded like it had turned into a nasty business indeed and Antal had little wish to be a part of anything involving the outlander. He shuddered a little to see him standing so prominently by their leader's side.

'I can't have you just working territories anymore,' said Lakatos, in reference to the duties that the lowly likes of Antal and the lame like Todor normally undertook. While the most thuggish acts of extortion, intimidation and outright violence were left to hardened veterans like Morden, Berzel or Lirbus (and now the outlander), gangers like Antal and Todor worked the gang's territories by scouting for scrap, harvesting valuable weeds, slimes and goos, or salvaging what working equipment they could find from the dome's derelict areas.

Rubik, on the other hand, was a man who largely avoided any form of turfwork at all and was pretty much excused from everything bar fighting on account of his esteemed position of heavy, and his inescapable habit for turning all situations into a fight. That he was being called upon was a surprise to Antal.

'Goddlesby is gone, and we're going to be collecting our own taxes from now on,' said Lakatos. 'We do it once a week, starting from today. Todor, you go with Rubik; Antal with Mero, and Galamb you'll go with Jurgen. Jurgen has lists of who pays and how much.'

At this, Jurgen stepped past Lakatos and handed out two, long thin parchments, one to Todor and the other to Mero.

'I can't read this,' said Mero. There was a pause before the last word, as though he added it afterwards, suddenly reluctant to admit he just couldn't read at all. It was hardly uncommon. He thrust the list into Antal's hand, for all the good that would do.

'I can't read either,' said Antal. Lakatos scowled.

'You?' he asked, pointing at Galamb. Galamb nodded eagerly.

'Okay,' said Lakatos, 'Galamb, *you* go with Mero, and Antal you can go with Jurgen.'

Antal cursed under his breath. He was hardly relishing the job of shaking down the townsfolk, and now he was stuck with the outlander. Emperor only knows what the outlander is going to do, thought

Antal to himself. He was quite sure Jurgen's powers of persuasion would be more unpleasant than they were subtle.

'Go on,' said Lakatos, 'go.'

ANTAL KEPT HIMSELF just behind the outlander as they marched down the street. He decided walking alongside him would only make it more obvious that he wasn't really talking to him, and that he had nothing to say. Jurgen stopped abruptly outside one shack in particular.

'Lorgan Dreg,' he said. 'Three credits. You do it.' The outlander was abrupt to say the least.

'Me?' asked Antal.

'Go on,' Jurgen said. 'I'll wait here. This doesn't need both of us.'

Antal approached the door, raising a fist to knock. He wasn't really sure he should be knocking, but then again, he wasn't sure that he shouldn't be. He faltered for a second, couching his balled fist in the glove of his other hand before finally making his mind up and rapping sharply on the door three times.

The door was a rickety old corrugated thing, and the sharp rapping of the knock disintegrated into nothing more than a rumbling clang as the door shook loosely in its frame. It had none of the staccato interruption of a good, sharp knock and Antal was actually a little disappointed. It did the job nonetheless.

A rather stringy looking man emerged from the doorway, dressed in rags. They were oily rags, though, and that meant he had at least some kind of trade; perhaps even a skilled one. He squealed at the sight of Antal and Jurgen and tried to slam the door shut immediately upon opening it.

That gave Antal confidence and he acted on instinct, jamming his foot in the door and forcing it open with his shoulder. He stepped inside as the terrified little man recoiled from the door.

'What's wrong, Dreg?' said Antal. 'Aren't you pleased to see us?'

The man gasped and scurried back across the room, halting with his back pressed up against some gigantic contraption of blackened metal that occupied most of the far wall. Antal was secretly keen to get this over and done with, but thought stretching the experience out a little might make future visits easier. He strolled over to the contraption.

'What, in the name of Helmawr's daughter, is this?'

Dreg said nothing, but scurried away from it as Antal approached. Now Antal could see that it was something built inside the shack, and actually a part of it. Only two of the walls of Dreg's humble abode were solid – the back wall and the one to the right of it – and the contraption was mounted in the corner between them. It was a mass of pipes, pistons, cogs and gears. It was blackened, though moist with oil in that way all working machines were. It appeared to be just the foremost tip of a much larger machine embedded deep in the wall.

Here and there, panels of shabby grey, once white, plasteel covered it, with arcane markings and numerals in turn covering its surface. Antal couldn't read them, but he was fairly sure that they were just part of a much larger covering that Dreg had stripped away to get at the machine.

It was a generator. Dreg had built his whole damned shack right over an old generator, hiding it behind walls so that no one would see him stripping away at its protective panels to get at the workings within.

There was no way Dreg could get at the bulk of the machine that lay deep within the wall and anterior structures as it was, but the exposed portion seemed pretty crucial to its operation and was probably enough for Dreg to keep it in some kind of working order. It looked in pretty fine working condition to Antal, and the dull *hum* coming from it suggested the same. Dreg was probably pumping power out of this thing to all those parts of the settlement fortunate enough to still have a physical connection, and no doubt charging for the privilege. A nice little earner that would be.

'That'll be four credits, then,' said Antal.

'What?' asked Dreg. It was funny how even the most fearful silence could be overcome when someone mentioned money.

'Four credits. Taxes. Now pay up.' Perhaps the outlander was wise in his abruptness, thought Antal as he tried to mimic it.

'Three,' said Dreg timidly, 'and I paid Goddlesby.'

'That was last week,' said Antal, though in truth he wasn't exactly certain that an entire week had passed. 'Goddlesby won't be collecting taxes anymore, we will. *I* will,' said Antal, hastily correcting himself for the sake of face. 'So you pay up like a good boy and I'll help you out.'

'Help me out?' asked Dreg. 'How?'

'Pay up on time, and you won't be having any problems,' said Antal, 'like a generator with a grenade in it. Now four credits, Dreg, and make them shiny ones.'

'Three?' said Dreg again, in one pathetic last attempt to avoid the increase.

Antal just scowled and folded his arms. Dreg slipped his hand into the leather apron tied around his waist and pulled out a couple of credits. Antal was sure there were plenty of credits stashed in there, but Dreg was careful not reveal too much of his wealth and pulled out the remaining two credits one at a time before dropping all four into Antal's open palm.

'A pleasure, Dreg,' said Antal. 'Same time next week.' Antal smirked and walked out of the little shack.

'Got it?' asked Jurgen.

'Got it,' said Antal. That was the fifth straight take in a row with no problems at all, and the third to have actually footed a rise in taxes. It seemed Goddlesby hadn't really tried to wring as much as he should have out of most of these wretches and now that Antal was there to see them in person, there were plenty, like Dreg, who clearly had more to spare. Antal toyed with the idea of letting some of the really poor ones off, but thought better of it. He didn't really see the point.

They marched down the street. They were getting much further out of town, and where the first takes had all been from the densely packed shacks and habs that lined the broad main street of Fall Sands, their targets now were the isolated holesteaders that littered the edges of the settlement. Nirin Hobb was next on the list.

Nirin Hobb's hole was a truly rank place. The only way out to it was across a bridge leading over a sewage pit. The pit was still used, but Hobb had divided it up into dozens of pens, each no more than a metre across. Within these pens festered – for that was the only word for it – the most unpleasant of the Underhive's denizens. Gigantic worms, bred large, grown bloated feasting on the sewage, writhed in pens barely big enough to contain them.

Their fanged mouths rose to the surface as Antal and Jurgen passed, clearly not averse to something more substantial than the repeatedly digested filth in which they languished. The odd boot to be seen floating here and there in the pit suggested that the worms were not entirely disappointed in that regard.

About halfway out, Antal noticed one of the worms writhing more strenuously than the others, and hardly dipping out of sight at all. As he drew nearer he saw it was engaged in some rather curious behaviour. It smashed itself into the wire of its pen, over and over, crumpling the fence little by little. It had clearly made advances and the edge of its pen extended well over halfway into its neighbour's.

Antal watched as a few more determined charges collapsed a small section of fence and the worm launched itself over the crumpled barrier and into the pen beyond. It disappeared beneath the brown filth for a second before rising again, another worm grasped between its teeth. It shook the worm violently and bashed its head against the fence. The struggle lasted for a few seconds before the aggressive invader – much larger than its unfortunate neighbour – disappeared beneath the now tranquil surface to digest its catch in peace.

Jurgen hadn't been nearly so fascinated, or distracted, by the spectacle and Antal suddenly noticed him with his arms crossed, waiting for him at the end of the bridge where Hobb's own hole nestled above the sewage inlet pipes.

Antal hurried across the bridge to catch up with Jurgen. Jurgen nodded up towards Hobb's place and Antal wasted no time in scampering up to the entrance, which was an upturned, badly rusted pipe.

Lowering himself through the pipe, Antal descended onto a mesh floor of a corridor above the maze of pipes that presumably regulated the pit's contents. Whatever they did, they didn't do it very well, and the only thing more revolting than the endless belching noise that the backfiring pipes unleashed was the rank stench that followed every such eruption.

Antal crossed the meshed walkway and entered the collection of dimly lit rooms beyond. Each was identical; nothing more than a tiny dorm for the workers that once must have been required to operate the pit. A walkthrough corridor connected all these rooms and Antal passed through them, one by one, in search of Hobb.

The rooms were either empty, or filled with all manner of junk. He passed five or six of them before finding one that looked even remotely lived in. A brightly glowing lantern perched on a stone bench in the corner and a cot that wasn't so completely covered in filth as to be unusable were the only signs of life, but they were signs enough.

There was, however, no sign of Nirin Hobb.

Antal moved closer to the bench, close enough to see that it was in fact being used as a makeshift desk. A scattered set of ledgers lay in the dim circle of light cast by the lantern. Antal turned one of them over and cast its cover open. He couldn't read a thing, of course, but he thought meddling was pretty much part of the job and began to flick uninterestedly through its pages.

'What do you want?' asked a voice from behind him. Turning, Antal saw it was Hobb.

'Taxes, Hobb, time to pay up,' he said, closing the ledger. 'It looks to me like you can afford plenty,' bluffed Antal. True, the holesteader's chambers weren't exactly salubrious, but his business seemed to be booming in its own filthy way. 'We'll call it twelve credits,' Antal said.

'Get out,' said Hobb, raising a shotgun that Antal hadn't noticed before. Antal's early successes had made him confident. He hadn't realised that those were just the easy jobs and he hadn't given a moment's thought to what he would do if anyone objected.

'You've gotta pay up,' said Antal unconvincingly, in one last attempt at genuine extortion. It clearly didn't work, as was indicated by the shotgun's barrels jabbing ever closer to his face.

'Whoa,' said Antal. 'Wait. Ten credits. Ten credits same as before, that will do.' Antal instantly regretted the move. In his panic, going back to what Hobb had been paying Goddlesby seemed like a good move, but now he realised the folly. He had shown weakness, shown that he could be budged on his demands, and now the resolute Hobb had the upper hand. He grabbed the back of Antal's robes with one hand and frogmarched him back out of the room, across the mesh walkway and back to the base of the pipe by which he had entered.

'Now get out,' said Hobb.

Antal decided to cut his losses and did as he was told, scrambling back up the pipe and out onto the deck above where Jurgen waited.

'Got it?' asked Jurgen.

'Erm, no,' said Antal.

'What?' said Jurgen.

'He won't pay. He's got a damned shotgun and says he won't pay.'

Jurgen just sighed and, without saying another word, kicked his coat tails up behind him as he leapt, feet first, into the pipe. Antal heard the clanging of his heavy boots landing on the mesh below and then the startled 'What the–?' from Hobb before a scuffling noise and the voices passed out of earshot.

It was only a momentary lapse, though, as Antal swiftly pulled a metal pick from the top of his boot and pushed it into his ear. He jacked the implant right up and focused on the noise coming from the pipe, homing in on every sound. That outlander was a nasty piece of work, Antal was sure of that, and he was certain Hobb was in big trouble, heading for nothing more than a brutal death at Jurgen's hands.

'Listen here,' came Jurgen's voice – or rather, came the clicks and crackles which Antal translated into Jurgen's voice – 'I don't want to have to bend you in half like I did that damned shotgun, so why don't you just pay up and be done with it.'

Antal wasn't sure the outlander even knew about his implants. He couldn't have guessed that Antal was listening in but Antal was surprised nonetheless at his reasoned course of action. There was a depth of thinking to this Jurgen that he hadn't imagined so far. He listened harder, curious to find out what Jurgen's next move would be.

He didn't hear another word, not so much as a crackle, or a click, or a ping. He recoiled in agony as a metallic *clang* rang out from the pipe. Somebody had smashed something, or dropped something very heavy, and the noise was agony to Antal's augmented, and currently overcharged, hearing. He dropped to his knees, covering his ears instinctively, but that only made it worse.

In his shock, Antal had dropped the metal pick and he had no way of turning down the implant or adjusting the frequency. His loss of concentration meant every sound from hundreds of metres around now flooded his ears and he wailed in agony. He scrabbled on the floor desperately looking for the pick.

He found it, encrusted with muck, beside his boot and wasted no time in jabbing the filthy thing into his ear and cranking the implant's volume and sensitivity down, all the way down. He breathed a sigh of relief and fell on to his backside, sitting panting on the deck.

That was how Jurgen found him, sitting and panting. Antal hadn't even heard him coming and the outlander emerged from the pipe as silently as ash falling on ash. Even his boots made no noise as he paced across the deck towards Antal, a look of utter bemusement on his face, his pistol drawn.

Jurgen's lips moved, but nothing came out. It was at that point that Antal realised he had turned the implant's settings to zero and was temporarily profoundly deaf. He pushed the pick back into his ear and jostled with it for just a second, hardly daring to raise the volume one iota. Jurgen's voice gradually drifted into audibility and Antal left it at that.

'Come on,' said Jurgen. 'We're going.' Antal was glad not to be quizzed more rigorously on his unusual behaviour, or why he was jabbing himself in the ear though he couldn't be sure that Jurgen hadn't already asked him for an explanation. He'd wait to be asked again, he decided.

'Got it?' asked Antal.

'No,' said the outlander. Antal was stunned. That the outlander had failed was astonishing, especially after he had apparently disarmed the man, and if he hadn't beaten his taxes out of him, what was the clanging noise?

'What happened?' asked Antal.

'He said he ain't paying,' said Jurgen, 'so I pushed a little harder.'

Ah, thought Antal, so he *had* killed him for not paying.

'Ah,' said Antal, unintentionally thinking out loud. Jurgen ignored him and continued.

'So I pushed a little harder, and it seems he won't pay, because he has already paid.'

'Yeah, but that was last week,' said Antal. That was the same stupid excuse he had heard from every single one of the day's takes.

'Oh no,' said Jurgen, 'it was yesterday. He says he paid Erket.'

'What?' said Antal.

'Exactly,' said Jurgen.

'WHAT?' SAID LAKATOS. 'What do you mean, you pathetic little wretch?' Lakatos sneered in Erket's face.

The juve tried to shy away but all he could do was turn his head. The heavy chains that bound his hands to the ceiling and his ankles to the floor allowed him little space for movement.

'I was taking taxes. Someone had to since you got rid of Goddlesby,' he whined.

'Yes,' said Lakatos, 'but you were taking them for yourself!' Lakatos turned and nodded to Morden.

Morden reached out and dragged the tongs from where they lay in the fire. He jabbed them into Erket's side, pinching at his flesh. The juve howled in agony. Antal shied away from watching the spectacle and took a step back. Even at this distance, Antal's eyes were dry and painful from the heat of the flames. Erket, suspended just metres in front of the fire, must have been in agony. Idiot, thought Antal.

'Don't make it too quick,' said Lakatos to Morden before turning and leaving, bustling his way past the assembled spectators.

'Come,' he said, as he passed Antal and Jurgen where they stood at the back of the crowd of gangers.

'You GOT THE others?' asked Lakatos, taking his seat in the rather less crowded and, rather cooler main room of the hideout.

'Yes,' said Antal, 'all of them.' He pulled a pouch from his pocket and hurled it to his leader.

Lakatos caught the pouch in one hand and shook the contents out onto his lap. He scooped the credits up a handful at a time and counted them back into the pouch. He paused once he had counted the last credit.

'Give me that list,' he said to Jurgen who immediately proffered the rather tatty strip of parchment. Lakatos's gloved forefinger skimmed down the edge of the sheet. He mumbled to himself as he went, an almost silent tally.

'I thought Hobb didn't pay?' said Lakatos.

'No,' said Jurgen. 'Not a credit. That's how we found out about Erket's siphoning.'

'But it's all here,' said Lakatos.

'Oh, some of them paid a little extra,' said Antal.

'There is enough here to have covered Hobb's share, you know that? You could have covered for Erket with this.' Lakatos raised his gaze to Antal.

'Hobb didn't pay,' was Antal's only answer. It was greeted with a raucous, booming laugh from his leader who leapt from his seat and strode across the room, slapping Antal firmly on the shoulders in congratulation.

'Very good, Antal, very good indeed,' he said. 'Taxes will be solely your preserve from now on. I am most impressed. I am afraid, though,' he went on, 'before that there is some rather more urgent business to deal with.

'Durn hasn't come back yet.'

'You want us to go to Fulcrum Spike and look for him?' asked Antal.

'I don't think there's much point in looking for him,' said Lakatos, his voice tinged with bitterness. 'But you must go to Fulcrum Spike and be sure the message got through.'

'We will go at once,' said Antal, buoyed by the reception his tax raising efforts had received, and keen to show his loyalty to his leader. It was a chance he was to be denied, however.

'No,' said Jurgen, 'I'll go alone. There's work to be done here still, and it seems I'm having more luck out there than most.'

'Very well,' said Lakatos. 'Go it alone, Jurgen. Emperor fare you well.'

Jurgen nodded and left the room, leaving a mildly disappointed Antal to nonetheless bask in the glory of his leader's admiration.

CHAPTER: THIRTEEN

'COME,' SAID ADDEC, beckoning to the stranger. He had heard of the outlander, but he had yet to lay eyes on him. He was greatly startled when he did.

'I am Jurgen, your leadership. It is an honour,' he said.

The stranger was tall and lean looking, his skin ruddy, almost red, though Addec thought it nothing more than the dyeing effect of the ash carried in the storm winds. He bore none of the garb of the Cawdor and was clearly a convert. He was also clearly a particularly hardy individual, having ventured here alone from Fall Sands at the height of Ash Season. These traits combined told Addec that this Jurgen might be rather more than a simple ganger, and perhaps a chosen convert working directly for Catafengi himself. Because of this, Addec was both openly welcoming and privately wary.

'Very well, Jurgen,' said Addec. 'You are welcome, but what brings you here in a season such as this?'

'Hmm,' said Jurgen, frowning. 'Then I take it you haven't seen Durn?'

'Durn?' asked Addec. 'I have not laid eyes on him for perhaps a year. What do you mean?' Jurgen seemed troubled by Addec's reply.

'Durn was sent here some days ago,' said Jurgen, 'bearing urgent news, Brother Addec. *Urgent* news.'

'Hmm,' said Addec, rising from his seat. 'Best you come with me, Jurgen.'

Addec held out his arm and gestured for the out-lander to follow him. Jurgen skipped the short distance across the floor in two purposeful strides and followed Addec off to the corridor at the right. As they passed the crowd of Cawdor at the edge of the room, Addec called out.

'Deeran. Deer–' but he was cut short as he noticed the figure perched behind his shoulder. His son was already at his side, following instinctively. The three of them hurried down the corridor and into a much smaller, and rather sparsely furnished room at its end.

'I am guessing,' said Addec, 'that this is not the kind of urgent news to be discussing in a crowded room.'

'Perhaps not, Brother Addec, perhaps not,' said Jurgen. He placed his hand in the breast of his jacket and rifled through his pockets. He drew out a parchment and passed it to Addec.

Addec unfolded it. *All well*, it read. Addec just frowned. Such a simple message was clearly no more than a foil. Addec gazed around, but he could see no canteen or trough. The best he could find was a puddle of murky, milky water in the corner, pooling on the stone where a steady trickle ran down from the pipes mounted on the ceiling above.

Addec stepped over to the puddle. With his old bones creaking he knelt and dragged the parchment over the water's surface. Instantly he was interrupted by a determined and quite unnatural-sounding cough from the outlander. Addec turned and looked back over his shoulder.

'Brother Jurgen,' said Addec, nodding in the direction of Deeran, 'I give you Brother Deeran,' he went on. 'My *son.*'

Jurgen nodded, clearly satisfied at the explanation and the indication of trust. Besides, thought Addec, he had no particular reason for thinking that even this Jurgen was privy to the secret of the parchments, though his reaction had clearly shown that he was. For Lakatos to have sent him when Durn was already feared lost, clearly marked Jurgen out as a man more capable than most. He knew of the parchments and of their hidden messages and so was not some mere hapless messenger. Addec's suspicion that Jurgen served a higher authority was growing rapidly.

He hoisted the damp sheet up out of the puddle and held it aloft.

The Scarlet Skulls are no moor. Lago is out for us. Be reddy.

So it read. Lakatos's dialect was crude, his hand cruder; not like Addec's own, cultured language learned in the higher chambers of House Cawdor's Hive City monasteries, but the message was clear enough.

'You have read this,' said Addec to Jurgen, more of a statement than a question.

'No, though I know its meaning,' he said.

'Very well, then tell me what you know.'

Addec listened as Jurgen recounted his nigh unbelievable tale. How he had found Handomel's gang slaughtered to a man, perhaps by their own hand, perhaps by another when distracted by some internal strife. Addec was shocked, but far from surprised. Handomel had been less than wise in Addec's view, and the discipline he bred in his gang was an insubstantial thing, a careful balancing act for which he relied only upon his own finely tuned guile. He had

always been confident of it in his own arrogant fashion, and convincing for it, but to Addec – a man
three decades his senior – this fragile discipline had
always seemed to be a thing destined to break down
just as soon as Handomel's tongue was silenced.

That it had turned out this way was no surprise, and
Addec felt precious little sympathy for any of them.
He'd seen a hundred ambitious fools come and go in
such a manner. He'd saved a hundred, too, but only
those who listened, and Handomel had certainly never
listened. He sighed as Jurgen concluded his tale, but
offered no more a sign of his feelings than that.

'And this Lago,' said Addec, 'tell me what you know
of him.'

So began yet another nigh unbelievable tale, that Jurgen was the author of the secret messages, and the
architect of their very fabric. That he had once served
the guilders with this expertise and that he had, by the
same means, fallen foul of their jealous secrecy. That
they had tried to kill him, that they had failed, and so
entrusted the task to a man named Lago.

'I do not think, Brother Jurgen, that if I were Lago, I
should be so keen to wipe out an entire gang that has
never so much as met the man I sought,' said Addec,
unsure of the relevance.

'Very wise, brother,' said Jurgen. 'I don't think that's
what happened. I don't even think Lago knows I'm
here. If he finds me, it'll just be blind luck on his part.
He's here for somebody else, or something else, and
that's about it.'

'Handomel?' asked Addec.

'He was after Handomel, yeah,' said Jurgen, 'but he
got him. Then he came back. He's after all of us, as far
as I can tell.' With that Jurgen pitched into yet another
chapter of the tale: of the body found out in the abandoned domes between here and Fall Sands bearing

Jurgen's wanted poster, of Deveres's disappearance and now Durn's. It all added up to a tale with much drama yet to come.

'Then Handomel's men are done away with, and we are his next targets, is that what you are saying, Brother Jurgen?' asked Addec, though he was already sure of the answer.

'Yes,' he said, 'and we've already wasted too much damn time working it out.'

'There is still no reason for it,' said Addec.

'Maybe there isn't,' said Jurgen, 'but at this rate we'll be dead before we fathom the reason. Seems plain enough to me he's out for us, and we should deal with it now or this whole damned scheme comes tumbling down.'

Ah yes, thought Addec. This, perhaps, was the real reason behind Jurgen's urgency in the matter, and the reason why Lago seemed to be engaged in such a systematic extermination of the Scarlet Skulls, and now the others.

Addec knew of many ways to spread the Emperor's word, to bring redemption to his struggling children, but Catafengi, and those that served him, were engaged in a particularly blatant mission to do so. Addec had never been entirely sure this was the best way.

His House, his own family, laboured as hard as any to do the Emperor's work, but always unseen, never drawing unwanted attention to themselves. House Cawdor was committed in its entirety to doing just this, and they were well advanced in those aims. They were populous, perhaps second only to the promiscuous litters of Orlocks in number. Certainly the Escher and Goliath couldn't match them in size, their numbers cut short by brutality and male infirmity respectively. The mysterious Delaque were impossible to pinpoint in all things, though they certainly never appeared especially numerous, nor did the Van Saar, whose great minds seemed little given to the matter of dynasty and dominion. Cawdor were numerous, strong and prosperous, and because of this it had long spread the word of the Emperor.

Every Cawdor acquisition, new trade agreement, or contract fulfilled was tribute to the steps taken one at a time towards achieving the Emperor's will. Was such slow, steady progress a bad thing? As a young man, Addec had been sure it was and wholeheartedly committed himself to the fiery revolution offered by men like Catafengi.

Now, as an old man, Addec was increasingly sure that his life would have achieved much more had he remained up there, working away unseen and unthreatened. House Cawdor had enemies, true enough, but there was certainly no Lago up there, threatening to upend the entire venture, root and branch.

Catafengi and his cult were secretive in their actions, but their existence was certainly no secret. Had their plot been uncovered, and their agents, too, then it was no surprise that men like Lago were after them. There would be no reward too great for bringing down a Redemptionist cult such as theirs, feared and loathed, as they were, by the hive's most powerful. Addec had long thought such a day might come, but he had long ago made his bed and now he had to lie in it. He breathed a sigh of regret as he pondered how to proceed.

'Tell me, Jurgen,' he said at length, 'what does Lakatos plan now that Lago is upon us?'

'If Durn is dead, then it's Lago who got to him. I'd bet a fistful of credits it was Lago,' said Jurgen. 'I lost Deveres out there, too, but that was further out, away towards Handomel's territory. If he got Durn this

past week, then he's out there someplace between
here and Fall Sands. That's where we can get them.'

'Them?' asked Addec.

'I don't think Lago is alone,' said Jurgen. 'We
already found one dead bounty hunter out there,
and if it was him who killed the Skulls, I don't think
he did it alone.'

'How many?' asked Deeran, suddenly interested.

'Impossible to say, but we'll outnumber them.
That's how we get them,' said Jurgen.

'How?' asked Addec.

'Lago's smart,' said Jurgen. 'He won't just go charging into town. He picked off Handomel, and let his
gang tear themselves apart before finishing them off
– if he even had to – and he's been picking us off one
by one just the same. He's taken Durn and Deveres
out there. It won't harm him any to take his time.
We've got to force his hand, flush him out,' said Jurgen.

'What are you suggesting?' asked Addec.

'Well, he's past here, well beyond Fulcrum Spike,
I'm sure of it, and probably holed up out on the edge
of Fall Sands,' Jurgen said. 'If you and your men can
run a sweep towards Fall Sands, and drive him
towards the town, we'll pick him off from there. Give
me a day's head start and we'll be ready.

'The edge of town is full of good spots, and its
almost clear of the ash. We'll be holed up there, and
can pick Lago's men off once you've driven them
onto us. They'll be trapped, they'll be surrounded,
and they'll be sitting ducks.'

'I'm not sure it will be so easy,' said Deeran.

'We've got to be precise about it and plan carefully,
it's true,' said Jurgen, 'but we can do it.'

'Go on,' said Addec, 'tell me every detail of your
plan.'

ADDEC HAD LISTENED to every word, hung on them even. He had repeated almost every word of it, too, saying it back to Jurgen for fear of leaving any single detail unaddressed. Even so, it had not been an easy decision to come to. Jurgen had been gone for a day, with Addec's promise that he would do as was asked, but even then Addec had fretted and could not be sure wisdom was on the side of this particular plan.

In the end, he had settled on it as the only plan. It was a necessary course of action, whether it was prudent or not. Addec worried that it was simply the lethargy of age that disinclined him to the plan, and since Deeran seemed keener on it, Addec had at last resolved that it truly was a vital action they would be undertaking. Vital enough, Addec had decided at length, that he would lead his men in person, for the first time in many years, and perhaps for the last.

He strolled at a gentle pace from his private chambers, striding through the heart of his domain on his way back to the rundown old ganghouse where he would impart his orders, and his blessings, on his men. Deeran had gone ahead to the hideout, so at least some of the plan would be known to them, and practical preparations would already be well underway.

At length, Addec reached the ganghouse. He entered the building with a reluctant sigh and a heavy heart, but a firm resolve.

'Brothers,' he said as he stepped inside, 'we have a fight, and this is how it will be.' Deeran nodded from across the room and stepped forwards into the centre of the crowd.

'We're going to fight out in the old dome around Fall Sands,' said Deeran. 'There is a man out there who is a threat to us all. His name is Lago.'

A gasp emerged formlessly from the crowd. The name had been whispered, rumoured for weeks, and now they heard it from their leaders. Their shock was of little surprise to Addec.

'He's not alone, but we will outnumber them, and we will be triumphant,' said Deeran. 'This is the plan.

'Every one of us will wear one of these, plus whatever other dark robes you can find.' Deeran flung a pile of black cloaks onto the table. Two more similar piles stood in the corner behind him. The robes looked exactly like Jurgen had said they must.

'The Union will be wearing black cloaks just the same. Do not fire on anybody with a black cloak. Anyone else, don't waste a second in bringing them down.'

A boisterous cheer greeted the mention of violence.

'We'll head towards Fall Sands,' said Deeran. 'Lago and his men are out there. We'll find them and take as many out as we can. The most important thing, though, is that none of them get past us and that we drive them towards Fall Sands. We'll have them trapped there and the Union can pick them off from the edge of town.

'The Union won't be leaving Fall Sands. Lakatos will keep his men behind a line on the edge of town, so you won't meet them out in the wastes, but remember the black cloaks, just in case.

'Stick together,' Deeran continued. 'We'll be fine as long as we don't get separated out in the wastes.'

ADDEC LED HIS men in the long march out of town. It seemed like an eternity since he and Deeran had finally gathered the men, but in truth it had been no more than two hours. It had taken two hours to ready the weapons and to have everyone dress in black robes. Each and every one of the gang that marched out into the wastes was dressed alike in plain black robes, just like Jurgen had told them.

In truth, quite aside from the ease with which the garb would allow them to tell friend from foe, these heavier cloth cloaks would serve them well out in the storms.

They were not underequipped by any means. Fulcrum Spike and the vast vents lying derelict at its edge had once been the lungs of the whole hive. In a lost age of industry, the dome's population had been engaged in maintaining the wellbeing of this intricate ventilation system. For a few, this had required venturing out onto the exterior of the vents, out into the ash wastes themselves, and the equipment required for such perilous work could still be found in Fulcrum Spike by a determined searcher.

It wasn't exactly archeotech, but as well as the grapnels used to ascend the high vents, Deeran had salvaged half a dozen respirator masks of the sort used by hive engineers. They were manufactured to the highest possible standard, far better than the unreliable, chemical filter rubbish you could buy in the Underhive, but they were aged and only three of them could be made to work. Addec himself had declined the offer of a mask, but beside him Deeran and his two heavies now wore the devices. They would be an unbelievable boon out amidst the raging storms.

For all this, Addec was still deeply wary. In his darker moments he contemplated leaving Lakatos and the others to their fate. He considered arriving – quite by accident of course – just a little too late. Addec would shed few tears for the end of Lakatos, and fewer still if Catafengi were to meet his doom. He was quite sure that he could go on spreading the Emperor's word without that damned cult drawing attention to them and bringing trouble to all of them. But, as he knew all too well, there was simply no way he could be sure it was Lakatos that Lago would come for first. He had no way of knowing if he or his men might be Lago's first target, and for that reason alone he was certain that he must do exactly what had been asked of him.

With that curious resolve foremost in his mind, Addec led his men once more into the raging storms.

CHAPTER: FOURTEEN

JURGEN CROSSED A shallow bluff. Its shape had changed since last he saw it, but its location remained familiar. Reaching its crest, he could see down the shallow incline to Fall Sands, its silhouette dimly visible through the ash storms that raged around him. It was a long journey, but a familiar one and it troubled Jurgen little. Truth be told he enjoyed it: the solitude, being alone in the wilderness. He had always been a loner, an outlander.

He would be alone again soon enough, he thought to himself as he descended the far side of the bluff and made his way once more to the less than welcoming lights of Fall Sands.

'ADDEC SAW HIM,' said Jurgen, his tone hushed and his face pressed close to Lakatos's ear as the pair huddled in the tiny alcove. This was news that Jurgen certainly didn't want to break to the others. 'Three days ago, so he made good time.'

'Then why the hell didn't he make it back?' asked Lakatos.

Jurgen frowned but gave no other answer. There was no need since it was written on Lakatos's face. Durn had died out in the storms, just like Deveres. Lakatos had sent them both on their way, sent them both to their deaths. That was true: Lakatos had indeed sent them to their deaths, no matter the manner in which they found it.

'This is the message Addec gave him to bring back,' said Jurgen, handing Lakatos a sheet of parchment folded into quarters.

'Have you read it?' asked Lakatos.

'Addec read it to me himself,' Jurgen replied. 'It isn't good.'

'IF DURN LEFT Fulcrum Spike but didn't make it back here, then Lago is close,' said Lakatos. Jurgen just nodded in grim agreement. Lakatos folded the parchment and passed it back to Jurgen, who returned it to a pocket inside the breast of his coat. Its contents had come as no surprise to Jurgen: that Lago was still at large, that he had killed Handomel and later wiped out his gang, and that he was intent on doing the same to the Union.

Lakatos didn't seem to care exactly how Addec had come to know this and without being asked Jurgen had little inclination to explain. Clearly Lakatos's mind was elsewhere, troubled more by the news than the method by which it had been uncovered.

'Damn it,' said Lakatos. 'What do we do now?' Lakatos seemed genuinely scared by this latest turn of events, as if suddenly realising that this Lago presented a rather greater threat than he had so far imagined. Jurgen, of course, had not for a minute underestimated the danger.

'You know this Lago. What do we do now, Jurgen?' Lakatos asked.

'Way I see it, we've got two advantages,' said Jurgen, placing a toxstick to his lips and sparking it. 'One... the ash storms. We're at home in them, or near as a man can be, and we know the lay of the land, which Lago doesn't.' He paused.

'And two… Lago is a fool. He's got no subtlety, no guile. He just can't resist a showdown. Chances are him and his goons are gonna stroll straight into Fall Sands, expecting us to meet them right out on the street. That would be a very foolish thing to do. We wouldn't stand a chance in a shootout with Lago, but we do have a chance if we ambush him. I bet he just won't be able to resist making the big entrance. We've got to ambush him out amidst the storms before he reaches town.'

Lakatos turned, taking a step away from Jurgen, his back to him. In the shadowy alcove, even this tiny distance was almost enough for Lakatos to vanish completely into darkness. Even then, it was clear to Jurgen that Lakatos's mind was racing, and that he was wracked with uncertainty. The noise of his hobnailed boots beat out a fast rhythm from the shadows as he paced frantically. At length, his mind was made up.

'Okay, Jurgen. I don't see any other way. Let's do it. Let's go and get the others,' said Lakatos.

THEY ALL CLUSTERED round him. Even Lakatos was no more than a spectator, another face in the crowd, thronging round the table across which Jurgen held court. All of them were there; at least, all those that remained. Morden, Lirbus, Hargitay, Antal, Galamb, Karman, Todor, Rubik and Mero. Ten with Lakatos, plus Jurgen himself. Todor was all but lame, and Mero was all but blind. The pair would be useless out there, but the plan would not be well served by leaving them behind. They stood and listened the same as everyone else. They were Union, and now was the time for them to show it.

Even Erket was within earshot, though he was clapped in chains, and had no part to play in what was to come. He *was* there, however, and he could hear what was being said.

'You've heard by now,' said Jurgen, his voice booming across the room, its timbre carrying every ounce of his stern resolve, 'that Lago is coming.' Each and every member of the assembled crowd exhaled and turned to look at his neighbour or hung his head to stare at the floor. They had known it was coming, but it was no easier to hear it said.

'Here's what we are going to do,' said Jurgen, unfazed. 'Lago is a stranger in these parts. The lay of the land, and the storms, are our greatest allies. We'll use them against him and we're all going to be fine.

'We're going to ambush him – as best we can in these storms, anyway – outside the settlement, out in the wasted part of the dome. If we let him get to Fall Sands, we're in trouble.

'We're not going to make ourselves obvious, either,' said Jurgen. 'We're not going out there like this just to paint targets on our backs. I want all of you changed, out of robes and into something he won't recognise us in. Nothing too Cawdor, nothing too Redemptionist, you get me? In fact, let's make sure it's something dull. The more we can hide ourselves in the ash the more chance we've got, okay?' A few scattered nods answered him.

'Lago is out there, somewhere between here and Fulcrum Spike. Durn never made it back, but I did, so Lago can't be that close, or he could have cut me off on the way back into Fall Sands.

'There's only one way into Fall Sands from that direction, so we'll ambush him there. We'll get far enough from the settlement to get under the cover of the storms, and to get out amongst the dunes, but not so far as to make it possible for him to get past us, you understand?'

Half a dozen nods, a couple of swift hand gestures and yet more grim silence answered him. That was enough and Jurgen continued with his plan.

'If there's no sign of Lago, we can wait it out, we've got time. We'll take up high positions on the dunes, and wait till Lago passes into one of the furrows where we can catch him in crossfire. He won't stand a chance.

'He got Deveres and Durn, and Emperor only knows what happened to Handomel and the Skulls, but this will all be over soon. There is no problem here, you all get me?'

Silence again filled the void left by Jurgen's commanding oratory. Still, it would do. They had all absorbed every detail, out of fear if nothing else. They were ready to begin, if 'begin' was the right term for an endgame such as this. No, thought Jurgen, they were ready to *finish* this, and he was more ready than any of them.

JURGEN HAD LEFT nothing to chance. He had moved the gang from their regular hideout to a crumbling shack some two hundred metres from the pipe, just in case their enemies should approach while they prepared. Thus, it was here that the Union gathered in silent contemplation, here where magazines were filled, spares pocketed, weapons checked, bandoliers slung and minds readied.

'Galamb, Karman, you ready?' asked Jurgen.

'Yes. I am,' said Galamb, while the younger juve at his shoulder simply nodded. Their arms were meagre – an autopistol for Galamb, a laspistol and knife for Karman – and they had needed little time to ready themselves. He presumed Galamb also had at least one blade, though he had so far chosen not to draw it. The pair of them wore nothing more than rags, but dull, khaki rags, which would do a good job of hiding them out there in the storms. Lacking enough rags for a new hood, neither Galamb nor Karman were masked at all and looked quite unlike their usual Cawdor selves. There were, of course, no black cloaks to be seen anywhere amongst the gang's new panoply. Jurgen was quite clear about this point.

'Go to the edge of town, no further than the first dune, and hide yourselves on opposite sides of the approach. If anyone comes, get right back here. Otherwise, do nothing until we get there, you understand me?' asked Jurgen. The pair nodded vigorously at which Jurgen raised his hands and ushered them out of the door.

Rubik was some way from ready yet. His immense autocannon lay in pieces on the table in front of him, and as fast as he worked, it would be the best part of an hour before he was ready. Earlier, he had seemed ready to rush, to abandon some of his familiar routines, but Jurgen had demanded that he calm himself and take every care he would at any other time. He had to be prepared as best he could, and if that took time, so be it. Even some of the others weren't yet done.

Ammunition wasn't in short supply, but it wasn't exactly plentiful either and Morden and Todor crouched in the corner, their hands hovering between a makeshift melting pot and the stone crucible from which they were churning out bullets. Another hour of that wouldn't exactly hurt them, and besides, Jurgen still had another matter to take care of first.

He crossed the room, those he passed hardly looking up they were so engrossed, and drew close to Lakatos.

'I have to go and see Catafengi before we do this,' said Jurgen. Lakatos looked up, surprised.

'You want to tell him about this?' asked Lakatos, clearly doubtful.

'No, but I must pass on a message,' said Jurgen.

'Send one of the others. Can't it wait?'

'No,' said Jurgen, firmly.

'Then I'll go with you if it demands such urgency,' said Lakatos. 'What is it?'

'It's a message from Addec. He wanted to speak to Catafengi himself, face to face, but until all this is over, I didn't see how he could. He gave me a message and made me swear to pass it on to Catafengi,' Jurgen said.

'What does it say?' asked Lakatos.

'It is a message for Catafengi himself, and for Catafengi alone,' said Jurgen. 'Please, I'm only doing as Addec asked, and I serve Catafengi, too, Lakatos. I mean you no disrespect.'

Lakatos nodded. Jurgen was gone.

PERHAPS THIS WAS going to be easier than Jurgen had thought. Preparations were not yet quite complete, but they were going smoothly and nothing had happened to make Jurgen think his plan might fail, or that he might be forced by necessity to change it. No, things were progressing very well, and once he had seen Catafengi, he would be ready to begin in earnest.

He had no time to waste with the goons on the door and shimmied off the ladder a metre or so short of its peak. He caught a hold of the underside of one of the adjoining walkways and, finding it suitably loaded with pipes and metal ribbing, swung himself along underneath it by his arms alone. At the end he squirmed through a tiny ventilation shaft that was barely wide enough to accommodate his shoulders. He needed to squeeze through for the metre it took him to get behind the deacons on the door. Emerging behind them, he was clear of the shaft and stepped out into the dome proper.

It had changed considerably since Lakatos first introduced him to the place. It had a sense of permanence that hadn't been there before. The Redemption seemed almost settled here, as monolithic as the stone walls that surrounded them. Perhaps Catafengi's plans for his fiery domain of the righteous were better advanced than Jurgen knew. Perhaps not.

Jurgen strode up the steps, flanked on either side by metal spikes bearing skulls: many, many more skulls, in fact, since Jurgen had first come here just two weeks earlier. Perhaps that was a good sign. Perhaps not.

Jurgen slid past the innermost of the two overlapping metal sheets, which served as an entrance to Catafengi's chambers. The room was busier than Jurgen had seen it before. Four robed and hooded acolytes knelt at the grand master's feet, his ministry to receive. Their devotion was plain, but it certainly wasn't a match for Jurgen's urgency and his purposeful stride was unbroken as he crossed the floor towards Catafengi's throne.

'I must speak, grand master,' he said. His voice must have sounded urgent, for Catafengi at once raised a bony finger and bade the acolytes leave him. They did so and Jurgen offered only the swiftest genuflection before coming to the matter at hand.

'What is it, Jurgen?' asked Catafengi.

'It's urgent,' said Jurgen. 'I've seen Addec, and he says Lago is coming.'

Catafengi gave the verbal equivalent of a frown, his actual expression hidden by his flame-red hood.

'Lago?' he asked.

'Yes,' said Jurgen. 'Addec wanted to be sure the message reached you straight away… and he also sent this.' Jurgen reached into his pocket, pulling out a crumpled parchment, its imprecise folding apparently indicative of its urgency.

Catafengi took it and peeled its edges apart. It was plain enough and he beckoned with his hand. Jurgen pulled his canteen from under his coat and passed it to the grand master. Catafengi pulled at its stopper, but it wouldn't give.

His patience didn't last long and, forced to drop the parchment on his lap, he wrapped both hands round the stopper, pulled it clear and flung it away moodily. He spilled the flask's contents onto the parchment and ran his hand over it to spread the pooling moisture.

Catafengi held the parchment aloft. He had wet it from the reverse side and the writing was a little dim. He raised the sheet above his head where a stronger ray of light piercing the shack's ragged roof shone through the paper and made the writing a little clearer.

Catafengi, you are a dead man it read. He raised his glare to Jurgen.

'What is the meaning of this?' he asked.

The bullet through his head answered him instantly.

JURGEN DESCENDED THE steps as purposefully as he had gone up them. He strode across the dome's floor, passing out onto the walkway between the two deacons he had gone to such lengths to avoid minutes before. He didn't care now; they never stopped anyone on the way out, no matter how much his sudden emergence from the inside might startle them. He pushed them aside with his bustling pace and disappeared over the walkway, quickly vanishing into the Underhive's murky shadows.

It might be hours before they found Catafengi's body and realised they were leaderless, and what would they be then? Nothing better than a frenzied mob: nothing more than a collection of the same bitter, hateful, worthless individuals they have always been, leaderless, discontent and of little accord.

They might possess the same zeal and lust for violence, and they might still retain their senseless vitriol and fiery tempers. They might still have their weapons and their cruel implements of torture, but they had none of the direction that Catafengi's demagoguery brought to them, and without that they presented no more threat than the raving madmen that hollered and yowled at passers-by in settlements across the Underhive.

They would be nothing more than disgruntled, petulant radicals, hating the world all the more for the realisation of their own inability to change it. They were nothing at all now. This was how it had to be.

JURGEN WAS pleased with his work, now that it neared its end. He passed the gang's old hideout, where Erket still lay clapped in chains.

Erket was a loathsome, snivelling wretch: a wicked, bitter little snake whom Jurgen had despised since first laying eyes on him, but he was ignorant and he was harmless. He was privy to nothing of consequence and responsible for nothing of note. He was a worthless creature, but he was no more deserving of death than he was of salvation, and he would find neither at Jurgen's hand. Were it not for his utterly detestable character, Erket might have been more a target for Jurgen's pity than his retribution.

Could Erket have imagined that the ferocious beating Morden had dealt him, the humiliation, and the hours spent clapped in chains had saved his life? Probably not. It didn't matter. He'd survived nonetheless. He had to.

Somebody would have to remain. Somebody had to tell the tale, to pass on the legend, to speak of the crippling fear that cowards like Erket deserved to carry in their hearts wherever they went. They were many across the Underhive: those who spoke the name and voiced the legend. Erket would be one more, and he would serve well in that regard.

Jurgen walked on.

He passed the building he had called home on and off
for three weeks, that dirty little place where his tricks had
been worked and his pieces forged. That was the place
where the poor, desperate girl had come to find him to
take whatever revenge her addled mind thought he
deserved. That was the place where Durn had followed
her, and where Jurgen had killed him.

He'd met a fate kinder than dying out in the wastes. Jurgen's lone bullet didn't make Durn wait for the end whilst
choking, dehydrating or wasting away out in the storms.
He hadn't let Deveres suffer, either. He'd come back to finish him off just as soon as he'd given him long enough to
get himself disoriented. There was no need to make them
suffer, not the ones who were going to die, anyway.

The girl had chosen a wise place to confront him,
though she would never have known it. As he walked past
the building, he thought of the maze of lost corridors running deep beneath its few remaining floors. They were the
reason he had chosen it, and they were the means by
which he had smuggled that poor girl to safety in some
distant dome where she would never be known. A handful of his best forgeries had given her everything she
needed to buy passage all the way to the Spire, if she
wanted it.

Jurgen walked on.

He passed the Pipe Under Mile, where it had first
begun, and where the holy had first given themselves
away as the loathsome hypocrites they truly were,
crowded round their liquor as if it was the salvation they
claimed to be searching for, though every single one of
them knew better. Still, it had started there and it had
been as good a place as any. He strode on, towards where
it would finish.

* * *

'READY?' ASKED JURGEN. He had been back in the room barely ten seconds, and had done nothing more than throw the most cursory of glances around the place, but he could tell that they were all waiting for him. Every one of them was a completely changed figure. Their faces were still covered, as ever, but no longer by the heavy hoods and thick leather masks. Now they were swathed in rolls of dull cloth, wrapped so tightly that their features could be made out by the contours.

Their bodies were clothed likewise. Heavy brown, yellow or dull green material had been hastily slashed into tunics, strips had been wrapped round and round their arms and legs forming layers six or seven sheets thick. They would serve them well out in the storms, both as protection and as disguise.

Even Rubik stood ready, his knuckles white where his big hands braced the autocannon's staggering bulk.

There was no reply to his question, but Jurgen knew they were ready to a man, and he was too.

The gang paced out onto the street, an ominous feeling hanging over them. Jurgen marched at the head of the pack, leading them the short distance down the dusty track to the very edge of town.

As the swirling storms enveloped them, Jurgen stopped. He cast his gaze out to either side where the shifting dunes rose like shadows around them. Away to his left, a single figure skidded down the flank of a distant dune, coming into view again as he crested a nearer peak and scampered towards the gang. It was Galamb.

'Anything?' asked Jurgen.

'Nothing,' said Galamb.

'Good,' said Jurgen.

The gang continued its advance, striding forwards line abreast. Galamb ran a short distance ahead, leading them out as far as he had dared go. Reaching this high bluff, the line halted, and a second figure appeared on the dunes away to the right: Karman.

'Nobody has passed this point?' asked Jurgen as the second juve rejoined the group.

'Nobody,' said Karman. 'Nobody got past me at all.'

'Nor me,' said Galamb.

'Okay,' said Jurgen, turning and raising his voice to address not only the juves but the entire gang. 'Here's what we're gonna do. We'll hold a line here. Morden, Lirbus, Hargitay and Antal here with me; Todor, Rubik and Mero across the gully with Lakatos. Karman, Galamb, you push on and scout out the land ahead and as soon as you see anything, get right back here and tell us, y'hear me?'

Both juves nodded before dashing off into the storms as the line of gangers gradually parted, Lakatos's group making its way across the gully and up the ashy slope to occupy the dune on the other side. They were invisible amidst the storm before they had even crossed the gully, let alone by the time they had reached their hiding place on the crest above.

Jurgen lay back on the dune beneath him. To his left was Morden who lay flat on his belly, his gun aimed out into the gully. To his right was Hargitay, doing likewise, and beyond him, Antal stood scanning the horizon, or at least scanned as far as he could see in the ferocious storms. Lirbus crouched just beyond him.

Jurgen was in no rush and tossed a toxstick to his lips, sparking it with the small slate palmed out of his sleeve, almost imperceptibly. It brought to mind Goddlesby, and the events of a few days ago. Jurgen had led the little man to this very spot before dealing with him as his actions deserved.

Jurgen ran his fingers over the scraggly flame motif crudely embossed in the lid of his toxstick tin. It was the same tin from which he had offered Goddlesby that small mercy, though the contents at that time hadn't been quite the same.

Goddlesby was a good man, weak, but well-intentioned, and he deserved no ill-treatment at Jurgen's hand. The toxstick had been a true mercy: a dummy, laced with sedative. That first puff had sent Goddlesby into a deep sleep. He would be disoriented when he woke up, but he would at least be far from here, down in the domes beyond the Falls where Jurgen had taken him to a safehouse. He didn't want to trick the little man like that, but he just couldn't have him asking too many questions, and he certainly couldn't have him finding his way back. Doping him and smuggling him out was the best he could do. Goddlesby had disappeared sure enough, that was all that was asked of Jurgen. He had just made Goddlesby disappear in a rather less gruesome fashion than the rest of the Union would have imagined.

Jurgen inhaled deeply on his toxstick. He exhaled, but it was imperceptible, the trail of vapours merging instantly with the equally toxic ash carried in the howling winds of these seasonal storms. The toxstick was nothing more than an affectation, anyway. The implants in his neck filtered out its toxins just the same as they did any other, and by the time the inhalant reached Jurgen's lungs it was nothing more than fresh air. It was an old habit, though, and one that died hard, no matter its ineffectiveness.

He finished the toxstick and readied himself. It was about time.

GALAMB ADVANCED CAUTIOUSLY, stopping and looking around almost every second step. Even then, he couldn't escape the feeling that he had gone too far, that he had lost his bearings and that his enemy could well have got past him.

He moved on again, his visibility improving unexpectedly as the wind took another of its restless turns and drove the thickest of the ash cloud away from him.

That was when he saw them: perhaps a dozen cloaked figures, crossing the dunes towards them. Lago and his men, it had to be. He turned, ready to race back to the others, but he had barely gone a step before he caught sight of another figure, way off in the distance. It was Karman.

Damn him, thought Galamb. It was hard to gauge relative distance out here, but he could tell instantly that Karman had advanced perhaps a hundred metres further ahead and was already far too close to the approaching bounty hunters. Worse still, it looked like Karman still hadn't seen them.

Galamb watched in horror as a flash of light pulsed out from the cloaked figures, tearing through the ash-laden air and dropping Karman's silhouetted figure to the ground without a sound. Shit, thought Galamb, too late.

On instinct he opened fire with his own pistol, unleashing two, three, four autogun rounds at the bounty hunters, though at this range, and in this visibility, he didn't stand a chance of hitting them. He should have run. He knew he should have run, but he had just seen Karman being gunned down and he was firing on impulse.

The ordered line of the bounty hunters broke apart and four or five of the figures faded from sight, presumably skidding down off the dunes and into one of the deep furrows that delineated them. The others turned straight towards him and a hail of fire rushed past his head. Galamb dropped onto his stomach and lowered his head to the ground as all hell broke loose around him.

* * *

ANTAL RAISED HIS head at the first sound of it.

'Gunfire!' he said, hollering across the line to the men crouched beside him. Hargitay and Lirbus dithered, their heads turning from Antal, to Jurgen, and back to Antal again, unsure of what to do. Jurgen and Morden showed no such indecision and the pair rose at once to their feet. A moment later, all five were dashing along the crest of the dune, advancing out into the storms but never once losing their precious elevation.

Luckily for them, the dune formed a great U-shaped ridge, and as they closed in on the sound of the gunfire, they found themselves on its highest spur, overlooking a rapidly erupting battle.

Two groups of cloaked figures could be seen below. In the distance, one was already engaged in a firefight, though Antal couldn't be sure who with. Below them, a second group rushed across a broad furrow, heading right for the base of the dune on which Antal and the others stood.

Antal raised his hand and without a sound pointed down at the men below. Jurgen and Morden nodded, Hargitay and Lirbus following suit a second later. All five lowered their weapons and unleashed a withering volley of fire on the cloaked figures below.

Two fell instantly. One rose again a moment later, hauling himself to his feet, before another cacophony of gunfire sounded and he was again felled, this time lying utterly motionless beside his equally dead comrade.

The other three scattered but they couldn't escape the open ground. Antal raised his sights, tracking one figure that raced away back down the furrow. His heart raced and adrenaline coursed through his body but he kept his nerve and didn't fire until he had matched the man's speed with the slow movement of his own aim. At last he fired, a scorching las-bolt shooting out and

striking the target square between the shoulder blades.
He fell to the ground, kicking up a cloud of ash around
him. Before he had a chance to see whether the man
was dead or not, Antal unleashed two more shots
towards his prone form just to be sure.

The smoke began to clear and Antal realised his mistake. The follow-up shots had missed their target
amidst the swirling ash kicked up by the man's fall, and
the target had got back to his feet and continued his
frantic dash away. Antal fired off another blast as soon
as he saw him, but it was a snap shot and it flew well
wide, and now his lasgun's power cell was overheating.
He rushed on across the crest of the dune, trying to
keep the man in his sights, but it was a fool's move.

Antal had strayed past the dune's highest point and
suddenly found himself skidding down its steep-sloped
side. He reached out an arm to steady himself but lost
his balance and tumbled awkwardly down the dune.
He came to a halt a few metres further down as the soft
ash broke his fall and then slowly pulled himself back
to his feet. He looked up, straight into the face of one
of the cloaked bounty hunters, just in time to see the
autogun pointed at his face. The last thing Antal ever
heard – in terrible, stark clarity above the normal loud
hiss of his bionic implant – was the crack of the shot.

TODOR ROSE AT the sound of gunfire. He looked around
but couldn't pinpoint its source. It flared up again, and
then another volley could be heard from another direction. Someone was returning fire.

Todor's gaze crossed the gully where five silhouettes
dashed away into the distance. It was Jurgen and the
others.

Todor called out. 'Lakatos! Lakatos!'

His leader turned to face him at once, already aware
of the sound of gunfire.

'Over there,' said Todor. 'Jurgen and the others have moved up ahead. They must have found Lago.'

'Good,' said Lakatos. 'Let's go.'

Todor trailed a little behind his leader as they crossed the gully. Todor was deeply uncomfortable out in the open and kept his wits about him. Lakatos didn't seem anywhere near as bothered and strode ahead, straight towards the sound of gunfire.

Todor stopped and turned, taking a good look behind him, fearful of ambush. It was then that he caught sight of a figure away to his right, crawling through the ash. He raised his autogun, ready to snap off a shot before the figure raised its head and revealed a bare face. It was Galamb.

Todor raced towards him but pulled up short ten metres from the juve as he realised that he was under fire. Todor quickly dropped to his belly and scrabbled across to Galamb, bullets racing over their heads all the while.

'What's going on?' yelled Todor over the noise.

'Lago… He's here.'

'I know,' said Todor, though in truth he hadn't been completely sure until that moment, 'but I saw Jurgen's men over there,' he said, pointing off into the distance. 'There was gunfire from over there. What the frag is this?'

'They shot down Karman,' said Galamb. 'I saw them, so I fired back. There was a lot of them, ten, maybe a dozen, and they split up when I fired.'

'Shit,' yelled Todor, suddenly realising that they may very well be surrounded. 'Let's get back to higher ground,' he said.

Galamb just nodded.

Todor raised his arms above his head and loosed a couple of rounds. The shots were woefully inaccurate but silenced their enemies for at least a moment. With that Galamb pushed up off his hands, leapt to his feet and dashed back, away from the gunfire. Todor fired another couple of shots and began to crawl backwards on his knees.

He stopped a moment later and glanced over his shoulder. Galamb had taken up a new position about twenty metres back. He raised his hand as a signal and Todor nodded in reply. Galamb opened up with his pistol and Todor got to his feet, taking the chance to dash back to the slight ridge that Galamb now occupied.

'This isn't high enough,' said Todor, frustrated to find their view no better than it had been before. 'We've got to get right back or we'll never see them coming.' Galamb nodded again and rose to his feet, dashing up the steep dune to their rear as Todor laid down some covering fire.

It wasn't enough. Todor stopped and turned as he heard a scream and then a dull thud from behind him. Galamb had barely made it ten metres before being shot down. Todor thought at first that he was dead but as the little juve rolled over onto his back, Todor could see that his face was twisted in agony.

Todor had no choice. He scrambled on all fours to where Galamb lay and thrust his arm under his neck to prop his head up.

'Can you walk?' asked Todor. As Galamb opened his mouth to speak, a rush of blood gushed out and his head rocked back. 'Shit,' roared Todor, but Galamb was dead.

Todor searched the terrain all around, desperately looking for a route he might take without exposing himself to fire. The noise of gunfire still rang out ahead of him, and from his right where he was sure Jurgen was engaged with the second group. He looked back towards Fall Sands and his jaw dropped in horror. A tall, cloaked figure approached. How the hell had they got behind him, Todor thought to himself as the final, fatal shot rang out and silenced his thoughts forever.

THE MEN DOWN in the gully below were sitting ducks. From his high perch, Lirbus had time to take careful aim and fire without leaving cover for a moment. When at last he did pull the trigger, it rang out good and true, passing straight through the neck of one of the cloaked figures, dropping him to the ground instantly.

To his left, Morden opened fire from his position a few metres away. He had moved round, following the curve of the dune and Lirbus watched as his position lit up with a blaze of fire, catching the hapless bounty hunters below in a withering crossfire.

Lirbus forsook his precise aim. The bounty hunters were in disarray, fleeing out across the dunes and a blanket of fire would be as effective as any aimed shot. He rose up, standing at the dune's edge and sprayed his autogun fire indiscriminately over the chaotic scene below. Morden's shots spiralled in from his angled position and a second figure fell, his body riddled with bullets. Two remained.

One seemed to realise that flight was pointless and stopped dead, turning and aiming his weapon straight up at Morden. He cracked off a couple of rounds and Morden's position fell silent. Lirbus was sure he couldn't have hit him, but he had at least driven Morden back behind the crest of the dune.

Lirbus took aim on the plucky bounty hunter and pulled the trigger. Nothing. The bounty hunter below caught sight of him, turned, and unleashed a few wild shots towards Lirbus.

'Damn it,' he muttered as he dropped to his knees and frantically pulled at the clip in an effort to clear the jam. 'Cover me while I reload,' he said to Hargitay, who was still crouching next to him. Nothing happened.

'Didn't you hear me? I said cover…' Lirbus's words trailed off as he turned to look at the crouching figure beside him. Hargitay was dead, a single bullet wound piercing his skull. The bounty hunter's wild shooting couldn't have hit him like that, could it?

'Jurgen!' said Lirbus, calling out louder than before. 'Jurgen, cover me!'

Again there came no reply. Lirbus had become too caught up in his own wild firing spree. The last time he had looked, Hargitay had been beside him, and Jurgen a short distance further along the ridge. Now Hargitay was dead and he couldn't see any trace of Jurgen. Lirbus was alone and in big trouble.

He flung his jammed autogun to the dirt and wrestled the lasgun from Hargitay's warm but rapidly stiffening grip. He rattled off a couple of shots towards the two remaining bounty hunters below before rising and sprinting along the dune to where he had last seen Morden.

The sound of gunfire rang out behind him and he leapt and slid across the dune, relieved to find himself crashing into Morden. Morden was fine, keeping his head down, and seemed just as relieved as Lirbus to find he wasn't totally alone.

Morden raised his hand, three gloved fingers extended in a familiar gesture. Lirbus nodded and Morden rolled onto this stomach, stretching over the top of the dune to fire down onto the two men below. Morden's shots silenced the barrage from below and Lirbus, too, poked his head above the crest of the dune.

One of the bounty hunters was limping slowly away while the other positively sprinted. Lirbus took careful aim and picked off the limping figure, knocking him dead with a blast right through the middle of his back.

'Come on,' said Lirbus. 'Let's get him.'

'Do it,' said Morden, and the pair rose, dashing down the dune in pursuit of the lone survivor. Their target would quickly disappear from view in the cloudy air of the storms and Morden clearly had no intention of letting him out of his sight. He holstered his pistol and sprinted hard in pursuit of the fleeing bounty hunter. Lirbus did likewise without another thought.

They chased the man across the gully, towards the opposite ridge. Lakatos and the others should be up there, thought Lirbus. Why weren't they firing?

Morden outstripped Lirbus for pace and was quickly ahead of him. Lirbus was still lagging fifteen metres behind as he saw Morden crash into the back of the fleeing man, sending the pair of them tumbling to the ground amidst a flurry of ash.

Lirbus carried on his own sprint, leaping straight at the scrapping figures on the ground in front of him. As he leapt, he saw a boot rise up from the scuffle beneath him and Morden was flung clear, wincing as he took a sturdy kick to the chest. Lirbus came crashing down straight onto the cloaked figure and in an instant he was in agony. He rolled off him instinctively and reached down to the source of his pain: a dagger buried deep in his guts. He groaned, coughed and closed his eyes, falling onto his back and into deep darkness.

MORDEN ROSE TO his feet. The bounty hunter scrambled towards Lirbus's prone form, struggling desperately to pull his knife from the corpse. Morden wasted no time and leapt onto the man's back, wrapping his arms round his shoulders and drawing his own blade across his enemy's neck. The man struggled on for a few seconds, desperately trying to fling Morden off, but

Morden held his grip tight until the man at last collapsed face forwards, blood streaming from his neck and forming a deep red stain in the filthy ash beneath him.

Morden sank to his knees, breathless and panting.

He barely had time to draw breath before a crackle of gunfire forced him instinctively to the ground. Mercifully, it wasn't aimed at him, and the reports peeled off into the distance, sounding very much like shots passing to his side. Morden raised his head but couldn't see the source of the gunfire and suddenly felt very alone and stranded out in the open.

He gazed around, but he'd already seen plenty of men – friend and foe alike – caught out in a desperate dash for cover and decided it was better to keep himself low to the ground.

This was insane, thought Morden. If this was meant to be an ambush, then clearly they had already sprung it, but the battle still wasn't over and Morden felt the whole adventure was slipping into chaos. Jurgen's plan had seemed like a good one, but now he wasn't quite sure what it was meant achieve, or that it would really achieve anything at all.

Morden lay vigilant for a minute or two longer before a number of figures – three as far as he could make out – appeared ahead of him. They couldn't have been the source of the gunfire since they were approaching from the wrong direction entirely. It was only at that point that Morden realised that the gunfire had died away to nothing, and the mystery deepened.

Morden raised his lasgun's sight to his left eye and peered down it, readying himself for a shot just as soon as the dark silhouettes up ahead came into range. The sight offered no magnification as such, but squinting and concentrating on them as intently as he was, Morden gave pause and drew his finger back from the trigger.

He allowed them to approach a little closer. He was sure they wouldn't see him anyway, not with him lying flat on the ground like that, but he couldn't wait for ever. They covered perhaps another ten metres before he was sure. It was Lakatos and the others.

Morden raised his lasgun and loosed three shots, clear and evenly spaced. Three shots, straight up in the air, just like Jurgen had told them: it was the only way to identify one another out in the storms. Sight was useless. Sound was everything.

A moment later and three shots rang out from the group ahead. Morden could just make out a single raised arm, firing what sounded like a bolt pistol directly up into the air.

Morden was reluctant to show himself, but if he didn't they'd never find him. He leapt to his feet and quickly fired off another three shots in noisy reply. He had no way of knowing if they had seen him, or if they could tell that it was him who had fired the shots, and that he was a friend, but he just couldn't waste any more time. He set off at a sprint towards the distant silhouettes.

'JUST TO BE sure,' said Lakatos.

Rubik nodded and trained his autocannon on the figure approaching through the dismal murk of the storms. Just to be sure, thought Rubik, just to be sure. He'd heard the three shots the same as everyone, but things were not going well and, truth be told, if it hadn't been for Lakatos alongside him, Rubik would probably have just gunned down the approaching figure anyway, just to be sure.

The figure continued to approach at speed. Oddly, it seemed to drift to the right as Rubik followed its progress with his readied autocannon. Perhaps it was an optical illusion, caused by the rolling storms, or perhaps it was just impossible for anybody to run straight in such winds.

Rubik didn't so much as blink as he followed the figure's approach. He could feel his fist tightening around the hefty trigger grip of his autocannon as the figure at last came in to some kind of clarity.

It was Morden. Thank the Emperor it was Morden. Rubik released the grip on his trigger and breathed a sigh of relief.

It was a premature relief, to say the least, as a bullet ploughed suddenly into his shoulder, a second grazing him just above the elbow and a third whistling past, wide of its mark. He fell to one knee with shock and pain, barely managing to steady his colossal bulk even with his equally substantial strength. He roared in pain and the approaching Morden dived to the ground, obviously having heard the bullets that whistled past him.

Rubik grabbed at the trigger of his cannon but a searing pain in his arm stopped him before he could unleash so much as a single shot. Howling in furious agony, he used what little strength he had in his wounded arm to heave the autocannon across his body and into his uninjured left hand. His wounded right arm possessed too little strength to steady the great weapon, and Rubik was forced to kneel and rest the bulk of the thing across his thigh before unleashing a spitting, ripping volley of bullets in the direction of the unseen shooter.

At his feet, Morden crawled past him. Lakatos and Mero knelt alongside him, loosing shots in the moments when Rubik's great weapon fell silent. Between them, they provided sufficient weight of fire for their enemy to seem unable to respond, even with the Cawdor stranded out in the open.

Morden rose up from the ground behind Rubik. Rubik felt the searing heat of a las-blast pass by his shoulder as Morden took up covering duties, taking over from Lakatos who fumbled on the ground, desperately trying to reload the empty magazine of one of his bolt pistols.

Rubik unleashed burst after burst of fire, each one just a few seconds apart, but he couldn't go on like that forever. Even if he didn't feel the pain in his arm growing in intensity with every second, even if he didn't feel the drowsiness of blood loss descending on him like night, he would eventually run out of ammo and he needed to make his shots count before that happened.

'They must have followed my shots,' yelled Morden from beside him.

'How many are there?' asked Lakatos from the opposite side.

'I'm not sure. We ambushed five, I think, from up on the ridge, but they're all dead.'

'There's more. I saw Galamb shooting at another group. They must've split up,' said Lakatos.

'Galamb? Where is he now?' asked Morden. Rubik shook his head before Lakatos had time to answer and Morden fell silent.

'Where's Jurgen, and the others?' asked Lakatos, as Rubik unleashed another staccato burst. 'Where is Jurgen, and the others?' he asked again, repeating himself now that the sound of gunfire had died down a little.

'Lirbus and I chased the stragglers down from the ridge. That's how I ended up out in the open,' said Morden. 'I didn't see Jurgen. He must still be up on the ridge.'

'Two more!' yelled Rubik, cutting in.

'What?' asked Lakatos.

'I've got bullets for two more bursts. Get moving.'

'Shit,' spat Lakatos before moving backwards behind the wall of fire. Mero knelt beside Rubik, stripping the bandolier from across his chest. Rubik winced in pain as Mero dropped the heavy belt down over his wounded shoulder.

'Move!' yelled Lakatos, loosing a couple of shots from his new position fifteen metres or so behind the others. They did as ordered and scampered back towards their leader, though Lakatos's meagre bolts offered scant covering fire and a hail of bullets raced past them from their still unseen enemy.

Rubik crouched behind Lakatos, letting his cannon rest on the ground and taking the opportunity for a desperately needed breather as, beside him, Mero threaded another band of ammo through the weapon's hopper. It was the last one, and the way things were going, it wouldn't last long.

Morden rose in front of Rubik and fired off a hand-ful of las-blasts, his gun held lazily at his hip. With his non-firing hand free, Morden waved the others back-wards, an invitation they wasted no time in taking. Rubik hoisted the autocannon back up off the ground, feeling the weight more than ever. He rested it against the wrist of his damaged arm that was numb with pain, and he could feel the exertion even more. He could barely keep up with Lakatos and Mero as they scampered backwards, heading for the safety of the ridge.

Lakatos fired off two rounds as Rubik reached them, Mero loosing two more as he set himself down between them. Morden turned, waiting for the signal to retreat and Rubik wasted no time in giving it. He hefted the autocannon up onto his bent knee to give Morden some covering fire and clamped down on the trigger grip with his good hand.

Nothing.

Rubik looked up in horror but Morden was already up and running. In desperation he squeezed again but there was no sound. The trigger was firmly stuck

down, depressed against the weapon and utterly useless until he could reset the jam.

He looked up again. Morden had covered maybe a
quarter of the distance between him and the others, but
even at that range Rubik could see the look of terror in
his eyes as he realised what was happening. Rubik
raised his hand, waving his palm in a frantic downward
motion. Morden didn't need to be told twice and dived
forwards, hurling himself to the ground as quickly as
he could, but it was too late.

Las-blasts arced past him and the air filled with bullets. Morden's dive brought him crashing down to the
ground in front of Rubik, but it was no controlled landing. His body slammed into the ash, singed with laser
burns, riddled with holes and utterly lifeless. As the
puff of ash thrown up by his falling body cleared,
Rubik could see the deathly grimace on Morden's face
and swallowed hard in a mixture of anger and fear.

Rubik looked across to see Mero gripped by that very
same fear, yet Mero's own terror was not tempered by
anger and Rubik saw him rise to his feet, instinctively
sprinting away. It was a miracle he got away at all as
bullets raced past the three surviving Cawdor, and
Rubik quickly lost sight of the fleeing Mero as he was
forced to consider his own safety and turned his gaze
back in the direction of the approaching gunfire.

At last he could see them: five, no, six cloaked figures
emerging from the storms. Lakatos dived across Rubik,
pushing him to the ground as he fired off two more
shots from his bolt pistol. Lying on his side, Rubik was
at least free of the weight of his autocannon and wriggled his good arm free of the harness to get his fingers
at the jammed barrel. Damn Mero, he thought. Damn
him for fleeing, and damn him for stuffing up the
reloading. Rubik wrenched a tangled mess of ammo
from the barrel to clear the jam.

He braced the weapon against the ground and used his elbow to bring his weight down against the back end, tilting the barrel upwards just enough to aim it at the approaching group. He unleashed a rash of fire and the six became five. Another burst and five became four. At this rate, they weren't going to get any closer, thought Rubik.

At this rate, he thought again, as he felt the dull click of his weapon's trigger. At this rate… He suddenly realised he was out of ammo.

'Damn it, damn it, damn it,' he yelled, rolling onto his back in a bid to draw his laspistol from the holster around his waist, but it lay on the same side as his bad arm and he couldn't prop himself up sufficiently to get at the thing.

Lakatos drew close to him, stooping over and pressing his face close to Rubik's.

'What the hell?' he said.

'Out of ammo,' said Rubik. Lakatos spat a curse in reply and slung his arms under the bulky man, half lifting and half dragging him backwards. With Lakatos supporting him, Rubik at last pulled his laspistol free of its holster and raised his gaze back towards the approaching figures.

Doing so gave him just enough time to see the las-blasts screeching towards him: the las-blasts that smashed instantly into his chest and made Rubik suddenly forget the pain in his arm and the bleary-eyed, drowsiness of his blood loss.

MERO HELD HIS lasgun to his shoulder, cradling the barrel with his left hand and staring straight down the crude sight on its top. In truth, he could hardly see a thing through the murk, but using the sight gave him confidence, and the Emperor knew he needed it now.

He cracked off one shot, and then another, before falling to the ground in a desperate attempt to hide himself from any shots that might come his way in reply.

Beside him, the hulking Rubik raised his hand and signalled for the waiting Morden to retreat – a signal Morden wasted no time in following. Mero watched Morden dash frantically towards him, just as Rubik raised his autocannon to provide covering fire.

It seemed like an eternity for Mero, waiting for the familiar *chugga-chugga-chugga* of the autocannon. He waited, but it never came. Mystified, he turned to Rubik, only to see the big man's face freeze in terror as he fumbled ineffectively at the trigger of his jammed weapon.

Mero turned from Rubik's horrified visage and looked straight into the eyes of another. Morden made a frantic dive to the ground as he realised that the covering fire he so badly needed was well and truly stuck halfway down the autocannon's barrel. Morden's terrified grimace turned into a deathly one as blasts and bullets cut through his diving form and sent his body plunging lifelessly to the ground.

That was enough for Mero. If he was thinking about anything at all, he was thinking that running was better than staying where he was, and that a desperate, every man for himself dash offered more chance of survival than this supposedly ordered retreat, which was falling to pieces as he watched.

He took to his heels, turning in an instant and dashed away from the approaching enemy, away from Lakatos and Rubik, and the body of poor Morden.

The bounty hunters must not have seen him at first, and Mero found himself ten, fifteen, twenty metres away before the hail of gunfire swung predictably towards him. He dropped to all fours as bullets whistled around him and continued his desperate flight by scrabbling along on his hands and knees.

Behind him, he heard more shots ring out, but much closer by: Lakatos and Rubik returning fire, he thought, though it didn't sound like the autocannon was doing the firing. Either way, it seemed to draw attention away from him, and Mero hauled himself back to his feet and continued his frantic dash as the hail of bullets passed him, their owners concentrating on another target altogether.

Mero dashed on. He thought of Rubik as he fled, and was touched by a moment of guilt for leaving him behind, but then he thought of Lakatos and it turned to fear. Lakatos would never forgive Mero for fleeing; he'd kill him. The thought of it made Mero run on all the faster, and he wished that Lakatos would die, Emperor damn him for thinking such things.

Mero reached the foot of the high dune that led up to the ridge from which their ambush had begun. The ridge on which, Mero thought, they should have stayed all along. More importantly, the ridge that would offer him precious cover.

Mero began to scramble up the steep dune as quickly as he possibly could, scaling its face. A spattering of bullets just above his head told him that it was a bad idea. Climbing up the exposed side of the dune would make him an easier target. He shrunk down to the ground, skulking through the ruts of ash that peppered the dune's base. Bullets still streaked past his head but at least he was afforded some cover.

Mero skulked on in this manner until he reached the edge of the dune. He thought he could dip behind it and ascend from the other side, keeping out of sight of the enemy as he did so.

He waited a moment, carefully picking his time, and then made one sudden dash, exposing himself for just a second before turning sharply and racing to safety behind the dune's imposing bulk. He fell to the ground as he reached the rear of the dune, hurling his back against the steep pile of ash. He breathed a sigh of relief. He was out of sight. He was safe.

Mero took a moment to catch his breath before getting to his feet and beginning the long trudge up the side of the dune. From there, he could work out exactly what he was going to do. He would be safe up there at least and could better ponder his next move.

He could still hear the sounds of gunfire below. Perhaps he could redeem himself by picking off the bounty hunters from up on the ridge and save Lakatos that way. Perhaps.

Or perhaps he could just lie low, watch the bounty hunters until they moved off, and then make good his escape and get out of Fall Sands forever. He could flee to Fulcrum Spike, to Addec's place. If Lakatos were dead, there would be no one to say that he had fled and he could go to Addec with his head held high. He'd be a hero, a lone survivor.

Mero's chain of thought cut off suddenly as he caught sight of a figure up ahead of him, crouching down on the ridge. Who the hell could be up on the ridge? Then he remembered the bounty hunters had split up into two groups. Lakatos had seemed sure they were pursuing the nearer group, and Morden said they'd encountered another group over at the far ridge. How the hell could they have gotten up on the ridge?

Mero realised he had become hopelessly disoriented in the chaos. It was only a fluke that they had found Morden out in the open and it was conceivable that the bounty hunters had surrounded them, doubled back on them or just plain got past them. He cursed his luck, but knew there was no going back.

Mero was sure the figure hadn't yet seen him, but for his part, Mero couldn't see past the figure on the ridge and had no idea if there might be more beyond him. He didn't dare use his lasgun for fear of alerting others nearby, and instead drew his knife and began a slow, sneaking approach towards the crouching figure.

He crossed the dune against the slope, bringing himself around behind the figure. From here he could see that, mercifully, the figure was alone. Summoning what courage he had, Mero rose from his stoop and dashed at the figure, leaping on its back, his knife outstretched.

He landed hard on the crouching man's back, but instantly recoiled. One touch of that stiff, hard body told him something wasn't right. He grabbed at the figure and rolled it over.

It was Todor, stone dead, his eyes glazed over, forever emblazoned with a last moment of fear.

'What the–?' said Mero to himself, but they would be his last words.

Mero's body slumped forwards onto Todor's. A single bullet was shot through his heart from a gun he never even saw, pressed to his back by a shadowy figure behind him.

LAKATOS THRUST HIS arms under the big man's shoulders, dragging him backwards, but it was useless. Rubik was already dead. The first shot had killed him, and the ones that followed would have done the same to Lakatos had they not slammed into Rubik's all too solid body. It was far from dignified, but Lakatos crouched behind the dead man's body. It was the only cover on offer now that Mero had fled, damn his eyes.

'Shit,' said Lakatos, though there was clearly no one to hear him. He was in deep trouble. He unclipped the magazine of one bolt pistol, and then the other, checking both were full. They weren't but it was a situation he quickly remedied as he sheltered beneath Rubik's gargantuan frame. He would have precious little time to reload later.

He stashed the fully loaded pistols back in the holsters at his hips and pulled a grenade from his belt. He pulled the pin and hurled it as far as he could, not towards the approaching enemy, but laterally away from himself, creating a huge explosion away to his right. It was a diversion and nothing more.

The explosion had barely sounded before Lakatos was on his feet and running, drawing both pistols as he went. The grenade bought him a few seconds and he heard several shots peel off harmlessly towards the site of the explosion before the approaching bounty hunters noticed his own sprinting form. He loosed several rounds from his pistols and carried on running, covering himself as best he could.

As bullets whistled past him, Lakatos saw a shallow dip in the ashy ground and took his chance. He leapt and skidded down its side, landing on his back. Pressed flat to the ground, even such a meagre trench as this offered him some cover.

Lakatos lay for a second, drawing his breath, but he knew he had no time to waste. He rolled onto his front and rose slowly, just enough to take a peek out over the furrow's edge. Four figures were approaching, and quickly. Somehow, they'd lost sight of him.

He drew his pistols up, arms resting on the ground, and waited. He wouldn't get many shots. It was near impossible to gauge range in this weather, but Lakatos was a master. The figures continued their approach, close enough for Lakatos to make out the heavy cloaks they were wearing, which billowed out in the wind where they hung loose at the back of their legs. They were well-prepared for the storm. They were professionals.

Lakatos followed their approach for a few more seconds. They weren't coming directly for him. Rubik's body was still sitting upright fifty metres away and the bounty hunters were closing in on it, perhaps unaware that it was nothing more than a corpse. It would take an age for them to come into range, drifting across in front of Lakatos's view rather than coming closer. At last, just as the bounty hunters closed in on Rubik, Lakatos reckoned he had a mark and opened fire.

He aimed his fire at a low trajectory, pistols pressed both together and spraying from right to left. It worked, and the bolts scythed through the line of four figures. Two fell to the ground, one remaining there lifeless. The second dragged himself gingerly back to his feet as the other two fled and rolled to the ground. It was just as Lakatos had intended. He couldn't guarantee fatal shots from that range, but at least cutting across their legs would hamper their advance. The wounded figure limped forwards and Lakatos took his time in lining him up, picking him off with another spray of bullets and sending him tumbling lifeless, head over feet, into the dirt.

A shot skimmed the top of the dip in which Lakatos hid and he instinctively ducked his head down. The two remaining bounty hunters were advancing on him, and they were clever. They had split up, standing perhaps ten metres apart, and advanced in unison so that Lakatos couldn't possibly cover both of them. They had clearly worked out that he was alone. He would have to persuade them otherwise.

He unclipped another grenade, fumbling with the pin in his gloved hands and dropping it to the ground just in front of him. Frik it, he thought, and he leapt to his feet, setting of at a sprint away from the hollow.

Bullets trailed behind him, but he replied in kind and bought himself a few metres before the sound of the exploding frag grenade rang out behind him. It seemed to work, and he heard the bounty hunters' fire close in on his former position. Perhaps they had mistaken it for muzzle flash.

Lakatos raced away across the dunes, but he was too eager in his flight. He stumbled and fell. One of the bolt pistols fell from his grip, tumbling from his right hand as he collapsed. Feeling no pain, he presumed he had merely tripped and rose to his feet. Then his leg gave way and, looking down, he realised he had been hit square in the knee by a las-bolt. He couldn't stand on it at all.

He dropped onto his good knee and thundered off three more shots from his remaining bolt pistol. The two figures seemed unperturbed and were sprinting towards him. Their fire forced him to the ground and Lakatos began to think he was doomed. This had seemed like such a good plan. What the hell had happened? Even if he survived, his gang was in tatters and Catafengi would not reward him for this debacle. He cursed as he cautiously raised his head once more, extending his arm to loose two more shots with his bolt pistol. Two more, and then he tried a third.

Nothing.

'Damn it,' said Lakatos. He slunk as far down into the ash as he could, desperate for cover as he tried to reload the pistol's spent magazine as quickly as possible. The bolts fell from his nervous, twitchy grasp and he scrabbled frantically in the ash, making terrible labour of a routine task.

A dark shadow, perceptible even in the dim light of Ash Season, fell across Lakatos and he looked up.

'Oh shit,' he said as he gazed straight into the eyes of the two cloaked figures. They stood over him with their lasguns aimed squarely at his head. Lakatos flinched and shut his eyes as he heard a *bang* ring out above him. He gasped, and then opened his eyes as he realised the impossibility of a lasgun going *bang*. He looked up just in time to see one of the two figures fall backwards, a spray of blood jetting up from his head.

The second figure looked up from Lakatos, suddenly concerned more with his own survival than Lakatos's death. He started to raise his lasgun, but a second *bang* rang out all too quickly for it to be of any use. Another shot, clean through the front of the skull, another spray of blood, and another cloaked bounty hunter tumbled backwards. Lakatos was stunned and breathless.

He looked up and turned his head slowly, half expecting a third *bang* to ring out and silence him too.

Jurgen. Dear Emperor, thought Lakatos, it was Jurgen.

Sure enough, the outlander stood no more than ten metres away, arm outstretched, stub gun still smoking.

'Jurgen,' he said aloud. Jurgen said nothing.

Lakatos hauled himself to his feet, injured as he was, and stood up on his one good leg. He hobbled over to where the two cloaked bodies lay in the ash.

Lakatos dropped to his knees and smashed his fist into the body lying on the ground beneath him, pummelling the body's ribs with punch after punch.

'Lago, you bastard!' he yelled, pulling the tightly wrapped cloth away from his mouth and spitting on the prone figure as he raised his boot and unleashed a crushing stamp on its motionless head.

'You fragging bastard, Lago. Pah!' He seethed with rage at the terrible, bloody mess this infidel Lago had made of his plans, but railed victorious that he had won, that it was over.

Lakatos wrenched the ventilator mask from Lago's face, desperate to look into the eyes of his slain enemy. He recoiled in horror as the mask came away.

It wasn't Lago at all. It was Deeran. He had hardly ever seen the man's face, but the gang tattoo on his left cheek made him quite sure that it was Deeran. He scrabbled over the body, to the second corpse lying behind it. This one bore no mask, and a square sheet of cloth merely hung across its nose and mouth, tied behind the head, with infrared goggles to cover its eyes. Lakatos dragged the cloth down with one hand, pulling the goggles away with the other. He ran his fingers gently over the face and was almost reduced to tears.

It was Addec.

JURGEN WALKED SLOWLY towards Lakatos where he kneeled over the bodies. He stopped just short of him and stooped to the ground. Lakatos's pistol lay where it had fallen when that first shot caught its bearer in the leg. He scooped up the pistol and examined the magazine. Three bullets remained.

Jurgen pressed his thumb into the tightly sprung magazine and pushed out the top bullet. He spun it round in his hand and reinserted it into the magazine, its tip facing the wrong direction. He clicked the magazine back into place and walked on towards the crouching Lakatos – he wasn't going to give Lakatos anything like the mercy of a swift end, or the satisfaction of having anyone to blame but himself.

'You dropped your gun,' he said as he approached within earshot.

Lakatos rose slowly in front of him, taking the pistol from Jurgen's outstretched hand. Lakatos didn't say a word. He merely turned his back and took a pace or two away from Jurgen, who remained motionless standing next to the bodies of his two most recent kills.

'I thought they had you there,' said Jurgen.

'Me too,' said Lakatos. 'Jurgen, I don't know what in the name of the Emperor has happened here, but whatever it is, it's your doing.' Lakatos raised his pistol, aiming it straight at Jurgen's head.

'You're trouble, Jurgen,' he said. 'Whatever you've done, you're trouble, and trouble follows you. Maybe this isn't of your making, but trouble followed you here. This whole damn mess followed you here and it has got too many people killed.

'You're just too much trouble, Jurgen,' said Lakatos, squeezing the trigger.

The pistol backfired spectacularly. The explosive bolts it fired each contained its own propellant and its own charge, and as Lakatos squeezed the trigger the top round propelled itself backwards into the rear of the magazine, detonating as it struck the rear of the barrel and sparking off an explosion that covered Lakatos's right hand side in a gout of flame. He fell to his knees, roaring in pain.

Jurgen stepped forward, leaning over the howling Lakatos. His right arm was in pieces. Gristle and bone were visible down its length, and it was horribly twisted and merged with the burned skin and singed cloth of his clothing. The whole limb hung lifeless by his side, and shrapnel lay embedded in dozens of bloody welts across Lakatos's chest, neck and face. He screamed in pain, his agonised howls turning into a single, breathless word.

'Jurgen!' he screamed as the outlander drew nearer still, holding his face just inches from Lakatos's pained visage.

'No,' he said, 'I'm *Lago.*'

Lago placed a toxstick to his lips. He lit it and within a moment vanished into the swirling storms of Ash Season. He was gone, just like the Union, just like the Scarlet Skulls, just like Addec and his men, and Catafengi and the whole damned lot of them. They were all gone, just as Lago had always intended, and with that, he was gone too.

Behind him, Lakatos crawled along the ground, a short trail of his blood sorry evidence of the pitiful distance he had covered, though it had sapped all his strength. He hadn't the strength to stand, or to cry out, or even to grip his ruined arm and staunch the bleeding. Above him, moving like dark shadows through the haze of ash, carrion eaters whirled and danced, their mournful cries sure signs of a coming feast. They would not have to wait long, if they waited at all.

ABOUT THE AUTHOR

Matt Keefe has worked extensively in the movie and games industries and was one of the developers who worked on the latest edition of the *Necromunda* game. He lives in Sheffield, England.

An Eyeful of Evil

Kirk wanted to scream, he wanted to jab hot pokers in his eyes. He didn't want to be here anymore. He wavered, staring at Sylvie as she looked around the room.

Sylvie urged, "You've got to resist him, Kirk. That's the only thing I can tell you to do. Resist! Don't let him take you. Don't!"

Kirk felt the turning, the worms eating his guts. He sank to his knees, trying desperately to turn his face away. Demon laughed, keeping his eyes open. "You want to watch, don't you, Kirkie boy? Go ahead, boy. Watch. You'll love it," Demon spat into his ear.

Kirk shuddered again. Sylvie backed away from him, afraid . . .

SINS
OF THE
FATHERS

Based on
THE OBLIVION

Sam Chupp

HarperPrism
An Imprint of HarperPaperbacks

This is a work of fiction. The characters, incidents, and dialogues are products of the author's imagination and are not to be construed as real. Any resemblance to actual events or persons, living or dead, is entirely coincidental.

HarperPaperbacks *A Division of* HarperCollins*Publishers*
10 East 53rd Street, New York, N.Y. 10022

Cover illustration by Joshua Gabriel Timbrook

First printing: October 1995

Printed in the United States of America

HarperPrism is an imprint of HarperPaperbacks.
HarperPaperbacks, HarperPrism, and colophon are trademarks of HarperCollins*Publishers*.

❖ 10 9 8 7 6 5 4 3 2 1

This book is dedicated to my three Fathers: may they all three be revered for all that they have given me and taught me:

My birth-Father, whose seed helped give me life, and who knows the pain of not knowing where his son is. Hi, Dad.

My life-Father, who gave me all he could afford; who gave me his cynical humor, his anger, and his sense of honor, who did the best he could with the feelings that the Marines left him with, a tough old cuss who could give the worst of Spectres a hard time.

My spirit-Father, that wild man, that Smith/Stag/Sage/Boy so long denied by us all, who has taken me in his hand and shown me what fathers used to be, and what they will be again.

I only hope to be worthy of their gifts, and to make them all proud of me.

SINS OF THE FATHERS

1

Ghost Story:
Chains Rattlin' Roof

You see, there was this guy, name of Kurt or Kirk or somesuch. He was one baaaad motha. He used to hang out at school, just hang out, rake in the dough with his beeper and his little plastic baggies. Heh. He'd stolen a key up to the roof of the school and he'd do his meetings there.

Well, one day they came for him . . . no, not the cops, but the big guys, the really big guys who didn't like him cuttin' into their business. No, they didn't. They poked a gun in his gut and finished him off up there, gore all over the place. They didn't find the body until a few days later, when blood from the corpse drained into an air duct and spilled out on Ms. Martin, the science teacher. Pretty gross, eh?

Yeah. They say that you can hear Kirk's ghost up there sometimes, cryin' for his skank girl-friend and playin' his electric guitar and, from time to time, he'll try to make you a deal. Heh. Pretty cool, eh? Wanna go up there?

———

Kirk hated school, hated it enough so that the fire from his hate kept him warm at night, filled his belly with a fullness that burned. Still, from his perch on top of the four-story school near Grant Park, he was able to see pretty far in the dark misty Shadowlands that he had come to call home. He was able to keep watch from any barrow-fires which might be burning through at any point—the fires of Atlanta that still burned here in this place, in his purgatory, in this hell. Kirk had spent long hours trying to figure out exactly what and where he was: as near as he could tell, he was not alive, not in any real sense. The bad dudes with the homebrewed automatic pistols had taken care of that little detail.

This demon landscape that he lived in was something like the real world he was used to, though: all the buildings were in the same place, all the places he used to hang with his buds and sell dope were still there. The world looked as if it was stuck in some kind of black-and-white movie: everything was dark, and the only color Kirk ever saw was the red fires of the barrow-flame, and he had learned long ago that the barrow-flame was a hungry fire, intelligent like a snake is intelligent, waiting to strike you, burning through you and consuming you. Kirk never wanted near the stuff again.

Kirk soon found that, although he wasn't solid to the rest of the world, the rest of the world was quite solid to him. People would walk through him if he was in their way (or sometimes walk around him mindlessly, as if they could see him but chose not to). It was disconcerting to be walked through, but not as painful as when someone slammed a door on him. When that happened, he jerked at the potential impact and felt a sharp pain all over his body. For a couple of seconds, Kirk felt lightheaded and wispy: he looked down at his hands to see them slowly fading and then, slowly reforming. The same thing happened when he tried to walk through walls. Soon, he learned how to get around without much trouble, avoiding heavy-traffic areas in the school.

Kirk had a ball, at night, walking through the corridors of his old school, walking through open doors and looking at all the crap that the kiddies left behind. He'd learned a few tricks himself, too. How to open doors. How to open lockers (which was even more fun, because it meant you could go through kids' stuff and see what kind of crap they were trying to hide: a box of condoms, dirty magazines, bootleg tapes, and unregistered pistols). How he did this, Kirk couldn't really tell: it was something having to do with moving stuff with his mind, although he couldn't do it on command. He had to think hard about it, and get a little pissed off, and then he could hit a locker and have it open in the land of the living. He could usually close the locker door enough so that the stuff wouldn't get found. To Kirk, this was one of his only entertainments. Kirk just assumed that Purgatory was supposed to be boring, and that's why he didn't make any move to do anything about his tedium.

During the day, Kirk stayed in the machine room on the roof and practiced flipping stones at the far wall, sitting on the old paint cans. He liked the darkness inside the room during the day. One day he had stuck his head out on a bright, sunny day to a terrifyingly stark world where the shadows were long but the sun burned like a great explosion in the sky and threatened to blind him permanently. It was too much to even walk around outside during a bright day. Kirk longed for the foggy, overcast days of fall, but this was spring, and it'd be a long, hot summer before Georgia's grey weather rolled in.

So, Kirk sat in his self-imposed solitary confinement, sitting with his back against the wall and watching for cracks in the ground while he kicked at rocks and trash on the floor, trying to make them move. The cracks were what really scared him. There was a crack that opened on the roof from time to time, and Kirk had fallen into it once. Holding on for dear life, he used all his strength to pull himself up. Kirk shuddered everytime he thought about what he saw in the pit that the crack revealed. Kirk wasn't sure what the cracks were, exactly, but they grew and closed up with a regularity that made them seem "natural," if anything could be natural here in Purgatory. Maybe they were doorways into Hell? They led down, and he'd heard voices and saw . . . things down there.

At night, it was okay to wander around. Kirk never felt like sleeping much anymore, although he was vaguely aware that he'd conk out every once in a while and "wake up," it didn't feel like normal sleep. Kirk was afraid to leave the school. Following his horror-movie logic, he thought that he should be confined to the place where he died. Kirk knew that there was some kind of mystic tug, a pull, something he couldn't quite pin down but kept him here. And, something that kept him from other places. He was afraid of what those places might be like.

Kirk knew that he was invisible to people: whenever he walked around the school during the day (down hall 4C, which had no windows and had a stairway leading up to the machine room), people would walk right past him and nobody could hear a word he said, no matter how loudly he yelled. At first, Kirk got a headache from hanging out with the living folks: he could hear them whispering all over the place, could hear everything with a sensitivity that he'd never experienced before. Standing at one end of the hall, he could hear the quiet whispers of passion two young lovers were exchanging on the other end of the hall, and even hear the teacher bitch one of them out when they walked into the classroom and closed the door. Kirk soon learned not to listen too hard to anything: it was difficult, especially when he began to hear whispers he couldn't shut out.

Kirk wasn't sure what it was that whispered to him. He thought maybe it was a demon assigned to torture him specifically. The demon whispered to him all the time, but Kirk couldn't see him: one time, however, he was in the boy's restroom and caught a look at himself in the mirror when the demon started talking. Something strange had happened to his face, then: a darkening, a shadowing of his face that caused his eyes to turn into hollow pits of green fire and his mouth to shape itself into a rictus of anger and hatred.

For a brief moment, Kirk looked at the demon that was constantly bothering him with whispered innuendo, accusations, and insults. Kirk thought that the demon looked much like him, only older looking and more feral. With a chill, later, Kirk realized where he had seen that face before: the pictures of his father that his mother had hidden from him since he was a baby, since Daddy had died in Vietnam. Kirk had dreamed about his father once a week for his final five years, terrible dreams. Kirk only ever forgot the black nightmares by popping a Quaalude and sleeping: those dreams dredged up the truth and made Kirk feel cold, vulnerable, and full of resentment. His father had treated him like the soldiers he had trained as a drill instructor for the Rangers. Kirk never told his gang or anyone he hung out with about the dreams. Kirk was glad to be dead, if nothing else, so that he wouldn't have those dreams anymore.

Still, his father was here in some kind of demon form, and Kirk knew that if he didn't occupy his mind with other things, the demon within him would wake up and start talking again. He'd had some luck with screaming at the demon to "shut up" before, but he got the feeling that, if it wanted to, it could ignore anything he said and just keep right on talking. It talked about things he did in life: the girls he'd had sex with; the drugs he'd sold; the things his mother had done; his sister's "job"; his little sister, who never said anything to anyone; and Jo, his parole officer, who he often wished he could hurt. And most of the things it said he didn't really want to hear anymore. After a while, he began to learn how to deal with his demon.

So he spent his time with the one thing he'd been able to find in the basement of the school: an old Fender electric guitar. He'd heard the story of the principal of the school burning the guitar in the incinerator many years ago. Well, here in Purgatory it was still there, sitting in the old incinerator, a little worse for wear (scorch marks on the finish; no structural damage) but usable. Somehow, in destroying it, the principal had sent it to Purgatory. Kirk thought that maybe those Egyptian fellas had the right idea about taking stuff with them when they died, and wished he'd had a pizza, or some weed, or a TV or something buried with him.

One night, as the heat of the summer resonated up off the street, Kirk decided to sit down and focus for a while on his new-found guitar. Kirk played with it, hearing the wires rattle without the benefit of an amp, having taught himself to play guitar a little last summer, when he had been alive and full of hope that his band would get him better drug connections and his drug connections would get his band a better place to play. So much for that.

Still, playing the music had a calming effect on him. It also helped to drive the demon inside him away. He ran through his band's play list: they'd been obsessed with heavy-metal dinosaurs and Southern rock, although Kirk liked the heavy techno and goth music himself. He played the favorite songs that every beginning guitar player learns: "Smoke on the Water," "Iron Man," "Freebird," and, in a moment of cynical humor, "Stairway to Heaven." Thoughts of playing turned him to thoughts of Cindi, his girlfriend. She was only seventeen, but she was the hottest babe he'd ever known. He wasn't sure if she was dating him because he could get her free shit, or if she really loved him. He paused and thought for a second. What was Cindi's favorite song? He began to play "Beth" by KISS, and played all the way through it before he realized that the guitar had begun to sing and 'verb as if it had an amp plugged into it.

Looking down at the guitar, he saw that it glowed with some kind of eerie light, a light that made Kirk feel a little queasy but excited at the same time. He'd been thinking of the last time he and Cindi had made love, about how they'd not had a condom, but she didn't care. About how she'd felt beneath him. That feeling, that raw emotion, was something that he couldn't deny, and it had poured out of him. Shouldering the guitar again, Kirk began to play, this time slamming into the lead part on "Through the Never" by Metallica. The sounds reverberated throughout the machine room, echoing off the walls. Although his fingers used to go numb and scream with pain while playing this song, which used lots of incredibly fast riffs in rapid succession, his fingers didn't seem to even touch the strings now. He gave himself up to the music, and somehow, the spectral guitar's music burned out of the pickups, which glowed with the energy Kirk put into the song and into the guitar. He realized that his whole body was serving as the speaker for the guitar, that he radiated the music from his skin.

Kirk turned around, still lost in the music he was playing, and nearly dropped his guitar.

Seated in a cross-legged position across from him was a young girl, nearly ten in age, Kirk guessed. She was black—Jo, Kirk's parole officer, would've said "African-American." Her hair was done neatly in cornrows, and she wore a plain white Sunday church dress. She smiled quietly at Kirk. "Don't stop on my account, mister. I just want to hear the music."

Kirk looked at her, felt the hot rage and lust that he'd been feeling drain away to nothing, and watched the guitar go from a brilliant red and white heat-lightning ax to a dull grey antique. Looking up at where she was sitting again, Kirk was surprised to see that she was gone. Where had she disappeared to?

Kirk put down his guitar and walked to the open stairwell door—he always left the door open to the roof, because he hated walking through anything if he could help it. He walked to the edge of the four-story school building and looked down to the street below, scanning in all directions for the girl.

She was nowhere to be found. Up one side of the building and down the other Kirk looked, straining his eyes to see everything. Although he was able to make out the license plate number of a car two blocks down the street, he couldn't see the girl anywhere.

"Hey, demon. This your doin'?" Kirk said, trying to sound brave.

"What do you think, Kirkie boy?" came the voice inside him.

"I think you're playin' with my head. Tryin' to get me to stop the music. You don't like my playin'," Kirk said, grinning a little despite himself.

Demon said nothing in return, and Kirk ran his hand through his matted crop of hair and shrugged his shoulders, still looking all around for the little girl.

Then, a half-second later, she was standing there, holding part of a little corn-husk doll. She smiled at Kirk, looking at him sideways. "How come you don't ever come out, like the other spooks?" she said, quietly.

Kirk looked down at her. "I ain't no spook, little girl. I'm a devil. Didn't you hear my devil music just now?"

The girl smiled. "There ain't no demons here, mister. Not 'less you bring 'em out of you. Or 'less they come up outta the ground . . . "

Kirk shivered, looking down at his feet for cracks. "Oh, yeah? What makes you so smart?" Kirk said, suddenly angry that this kid was trying to tell him what was what.

That smile again, nearly ubiquitous. "Because, mister, I've been around Marthasville for a long, long time, ever since it was Terminus. And I know a lot about it. A lot. You'd best listen to your elders, mister," she said, almost laughing.

"Shit. You ain't my elder. You're a little kid, and I ain't gonna take this crap from a little kid. See ya."

Kirk turned around and stalked back into the machine room. He turned around a few times, looking to see if the girl was following him. But she had vanished again.

Kirk felt anger welling up inside him—the girl couldn't be just a trick of the demon. She was too detailed, too real looking. So, she was someone like him. Why did she have to put on airs, callin' herself an "elder" and all? Kirk let his frustration overflow, and he turned around to kick at a paint can. With a flash of fiery-red light that burned down his leg, the can toppled over and began to roll across the room. It rolled down the stairs, stair by stair, picking up speed. Finally it slammed into the door at the bottom of the stairs, making a loud spanging noise, and Kirk watched as the beige paint began to slowly pour out of the can, glooping on the floor and flowing under the door.

"Shit," Kirk swore, looking at the mess.

Demon spoke up, "Oh that's just great Kirkie-boy. You just screwed up major big-time. Wonder what they're gonna do when they find that little puddle tomorrow morning? Huh? I'll tell you what they'll do, they'll lock this place up tighter than a drum and you're not going to like that, no boy. You're too much of a sissy boy."

Kirk ignored Demon's taunts and walked back outside, out on the roof, sitting down on the ground and watching for cracks, his favorite meditative activity. He felt Demon rattling his cage inside him— it felt like a rabid rat trying to eat its way out of his guts. He felt that peculiar feeling of fear, anger, and dread burn through him that meant that the demon was flexing his muscles. Kirk did what he could to hold on, but Demon knew when to strike, when Kirk was weakest.

He felt the slithery feeling of Demon sliding its tendrils into place all over his body, watched as the greenish grey opaque smoke billowed through his body, slowly covering it. He tried to scream as he realized what was happening, but couldn't. Demon took him. Clutching its dark tendrils around his heart, he laid siege to and broke the defenses of Kirk's mind. Demon was in control.

Demon laughed, and Kirk realized that he was going to be forced to quietly watch everything Demon did.

Demon walked over to the cans of paint and paint thinner, grinning to himself, and knocked a can of thinner over without even trying hard. The can fell over and broke open and streamed down the stairs like an acetone waterfall. Kirk could smell the bitter bite of the chemicals. Then, grinning (Kirk felt his face freeze in the rictus of a grin, against his will), Demon reached down with his hands and rubbed his fingers lightly together over the acetone. There was a curl of smoke at first as Demon rubbed, and then, suddenly, there was a spark, a tiny burst of fire. With a roar, the paint thinner caught, burning rapidly in a blue-green sheet across the floor, down the stairs, to the door, where it fanned out. The plaster began to smoke. Kirk saw licks of flame begin to dance up the wall and realized that the school, old as it was, was one huge firetrap.

The flames began to dance up the walls and spread to the rest of the paint thinner cans, which were already bulging from the heat buildup. Demon forced Kirk's body out the door, over to the edge of the roof.

Demon hissed at Kirk inside his head. "If you weren't such a friggin' freak, you'd jump, boy. That's the smart thing to do. But you're a sissy. Ain't never jumped noplace. No guts, no glory, craphead!" it yelled at him.

Kirk felt its control slipping away as he stood on the lip of the roof looking down. He saw the fire start to spread through the walls, saw smoke rising from below him. Time must have passed that he hadn't known about, or else something the demon was doing was making the building burn faster and faster.

Kirk felt a sharp pain in his middle as he realized the building's burning was hurting him—it felt like he himself was on fire. Panicking, he closed his eyes and jumped.

The fall took forever, as he knew it would, and when he hit the street he felt his vision swim as, for a second, he felt his body enter the pavement, then bounce back. He shook his head to clear it, watched as his body reformed from the impact. It was disgusting to watch: the grey plasm slowly seeping back together to form coherence under his clothes. He knew he had no bones and yet he could "feel" his skeleton inside him reknitting, could "hear" the bones cracking and popping back into place. He slowly stood on his feet, looking up as another pang of pure fire in his chest wracked him. He knew that, somehow, the pain was associated with the building, that the building itself was important to him.

Kirk wanted to scream, but didn't. He hated that school building more than anything, and now, here in death, he was cursed to protect it. What for? He wanted to grab whoever it was that was in charge of this place and shake him. Then another pang wracked him as he saw the entire fourth floor of the school in flames. Kirk put a hand over the middle of his chest, winced, and began walking down the street.

"Come on, where are you fire dudes?" he whimpered to himself as he began to run. He remembered a fire call box down the street, one his buddy Rick had pulled once as a joke. He began to run, looking for it, found it open and the handle already pulled: another joker, another false alarm.

Then, looking up, he saw an old lady sitting with her pit bull in an all-night Laundromat. Stumbling through the door, as another pang shot through him, he held himself up by grabbing the doorframe. The glass in the window was riddled with cracks but somehow stayed intact. He looked down at the old lady. She was knitting something and had a revolver on the seat next to her, probably loaded. Smart lady. As he stepped closer, the pit bull woke up from its snooze and looked in his direction. Kirk was glad for a change that he was invisible. He smiled at the dog.

"Hey, nice doggie. Nice dog," Kirk said, grinning for a second, then another pang wracked him and he knew he had to do something.

Looking at the woman, he passed his hands in front of her eyes, trying to get her attention. Why couldn't she see it? The light from the fire was clearly visible out in the street. Then Kirk realized that the school was quite a few blocks down the street, and it was only his own heightened perception that let him see from there. Still, couldn't he get this lady's attention? He tried touching her. The dog began to growl, low, looking directly at him. Could the dog see him? Kirk growled back at the dog, just to see. The dog stood up on its stubby little legs and growled louder this time, showing some of its fangs. Kirk froze in place as he realized the dog was about to pounce.

"She can't see ya. But he can," came a voice from behind him. He turned around. There was the little black girl again.

"You again? Well, you can just go ahead and do your vanishing act, cause I'm busy. . . . " Kirk felt another wave and nearly doubled over at the pain rushing through his body.

"The school's your fetter too, eh?" The girl said, wincing as well. "I didn't think anyone else cared about it."

"Fuck no, I don't care about it. But I'm stuck with it. Why does it hurt me when it's the one that's burning?" He divided his attention between her and the growling dog.

"It's your Fetter—one of them, anyway. We're tied to things, people, and places that were important to us in life. When those ties are broken, it takes away what we are, who we are. It hurts," the little girl said, wincing in pain herself.

"Damn straight it hurts! Now, if you'll just be so kind as to help me with the pooch, we'll see what we can do about getting the old bag up and callin' the fire trucks," Kirk yelled at her, feeling Demon grinning inside him. Demon wanted him to take control, tell her exactly what to do, Kirk knew that. He shook his head. "Look. I'm afraid the pooch is goin' to chew me up. I don't know how he can do it, but I just don't feel like trying him out. Capiche?"

The little girl nodded. She whistled to the dog, who looked up in her direction. "Come here, boy. Come here," she called to him. The dog began to whine, looking at Kirk and the little girl. "Come on, boy," the little girl said pleadingly, holding out her hand like she had a treat in it.

Kirk saw a flash of light inside the girl. The dog looked at Kirk one last time, scrunched his legs up and jumped to the ground, waddling over to her. Kirk took this opportunity to heave back with one hand and thrust his hand into the woman's face, hoping that it would have some effect.

The woman's glasses jumped off her nose and fell onto the floor, making her drop her knitting. She looked up, blinking, in Kirk's direction, as if she saw him for a second.

The little girl's quiet, melodious voice spoke up. "The old are closest to death and can sometimes see us if we're not careful," she whispered to Kirk.

Kirk nodded and took a step back. Getting on his hands and knees, he flicked his finger at the glasses, making them jump nearly a foot toward the door.

"Careful, don't break 'em," the little girl said. Her hand was resting comfortably on the dog's forehead now. The dog was calm, seated, resting with his head on his paws.

The lady followed the glasses, bent to try to pick them up, and Kirk flipped them again, moving them closer to the door jam. She swore once and said something about "ghosts" to herself. Kirk flicked the glasses one last time and watched them tumble out into the street. He then got up and quickly stepped outside, around the woman as she was passing through the door.

She bent to pick up the glasses, and this time Kirk put his lips to her ear and screamed at her. She looked up, shocked, looked around, and found nobody anywhere nearby. She looked at her revolver sitting on the bench inside the Laundromat and obviously wished she had it in hand. She bent down one last time to get the glasses and put them on slowly.

"Listen, *lady*!" Kirk yelled. "*Call the fire department!*" He screamed as another pang of fire shot through his heart. Kirk saw a red light go off inside him like fireworks on a summer night.

Looking down the street, she saw the orange-red glow of the fire in the school, smelled the smoke. She walked back into the Laundromat, got her dog, got her revolver (which she put in her purse), and walked out, moving across the street slowly and carefully, looking all around her. She picked up an ancient, battered public telephone and dialed 911.

Kirk relaxed, watching her talk to the fire department. He turned around and looked for the little girl: true to her style, she was gone.

Kirk shrugged, cursing to himself as the pain kept coming, but less now that he knew help was on its way. He walked back to the school, swearing under his breath. He looked up at the building and hated it, wishing somehow it would burn, if he could just get out of this curse of being tied to it.

Kirk heard Demon whisper, "Go ahead. Let it burn. Make it burn. I have the power. You do, too. I could just give you what you need, Kirkie boy. Ever see napalm go up? I love the smell. Let's make the whole thing burn, shall we, Private?"

Kirk hated when Demon called him Private, like he was some army soldier that the demon issued orders to. Kirk tried not to let the things Demon said bother him, because if he did, it always came to no good: witness the paint cans and the fire.

Kirk leaned against a light-post that had long ago been turned off to save money and now stood like a dead steel tree, never dropping its light-bearing fruit. He heard the fire trucks off in the distance, their high-pitched whine, their horns blasting as they moved through heavy after-bar traffic in the middle of the city. Kirk wished he had a watch: the one he'd had didn't come with him when he came to Purgatory. Kirk figured it was just another punishment.

Then, suddenly from the direction of downtown, Kirk heard the clippity-clop of a horse's hooves on the street. He felt a hand on his arm—the little black girl again.

"Come on," she whispered, tugging on his arm. "We gotta hide." She pulled him into an alleyway, almost against his will. But the girl seemed to know what she was doing, so Kirk let her drag him into hiding.

"He'll see us here!" Kirk whispered.

"Shush. He won't see us if you be quiet. I'm vanishin' us both. Now keep quiet," the girl whispered, almost hissing her words. Kirk was quiet, although Demon muttered something about taking orders from black kids.

A tall man on a horse, clad in black metal armor that didn't shine or even seem to clink together as he moved, was the first on the scene. He had a Confederate officer's sword on his belt. Clearly visible in a saddle-holster was a shotgun with some kind of lightbulb attached to it: Kirk saw a tiny glow coming out of the little half-sphere attached to the butt of the gun. Strung in a special harness across the rider's back was a large scythe, of the kind Kirk's country uncle had hanging up in his living room: it had two handles. The rider's face was covered with an iron mask that hid his features and made him look rather piggish: like a hungry pig looking for food. The mask was attached to an immense helm that covered the man's whole head. Kirk thought he looked like a strange Disney version of Darth Vader, and almost laughed to himself at the concept, but decided against making any noise.

Following the rider were several men in combat gear with guns that had lights on their stocks, and two men who weren't wearing shirts but were carrying several sets of heavy-looking iron chains. The rider slowed to a stop next to the burning building and directed the soldiers to split up into two patrols: they soon disappeared around the corner of the building.

It was quite clear to Kirk that these men and the horse were all like him: grey, quietly moving. They had an eerie presence. They were all dead, like him. Kirk marveled at the horse: where do you get a dead horse to ride on around here?

Kirk strained to hear their conversation. "Doubtful we'll get any souls this time out, but check around anyway. Don't want to lose a chance. Monitor! Sense the building, if you will. I have a feeling about this place."

Kirk looked over to the girl, who put a finger in front of her lips. The world flickered around them both: for a second, Kirk felt an icy cold and then everything was right again, except this time they were standing atop a warehouse across the street from the school. Kirk looked at the girl questioningly, and she just smiled and shrugged.

Kirk focused his hearing on the group of ghostly soldiers again. One of the soldiers was speaking to the rider. "Dread Knight, I report that this structure seems to be the Fetter of two wraiths. One, a newly dead wraith, and another one we know to be named Sylvie—a Renegade, master."

"Interesting. A newly dead wraith? An Enfant? Fascinating. Monitor, can you sense anything further about this Enfant?"

The little girl closed her eyes and stayed very still, while Kirk looked at her inquisitively.

"No, milord. My senses are blocked by some greater force. Perhaps the use of an Arcanos?"

The black knight laughed cruelly behind his helm. "Ah, Monitor, that is always your excuse if you cannot get your art to do what I wish. Still, the Renegades could be protecting this new wraith, having gotten to her first . . . "

"Him, sir. Very definitely a he."

"Very well, then. Him." The black knight sighed. "It's a shame that the Hierarchy cannot be everywhere at once. I would have liked to have gotten hold of an Enfant during these times. One loyal to the Hierarchy could be very useful right about now." The black knight turned his attention back to the Monitor. "Monitor! Send a message: I would like a soldier well-versed in the Arcanos of Masquers and of Harbingers to be posted to this Fetter, to await the possible return of our new wraith. It's not too late to give up on fresh blood, as it were."

A soldier approached and saluted the knight. "Perimeter secure, sir!" The other soldiers had returned from their patrol and were slowly filtering back to the street as the large red fire trucks pulled up, a flurry of firemen getting out, attaching hoses to the trucks and to fireplugs, and starting to blanket the upper floors with powerful streams of water. The grey patrol moved out of the way as more trucks screeched to a stop.

The knight nodded to the soldier, edging his horse over to the other side of the street. "Excellent. Well, too bad it's not going to burn to the ground. I wouldn't mind harming the Renegades a bit. Troops, let's move out. We've got a full third of our domain left to patrol," the knight said, and clucked to his horse, which took off at a walk, the troops and slaves following along behind.

As soon as they were out of hearing range (even for a ghost), the little girl dropped the cloak of darkness from around them both and smiled at Kirk. Kirk shook his head, running his hands over his chest, where he felt the soothing water starting to ease the pain of damage to his Fetter.

"You Sylvie?" Kirk said, grinning.

She nodded yes.

"They're lookin' for you, I'd guess, eh?"

She smiled. "They're looking for all us Renegades. But who ain't?"

Kirk shook his head again, not knowing what to think, or who to trust. Demon spoke up within him: "Oh, yeah, that's the way, Kirkie. Trust a little kid. Trust a little jungle-bunny girl. What is it? Got a little jungle fever?" the foul thing whispered in his head.

He looked up, grinning. He was starting to learn that anyone Demon didn't like must be good for him. He put his hand out to shake Sylvie's. "Nice to meetcha. I'm Kirk. I don't know where it is that I am, Miss Sylvie, but wherever it is, you've been the nicest person I've seen so far, and besides, anyone Mr. Demon doesn't like, I have to give a second chance at likin'."

"Mr. Demon?" Sylvie asked, amused.

"Yeah. Talks to me in my head. You know, used to be I'd've thought you was crazy if you'd come to me and told me that you had a man talkin' in your head—but that was last month. Now that I'm dead, I can kinda see where it might happen." Kirk grinned and scratched his chest again, still feeling the cool water's effect.

"Mr. Demon, Kirk, is what we call the Shadow," Sylvie said quietly, as if she were reciting something she herself had once been told. "He's an evil force inside you, contrary to all you are. It seeks to strip away what makes you you, and force you to become one of the mindless servants of Oblivion . . . of the nothing," Sylvie said, the words sounding strangely chilling in her mouth.

Kirk shuddered, laughing. "Damn, girl," he said, grinning. "What *is* that supposed to mean? Servants of the nothin'?"

Sylvie looked at Kirk with a deadly serious glint in her eye. "Don't laugh. It's everywhere. It's inside you. Mr. Demon— my mama . . . Inside of us all. All us Restless, anyway. Not like the lost souls or the drones."

"Oh, you mean we're a special kind of ghostie?" Kirk said.

"Very special. And very . . . caught. Other ghosts are thin and ain't worth nothin'. But a Restless like you and me, we got smarts, and powers. We got Fetters, and we got our own feelin's. Feelin's that make you strong," Sylvie said, her eyes big and round.

"Like when I get pissed off about school?" Kirk said, suddenly remembering his guitar.

"Yeah. Like when I see dollies. Like, when I can feel again. It's a pretty thing, and ya gets light for it. Light, you know—juice? Stuff. Inside you. Like this," Sylvie said, holding up her hand, which briefly glowed a cool blue-and-purple color.

Kirk nodded. "Yeah. Light. I getcha. So, all I gotta do is get pissed off. That's good."

"You can't just get pissed, Kirk. You gotta think about things and know what you're doin'. Like when you knocked that lady's glasses off. You must'a been practicin' that," Sylvie said, smiling.

"Yeah. Like when you carry us around so quick. How you do that?" Kirk said, looking at her sideways.

"Miss Cindy used to call it 'Argos'—it's the fancy word for it. I just call it travelin', cuz it can get you around places. Quick, like ya said. She's the one who kenned me out, found all the things that I could do. Taught me 'em."

"Kenned you out?" Kirk said.

"It's like, she looked at me with these pretty blue eyes and she looked through me, and then she knew all the things I could do. As a ghost. All my powers," Sylvie said, chewing on one of her braids.

"All of them, eh? Can you do kennin'?" Kirk said.

"Nope. She said it was easy for her, but it ain't easy for me. I can do a little divinin', but no kennin'."

"What other powers do you have?" Kirk asked, looking down. He wanted to know what he could do. He liked the idea of having powers, like having superpowers in a comic book.

"I can sing some, and dream some. I like to do dreamin'. It's fun. I can travel some, and give folks juice. And some divinin'. But not like Miss Cindy!" Sylvie said, grinning.

"Sing? What good is that?" Kirk said.

"You can make people feel stuff. You know, get 'em in a mood. Like that dog—I made it all happy. I like makin' things happy. I do it all the time. There's too much sadness in the world. I betcha you could do singin'. It sounded like it when you were playing your git-fiddle," Sylvie said. "And, you got the 'rage, too. That means you can hit stuff in the land of the living. Open doors, knock people's glasses off—"

"Start fires?" Kirk said.

"Yeah, if you know what ya doin'," Sylvie said. "That's a powerful power. Can you do that?"

Kirk focused on his fingers and rubbed them together like he remembered the Shadow doing. He rubbed and rubbed, but nothing happened. He looked up at Sylvie. "Ain't somethin' supposed to happen?"

Sylvie grinned. "Hey, you gotta let loose some feelin's. Some juice."

Kirk grinned. "Oh, yeah!" He got a serious look on his face and started thinking about the pain he'd felt, the school on fire, the scary man on horseback, the strange pain as the building burned. His hand began to glow red, like a heat element on a stove that just got turned on. He started rubbing his fingers together.

"You can't do that without me," Mr. Demon said, chuckling. "Of course, you've never been much without me, boy. Want some help?"

Kirk looked pained and looked up at Sylvie. "Mr. Demon says I can't do that without him. He's offerin' to help."

Sylvie shook her head. "Don't you go makin' a deal with the devil, Kirk. If he says he can help, don' believe him. He ain't never gonna help you 'less it's gonna help him. And what helps him, hurts you. Miss Cindy said that, and I believe it. I ain't never let Mama do nothin' for me, and she stays quiet about it now."

Kirk looked at his hand, glowing bright hot, and then shook his head and watched the light slowly die. "Damn," he said. "Oh, well." He looked up. "Do you think it's safe to go back over there?" He got to his feet and looked across to the school building. It was smoking, but the fires had mostly gone out.

"I guess so. What for? I don' want to see no Legionnaire over there." Sylvie stood on her tiptoes looking across at the school.

"Legionnaire?" Kirk asked.

"That guy with the horse and his soldiers," Sylvie said. She squinted. "But I don' see 'em."

"I wanna get my guitar," Kirk said. "That's all. We don't have to hang around. Say, what would they do if they caught us? They like the cops or somethin'?"

Sylvie smiled. "Somethin' like that. They're lookin' for new dead folks, just in case. They collect 'em all, and take 'em to the Citadel. From there they ride the rails to Stygia, where the Big Devil lives. Unless you Restless, like me. Like you. Then they make you swear oaths and stuff, and then you get to walk around with a Centurion and do everythin' your boss says, or you get yourself put in chains. Like those Thralls you saw—the ones in chains."

"Sounds great. Not," Kirk said. "Who died and left them in charge?" he added, grinning. "Or do they work for God?"

"Nah. They work for Charon, the Big Devil. He's dead, or gone, or somethin'. Miss Cindy used to know, but I never listened to her when she went on about them Archy folks. Scuse me, it's 'High-er-archy.' Hierarchy."

"Where's Miss Cindy now?" Kirk asked quietly.

"She's gone. Down there. Down in the nothin'," she said, looking glum.

Kirk ran his hand through his hair. "I ain't never seen this nothin' you keep talkin' about."

Sylvie climbed up on the edge of the roof. "You don't wanna. Come on, we gotta get your guitar." She held out her hand.

Taking her hand, Kirk felt a flash of total cold and pure black, and then he was through the other side, standing next to the charred remains of the machine room. Leaving Sylvie behind, he stepped inside and saw his guitar leaning up against the wall. A fireman was poking around the machine room, looking at the spilled paint cans, writing in his notepad and holding a lantern.

Mr. Demon spoke up inside his head. "See what I mean, boy? It's over for you here. Shoulda let it burn. Oh well, gimme another chance, and it will."

"Fuck you, Mr. Demon," Kirk whispered, and picked up the guitar, which seemed none the worse for the fire. Kirk inspected the strings, wondering when one of them would break—and where he'd get more when they did.

Sylvie stood at the doorway. "Want to go someplace else? I can take you."

Kirk looked back at her, then at the fire inspector looking over the burn markings. "Yeah. I do. People walkin' around make me nervous."

Sylvie nodded and extended her hand. "Okay. We'll go see some folks I know. They Renegade like us."

"I didn't know that's what I was," Kirk said, grinning.

"Renegade? Oh, everybody Renegade, unless they are with the Hierarchy. Or 'less they're with the churchy types." Sylvie grinned.

"What churchy types? Angels and stuff? I wondered what God had to do with all this," Kirk said.

"God ain't said yet. The churchy types think He has, but I ain't heard from no angel yet. I seen angels that say they're angels, but even my pitiful divinin' can tell they ain't angels. Just Restless like us, only with wings and glowin'."

"Maybe there ain't never been no angels. Maybe there ain't no God," Kirk said.

"Maybe. I dunno. Miss Cindy believed there was a God, but she didn't never say how she knew. She wasn't no churchy, though. Those churchies get strange—rantin' and ravin' and sermonin'. Lucky enough they keep to themselves," Sylvie said.

"Who we gonna go see?" Kirk asked, feeling drained, almost tired. He wanted to sleep, but the building seemed foreboding now. He couldn't sleep here.

"Duke's Circle. He's a nice man. Has a few friends. I guess we can hang with them, if it's okay with them. They have to say when they sees you. Duke has the kennin' somethin' fierce, and so he'll be able to tell ya more about your powers," Sylvie said, somehow seeming to know that would be all Kirk needed to hear for him to decide to go with her.

Kirk grinned. "Okay—can I take my guitar with me?"

"Sure. Don't weigh nothin'," Sylvie said, holding out her hand and twirling a braid in her fingers. Kirk grabbed onto her hand, holding tight this time.

With a lurch, they plummeted down—into darkness.

For a moment, all Kirk could see was blackness punctuated by skirling storms of purple—although the sense of incredible velocity wasn't lost on him. He almost trailed off behind Sylvie, but the girl's grip was firm and strong, and there was considerable power in her will.

Then, almost a second later, they were standing atop an ancient hotel, looking down. Kirk heard a gunshot go off below him.

"What was that?" Kirk asked, surprised.

"Shh." Sylvie said, bending down. "Bad news." She pointed over the lip of the building into the alley below.

Looking down, Kirk saw what had been a familiar scene while he was alive: a gang of his age faced a team of scared, but relatively well-trained, uniformed police—except that, in this case, they were

all Dead. Kirk saw that the gang's weapons were out-
lined in the darkness with light that seemed to come
from their hands, and the cops had guns mounted
with tiny starlike jewels burning furiously red.
Almost immediately, Kirk found himself appraising
the scene from a strategic point of view, muttering
under his breath, "Must be a low-ammo situation:
they're taking their shots carefully. Of course,
they're wiped if they don't watch their rear flank. If I
were the cops, I'd send two men around the building
to nab 'em from the back. Of course, the cops are
scared shitless; I'd think a little distraction would go
far in taking care of them." Kirk grinned as he felt
his anticipation of the fight. He looked up at Sylvie.
"You think they could use some help?"

She looked down. "I think so, Kirk. It'd be your
choice."

Kirk knelt down beside her. "What do you mean
by that?"

Sylvie looked up at him. "Kirk, those cops—
they're from the Hierarchy. If you throw in with
Duke's gang, you'll be marked by the Hierarchy for
imprisonment. This is where you decide whether
you're a Renegade for sure or not. There ain't no
goin' back."

Kirk shook his head, looking down at the gang,
which was losing, bit by bit. "Sooner or later, it's
gonna happen. I'm just not cut out to follow the
rules." He watched as one of the Hierarchy cops
nailed a guy in the arm: they might be dead, he
thought, but the bullets still looked painful, maybe
even fatal. Kirk wondered what would happen if he
was hit too many times.

"We're already dead, Sylvie—how are those bullets going to hurt us?" Kirk asked.

"They hurt a lot. And Kirk, there's more to worry
about than dyin', here. If'n you get hurt too bad, you

go to a very bad place. It's hard ta come back. Sometimes, people don't."

"Where do you go? The nothin'?" Kirk said, watching one of the gang members try to rush the line of cops. A bright red bolt shot into him, and he fell, clutching his shoulder. Kirk watched in horror as the kid screamed and dissolved, flowing like water down a crack that seemed to open up and consume him. A second later, there was no trace of him.

Kirk looked up at Sylvie. "You go into the Harrowin', Kirk. A place that's controlled by the Shadow. And if ya don't watch it, you're gonna go straight to Oblivion."

Kirk screwed up his face. "Oblivion? The nothin'?"

Sylvie nodded. "The nothin'."

The gunshots quieted quickly. Kirk saw the gang moving down the street, backing up, taking shots as they went. He nodded to Sylvie. "Okay. Important safety tip. Don't get hurt," Kirk said, grinning to himself. He watched a few seconds more, feeling the call of battle, shaking his head as he saw the gang expertly retreat, taking shots at the cops pressing them.

He made a decision and looked Sylvie in her eyes. "Can you get me across the street into that alley, down next to that shoe store?" Kirk said as he saw the gang break up and make a defensive rear action—in other words, they ran around the corner of the building and ducked into a nearby alley.

Sylvie smiled. "Sure." She took his hand. "Beam me down, Captain!" she said, and there was a brief moment of cold discontinuity before Kirk's vision reformed.

Suddenly three gun barrels were pointing at him as he heard the word "Harbinger!" yelled. Kirk slowly raised his hands, as did Sylvie. The gang members looked at each other, then at him. Their faces were strange—it was only a second's thought before Kirk realized they all three wore masks: one a lion's head, one a wolf's head, and another looked like a monkey.

Kirk grinned. "Um, I guess you don't need no help. Ahhh, could I convince ya that I'm one of the good guys?" he said, whispering, still grinning.

The wolf-head ran to the edge of the alley and looked down the street. "We've got to go, Duke, they're coming," came a feminine voice from under the wolf mask.

The lion-head turned back to Kirk and Sylvie, shotgun still trained on them. It glowed red. "Nah, you're too stupid to be an 'arch. Anyone who'd jump down next ta some armed folks without a gun's got a screw loose, in my opinion."

The monkey-mask started giggling, crouched down as he was, but said nothing. Kirk saw that he held a grenade, the pin still in it. It glowed with a white-hot radiance.

The lion-mask turned his head back and forth between the wolf-head and Kirk, checking every few seconds. "Look, buddy, I don't know who you are, but if you'll get your Harbinger there to get us the hell out of here, I'll be glad to have a nice, long conversation with you."

Sylvie shook her head. "I can't carry you all. I don't got enough juice."

The lion-head looked down at the monkey-mask and nodded in Sylvie's direction. A spindly hand fanned open under his mask and offered a finger. Kirk thought, for a moment, that he looked like E.T. with his long, thin finger glowing red. Sylvie took his hand, and Kirk watched as fiery luminescence washed from monkey-head's fingers into her body, illuminating her from within.

Sylvie giggled. "Okay . . . I have enough now." She grabbed hold of Kirk and the man in the monkey mask.

The lion-head grabbed Kirk and stretched his arm out to grab the woman in the wolf mask, who was already leveling her pistol and starting to fire down the street. Kirk watched in amazement as the lion-head's arm snaked out, longer than it could've possibly been, to touch the wolf-mask's shoulder. As soon as Sylvie saw the contact, she raised her hands, and Kirk saw them all, one by one, fall through a hole in the ground that irised open. There was the brief sensation of falling, and then, suddenly, velocity.

Kirk opened his eyes and saw a straight, flat desert all around him, red sand, and a single black-top road. Sylvie was flying along, her braids streaming behind her; the chain of ghosts she was tugging was nothing to her. Her face was contorted in a grimace of concentration. Finally, she lifted her head up and Kirk felt the ragtag wraith-chain fly upward. There was darkness again—the nothin', Kirk guessed—and suddenly they were all standing next to a beautiful old oak tree. There were no Hierarchy agents in sight.

"Freda, can you check to see if we were followed?" the lion-head asked. He took off his mask and smiled at Sylvie. "Thanks for the save, Sylv. I didn't recognize you at first—normally you go it alone."

Sylvie nodded. "No problem, Duke. This here's Kirk. He's my friend. We share a Fetter."

Duke nodded. "Anyone who's a friend of Sylvie's can't be too bad. How are you doin', Kirk? Ain't it great to be dead?" Duke smiled, his mane of hair all white.

Kirk smiled, looking at the lion mask, and shrugged. "God, I wish I had a cigarette. Other than that, I'm okay I guess," he said, stomping his feet from the sudden cold that gripped him from his travel.

He turned away, looking out across the street. Duke was silent, but when Kirk looked up at the tall Renegade ghost, he was proffering something with his hand. "Smokes. It's not the best, but it's something," Duke said, grinning.

Kirk shook his head and put the hand-rolled cigarette in his mouth. Monkey-mask held up a finger (the same one that had glowed like E.T. earlier), and his cigarette briefly caught on fire.

"Puff on it quick, or it'll go out," Duke said. Kirk winked at Sylvie, who wrinkled her nose at him.

Kirk inhaled the sweet but bitter smoke, felt a cold chill go through him as he held it in what used to be his lungs. He realized that the smoke was moving through him, billowing out around him, illuminating him from within. Still, it gave him what cigarettes used to give him: a tinge of something crisp and something to do with his mouth while he was thinking.

Duke smiled. "So, what brings you here tonight to save our asses, Sylvie?"

Sylvie smiled. "Oh, I'm just out and about. Not doin' too much. Just givin' Kirk the tour."

"Ain't thinking he's just gonna get cut into the Circle are ya, hon? Hate to disappoint you," Duke said, grinning. He lit his own cigarette and started smoking. He pointed at Kirk. "What sort of thing are you lookin' to do for the rest of your afterlife? Hang out? Try to screw with the skinbags? Avenge your death? Find God? What?"

Kirk blew the smoke out into the dark air and spread his arms. "I dunno what to tell you. I don't want to just sit around. I want a piece of the action— I want to be out and runnin' with a gang. I'm good, but how can you know that? I'm good at the kind of stuff you guys do. I notice you're down a man. You could use me."

The wolf-masked woman turned to Kirk and picked him up by the collar of the jacket he was wearing. With one hand, she held him suspended in midair.

"Look here, smart boy. That guy was our friend. Derek was the best Breaker I've ever known, and he was ten times smarter than your pansy ass." Kirk hung there, kicking a little, looking down at Sylvie worriedly. His cigarette had bounced out of his mouth and had rolled somewhere in the grass.

"Put him down, Freda," Duke said. "He didn't mean anything by it. Did you Kirk?"

Slowly Freda, her wolf mask seemingly grinning at him, put him down.

"So . . . Kirk. Kirk who?" Duke asked. Kirk looked at Sylvie out of the corner of his eye, but she wasn't giving out any clues.

Kirk's eyes darted to Sylvie and then back to Duke. "Kirk Rourke. You wanna check my job references?"

Duke shook his mane of white hair. "Naw. This is Freda, and this guy in the monkey mask is Jojo."

"Why were those cops messin' with you?" Kirk asked.

Duke put his lion mask back on. "They caught us near one of their secret caches of equipment and stuff. We were trying to rip it off, maybe get in with the Greymaster and his gang. We ain't doin' too good by ourselves, especially now that Furman's gone. Jojo . . . can you sense him anywhere?"

Jojo shook his masked head. "No. Furman gone. Bye, Furman."

Duke slammed his hand into the oak tree so hard he went fuzzy for a moment, and then turned back to Kirk. "What can you do for us?" he said.

Kirk looked down at Sylvie, who smiled at Kirk. "I can push things around. A little singing, too."

Freda swiveled her wolf mask in Kirk's direction. "How do we know he's not an Archy plant? They've been gettin' pretty smart lately."

Sylvie shook her head. "No. I divin'ed him out. He ain't with the Hierarchy. He's a baby. I was surprised to see his Caul gone—someone musta already Reaped him. Don't know who."

Kirk turned around to Sylvie. "Hey! I ain't no baby! I'm twenty-six!"

Sylvie grinned. "You're a baby ghost, Kirk. Ain't been dead for more than nine months. Ain't even seen a Halloween yet. Heck, Miss Cindy spent four months teachin' me powers and stuff."

Freda looked up and down the street. "Um, folks, I hate to break up this party, but all we need right now is some wastrel to see us and report us, and we'll have a bunch of Legionnaires on our asses. Let's go someplace safe."

Jojo looked up suddenly. "The World is safe. Meany will let us in for free."

Sylvie clapped her hands. "Oh goodie! The World!"

Jojo danced around. "Yeah! The World. We say good-bye to Furman! We ride the Merrygo."

Duke looked at Freda, then Sylvie, and asked "Can you carry us there?" Freda shrugged her shoulders, and Duke caught her eyes rolling skyward behind her mask.

Sylvie nodded at Duke. "If you got the juice," she said.

Jojo grinned and touched Sylvie's hand again. A flash of light burned like a magnesium flare between them. Sylvie glowed all over like an industrial angel for a second, and she giggled at the power.

They stood in a circle this time, holding hands: Sylvie liked it best that way.

2

Ghost Story:
Justice Burning

And this, ladies and gentlemen, is the portrait of Magistrate O'Rourke. Jebediah O'Rourke was a prominent member of the community. Served in the Civil War as a colonel in the Georgia Volunteers and rode with Stonewall Jackson. Believe it or not, he was actually murdered here in Dekalb County Courthouse. As you see by this commemorative plaque on the wall, Jebediah was appointed magistrate of the Superior Court in 1856 and served for several years. He was supposedly killed by a group of Ku Klux Klansmen in his chambers, stabbed thirty-six times in the back and burned at the stake for refusal to cooperate with the Klan.

The really interesting part of Jebediah's story is that it's said at certain times when the light is right you can see him still sitting up on his bench, dispensing justice with a stern hand. Some claim to have seen him stalking the great

hall of the courthouse, looking out the great win-
dows and brooding over the state of the city. I
wonder what he would think about Decatur now?
Well, ladies and gentlemen, if you'd like to step
this way, I'll show you our collection of Civil War
relics. . . .

Jebediah loved his little courthouse. Loved the windows that looked out onto the street. He loved the
shadows that were so cool in the day. He hated what
he had to do here, hated to have to send free people
into bondage, but it was the way of things. He was a
judge: he was not to make laws, but to judge them
fairly.

Jebediah would stalk the halls of his courthouse,
climbing the spiral stair to the utmost tower room,
and watch the Shadowlands of the city, watch the
purplish red fires that lit the city from below and
made the dark sky glow with streaks of magenta.
From the top of the tower, Jebediah could almost see
the nightly battles that took place in Oakland
Cemetery, not too far away. He often walked down
to the graveyard to see the Northern soldiers, who
had been buried in Confederate graves, drag
Confederates from their open crypts and do battle
mindlessly. They had long since abandoned gunfire:
they possessed no bullets. Still, many of them still
aimed their guns and "shot," while more had come
to understand that only the bayonets on the ends of
their weapons mattered now. Every night there
would be wholesale slaughter, and the next night the
Drones would rise again to do battle once more.
Jebediah watched these fights more to assuage his
own Shadow, which was a bloodthirsty sort, than to
satisfy his curiosity.

Still, he was always excited when the South rallied

and "won" the nightly battle. It was one such night, the same night that Kirk met Sylvie, that Jebediah used his Argos powers to travel from his beloved courthouse to the cemetery to watch the festivities.

Jebediah was troubled, because his Shadow had grown quiet in the last few days, and his dreams had turned into things of true fear: fiery maelstroms that swept the city, taking all the Restless with them in their relentless paths; a dark demon coming to him to demand payment of some kind; a familiar but strange old woman; his grandson James. Jebediah's dreams had become dire, and he felt the need to let the Shadow out for catharsis to keep it from overcoming him while he was rendering verdicts.

So he sat and watched the carnage, feeling the dark, old cloak of the Shadow mantling him, and it wasn't until the fighting was nearly over that he came back to himself to see a woman resting on one of the benches. One of the dead, Jebediah was certain—a noncombatant. Some of the women buried in Oakland were as fierce as the men, but this one was docile, quiet, her hands folded as if in prayer. She looked up at Jebediah from afar and nodded to him.

She was wearing an exquisite black mourning gown, a black neck draping and veil, elbow-length sleeves, and black lace on her kirtle. She looked ancient, one of the Travelers, obviously—one of the ghosts who had come over the sea with her family.

Jebediah was suddenly shocked as he recognized Mary Riorche, who was not only his great-granddam but also a known Heretic in the area. If he was seen with her, he would be duly censured. The Hierarchy was firmly against the Heretics, who in ancient times tricked Charon into sending them their souls only for personal gain. Although secretly Jebediah still believed in God, he would never have voiced that belief to his Hierarchy friends—then he would also be branded a Heretic and cast out.

Drawing on his Mask of Privacy (an owl's-head mask made of Stygian iron) he strode across the battlefield. Drones were known to avoid their more self-determining Restless "kin," avoiding their presence much like mortals avoided their presence. Jebediah and the lady would not be disturbed.

He bowed low to the lady in black, and she inclined her head at the same time. She wore no mask, as was customary for Heretics, but her mourning veil was firmly in place.

"What brings you to this awful place, dear Mary?" His thick Southern drawl came from behind the owl's beak.

"I come, as ye know, Jebediah, as a bearer of prophecy. From our most holy Laird. As it has ever been. I come here, knowin' as I do that you frequent this place," Mary said, crossing herself.

"I see. What prophecy do ye bring to me this time, most respected dam of my father's father?"

"Ye are to know that the Firebird has arisen. That the Curse of our line has claimed the last son of the Riorche: Kirk, his name be. That he has stepped forth from the Caul to claim his destiny, and I cannae be sure what will befall him," Mary said quietly, her melodic voice carrying to Jebediah's ears over the sounds of men fighting.

"Mary, say it cannot be! I promised I would not continue the Curse of the Dead, and yet you say it's continued without me?" Jebediah looked shocked.

"Aye, and before this it has. The Curse has been fulfilled twice since."

"Twice? Another Riorche lies now in this eternal turmoil! Give me his name!"

"James. Thy son's son."

"Then surely the Kirk-boy isn't a product of the Curse—which is said to skip a generation, from grandfather to grandchild, through the male line," Jebediah said.

"James Rourke lives on, without rest. And his pain, and his fear, and his anger live strong in him," Mary said, her head impassively turned toward the battle.

Jebediah looked up as the call for a Charge was bugled out over the gravestones. He shuddered involuntarily.

"Surely this boy Kirk has no get? Thus ends our line. Thus ends our curse." Jebediah's voice was pleading.

"Aye. And I not be the one you plead to. Plead to God, if such you must do, or to the black-hearted Celt who cursed the Riorche with Restless death so long ago. I only see God's will as described by his great Plan," Mary said, folding her hands.

Mary stood up to leave. Jebediah rose with her at once. "You must tell me more. Where is Kirk? Where is James? Sweet, young James, so strong and brave. I could not claim him as my grandfather claimed me, Mary. I do not know why he is a Restless."

"He was in a great an' terrible war, or so the angels hae told me. It claimed his very soul. Now, I must be going, Jebediah. Likewise, I think ye can set your Monitors to tracin' their places in Purgatory. For me, it is not my place. God gae with you," she said, and turned from him, her fiery red hair streaming out in the wind from under her veil. She made her way out of the graveyard and soon vanished from sight, leaving Jebediah to watch the rest of the battle alone.

Jebediah took a parcel that he always carried in his greatcoat out of the deep wool pocket and unwrapped it, checking the contents. He ran his hand across the mother-of-pearl hilt of the sword, up the blade, to the ragged tip where it had been broken. Would the Firebird come to claim it? he wondered. And what shape would its weapon take this time?

Ghost Story: The Haunted Gun

"No, man, it's not that I'm scared . . . I don't care about no stupid ghosts. I just don't want to clean the armory, that's all. So, if you do it for me . . ." Squire said.

"Me? But Sarge said for you to do it. Besides, it's a haunted gun, not a haunted armory. Just don't mess with the gun, and you'll be fine," his pal, Griff said, grinning. "Look, I'll hold your hand while we go back there . . . "

"Fuck you, man. What do you think I am, a fag?"

"Don't ask, don't tell, Squire."

"Fuck you. All right then, you . . . you stay out here, and hold the light . . . "

"Yeah, it's a good thing you don't believe in ghosts, Squire. 'Cuz the guy who used to own the haunted gun . . . Colonel Jim Rourke I believe his name was, well, damn. He was a mean bastid. I mean, just a hellacious DI and an Army Ranger and he'd as soon rip your heart out and show it to you as shake hands. And, you know about the curse, right? Anybody who goes into training with that rifle gets a medical discharge before too long: funky things happen to them. They get wonky. But you don't believe in that shit, so I'll just leave you here in the dark. . . . " Griff grinned in the doorway of the armory.

"Griff! Dammit, I'm trying to sweep here!"

His men called him the Greymaster, themselves the Grey Wolves. In the twenty or so years since his death, James Rourke had become proud of the wraiths he'd gathered from battlefields all over Southeast Asia, Korea, and even across the Persian Gulf in Desert Storm. One by one, his unit of crack troops (trained as they were in several powers of the dead each) plowed through the Shadowlands of the tropical islands, looking for the dead, the disenfranchised, the lonely soldier-wraiths who would never see their units again. He was able to give them a place, a soldier's job, which is all the Heaven a soldier needs.

His soldiers were from nearly every era. Jameson was a Confederate colonel who was killed just north of Atlanta in a skirmish, one of those that damn fool General Hood ordered. Adams was a doughboy in the Great War, who died nameless in a trench. He'd have no Fetter at all except for the memorials that dotted the French countryside. Collins was a Marine in World War II, one who fought and died on the beach at Iwo Jima. Becker was a riverine patrol officer in the 'Nam, who ran the "cruise ship Oblivion" back in the day. One or two of the men were former Legionnaires, although none of them were older than the modern age. Except maybe Dr. Teeth, but he wasn't what you'd call a soldier. He wasn't what you'd call a doctor, either.

The Grey Wolves numbered forty-three: three highly trained teams of ten, plus administrative support. What Arcanos they needed to know, they were taught. What the Greymaster asked them to do, they did, without question. That was the way of things. The Greymaster could've just as easily gone to work for the Hierarchy, except that they had pissed him off when he'd died. Some backward filing clerk in some embassy over in the 'Nam had forgotten to pick him up, so he'd had to spend two years in the Jade Empire's Hell of Burning Embers, a special Hell they reserved for the spirits of their dead enemies.

Becker and Grim (another wraith, a tall black fella who had since passed on to Oblivion) had broken him out of the Hell of Burning Embers using Becker's riverine boat (they were, as Rangers, sworn to get the last man out of there) to escape down the River. For that reason, Becker was his right-hand man and would, if anything ever happened to him, take over his position as leader.

They called James the Greymaster because he was a master of the quick fade with all his troops, leaving behind nothing but a fog. He was adept at bringing up a fog of grey smoke in the Shadowlands to cover their pursuit, and good enough at Argos, the traveling power, to move his troops through the Tempest if need be. That, and he wore an unmistakable, mirror-helm.

His troops even respected Greymaster's Shadow, which had a known Relic attached to it. When his Shadow was dominant, he would draw a black-bladed machete seemingly from thin air. None had ever been able to best Greymaster's Shadow in a fight and take the machete away from him. No one was that suicidal, not even the worst of the Martyrs, who James suspected secretly worshipped Oblivion.

They had made a headquarters for themselves in a fairly nice place. A MARTA train ran overhead, so there was instant, cheap transportation relatively available. It was an ancient warehouse, one of the many hundreds in Atlanta, a city of rails. It had been condemned several years ago, but one of Greymaster's teams had gone in, possessed the necessary clerks, and made the necessary changes. The warehouse didn't exist anywhere anymore—not even in computer records.

Greymaster had made—just for effect, mostly—a throne made out of a barrel, backed by one of Sherman's neckties. A Sherman's necktie was quite clearly a steel rail twisted into a loop, usually heated on the roadbed and beaten around a nearby tree. General Sherman left quite a few on the trees around Atlanta as he destroyed the rails, and to Greymaster, this symbolized many things at once. For one, it made clear his position on the Greyboys and their Klanriders: he'd have none of that racist crap in his organization. Becker was black, as were a few others of his men, and he couldn't afford to lose any of them. It also signified his other main goal: crippling the rails, specifically the rail line that ran from the Shadowlands to the hub of the Hierarchy, Stygia. It was a stratagem worthy of Sherman: disable the enemy's ability to make war, and he would destroy them. Without the regular supply of soulfire to Atlanta from Stygia, the Hierarchy would just be another group of trained soldiers fighting a losing battle against his better-trained troops.

Greymaster hungered for soulfire. He didn't know exactly where it came from: he was sure it wasn't an easily stomached process. Tales had been told that soulfire was the distilled essence of souls: kind of a spiritual version of Soylent Green. Soulfire was energy, passion, what the Hierarchy called "Pathos," and it was contained in special crystals mined from some hellish hole in Stygia. The crystals fed guns, cars, whatever you needed energy to run. This allowed the Hierarchy Legionnaires to use their Arcanos, their powers of hiding, moving, and magic, and their rifles at the same time.

This was an unacceptable tactical advantage to James, one he must deny the enemy. Besides, there were many other uses soulfire could be put to. It was a more ready currency than oboli. It was also needed to operate not just weapons but radios, computers, anything that once required electricity in the living world. It could also be used to drive a vehicle, sometimes a critical advantage in the lands of the dead. Attach enough soulfire to a bomb in the Shadowlands (oh, that rarest of commodities!), and you would see an explosion the likes of which the Hierarchy had never seen. Oh, how Oblivion loved a bomb, how it hungered to take the fiery power of its explosion and magnify it.

Greymaster had, understandably, become quite adroit at discovering when the Hierarchy shipment of soulfire was to arrive in town. He had operatives on the outer rings of the Hierarchy defenses in downtown Atlanta for many months, testing their response time and readiness. He had informants within the Hierarchy who themselves wanted a cut of the soulfire. He had trained his own men in several soulfire-gathering exercises. Now, all that he lacked was enough weaponry—enough guns to take the Hierarchy by storm and make off with as much soulfire as he could.

And as for that, well, Greymaster had a plan. His Wolves were incredibly efficient, but sometimes measures called for more . . . expendable instruments. James put on his Greymaster's helm, a shiny, smoked-mirror helm which reflected a distorted view of those who looked him straight in the eyes, and strode out of the tent he had erected in the main receiving area of the warehouse. Within seconds, his commands were being followed.

When the cold of the Tempest was done, Kirk and his new-found circle of the dead stood at the bottom of a huge escalator, the bottom-most part of it boarded up. The escalator reached up many stories to the World of Krafft, originally an indoor amusement park that never made it financially.

"Damn. That's what you were talkin' about. That place closed down years ago," Kirk said, shaking his head.

"Not to us," Sylvie said, smiling. "Meany runs it now. He's a clown." Sylvie looked up at the others, as if sharing a secret joke.

They climbed up onto the partition which blocked off the entrance to the escalator and started climbing the frozen metal stairs to the World. Kirk felt dizzy as he rose in height, looking down off the side. He remembered reading that this escalator was one of the largest escalators in existence, when it had been operating. It was even higher than the one in the Underground MARTA station, which took people several stories down.

A few minutes later, Kirk could make out a man standing in a blood-stained clown costume at the top of the stairs. Turning around to face his companions, he realized that this was nothing strange to them. He tried to be cool, but kept avoiding the man's gaze. It was unnerving.

The clown stood there, fingering a rusty razor blade and grinning at him as he reached the top of the stairs. Somehow his companions had maneuvered him so that he was walking in front. Just before Kirk took a step off the escalator, the clown spoke up.

"STOP! Who goes here?" he said in a high, squeaky voice.

Kirk looked back at his friends. Sylvie whispered, "Tell him your name."

"Kirk," Kirk said.

"Ah-ha! Kirk! Are you a first-time visitor to the World?"

"Yes," Kirk said.

"Ah-ha! Then your friends get in free. Come on, friends, come on," the clown said, ushering them past. Kirk started to follow them. "Now, now! Not so fast!" the clown said, interposing his rusty razor blade. "We need to have a chat. You see, everyone who comes into the World has to pay one way or another. If it's your first time, it's easy to pay. Just agree to look in Meany's Mirror in the Hall of Mirrors. Easy enough, no? Everyone here has done it. Why can't you?" the clown said, grinning at him.

Kirk shot daggers at Sylvie, but she looked very seriously at him. "If you want to be one of us, Kirk, you'll do it."

Kirk nodded. "Let me see this mirror."

The clown laughed. "All right then! Follow me, Kurt!"

"Kirk! My name's Kirk."

"Oh! Sorry!" the clown said, rushing ahead of Kirk toward the Hall of Mirrors, which was right next to the entrance. He stepped up to the door leading inside. "Do you have a green ticket?" the clown asked.

"No. I don't have any damn tickets," Kirk said, putting his hands on his hips.

"That's too bad. I always love asking that question. Nobody ever has any tickets. Okay, you can go in," the clown said, opening the door.

Kirk turned and looked at Sylvie again, who mouthed the word, "trust me" back. He turned and confronted the darkness of the Hall of Mirrors.

"Can't see anything in there," Kirk said, looking back at the clown.

"That's the idea," the clown said.

"Can't see anything. How am I supposed to find Meany's Mirror?" Kirk said.

"You'll know it when you see it. You will. I promise," the clown said, grinning wildly.

One of the mirrors in Kirk's view began to writhe.

Freda spoke up from behind the fence leading to the attraction. "Hey, Kirk—what's wrong? Afraid of a little darkness?"

Kirk ignored her. He looked at the clown, looked at his bloody costume, his knife. He wanted to kick the bastard's nuts in and run. Fear and desperation gripped him, nearly suffocating him. The darkness beckoned to him.

Closing his eyes, ignoring the taunts, the anger, the fear, Kirk took a step into the darkness. Almost immediately, the clown slammed the door to the hall. Somehow this place existed entirely in the Shadowlands, in the realm of the dead. Looking at the cracks in the mirrors and the scorch marks on the walls, Kirk guessed that, somehow, this entire place was like his guitar: part of someone else's life, so important a part that it came over with them.

Slowly his eyes adjusted to the utter absence of light, and he began to see movement on the walls around him. Fragmented mirrors, shattered long ago, danced around him, taunting him with different sizes, shapes, distorting his body as he walked by. And as he walked, he saw a dark cloud start to form around him, a dark cloud that contained within it fiery red motes of light that danced. The cloud had his father's face, a face Kirk had seen only in home movies, in pictures in photo albums, and in his dreams. The cloud was Mr. Demon, his Shadow, Kirk knew somehow. And the cloud mocked him, called to him from the other side of the mirror, beckoning him. It flitted from one shattered mirror to another, yelling at him soundlessly, as if the glass kept the voice from being heard.

Kirk walked through the maze, glad for the sturdy feeling of his guitar strapped to his back. He pulled the ax around to his front and held it by the neck, ready to bash anything that came at him.

In the center of the maze of mirrors, he came to a room with six mirrors in it, all six of them perfect except one, which had been painted black. Kirk felt strange, like he had entered someone's dream. Everything sounded hollow, and everything looked out of focus.

"Kirk. You gotta come home, Kirk. I'm really worried 'bout your momma," came a voice from behind.

He turned slowly around. Standing in the mirror behind him was Desiree, a prostitute who worked for the pimp that his mother used to date. Kirk tried to look her in the face: she was wearing nothing but a black lace bustier, and she looked real. To Kirk's eyes, however, her lungs were filled with black energy, her veins running with grey-green foulness.

"What about Momma? She smokin' again?" Kirk asked, compelled by the reality of her image.

Desiree nodded. "Smokin'. Bad. Spent all her AFDC on crack, then had to go work for J.T. for the trailer payment. Anna's sick, too."

Kirk winced. His little sister sick meant that Anna would probably linger on for months, now that Kirk was gone, before she got help. Kirk used to take her to the doctor, because ol' Mom would never do it. Even if it was free. Of course, Anna would only talk to Kirk: she'd not spoken a word to her older sister Kristy or to her mother since she was three. She was out of school most of the time because she was sick, and was constantly being held back grades because of absences.

"What about Kristy?" Kirk asked.

"Kristy's working full-time for J.T. Shootin' up, too. Only, Kirk, she can't afford a hotel room like most of us. She takes her johns home, to the trailer."

Kirk shook his head; he turned away from Desiree. "I don't want to hear this. I'm dead. Can't they take care of themselves?"

Another voice came out of another mirror. It was a strange voice, but one he'd heard over the phone and coming from his mother's bedroom many times: J.T.

"Now, Kirk, don't you worry about them girls. I take good care of them." J.T. grinned. J.T. was an immense white man with a cheap polyester shirt and black jeans bought at Wal-Mart. His rolls of fat were barely contained by the plastic buttons on his shirt.

"You fuckin' leave Mom alone, you hear me, bastard?" Kirk said, feeling his voice get hollow, feeling the black cloud start to congeal around him. He felt burning sensations inside him and saw fiery motes start to dance inside him in another mirror.

"Oh, now, come on, Kirk. Don't you know that she's my best whore? I couldn't leave her now. She'll do anythin' I ask. Anythin' for another pipeful. And you can't tell me you hadn't thought about your sister goin' into the business with me? I know for a fact you've been lookin' at her the past year or so. Just 'cause you're dead don' mean you're dead, boy. And when Anna grows up, just a little bit more, well, she can start earnin' her keep, too." J.T. grinned, showing his cracked teeth.

"You foul fuckin' bastard, I'll rip your fuckin' heart out if you so much as touch Anna, you hear me?"

J.T. laughed and shook his head. "You can't touch me, boy. You dead. Gone. I think I'll go take a piss on your grave."

Another voice: thin, quiet, hoarse, soft. "Kirk? Is that you? Kirk? Oh God, Kirk, it hurts. Can you make it stop hurting?"

The figure was lying on a bed, her arms strapped down, her tattered, straight black hair covering her shoulders. She was thin, bony, wearing a hospital gown that was soaked with blood, her knees up in stirrups.

"God, Kirk! It hurts! I can't take it," came the voice again, and Kirk realized it was Cindi. Cindi on some kind of operating table. They weren't giving her anesthetic. What were they doing?

"Cindi? I'm here. Cindi? Can you hear me?" Kirk called out.

"Oh, shit, Kirk, it hurts. It hurts. Make them stop. Make them stop it, Kirk!" Cindi called out, twisting in the straps. A nurse blew on her face.

"You're forgetting to breathe, Cindi. Breathe, dammit. Breathe through the pain."

"What the hell's going on, Cindi? What the hell?" Kirk screamed at her.

Cindi looked up at him. "Kirk—where are you? You're supposed to fuckin' be here. You did this to me. Damn you to hell, Kirk Rourke," Cindi called out, gritting her teeth as another wave of pain crashed over her. Kirk could feel the pain, stabbing deep in his bowels.

"I didn't—what the hell? I didn't do anything— that's not my baby you're carrying," Kirk said, his voice cracking. He wanted to believe it, but he couldn't.

"Just shut up. You can't help me. You can't do shit," Cindi hissed, and she bucked against the straps. "Shit, I just want one shot of Demerol. Just one. Come on, dammit," Cindi said to the nurse, pleadingly.

The nurse shook her head. "Judge's orders. No painkillers unless absolutely necessary. The doctor hasn't authorized it. Part of your probation. Besides, don't you think your baby's gotten enough drugs?" the nurse said. "Now, breathe."

Kirk put his hands over his face. He didn't want to watch the blood on the sheets. The nurse was bending over her, telling her not to push. Not to push yet.

Mr. Demon spoke up. "See, what did I tell you? No guts. No glory. Just a fuckin' sissy, that's what you are, Kirkie boy. Why don't you suck your thumb a little bit? That'll make you feel better. Come on little boy. Suck your thumb."

"Shut *up*!" Kirk screamed, throwing up his hands.

He swung his guitar around and started breaking mirrors—first Desiree, then J.T., then the mirror showing Mr. Demon clouding around him. Glass flew everywhere. He poised the guitar to smash at the mirror containing Cindi, and stopped. She was crying. She never cried before, never once.

"Oh God, Kirk. Can't you do something? Something. Make them give me something. Oh God. It hurts so much," Cindi screamed out loud, her head thrown back in pain.

Kirk put his hand on the mirror, trying to touch her. Instead of feeling her warm, soft skin, all he felt was the cold glass. Cindi screamed as another wave of pain shook her. Kirk's fingers loosened on the frets of his guitar, and he reversed it in his arms. She opened her eyes as Kirk began to play for her.

"'Beth—I hear you callin'—'" Kirk sang, playing her favorite song, and she nodded her head, listening, smiling weakly. His hands played over the strings, moving in proper time. He'd never played that way before. Grey light was dripping from his fingers, making the guitar vibrate, making the sound resonate against the mirror.

She tried to put out her hand to him, but she couldn't move. He watched her face as he played through the whole song, and when he reached the end, he started on it again, this time without the words. She hummed along, singing, thinking only of the song as she pushed, pushed, breathing like she had to, breathing with every push.

A piercing cry shattered the darkness, light surrounding Kirk's vision wherever he looked. The light was intense. It almost burned him. The light blossomed up from between Cindi's legs, burned into the room. Kirk felt the light as a tangible thing, burning him like the sun burned him. Then the light died down into a tiny, small pinkish light: faint, but steady.

Then they were releasing Cindi's arms and putting a tiny bundle into her hands. It was small, covered in blood, weak, and hungry for crack more than for his mother's milk. It was a boy.

The mirror fell silent and vanished. Only the last mirror, a single dark mirror that stood quietly there, challenging him, remained. Kirk looked down at his body, at his hands, which were still glowing from the light. He wanted to see his son—his new baby boy. He felt more attached to him than anything else, more than the school, more than Cindi. He wanted to see Anna again, see if he could protect her from that bastard J.T. He suddenly felt responsible, some-how, as if he could and should do something.

The dark mirror confronted him, and he was afraid, given what he'd seen in the others, to look into it. He felt a tap on his shoulder.

The clown stood there. Meany. He grinned. "Having fun?" He asked.

"You bastard," Kirk growled. "Did you put me in here to torture me?"

"You're doin' this to yourself, Kirkie boy," Meany said.

"Don't call me that."

"You've got one mirror to go, Kirk-me-lad, or else you'll never leave this place. And I wouldn't break that glass. Oh, no. You've already got twenty-one years bad luck with the three you've already bro-ken," Meany said, giggling.

"What's in there?" Kirk asked.

"Your Shadow. Your darkness. Your life, your death, your regrets. All that you are on the inside, Kirkie boy."

"I said not to call me that! Fuck you. Get me out of here," Kirk demanded, grabbing at the clown.

"Tsk, tsk!" Meany said, and vanished, leaving behind a curl of smoke.

Kirk stood at the edge of the dark mirror, looking into its depths, seeing nothing. He put his hand up to its cool darkness, touching it. It was cold at first, growing warmer. His hand slowly moved into the mirror, like in *Alice Through the Looking-Glass*.

Shouldering his guitar once more, Kirk put his hand farther into the mirror and took a step through. He fell into darkness, into a nightmare, reexperiencing his death.

Rosario was mad. Well, he had a right to be. His dad owned the city's drug trade, and Kirk—well, Kirk was always the independent kind. Kirk thought he could take Rosario in a fight, but he wasn't sure. Rosario grinned at him on the roof of the school, in his nice Armani suit, his beeper attached to his pocket.

"So, Kirk. Kirkie boy. What sort of business you been doin'? I told you to stick to nickel bags and the small shit. What's this I hear about you sellin' C?" Rosario put one of his big, broad hands on Kirk's shoulder. Kirk could feel his buddy move into position behind him, and he knew that the two weren't playing this time.

"Nah, not really. Just a little bit. For a friend. Nothing big," Kirk said, trying to sound like it was true.

Rosario grinned and winked at his friend. "There, you see, Richard, he's a reasonable man. Wouldn't go back on his word to us, would he? No, no. He's a nice boy. A good man. We can count on you, can't we, Kirkie?"

Kirk grinned and nodded. "Sure, you can."

Rosario nodded again. "Count on you to fuck us over as much as you can. You see, Kirkie, I understand you've been on the phone to Miami. Trying to get a shipment in. Smart boy. Close, but no cigar. My dad's already purchased the whole load out from under you, and you ain't got nothin' comin' in on Monday."

Rosario grinned and continued. "Now, I would've gone ahead and let you get caught by the Atlanta DEA, but you know what? I'm gonna be nice to you. You see, the way I figure it, you're gonna keep gettin' out on probation and gettin' back into my supply lines, and keep showin' your grubby-ass white-boy face back in my business. And I don't like that."

"Whoa, Rosario! Let me explain. I can just tell you what's goin' on—" Kirk said, grinning, trying to move away.

Rosario shook his head. "You a fuckup, Kirk. A serious fuckup. And I ain't gonna let you keep making the same mistakes. Bye," Rosario said, turning his back on Kirk.

Kirk felt a cold muzzle pressed against his back and felt Richard pull the trigger on his bootleg automatic SMG. The bullets ate through Kirk's spinal cord, and as the gun bucked, shot through his rib cage, his skull, his heart. He fell forward onto the roof, dead.

And he fell into darkness . . .

. . . of the prison cell he'd spent a month in, the first time he was busted. He remembered the dreams he had, the dreams of his father coming to him there. . . .

The ride in the sheriff's patrol car was short. Kirk thought for a moment about kicking, about throwing his legs against the window to try to break the glass out. He seethed inside, wanting to scream out all his hatred and anger, but realized that he was bound by something stronger than the metal bands that secured him. He heard a laugh inside his head. Mr. Demon?

It was nightmarish, watching the shadows fall across his face as he rode in the back, wishing he knew where they were taking him. He caught sight of granite walls and the car slowly came to a stop. He heard the cop talking to someone else. Two deputies with truncheons opened the door and grabbed him. He blinked in the sunlight as he was dragged to the door of the prison: for some reason there were a few photographers here, catching flash pictures of him—some kind of special-interest drug story, perhaps.

Nausea gripped him as his nose breathed in the foul stench of the indoors. He was thrown into a room with a wooden bench, all of the walls covered with graffiti. He waited there for hours before someone came for him: a blue-uniformed prison guard. The guard unlocked his foot shackles and let him walk to the processing area. They asked him to remove his jeans and T-shirt and underwear: his underwear, they explained, would be returned to him after it had been washed. A trustee sprayed his crotch with some cold liquid. "What's that shit?" Kirk said.

"Crab juice," the trustee mumbled.

They gave him blue prison fatigues and fitted him with a bright red armband.

"Red for felony . . ." the trustee said, grinning. "You goin' to be with the big boys." He had a white band. "Don't take off your band, or they'll put you in solitary."

Several electronic doors opened, and they threw a bedroll at him. "Carry that thing right through there," a guard said, and Kirk walked past the main guardroom and into a long line of cold, iron bars.

Yard lights cast shafts from windows high above the floor: even those had bars on them—it had gotten dark since he last saw the sky. The stink from fifty men in close quarters assaulted him, and some of the cons began to hoot at him as he walked by. They made their way down the row until they got to a single cell, pitch-black inside. He pushed his way into the cell and tripped, slamming his roll onto a bunk.

"Y'all have a nice sleep, now, ya heah?" the guard said, smiling. The door to the cell slammed shut electronically, and the light above went off. It was dark except for the pale red light above the far door.

Kirk dreamt.

"Why did you desert your troops boy?" Captain Rourke bellowed, looking down at him, shaking his head. Kirk had run when the rest of his gang had stayed behind in the house, when the Red Dog drug cops broke down the door. "You should've stayed with them. Never desert your people. You lost them to the enemy!"

Kirk, kneeling in front of him, looked down. "I'm . . . I'm sorry, sir."

"You are sorry, son. A sorry example of a soldier. I hope no one ever finds out you're my boy. I'll have to say 'Who? Who that? Oh, no, most be someone else's fuckup of a kid.' Just you tell me how I'm supposed to stand up and be proud of a screwup like you? A wimp? A momma's boy?"

"I'm . . . no excuse, sir."

"That's right. No excuse. You no-account, no-excuse, useless piece of bird shit. Ah just a'soon get rid o' ya and start over. But I can't, now that your momma's become a worthless junkie. Of course, you had nothin' to do with that, noooo, not you. You little shit."

Kirk tried not to flinch as the captain kicked him. He felt the boot, felt the crack of bones under his nose, felt the blood running freely down his face. He looked up, his face a mess. He knew better than to wipe the blood away—that would just get him another kick. He'd grown used to these visits, in his dreams, in his sleep.

"I'll . . . do better, shur," Kirk slurred as his lips puffed up. He felt as helpless as he had when he had been paralyzed earlier in the day.

The captain lit a cigarette, grinning. "Oh, now, son, don't you take it so hard. It ain't like you're a total failure. Hell, you ran away pretty good from those ossifers. I tell ya what. Find a razor blade, somethin' nice and straight, and off yerself, okay? Save me the trouble of havin' to do it myself. That'd be real nice. Might even get ya a promotion."

The captain threw the cigarette down. "Posthumously, of course," he said, grinning even wider. He held out his hand. In it was a rusty straight razor. "Go ahead, boy."

Kirk drew cuts on his wrist with the blade, and fell back, into darkness . . .

. . . black singing darkness,
darkness that grasped,
sucked at him, darkness that wanted him . . .
he was surrounded in it,
he was being eaten by it . . .
he saw faces in the darkness,
twisted things that had no
shape or symmetry but reached
out to him.

Something stopped them, moved them aside, took his hand . . .
He heard whispers
whispers within him,
whispers echoing through him,
whispers from his past,
whispers from his future . . .
. . . and moved, as if in a nightmare,
through the tragedy of his life . . .
. . . he felt a dark hand, gloved, take his,
leading him through the darkness.

Many things moved past his eyes, not all remembered:

He saw his own grave, a space no bigger than a file drawer in a state-run crematorium. . . .

He saw his old trailer home: still business as usual with his older sister Kristy, who had found another trucker to trick with, taking his money for an hour in her bedroom. . . .

His mom spending her time planning her lottery buys for the next day and nursing a new vial of crack she'd gotten, presumably to celebrate Kirk's death. . . .

He saw his little sister Anna, who was too tired to cry, too afraid to have tears roll down her cheek, who clutched her teddy bear close, the same teddy he'd given her so many years ago. . . .

He saw his girlfriend Cindi, her face still wet with tears, slugging down hits of Jack Daniels straight and looking very long and hard at a sharp knife she had balanced on the side of the tub. . . .

He saw the roof of the old school building, where he'd spent the last months. . . .

He saw the shell of the burned-out cathedral his gang had burned to the ground when the Dragons had tried to take it over, and remembered their blind hatred of him when they'd found out he'd done it. . . .

. . . and, finally, he saw his old '67 Harley warthog motorcycle, the last remaining gift from his father, the only legacy he was ever to have. He saw it on the back of a pickup truck, burning rubber down I-20, heading toward Conyers. Out in the boondocks, where there were still trees and grass and farmland, to a place they called Competition Hills, an ancient subdivision that had failed due to the fact that the hills were too steep to build on. Now there was nothing but cracked asphalt streets and lightposts that would never see light . . . and hills. His friends drank themselves into a stupor, rigged the motorcycle to go by itself, started it rolling,

and set the thing on fire. As it burned, it fell down the ravine, trailing smoke. When it hit the bottom, it exploded, completely destroying it. . . .

The last thing Kirk remembered was a kiss, and a hand pressing something dark and hard and cold into his hand, something that slung onto his back.

Then, a hand grasped his, a small hand. Kirk stepped into the light.

Sylvie grinned at him. "Kirk! You made it through! You're one of us now! You're a Renegade!" She was hugging him. He felt somehow lighter, as if the whole experience had caused the Shadow inside of him to become weaker, drained.

"Welcome to the Circle, Kirk," Duke said, stepping forward to shake his hand. "We all said that if you came out of there, we'd let you be in the Circle. Anyone who can endure Meany's Funhouse is okay by us."   .

Kirk squinted in the light. "What does that mean? In the Circle?"

Sylvie smiled. "The Circle, Kirk, is what we call our family. We're all dead and, well, there's nobody to look out for us but us. You know what I mean? So we look out for each other. We're a group. Compadres."

"A posse," Jojo said, nodding, looking up from some work he was doing with his hands. Sylvie grinned at Jojo and stood in front of him as if hiding what the small monkey-masked man was doing.

Freda turned her wolf-masked head to look back at the World's entrance. Kirk now saw that other wraiths were hanging out on the old amusement rides, draped over old chairs, riding on a rickety old rollercoaster, seated on the merry-go-round.

Freda pointed at the entrance. "Looks like we got

some company." Three ghosts stood at the entrance, bargaining thick black coins with Meany for entrance. A few moments later they were admitted, Meany vanishing off to wherever he hid his wealth.

They all three dressed the same, in grey cloaks, wearing wolf masks that were quite different from the one Freda wore. She sneered behind her mask. "Grey Wolves. Greymaster's moving again. Wonder what's up."

"Play it cool, Freda. Let's let them come to us," Duke whispered.

Freda nodded, keeping her hand on her sidearm, but not lighting it with the glowing energy needed to fire it.

Kirk looked at the Grey Wolves and marveled at the effect they had on the other ghosts hanging out in the park. As they moved through the loose clump-ings of wraiths, they parted the traffic like Moses parting the Red Sea. They had a presence about them that seemed to seethe with quiet power.

The three Wolves made their way slowly around, and Kirk was distracted watching them. Jojo whis-pered to Kirk, and Kirk bent his head down to speak with the small man. Jojo's quick hands slid a mask onto Kirk's face and he said, "Surprise. It's a pre-sent. Our Circle wears animal masks, so you get one. It's a Firebird mask. Shhh. Don't talk, here come the Wolves."

Kirk felt the mask with his fingers, but couldn't picture how it looked. There was no time: one of the Wolves strode right up to Duke and saluted smartly.

"Sergeant. It's been a long time," came a voice from behind the lead Grey Wolf's mask.

"Yeah, it has. Who are you?" Duke answered. Kirk could almost hear the cocky grin in Duke's voice.

"Inconsequential. I'm here with oboli and a job for some smart Renegades," the Grey Wolf said.

"What do I need with oboli? You think the Hierarchy's gonna let me spend them? I don't need no damn Stygian coins," Duke said.

"Then there's somethin' you do need, and we can get you that, too," the Grey Wolf said.

"What's the job?" Freda interceded.

"A simple skinriding mission. Nothing big. The way's already been primed; we've been working with these as Consorts for many months. They love to be ridden. Really get a kick out of it. And they'll do anything you want. Anything."

"So, what do you want them to do?" Duke asked, crossing his arms.

The Grey Wolf's permanent grin seemed particularly appropriate. "I want them to break into a weapons bunker. There's an old gun there, a relic, that we can't get at. Someone's warded the place."

"All of this for one gun?" Kirk spoke up. The Grey Wolf looked at him closely, silently. A moment or two passed, and Kirk wondered if he'd just blown their chance at getting the job.

"I don't believe I know you, Lemure," the Grey Wolf said. "Are you new?"

Freda took a step in front of Kirk. "He's new. Just arrived from out of town. One of our Circle, though, so you can't have him."

"My dear Freda, I would never think of stealing your Firebird friend. I was just very interested in his rather beautifully crafted mask. Where did you get that? I would like to commission the artificer myself," the Grey Wolf said, mellifluous tones in his voice.

Duke spoke up. "None of your business, Wolf. But you could do me a favor and answer his question for him."

"My, my. Touchy, touchy. All right, then. Yes, this operation is to recover a single relic pistol, very important to my master. But we need the skin-puppets to open the door for us. We've arranged to have the proper keys available. These Consorts are very easily guided—even if you've never skinridden before, you should be able to easily take control. As I said, it gives them great pleasure. They think they're some kind of superheroes or something," the Grey Wolf leader said. Then, he noticed Sylvie and bowed a little.

"Miss Sylvie. I'm sorry, I didn't see you here. I heard your schoolhouse was nearly burned. I'm dreadful sorry. You need help tracking down the arsonist?"

Sylvie shook her head. "No, thank you, Wolf. I'm perfectly able to take care of myself."

The Grey Wolf nodded. "Ah yes, but Greymaster always tells us to respect our elders, and I and my men are always willing to help out such an honored and revered Gaunt as yourself."

Sylvie smiled. "Well, thank you, sir. But I do believe I'll be just fine."

Duke spoke up. "What, exactly, are you sayin' you'll pay, Wolf? We can do this job just fine. If it's all that you say it is."

The Grey Wolf leader grinned. "Oh, it is, it is. What I'm sayin' is that the Grey Wolves will be in your debt, and we'll be perfectly willing to work out a deal for whatever you want—"

Freda spoke up. "Even souled weapons?"

Grey Wolf laughed. "If all goes according to plan, souled weapons won't be quite as rare as they are now. But if that's what you want, then that's what you'll get."

"Ooh. Ooh. Soulfire?" Jojo said, dancing a little.

Grey Wolf nodded. "Definitely soulfire. I can even provide you with some right now, if you desire a down payment."

Duke coughed. He looked at his circle, but he didn't have to. He could feel their interest and curiosity and need. His lion mask swiveled back to the Grey Wolf leader.

"Sure, we'll do it. Let's see the color of your crystal," Duke said.

Holding out his hand, Grey Wolf gestured to one of his two companions. From beneath his full, grey cloak came a small army green pouch. He placed the pouch in Freda's waiting hand. She opened it, counting to herself.

"Four shards," she reported.

Duke nodded his lion mask. "Yes, that'll do just fine. How much more can we expect once the run is done?"

"Ah, we have a prism or two for you then. Much larger. There's one stipulation, however," the Grey Wolf leader said.

"Which is?" Freda said with an "oh, boy—here it comes" tone to her voice.

"The Grey Wolves get to keep any salvage from the run. Relics, Thralls, whatever you get. Deal?" said the Wolf.

Duke glanced at Freda, who nodded almost imperceptibly.

"All right, then. It's a deal. Where are these skin-puppets?" Duke said, shaking the Grey Wolf's hand.

The Grey Wolf's directions showed them how to get to a place Kirk already knew about. Sylvie picked up the location from Kirk's head and was able to get them near it: Joe's Bar, a cheap dive just outside of Cabbagetown. Kirk was feeling woozy by the time they traveled all the way there, holding on to Sylvie through the bitter cold and dark of the Tempest. It was just one more mind-numbing feeling to add to the hundreds of emotions he'd already felt that day. Kirk was feeling empty, emotionless, despite the looks of triumph Sylvie gave him from time to time. He kept thinking about Anna and his new baby son, wanting to see them, wanting to be near them, to protect them, somehow, from the world around them. He didn't know when he'd see them again.

Behind all that feeling was the sense that the Shadow inside him, Mr. Demon, was building up energy, waiting to strike like a cobra. He felt different somehow: changed. His memory of his death was starting to come back. He found himself staring at people and places most of the time, looking through his hands at them.

"Hey, Kirk! You look a little fuzzy! Let's fix that!" Jojo said, touching him. Suddenly, like a flush of cool water all over him, he felt his vision sharpen, his wits come back to him. "You were nearly outta meat, Kirk. I'd watch that. Didn't your Reaper teach you how to heal yourself?"

Sylvie looked at Jojo sternly. "Now, Jojo, Kirk didn't have a normal Reaper like everyone else. She found him and released him. Didn't stick around to teach him nothin'. Kirk: your body, even though it's dead, is still there. It's just more solid energy now. Miss Cindy used to call our bodies 'Corpus,' but that sounds too much like 'corpse' to me, and I don't like corpses too much. Anyway, when you get tired like that, you just need to fill out yourself body-wise. It's pretty easy. Just relax and think about a full stomach, let that feeling guide you."

Kirk nodded. "Thanks, Jojo, for the jolt. I needed it. Hey! Look in there! Some of my old buds."

Freda peered inside the dusty window of the bar and nodded. "Yeah, those are our skinbags for the evening. They're wearing the Metallica jackets. You know them?"

Kirk nodded. "Yeah. I used to . . . well, I used to kind of tell them what to do."

Duke smiled behind his mask. "Well, there you go. You should take to Puppetry easy."

Sylvie put her hand on Kirk's arm. "Puppetry is the art of getting into someone's skin and makin' them do what you want them to do."

Kirk looked down at Sylvie. "You kiddin' me? Well, why didn't you tell me that? I could've puppeted that woman over to the phone to call the fire department!"

Sylvie grinned. "It's a little harder than that, Kirk. Besides, I didn't know if you had it in you or not."

Kirk said, "Huh. Just give me a chance. Tell me what to do."

Duke stepped slowly through the front door and turned around to face Kirk. The din of the bar was starting to become clearer, but he could still hear Duke easily. "Come on in, Kirk. I'll show you," Duke said.

Duke stepped into the body of the nearest boy, a guy Kirk knew as "Big John." Mimicking Big John's movements, the differences between Duke and Big John slowly disappeared, and Duke faded into Big John. Instantly, Big John began to giggle.

"Guys . . ." Big John said.

"What is it, you big ass?" Tony, a short, squat kid with an attitude asked. Tony was drinking a beer. "You drunk?"

Big John shook his head.

Kirsten, a miniature amazon in a black leather skirt, spoke up. "What is it, Biggie? You got somethin' in your head?"

Big John nodded slowly, grinning.

Monica, an even taller, darker-haired version of Kirsten, sighed. "Oh no, not more funky shit. I hate this crap. Kirk should be here—he always knew what to do."

Tony giggled. "Hey, maybe Kirk *is* here. Maybe Kirk's takin' Big John over." Tony always was a very morbid asshole—he loved to screw with other people's heads.

Then Kirk looked up and saw Rick walking to the table, his pool cue in his hand. "What's up?" He said. Rick was his old second-in-command, his best buddy.

"Big John's getting giggly. Must be something in the air," Tony said.

Rick nodded and sat down. The gang looked at each other across the table. Monica almost stood up to leave, but Kirsten shot her a look.

Sylvie stepped up to Kirk's side. "Go ahead. You take Rick. You know him, right?"

Kirk felt funny about it. Getting inside his old best friend? That wasn't something he ever wanted to do. Still, it was time, and this was the deal. Kirk slid his hand slowly inside of Rick, moving to sit down in the same chair as he was. For a second he felt like he couldn't breathe, and he almost jumped up. He felt himself sliding into place, felt his vision blur. Then, a second later, he was in Rick, using Rick's eyes, feeling Rick's body around him. Rick was smoking. It tasted so good to get real smoke in his lungs. He looked out of the corner of Rick's vision at Kirsten, who'd only sort of turned him on before, but looking at her now . . . ! So many curves! Such a hot, sexy babe! He wanted to shake his head to clear it, but found he couldn't.

Then, something clicked. His control was not total and absolute—he still felt Rick's identity just below his, watching. Still, he knew that Rick would never remember the details of the night past the moment Kirk took him—something told him that Rick would only remember this as if it were a dream.

Rick/Kirk grinned. "Yeah, I think it's going to be party time tonight, boys and girls."

Monica looked shocked. "Rick? That's not your voice. That's Kirk's voice!"

Rick/Kirk looked down at his hands. "Huh. Who woulda thunk it?" Rick/Kirk looked up at Monica. "I guess it is."

Sylvie turned to Freda. "He's got more Puppetry than I do, with no training! He's got full possession!"

Freda shrugged. "It happens sometimes. These guys are his friends. They're looking for him. Of course it's gonna be easy for him. Let's make the best of it.

Kirk/Rick smiled. "You folks miss me?"

Tony shook his head. "Rick, stop it. You're scarin' Kirsten."

Kirsten kicked Tony under the table. "I'm not scared. If that's you, Kirk, when's the first time we ever had sex?

Kirk/Rick grinned. "You know, Kirsten. Stone Mountain. Just off the walking trail. Under the stars, at night. You don't remember?"

Kirsten grinned. "Ahh, Rick, I forgot. You boys told each other everything. Probably sucked each other's cocks, too."

Rick/Kirk said, "Fuck you, Kirsten. We never did that."

Tony grinned. "Ah, there! You see, Rick! You can't keep that Kirk accent. You're fakin' it."

Rick/Kirk shrugged. "What say we go have some fun? There's supposed to be an envelope waitin' for us at the Y. Let's head over there and figure out what's goin' on. What say?"

Freda stepped into Monica, the tall one, riding along with her. Jojo leaped into Tony. Sylvie, smiling, eased herself into Kirsten. She stuck her head out of Kirsten and winked at Kirk. "Ain't never been a hot, sexy, white girl before. You think you'll take me out to Stone Mountain after this?" Sylvie said, grinning.

Kirk/Rick rolled his eyes as the rest of the group started giggling. Monica/Freda growled. "Oooh. I feel like kickin' some major butt."

Tony/Jojo shrugged. "Me, too. I guess. I feel kind of weird, actually. But okay."

Big John/Duke said, "Let's get goin'."

It was a hell of a lot of fun for Kirk, riding motorcycles again. They rode in perfect formation, his gang. He loved that. They were so cool. Kirk thought about his motorcycle . . . the one that was destroyed, wondered where it was. Unbidden, the motorcycle flashed in his mind's eye: hidden behind some trash somewhere. He wasn't sure. It was there, though. All grey, the headlight cracked, but there.

The rode across town to the Y, where Big John/Duke went in and got the envelope. Inside of the envelope was a set of keys and a map.

Tony/Jojo giggled. "Shit, man. This is Fort Gillem. That's not far from here. Shit. The big time."

Rick/Kirk grinned. "That's right. Big guns. Really cool."

Kirk couldn't help but feel that someone—something—was listening to them. He looked around, searching for the source of the feeling, but found nothing. Kirsten/Sylvie looked up.

"I don't know, Rick. I have a bad feeling about this . . . but what the hell."

Kirk/Rick laughed. "Don't worry. You guys stay here. I'm gonna go in and get somethin' out of my— I mean, Kirk's locker. It'll help." Kirk laughed to himself. Stealin' from the Army! Damn, this was going to be the biggest move since the Dragons busted into an old cop warehouse and snagged a bunch of revolvers.

A few moments later, Kirk/Rick came out of the YMCA wearing an old battered Army jacket, with the name "ROURKE" stenciled across the pocket. "Hey, what do you think? I'm Private Rourke. This is my—Kirk's dad's from boot camp."

Big John grinned and started his motorcycle. "Let's rock!" he yelled over the noise, and the gang, with their spectral puppeteers, rode off into the night.

3

Ghost Stories:
Inquest

Q: And who, do you think, had access to the files as to where the armament was?

A: Only myself, Captain Watson, and Sergeant Bailer, sir.

Q: I see. And yet, you report some kind of computer malfunction interrupting the system at 0413 hrs?

A: Yes, sir. It seems that we have some kind of cross corruption from the /dev/null area of the disk. "The Ghost in the Machine," sir.

Q: Private, what are you saying? How would security be circumvented that way? What is the "Ghost in the Machine"?

A: Sir, I don't know, sir. It's almost as if the hacker came in from the blank parts of the disk, trashed a few security sectors, and opened the file from a machine-level interface. I can't see how else it could happen. It's happened before,

*though. Computer jocks call it "the Ghost in
the Machine."*

Q: *You're saying you've had a physical security
breach on a machine that's in an underground
concrete bunker in Langley, VA?*

A: *Sir, that's the only way I can explain it. That,
or some seriously freaky kind of hardware
glitch.*

Q: *Thank you, Private. You're dismissed.*

Who sees a shadow? Who notices its passing? When
the darkness is besieged with them, how can you tell
when one breaks free and runs past? Sergeant Brian
Whittaker couldn't, certainly, sitting in his post
house on the grounds of Fort Gillem, an army depot
in Atlanta. He smoked another cigarette and threw it
out into the darkness, watching it fizz as it hit the
cold, wet grass. The young shadows (with their
secret skinriders) stole past the watchful eyes of the
Army and off into the woods on the base, grinning
to each other in the rush of danger. These young
lions felt like real commandos as they made their
way, in pairs, across the base, eluding the sleepy
security.

Rick/Kirk led them, his left hand clutching an old
Fort Gillem map that he kept tucked into a black
trenchcoat of Rick's—army-issue, of course. He'd be
the one to "play soldier" if they were discovered. He
ran to the top of a ravine and suddenly remembered
the silhouette that his gang would make when they
topped it. He shot out his hand, fixing them all with
a single gaze. They froze. Big John/Duke was grinning, Kirk noticed—the stupid grin that meant he
was either angry or ecstatic.

"Down!" Rick/Kirk hissed.

He looked over the edge of the ravine at the

bunker—their target. It was short and squat, piled up with green grass on both sides. The gravel road around it was for patrols—Kirk/Rick knew from the instructions that the Hummer would be around shortly, in about twenty minutes, and that he had just missed the last patrol.

Rick/Kirk gave his lions the "two-by-two" symbol with his hands and rolled over the crest of the hill, getting up and dog-trotting across the intervening space. He felt the gentle weight of Rick's .38 Special riding along in the big pocket of the trenchcoat and turned to see Big John/Duke loping down the hill after him. Then Monica, Kirsten, and Tony, all very quiet. Even Big John had managed to stay quiet, although it looked like he was going to break into a giggle at any moment.

Walking up to the bunker, Rick/Kirk inspected the lock. He motioned to Tony/Jojo to hold the penlight beam on the letters stenciled just above it: A13. Without looking back, Kirk began to count out the keys on the keychain: looking for the one that was marked A13. Looking up at Tony, who had gotten his dad's shotgun and now had it hidden under his coat, Kirk thrust a key in the lock and turned it.

There was a tremendous lurching sound within the door itself, and suddenly the whole gang started as the red light on the outside of the building began to flash.

"Wait . . . that's normal. It's okay. Monnie, put that garbage bag over it," Rick/Kirk whispered.

Inside, the red glow of emergency lights beckoned the gang like the glint of gold off of a treasure. Monica wrapped the light in the bag, and soon there was nothing but a dull red dimness glowing within.

They stole quietly into the bunker. It was beautiful to them. In the living world, along one side of the wall were a row of AK-47's in excellent condition. Kirk's mind inventoried the ammunition, the grenades, even the coffin-shaped box of LAW rockets stacked to one side. Beside it was a large vehicle-mounted machine gun with its mounting assembly. On the other side were black plastic cases that he knew, somehow, had laser sights packed in them, and other high-tech toys. What really grabbed Kirk's attention and held it was the large backpack in the corner which, Kirk knew, carried enough C4 explosive to make a city block jump. Rick/Kirk looked up at his gang. They were smiling, opening up crates, examining guns, grenades, toys. They looked like a bunch of kids on Christmas morning.

Then, the strange feeling that he was being watched came again. Kirk looked up quickly, sliding Rick's head aside like one might move aside a mask—looking around desperately for the gun that was supposed to be here. This "special" gun. All he could see was an old Confederate-issue revolver hanging in the darkness, and so he tucked that inside his own ghostly pocket.

As he slid back into Rick, he suddenly became aware of the sound of a motor and tires moving across gravel outside. He ran for the open doorway and, turning around, whispered, "I'll be back. There's a car." Kirk/Rick slammed the door closed, turning the lock on it, while settling the army cap on his head and hoping that the patrol wouldn't notice it wasn't real.

A Hummer was indeed slowly making its way down the road, bouncing through the pocks in it. Suddenly its searchlight went on and shone out to hit Rick/Kirk, who saluted smartly.

"What are you doin' here, son?" the MP asked, driving the Hummer a little closer, shining a flashlight into Kirk's face, on his hat and trenchcoat. "Private . . . Rourke? I ain't never met you. What do you think you're doin'?"

Rick/Kirk looked back at the bunker, and then turned back to the MP and grinned. "Sergeant, I have no excuse, but I thought I saw some perpetrators entering the area. Civilians. I walked over to have a look, sir, but found nothing. I—"

Suddenly there was a pounding sound on the inside of the bunker, the hard sound of metal against metal, of frantic screaming muffled through the steel and earth. Kirk saw flashes of darkness rise up out of the bunker, but he knew Rick couldn't see them. Then, the entire bunker erupted in a huge gout of fire. Kirk felt himself picked up and thrown by the blast: he watched the safety glass on the Hummer shatter and the MP inside thrown back. Kirk leapt out of Rick's body as he felt the entire left side of Rick's face turn red from burns.

The fireball continued to expand up and mushroom, covering the grass around the bunker with smoking, burning debris. Kirk looked down at Rick, his body badly burned from the blast. He looked up at his Circle, who were floating just above the bunker, watching the pillar of black smoke rise up.

"What the hell happened?" Kirk yelled, stunned at the death of his friends in life.

One by one the misty shadows slowly began to materialize again. Kirk watched as the sergeant in the Hummer called the explosion in and asked for hospital assistance and the local police to come out immediately. Rick was unconscious, lying there on the ground, and nothing Kirk could do could keep him out of jail now.

Sylvie touched Kirk's arm. "Big John started playing with the grenades, Kirk. There wasn't anything we could do."

"Why did he do that? He's not that stupid. Duke?" Kirk almost yelled at Duke.

"Duke, why the fuck didn't you stop him?" he yelled.

"I tried. It was . . . it was like someone else was tugging his strings. Not me. Like he was resisting . . . but I don't know how. Like he was doing what someone else said. I'm sorry, Kirk." Even Duke's lion mask looked a little sad.

Jojo became solid and spoke up, "Eh. I've got a feelin'. Grey Wolves on the way."

Suddenly, out of the Tempest, six grey-cloaked figures emerged and materialized. They were carrying their weapons "lit," that is, charged with the energy needed to shoot. They obviously expected trouble.

Duke turned to the leader. "Are you the same Grey Wolf we spoke to earlier?"

He bowed. "I am. You folks have done a wonderful job. Thank you very, very much. Here is your payment in full." The Wolf threw down a black plastic vinyl bag with a zipper. "Soulfire for everyone," he said.

Jojo scrabbled down and grabbed the bag, grinning.

Kirk watched as, one by one, the Wolves shimmered with their own energy. Their cloaks became mirror-bright, almost reflective, and they walked slowly into the flames, searching for debris.

Kirk bent down to Sylvie, who was also watching them. He asked, "What are they doin'?"

"Looking for Relics. Stuff brought over by the dead. And for souls," Sylvie whispered back in the ultra-quiet voice that only another wraith could hope to hear.

Kirk, beside himself with anger, strode into the fire, feeling a tingle and a shock, watching as his body discorporated. He was screaming at the Grey Wolves, but his voice was as insubstantial as his body. One of the Grey Wolves gestured at him to leave. As he grew solid again, Sylvie grabbed him and pulled him out of the fire.

"Smooth move," Duke said. "That's not going to get you anywhere. Kirk . . . your friends are dead. There's nothing you can do for them now."

Kirk felt the bottom drop out of his soul, felt darkness overtake him. His eyes burned like cinders. His hand clutched around the Confederate revolver in his pocket, and he took it out and aimed it at Duke's mask. But it wasn't his voice that spoke. It was Demon's. "I want to get them, you see? Never leave your team behind, Private. Never desert your people. Understand?"

Duke shook his head. Looking down at his own hand, he watched as it began to glow with a fiery-red energy. Duke slapped Kirk across the face.

"Snap out of it, cheesehead!" Duke yelled. He slapped Kirk again.

Kirk shook his head, the blackness dropping away instantly, Demon's control broken.

"What did you do?" Kirk asked, incredulous.

Sylvie grinned and took Kirk's hand. "Duke's a Pardoner among other things. He slapped th' Shadow outta ya."

Kirk looked back at the Grey Wolves in their mirror-bright cloaks and watched them emerge from the fires carrying several boxes of equipment from within the bunker. He turned around and saw Rick being loaded into an army ambulance, the MP's having arrived. He watched as the door to the ambulance slammed closed and it slowly drove away.

The leader strode up to the Circle. "You folks still here? We had a nice haul from that little venture. Too bad about the skinpuppets, but then again, these days they're a dime a dozen. Say, Firebird! I see you found the revolver. Very good. I'll just be taking that," he said, holding his hand out.

Kirk grudgingly turned the revolver around and gave it to the Wolf. He knew it was the object they'd been sent to find, at least ostensibly, but he felt that, somehow, the revolver was his. That, at the very least, he'd earned it through the blood sacrifice of his friends.

"Now, we were about to go have a victory celebration at the Den. Would you like to come along?"

Freda coughed. "No, we'll just be going, actually."

Kirk turned to Sylvie. "I want to go with the Wolves.

Sylvie looked up at him. A smile creased her features. "I thought you'd say that."

Freda shot daggers at Kirk with her eyes. Duke, ever the peacemaker, spoke up. "Ah, Sylvie, why don't you go along with Kirk? We'll head on back to the hole and rest up. We can even ride the bus. That'll be a decent change from swimmin' through the Tempest."

Sylvie nodded. "Okay, Duke. We'll meet up with you tomorrow night?"

Duke nodded. "Come on folks," he said, and began walking toward the gates of the base.

When they had vanished over the hilltop, the leader looked down at them. "My Harbinger or yours?" he said, his voice silky.

"Yours," Sylvie said, smiling.

The Thompson Railroad Warehouse was built in the early 1920s. Then it was a sturdy brick-and-steel structure, built to last. Now, however, the warehouse had gradually eroded over the years, and several load-bearing girders had begun to buckle and bend from the weight. Still, it was a highly defensible structure with many windows, and the Grey Wolves had made it their headquarters, training grounds, and communal Haunt.

In July 1977, Thomas Heck had killed three teenagers, the Stanford brothers, in a rather brutal and perverse way (the investigator found genital body tissue stuffed into every available orifice), and ever since that brutal act of mindless violence the warehouse had gained the reputation of being "haunted."

The other strange thing about the place was that a fog would invariably rise up around it at sundown and wouldn't go away until the sun rose again, every night, even on the hottest, clearest nights of the year. Folks in the area stayed away from the Thompson Warehouse, which was just the way the ghosts who lived there wanted it.

Jameson's Wolf patrol, back from the raid at Fort Gillem, materialized out of the Tempest, the dark holes temporarily created by their travel closing as they appeared. Six Wolves, plus two "passengers."

Instantly the Wolves' security routine went into action. Three Wolves strode out of positions around the arrival zone to examine the passenger-wraiths and get a report from the leader. Jameson smiled to the boys on guard duty. They examined Kirk and Sylvie, took a small black knife from Sylvie and the guitar from Kirk, and the officer of the watch nodded Jameson onward as the other Wolves in the team began to carry the armament they'd gleaned from the explosion into the warehouse by a different route.

They walked across the remainder of the field toward the warehouse. Kirk couldn't help but notice the layers of defense the Wolves had set up: what looked like old, discarded cars and railroad ties stacked haphazardly became a maze which any ghosts attacking the warehouse would have to negotiate.

Several times Kirk got the sense that they were being watched, examined by hidden eyes, but no one challenged their progress toward the building, walking as they were in front of the Wolves. Kirk felt like he was entering a military installation, not a

haunted house. Still, the overall effect of the place—
a rotting warehouse with the stench of bad chemical
spills and death running through it, the slight fog that
wreathed the building, the thousands of watching
eyes—had their effect on Kirk, who had not yet gotten used to any of it. Kirk couldn't help but continue
to think of his dead friends, of Rick (was he still
alive?), of Cindi and his new son. He couldn't help
but wish he was anywhere else. But something compelled him to continue moving forward, something
told him that it was important for him to go through
the giant warehouse doors and confront whatever
was inside.

Sylvie helped: she was always by his side, quietly
walking. The other ghosts seemed to defer to her quietly. They didn't like to have to show such courtesy
to what appeared to be a child, but every single ghost
they walked past on their way to the entrance turned
his head in deference to her. Kirk wondered if there
was something beyond her apparent age that caused
her to have such respect among these wraiths.

They stopped in front of two huge double doors,
and when a word was given from within the building, the doors slowly slid open, somehow operated
in the living world by an unseen operator. Perhaps it
was something as simple as a ghost punching an
"open" button like Kirk used to knock people's
glasses off. Or perhaps it was some magical power
these ghosts had that Kirk had never seen.

The doors opened slowly, but Kirk began walking
as soon as there was a large enough opening to do
so. He was impatient. Something inside him was
ticking off the seconds, watching, waiting. He knew
Mr. Demon had a hand in this, but didn't know
exactly what.

The light inside the warehouse was minimal,
although Kirk could see several small lights placed in

various parts of the room. At the far end was a strange-looking chair, a throne almost, with a large rail of steel twisted into a loop behind it.

Kirk looked at Sylvie several times in the intervening space, walking the length of the large warehouse, to see if she would give him a sign as to how to act. Kirk refused to look at the throne, knowing that the one who sat there was the reason he was here. He looked at Sylvie, who smiled at him: quite a child's smile, a smile which didn't acknowledge the fear boiling up inside of Kirk's gut. The fear which threatened to consume him. Kirk felt icy cold shiver through him as he looked at the throne, finally seeing the man sitting there.

He was a tall, immense man, with a well-defined but not overly developed musculature. On his head was a helmet that was also a mask: a grey-steel thing that was shined to a mirror polish, reflecting Kirk's image back at himself. The two wolf masks standing next to him were also fully articulated heads, with mouths that moved as they talked and ears that twitched like a wolf's does, ruby eyes, and a foggy breath which issued from their mouths whenever they spoke. One of the wolf masks bowed to Jameson, who bowed back, saluting the man. "I've brought someone for an audience with the Greymaster. Is that possible?" Jameson asked.

"I believe it is, Jameson. You're dismissed," came a chillingly cold voice from within the mirrored mask. Kirk felt Demon inside him start to rattle its chains, laughing to itself.

Jameson stepped forward and offered the Confederate pistol to one of the wolf masks, who inspected it and handed it to the man in the grey mask.

The Greymaster turned to look at Kirk. "I understand that you played a part in our raid tonight. Very well done."

Kirk shook his mask. "I . . . wouldn't describe it that way, sir."

"What do you mean? The team recovered my pistol, and managed to pick up a few guns and ammunition. I would term that a success."

"Sir, I lost several friends in that explosion. I would like to know who was responsible," Kirk said, his voice rising as he spoke.

"Now, boy, don't go usin' that tone with me. You'll keep your respect or leave here without your tongue," the Greymaster hissed.

Kirk shook his head, looking down at Sylvie, who looked back at him in alarm. He turned back to the Greymaster.

"Sir, I just want to know why they had to die, and who killed them," Kirk said quietly.

"They died because they were stupid, boy. They died because they liked to play with guns where they shouldn't be played with. They died because kids like them don't have enough sense to pour piss out of a boot before putting it on. That's why they died, and if you don't like it, boy, then well, I guess you can join your pals in Oblivion, because that's where they've gone," Greymaster whispered, his voice full of cynicism and hatred.

Kirk nodded. "Well, sir, that's what I wanted to know. Thank you for your time."

Kirk turned around and began to walk out.

"Wait." He heard.

Turning slowly, he said. "Sir?"

"I didn't dismiss you, son," Greymaster said, unmoving.

Kirk turned around. "All right." He bit down on the anger that flared up inside of him.

"Who are you, boy?" Greymaster asked, standing up and stepping down from his throne. "When did you die?"

"I died . . . I don't know, sir. About nine or ten months ago, I guess. But I don't believe I should tell you who I am, since I don't know who you are, sir," Kirk said quietly.

The Greymaster swiveled to peer, faceless, at Sylvie. "You've trained him well, Miss Sylvie. I wondered when you would repay the debt you owe Miss Cynthia by takin' a Lemure under your wing. Now I see you're coddlin' street thugs. Not the kind of people a nice girl like you should be hangin' out with, don't you think?"

Sylvie smiled. "He's a nice boy, sir. I enjoy teachin' him."

The Greymaster put a finger under Sylvie's chin. "You always was the cutest little thing. Anytime you want a place in my organization, you've got it, ya heah?"

Sylvie smiled, but it was the fake smile that children wear for their aunts and uncles at Christmas.

Greymaster turned back to Kirk. "Where'd you get that mask, boy? It's awful pretty."

"A friend of mine made it, sir," Kirk said.

"Boy, do you know what the Firebird means to us Wolves?" Greymaster whispered quietly to Kirk.

"No, sir, I don't," Kirk said. He tried not to shake as he felt the man's presence move closer.

"There's a prophecy that the Firebird will return to this place, and cause the whole city to burn. Last time the Firebird was here, the native ghosts were driven out by the Hierarchy. The Firebird is a harbinger of change, boy. Great change. Now why do you reckon your friend gave you that mask?"

Suddenly, out of nowhere, Mr. Demon spoke up. "Because, boy, you is gonna bring destruction and Oblivion to everyone. Ain't ya?"

Kirk jumped, as if someone had shocked him with a bolt of electricity. He looked around, looked straight at the man in the grey mask.

The voice within his own head, his own Shadow-voice, was that of the wraith in the grey mask. Without question, Kirk knew it to be true.

"I–I don't know, sir," Kirk said.

He could almost feel the smile coming from behind the grey mask. What did it mean? Mr. Demon sounding like Greymaster, Greymaster sounding like Mr. Demon. Kirk was afraid and intrigued at the same time. Did he know Greymaster from another life? Did Greymaster know things about him that he didn't?

Greymaster said, "Well, maybe one day you'll find out, boy. Thank you again for gettin' my gun. This gun was my father's gun, given to him by his grandfather Jebediah. Pretty ain't it?"

Kirk nodded, looking down at Sylvie who, despite her normal maturity, had begun to fidget.

The Greymaster paused for a moment, and no one filled the space with words. Looking at them both, Greymaster shrugged his shoulders. "Well, I guess that's it. You've been paid, haven't you?"

Kirk nodded.

The Greymaster whispered something to one of his guards, then turned back to Kirk. "I would like to offer you a place among us, Firebird. As a good luck token if nothin' else. You see, we're about to make a major raid. I'd like for you to be in on it. Lots of loot, lots of fun. Could be that our troops would like to see the Firebird out there with us, fighting alongside us. Just might shake the Hierarchy up a little bit." Greymaster paused for a second, obviously waiting for Kirk to accept.

Kirk spoke up slowly, carefully. "I-I'm sorry sir. I'll need a little time to think about it, if that's okay."

Greymaster ground his fist into his palm. "What's to think about?"

Sylvie looked up at him. "Now, sir . . . that was a legitimate answer don't you think? Firebird's still young. Let's let him make up his mind on his own time."

Greymaster nearly growled. His aura changed to a cool, dark blue. He smiled slowly behind the mask and nodded. "Well, Miss Sylvie, if you think so, then I don't see what the harm is in lettin' him have a few days to think about it. Son, the raid has to be fully planned out and practiced by the next new moon. Keep a watch for the dark of the moon, and when it happens, come back here and tell me your answer."

Kirk nodded. "Yes, Captain," he said without thinking.

Greymaster paused for a moment. "How did you know I was a captain, boy?"

Sylvie smiled and spoke up. "The boy's got a bit of kennin' to him, sir. Doesn't know how to use it yet, 'sall."

Greymaster nodded slowly. "I see."

Sylvie curtseyed to Greymaster. "Can we go now, sir?"

Greymaster nodded. "Remember, Firebird . . . the dark of the moon!"

Kirk nodded, then turned with Sylvie to walk out. As they walked, her hand in his, they slowly slid into the Tempest and were gone.

The Wolfguard to Greymaster's left spoke up. "You want me to find out who he is?"

Greymaster shook his mask slowly. "No. No, no need to waste time and effort on an unknown Lemure. Turn your attentions to finding the site and drilling the patrols!"

As the Wolfguards left, Greymaster reclined on his throne, his hand on his chin. He thought for but a moment longer, shrugged, then turned to address other, more pressing problems.

———

Kirk and Sylvie jumped to a building across the railroad tracks, far away from the Wolves' warehouse. Sylvie smiled at Kirk as he sat down on the roof, looking out across the city. "What's wrong, Kirk?" Sylvie asked.

Kirk looked up at Sylvie. "Sylvie, things have been happenin' left and right. I don't know what to do." Looking up, he saw the sun peeking over the edge of the horizon. *What a night,* he thought to himself.

Sylvie blinked, dazzled at the sunlight. "That's the way things happen sometimes, Kirk. You just have to accept them. What do you want to do now? We don't have to sleep if you don't want to."

Kirk looked at her. "There is one thing I really want to do."

"What's that?" Sylvie said, smiling, as if she already knew what it was.

Kirk smiled. "What?"

Sylvie shook her head. "Go ahead."

Kirk grinned. "Ah, I was hopin' to go visit my little boy in the hospital."

Sylvie grinned back, nodding her head.

Kirk looked puzzled. "How did you know about my son?"

Sylvie put her hand over her mouth. "I . . . I don't know, Kirk. Ahh. Oh, heck. I can't lie to you. I was with you, the entire time, when you were there in the mirror room. I had to see what happened to you. Are you mad?"

"No. I ain't mad. That's okay, Sylvie. I like you a lot. You've helped me out a lot. What do you get out of it?"

Sylvie grinned, looked down. "Nothin'. I just . . . Kirk, like the man said, I got a debt to pay. I don't mind doin' this for ya. If it weren't for Miss Cindy, I would still be a clueless spook."

Kirk nodded. "You must be pretty damn old. Most spooks like you a lot."

Sylvie put her legs together and smiled, looking down. "Yeah. Well, I am a lil' old. But the old folks, they think if you've stuck around, you is wise and powerful. I ain't powerful. I'm just Sylvie."

Kirk shook out his hair and looked hard at Sylvie. "Don't you be lyin'. I know you're powerful. You do all this travelin' stuff, and kennin'. Stuff I ain't never heard about. Say, why did you lie to that Greymaster guy for me? About the captain part?"

"Because, Kirk, you don't know who Greymaster is. And you don't want him to find out who you are, yet," Sylvie said, her voice sounding hollow and resonant.

"What the hell was that?" Kirk said, stepping back.

Sylvie grinned. "That? Oh, that was my voice-o'-reason, I call it. It's my kennin' voice. You see, Kirk, when you gots kennin', you just lissen to your heart. That's all, that's it."

Kirk grinned. "Oh. Do I have any kennin'?"

Sylvie peered at him. "Not a lick."

Kirk nodded. "So no fortune-tellin'?"

Sylvie grinned. "Maybe I'll teach you. One day. Not today. Oh, Kirk, ain't the sunrise pretty? Makes you feel good."

"Makes me feel good to be dead," Kirk said wryly.

Sylvie looked sharply at him. "You can't be talkin' like that. Just because you dead doesn't mean that you gotta be a sourpuss." She punched Kirk on the arm.

"Ow," Kirk said, rubbing his arm.

"You want to go see your baby now?" Sylvie said, her braids flipping around as she tossed her head.

Kirk nodded and yawned sleepily.

Sylvie grinned. "Oh, boy. Baby ghost all sleepy?"

Kirk shook his head, yawning again.

Sylvie touched Kirk and a flash of light shot into him. He jumped.

"How's that?" she asked, grinning.

"What did you do?" Kirk said, now wide awake.

Sylvie smiled, slipping into her old-life dialect. "I calls it 'ghost coffee.' It's just a little wakeup call. Nothin' big. Part of the dreamin' powers," Sylvie said, shifting her weight from foot to foot. "Let's be goin' on," she said, looking expectantly at him. "I love babies," she admitted as Kirk extended his hand to her outstretched fingers.

Then they vanished.

The morning sun was painting golden colors on the red brick of the hospital and shining in through the high skylights, making shafts that pierced the inner gloom and somehow made the antiseptic interior welcoming. Out of the shadows stepped Sylvie and Kirk, Kirk still shivering from the cold of the Tempest.

He looked down the hall one way and then the other. "Where is he?" Kirk asked.

Sylvie smiled. "Just listen to your heart, Kirk, like I was sayin'. Follow your nose. Just walk, you'll find him."

Kirk began to walk down the hallway, out of the bright sunlight, which dazzled him. He walked past rows and rows of doors with charts tucked next to them. The floor smelled of antiseptic wash and the air stank of hospital smell, which almost made Kirk gag. He looked down one corridor, then back down another.

Then he heard a tiny, shrill cry. The sound made his whole body quake. He looked down at his hands, not realizing to what depth his feelings reached. For a second he felt filled with energy, as if the sound alone filled him with light.

Kirk turned and entered a room with its door open, followed closely by Sylvie. There was Cindi with a tiny, utterly tiny, baby in her arms. She looked so frail, so thin. Sitting there in the darkness of the room with its drawn curtains, Kirk thought for a moment that Cindi had already died and that she was a wraith like him. Her hollow eyes looked as though she had just about given up.

She held the tiny baby woodenly, although Kirk could instantly see that her touch was helping the baby. He was calming down, moving his tiny fists against her cheek, her swollen breasts.

Kirk moved aside as a nurse stepped into the room. "It's time for a check. And medication for you," the nurse said.

Cindi nodded like a robot, letting the nurse take the child from her arms. The nurse weighed him, checked his blood pressure and heartbeat, looked in his eyes.

"He's doing fine. Has he slept much?" the nurse asked.

Cindi shook her head "no," looking down at the floor. The nurse nodded. "Well, you're going to have to take your pills. This is an iron pill: you're very anemic right now. And this is a pill which will help dry your milk up."

Cindi looked up at the nurse, moving a strand of her hair out of her eyes. "I can't breastfeed him?"

The nurse shook her head, giving the boy back to her. "Normally we'd let you have a choice. But the doctor wants to be sure that the baby's not getting any more contaminants. I'm sorry."

Cindi nodded woodenly and took the pills. Satisfied, the nurse turned and moved to leave. "You want the door closed?" she asked.

"No. I don't care. Whatever," Cindi said, still holding the tiny baby.

The nurse stopped for a moment. "Have you named him yet?"

Cindi shook her head. "The doctor says he might not make it past a week. I don't see that there's much of a point giving him a name just yet."

The nurse turned wordlessly, shocked, and left the room. Cindi held on to the little boy, who began shivering in her arms despite how warm it was in the room. Cindi closed her eyes and held on, waiting for the baby's wail. He cried out, as much as his little lungs could scream, throwing back his head in need, wanting something that he couldn't have, something he'd never tasted.

Cindi sobbed as she held on to him, but she didn't have any tears left. She tried to offer a tiny bottle of sugar-water to the boy, but he wouldn't take the nipple.

Kirk sat down next to the caterwauling child and his mother, on the chair opposite them. Her eyes went dull, glassy, looking out to the middle distance as the baby screamed, weakly trying to reach out and grasp what it needed.

Sylvie shook her head. Kirk saw a little drop of light at the corner of Sylvie's eye, and watched as she wiped the tear away. "What do you think, Kirk? Do you think he'll live?" Sylvie whispered.

Kirk looked at the boy. His boy. He could almost feel every heartbeat of the boy—a rapid thrumming which seemed to echo through his tiny rib cage. Kirk looked closely at him, touched him on the back. The boy instantly stopped crying, tossing his head around a little, lolling over to the side.

The boy hungrily sought the nipple of the glass jar with the sugar-water in it, and began to drink the glucose solution thirstily.

Kirk drew back his hand from the soft, exquisitely delicate skin and saw a strand of light drip from his fingertip. Sylvie looked up, eyebrows raised, eyes large. "Kirk! Kirk! Look! Your lifeweb! Look at it!"

Kirk looked down and took the strand of light in his fingers. "What is this?"

"That's your lifeweb. It's so close to your boy that you can see it. You can see the energy streaming down it to you. Look at it. That's your connection to him," Sylvie said, smiling.

"You mean . . . I'm connected to him like I'm connected to the school?" Kirk said, his voice belying the confusion he felt.

"Yes. Yes. Exactly," Sylvie said. "You have to protect him now, Kirk. Your Fetter's moved from mother to son."

Kirk looked up at Cindi. "You better treat him right," he said to her.

Cindi blinked. "Fuck you," she hissed.

Kirk looked surprised. "You can hear me?"

"Where the fuck are you? Not here. Had to be some goddamn cowboy, movin' in on Rosario's turf. What the fuck did you think he was gonna do? Send you a fuckin' engraved invitation?"

Kirk swallowed and looked at Sylvie. "Can she see me?"

Sylvie shrugged her shoulders. "Mothers are funny folks. 'specially new ones. It could happen."

Kirk turned back to Cindi. "I—I don't know what to say, Cindi. What do you want me to say?" Kirk said.

Cindi shrugged her shoulders. "It don't matter. Maybe I should smother him and jump out the fuckin' window."

"You better not!" Kirk yelled.

"Who's gonna stop me?" Cindi said, her eyes bloodred and starting to tear up in.

"I will, Kirk said, his voice turning hard. "You don't want to be here. This place sucks."

Cindi laughed. "Anyplace has to be better than this place."

As if on cue, the boy stopped drinking his water and started to scream again, screaming like someone was pushing a needle through his tiny foot.

Kirk shook his head. "He screams a lot, don't he?"

"It's the crack. He wants some. Wants more. Fuck, I know how he feels, Cindi said, laughing humorlessly. "Maybe I should get him a little baby-pipe, she said, continuing to laugh.

Kirk shook his head again, looking down. "Just . . . hold him."

Cindi held the baby close. "It doesn't help."

The boy screamed again, and again, each breath expended completely before he screamed again. Cindi heard his voice start to go harsh on the end of the scream.

Kirk reached out with his hand, humming as he did. There was no song, nothing he could think of, it was just him, his hand shaking, wanting to do anything to calm the little boy down.

"Ain't that sweet, Kirkie boy? Why don't you breastfeed him?" Mr. Demon said, his voice dripping with hate.

Kirk growled. "Shut up, Demon. Shut. Up." Kirk's fists clenched as he shoved the demon back deep into himself.

The demon was silent. Kirk relaxed, humming, humming a tuneless melody, reaching over and touching his son, feeling his tiny hummingbird heart through his skin.

The boy instantly quieted. Kirk hummed a song, which was not so much a lullaby as a gentle song of hope, born out of the driving need to see him calm, alive, happy. Kirk could feel his insides churning. As he touched the boy, he saw light streaming down his arm. He looked at him, watched his reaction to the tune.

The boy yawned a large yawn, squeezing his eyes closed a few times. His head lolled over to the side and his mouth groped on Cindi's collarbone, looking for a nipple. Cindi put the plastic bottle nipple in his mouth and watched as he sucked. She held him, rocking him slowly back and forth, cooing to him now that he was quiet. She was shaking, but at least the baby was quiet now.

She put the baby down in his crib and tucked a blanket around him. She lay back on the bed, looking nearly dead herself. "Kirk. I want to die. Please," she said, looking up at him.

"No, Cindi. No. You have to stay alive. Not for me. For the baby. For the boy." He looked down at the child, who had already snuggled down under the blanket, quiet, asleep.

Cindi looked up at him. "I love you, you know, Kirk. I really love you."

Kirk nodded. "I—I love you, too, Cindi."

Cindi laughed. "Don't lie to me."

Kirk shook his head. "No. I'm not. I—"

"I know you were fuckin' Kirsten. That's okay. You're dead now, not much I can do, is there?" Cindi laughed bitterly.

Kirk shook his head. "Not much." He felt a wave of guilt wash over him, felt cold, icy despair building inside of him. Cindi laughed again.

Kirk turned to Sylvie. "I think I want to leave now."

Cindi sat up slowly. "No, Kirk. Don't leave me. Don't leave me again, dammit."

Kirk looked at Cindi wordlessly.

"Kirk, you have to promise you will come back," Cindi said quietly. She looked like she was about to cry again. There was a manic edge to her voice.

Kirk looked at Sylvie. Sylvie whispered, "Watch what promises you make to the living, Kirk. They have a way of binding you. It's bad luck to break your promise to a mortal."

Kirk looked down at his baby son. He saw lines of

grey streaming through the boy's skin, grey that threatened his life, grey that wanted to grow and consume him, snuffing out his tiny light forever. He looked up at Cindi, saw perhaps for the first time that same light echoed in her: the light of life, the light of love that she must feel for him, despite her bitterness and pain. He looked through to her heart and saw her lonely and alone, terrified.

Kirk looked back at Sylvie for a second, searching his young-looking mentor's face for some hint of what to do.

Then, something within Kirk shifted. He didn't care anymore, didn't care whether or not it was wrong. It felt right.

"I promise. I'll be back," Kirk said quietly.

Cindi nodded and began to cry again, dry sobs wracking her. "Oh God, Kirk. I'm dying here. God, I want a smoke so bad," Cindi said, shivering.

Kirk put his hand on her shoulder and she shivered at his touch.

"Kirk . . . could you . . . could you do what you did to Jeb to me?" Cindi said, looking up at him.

"Jeb? You've named him? I thought—" Kirk started to say.

"An old lady came in this morning, wearing black. Said he was a beautiful child. Gave me a flower. She asked me what his name was, and I—I didn't know what to say. She told me to name him Jebediah. Jeb. That was a good name for him, she said. Since then, that's what I want to call him," Cindi said, sniffing, blowing her nose on a tissue.

Kirk nodded. "Jeb. Sounds good to me."

Cindi shivered again. "Please?"

Kirk nodded again. He began to hum, putting his hand over Cindi's forehead. Sylvie smiled, climbing up on the bed, and put her hand on top of Kirk's, smiling at Kirk.

Cindi gently let out a deep, deep sigh as Kirk fed her the same quiet, gentle, nervous hope that he had given little Jeb. Sylvie seemed to be growing less distinct as she touched Cindi, but Cindi's aura began to lose the blackest of the dark streaks. Soon she fell into a deep sleep. Kirk stood up to go quietly, but Sylvie stayed seated.

Running her fingers over Cindi's eyes, she blew a soft breath onto her face. Kirk watched, wild-eyed, as Sylvie gently pulled a dim image of Cindi up out of her body. Sylvie hugged the filmy spirit-version of Cindi, and whispered something into Cindi's spirit-ear.

Cindi's spirit nodded, then slowly sank back into her body.

Sylvie got up off the bed and looked seriously at Kirk. "Now, don't we have some other places to go?"

"What did you do?" Kirk asked.

"I told her soul to have peaceful dreams only. It's part of the dreamin' power. Don't pay it no mind. She's going to be just fine," Sylvie said, smiling, another tear forming in her eye. "That's a pretty little baby. Looks like his daddy," Sylvie said.

Kirk looked down at the sleeping Jeb. "Yeah. He's a cute thing. Tiny, though."

Sylvie shook her head. "Babies are strong, Kirk. Very strong. He'll live. I know he will. Now I know he will."

Kirk nodded. "Where else do we have to go? I'm bushed."

Sylvie smiled. "Oh, that's right. Little baby ghosts have to sleep a lot, too. I tell you what, why don't you sleep here? I'll pick you up tonight."

"I—I want to go see Anna. As soon as possible," Kirk said, starting to leave.

"No, Kirk. No. Anna's in school now, anyway. Let her have a full school day. She's just as likely to see you as Cindi is: kids are like that. You have to watch it around them."

Kirk nodded, yawning again. "Okay. Okay. I'll sleep here. On the floor or something."

Sylvie smiled and hugged Kirk around his waist.

"Hey! What was that for?" Kirk said.

"For doing the right thing. For once," Sylvie said, grinning.

Kirk looked down at Jeb again, nodding. "Geez. I guess I'm a daddy now."

Sylvie smiled. "Yeah. I guess you are," she said.

Kirk turned back to thank Sylvie for helping him, but she was already gone, vanished into the Tempest.

Kirk dreamt.

Warmth. Lights. Cookies. Tinsel. Candles. A fire in the hearth. Mistletoe. Holly. Ivy. The pungent scent of a young Georgia pine. Softness. Music, drifting through the house. The cinder block family housing on the base was tiny, but better than anything else they'd had.

Outside, it was raining a bitter cold rain, one that could turn to ice at any moment, but inside the smell of nutmeg and cinnamon permeated the house. Kirk lay awake on his bed, listening to the rain, listening to someone sing a song about a White Christmas he'd never known. He tried to sleep, knowing that the next day he'd wake to a floor piled high with presents but, most importantly, he would see his father the captain. He had been due to come home, away from the jungle and the fighting, and be with his family for the whole Christmas season. Although the date had been put off, time and time again, and it had begun to look like he'd not be there at all, the Marines had called that morning to say that Captain Rourke would be there as scheduled, on Christmas morning.

Kirk snuck out of his bed, quietly creeping into the living room, hoping to get a look at the presents that were laid there for him. Looking up at the fireplace, he saw his favorite teddy bear resting in the stocking there—Bearegard—only looking new, with a bright red ribbon under his stocking with the glitter-cursive "Kirk" written on the white band of fake fur.

Kirk hid behind the tree, pretending he was his daddy, who he knew was famous for hiding behind trees and sneaking out and killing everyone. He was good at that. One day, Kirk would be good at it, too.

The doorbell rang, and his mom came out of the kitchen like a rocket, trying to not look excited, trying not to anticipate anything. She threw the door open.

Out of the rain, the blackness, two men stepped. They were dressed in their shining dress blues underneath their rain gear, the blues that always excited Kirk because of the beautiful Marine sword that went with them. He stood up.

"Daddy!" he yelled, and ran for the door.

His mother's shaking hand pushed him back. "No Kirk, no, no . . . just go . . . just sit down . . . just . . . no, no honey, no."

They were speaking words he could not understand, words that were black and heavy with iron and the tang of gunpowder, the stench of the jungle and the sickly-sweet smell of orchids on the altar. They were words that carried daggers that thrust into his heart and made his mother cry. He wanted to make his mother stop crying somehow, but even trying to hug her wouldn't help.

The door closed, and Kirk watched his mother fall to the floor, crying, beating her fists against the floor until her nails cracked and her hands turned black.

Kirk woke with a shock. Looking at the window drapes in the room, he saw daylight still illuminating the edges of the curtains. He shook himself further awake and felt another shiver go through him. In his sleep, he had floated down through the floor. He remembered Sylvie telling him to follow his heart to find his son before, so he decided to walk aimlessly for a little while.

Turning the corner, he found himself in a red-walled area that was clearly the Intensive Care Unit, and looking up, saw a name that instantly captured his attention: Rick Lehrer, his buddy. The federal marshal posted outside his door confirmed it.

Kirk walked into Rick's room quietly. Rick wasn't in good shape: much of his body was burned. He had apparently inhaled some flame: he was on a breathing machine. Kirk looked closely at him and saw the black streaks of death all over him. His life-light was slowly dying out.

Kirk took off his mask, holding on to it. "Hey, Rick . . ." Kirk whispered in Rick's ear, trying to get Rick to wake up.

Rick's eyes fluttered open, although his mouth was stuffed with apparatus. Kirk felt Rick's pain as his drugged brain swam into consciousness. Much of Rick's face had been badly burned: he couldn't move his jaw or talk. Kirk looked down at him, seeing the death in him and wondering if he would survive this. Reminding himself that he was the cause of Rick's burns—that if he hadn't have been so willing to use his friend's body, this would never have happened.

Rick slowly smiled at Kirk, his facial bandages moving a little. Kirk tried humming his little ditty, trying to calm Rick down. But Rick wasn't having any of it: he knew he was dead already. Knew that nothing would prevent him from being a vegetable. Rick had already given up and was just waiting to die.

"Do you have the guts?" Mr. Demon asked. "Do you have what it takes to put him out of his misery, Kirk?" Demon taunted.

"I thought I told you to shut up," Kirk said quietly.

"You did. I'm back. Did you miss me?" Mr. Demon said.

"Miss you? Fuck no. I want you to go away forever," Kirk muttered under his breath. Kirk put his Firebird mask back on and turned to the heart-lung machine.

Kirk put his hand on the heart-lung machine, looking at it, watching the dials move. One flick of a switch, and it would flip off.

"Not good enough," Mr. Demon said. "Heroic measures. They'll take heroic measures to restore him. No, you have to hurt the machine that's keeping him goin'. Reach in and shock the heck out of it. That should do it."

Kirk's skin crawled with the thought of how he was listening to Demon, but this time what Demon said seemed to make sense. He wished Sylvie was there: she would know what to do.

Rick moved a little and moaned as the pain from moving wracked his body.

Kirk moved his hand slowly inside the heart-lung machine. He could feel the moving parts, the electronics zapping their tiny currents through the silicon chips. He clenched his fist and pulled, giving as much energy to his hand as he could muster. He watched as the indicators suddenly froze, looked up at the heart monitor and saw that Rick's heart was already beating slower. But no telltales went off: those, too, had been short-circuited.

Kirk watched as Rick's lungs began to fill with liquid, his breathing became ragged and shallow, burbling as the lung machine stopped making him breathe correctly. Rick began to shake in his restraints. For a second his eyes flew open again, and Kirk thought Rick recognized him standing there.

Suddenly, a doctor with a white lab coat and a clipboard strode into the room. Instead of rushing to his side and attempting to revive Rick, however, he simply watched as Rick died, as the black veins in his aura covered him, finally reaching his brain.

As Rick closed his eyes, the doctor bent over and grabbed up his soul from his body, like Sylvie had done earlier with Cindi. Rick's soul was covered in a kind of body bag of blackish, greenish slime, but it was definitely Rick. This doctor was dead—a wraith—like Kirk!

Then, a group of nurses, orderlies, and the marshal charged into the room, trying to save him, to no avail.

"What the hell are you?" Kirk said, looked at the "doctor" incredulously.

The doctor turned around, surprised that Kirk had spoken, and nearly dropped Rick as he did. "Oh, no! I thought you were just a relative. I didn't realize you were dead. Are you his Reaper?"

Kirk looked at Rick, whose eyes were still closed inside of the slimy body bag. He looked down at Rick's dead body. He looked up at the doctor, considering what the word "Reaper" meant. Had he Reaped Rick? He wondered for a moment, and then made up his mind.

"Yeah. I'm his Reaper," Kirk said, quietly.

"Good! Good! I was just about to call up the Hierarchy Reapers, but since you're here, I guess you get claim to him, eh? Where's your chains?"

"Chains?" Kirk said.

"We want to keep him from slipping into Oblivion—these Cauls sure are slippery," the doctor said.

"Oh. Yeah! Well, mine are currently tied up. Could you lend me a set?"

The doctor nodded, smiling. "Okay, but you'll have to bring me a cut of the oboli when you get paid for him. I don't mind lending out chains as long as I get them back. You stay here, and hold on to him real tight. I'll be right back."

Kirk grabbed ahold of the very slippery, slimy shell of Rick's soul. Looking through the greenish transparent slime, he saw Rick's face, still asleep, but healed of its burn damage. Kirk wondered what he was getting himself into, but he wasn't about to turn his friend over to those Hierarchy bastards.

The doctor came back with a set of black chains and linked them around Rick, locking them with padlocks of strange manufacture. Then, smiling, he looked up at Kirk. "So, are you a Harbinger?" the doctor asked.

"Harbinger? Oh, you mean, those guys that travel around? Nah," Kirk said.

"Oh, well, okay. I'll take you to the Citadel. But you'll have to cut me in for a little more, eh? This is gonna be great. Maybe they won't turn down my application to become a Reaper when they see me help bring in a soul like this. This is great. Let's go!" the youngish doctor said, smiling at Kirk, and reached out to grab Kirk's arm where he was holding onto Rick.

Before Kirk could speak a word, he, Rick, and the doctor were already in the Tempest on their way to the Hierarchy Citadel.

Jebediah stirred in his attic room, where he stayed in the courthouse during the day. His Legionnaire sentry coughed and waited to be recognized. "A Centurion to see you, sir," the sentry said. "Are you awake enough to receive him?"

"Certainly, Legionnaire. Thank you," Jebediah said, pulling on his stern Mask of Justice, the badge of his office.

The Centurion was a man who had fought with Jebediah at Leggett's Hill against the Yankees—the bonds of esprit d'corps made the man something of an informant to Jebediah about goings-on around the city of the dead—the Necropolis of Atlanta.

The Centurion saluted smartly. "Sir. An entire weapons bunker was destroyed last night, presumably many of the weapons will be gatherable. We have reason to believe that the perpetrators used skinpuppets to move past our Monitors there."

Jebediah nodded slowly. "Yes, well. I do believe we're seeing more Renegade activity these days: we shall have to take steps against them. Is there anything else, Centurion?" Jebediah asked.

"No, sir. No souls were gathered as far as we know. We have reason to believe that the Grey Wolves perpetrated this crime, although there have been some confidential reports by snitches that an unknown Renegade Circle was involved."

"This is very interesting, Centurion. " Jebediah shook his head slowly.

"You know I wouldn't have come to you, Jebediah, if it hadn't been important," the Centurion said quietly.

"I thank you kindly, brother Centurion." Jebediah bowed to the grey flannel-clad warrior as he spun on his heel and left.

So James, did you finally make your move? Jebediah thought, his brow creased. Opening up a pouch at his side, he removed a pack of cards wrapped in a white cloth. Closing his eyes, he opened himself to the lines of Fate, the possibilities of the web of life and death and all that lies in between.

He had learned this particular art from a visiting vagabond in exchange for her continued freedom: he knew that it would only be a matter of time before she was brought before him again on similar charges against the Code. Justice would eventually be served. He normally hid the talent from his Hierarchy friends, as he was certain that it was against some obscure portion of Charon's Code to know and use it. The cards had been a gift from Mary, of all people, who had given them to him without word or comment.

Jebediah laid out the cards in silence, looking at them for a moment to confirm his suspicions. The Monument was reversed in the Future position. The Charon card, reversed, was in the Final Outcome position. Jebediah's art read not just the cards, but the pattern of Fate that ran behind them.

Mary had been right. The Curse was not over. Jebediah sensed a great change coming. He knew that nothing would be the same as it was before.

He had wanted to wait before looking for James and his son Kirk, but now he realized that they had something to do with this great change. He knew that he would have to act quickly, or all that he had ever worked for, fought for, believed in, would be lost to the nothingness that hungered for it.

Jebediah put aside his Mask of Office and picked up his Mask of Honor, the one he had earned in the Fifth Maelstrom when he and many other Hierarchy wraiths fought for days against the Spectres that the storm had brought. The mask was deep black Stygian iron, marked with symbols of his prowess and honor.

As always, whenever he put it on, his Shadow laughed and attempted to frighten him with scenes of the Maelstrom, which had been caused when the atomic weapons were detonated at Hiroshima and Nagasaki. Suddenly, for the first time, people began to believe that everyone in the world could die at once, and Oblivion loved that.

Jebediah stood still for a moment as he watched the scene of the great purplish black wave of

Oblivion-energy crashing across the Necropolis of Atlanta, watched as it saturated the streets and made even the Shadowlands friendly to the Spectres who swept toward the Citadel like a cavalry charge. The Shadow within him was using its power to show him these scenes, and they affected him as if they were real. He shuddered as he remembered the utter chaos of the Maelstrom. If he could have broken a sweat, he would have. Then he felt a little sad as he remembered the brave members of his own Circle who had been swept out with the Maelstrom, or who had died later in the hellish barrow-fires that had raped the land after the Maelstrom had left. Then, slowly, the vision faded, and Jebediah settled the mask comfortably on his face.

Stepping outside, he spoke to his sentry.

"Take me to the Citadel, Legionnaire," Jebediah said." There is much to be done before the sun goes down."

TRAVELS AND TRIBULATIONS

Sometimes God just doesn't come through . . .
                                        —Anonymous

Ghost Stories:
Hewitt's Folly

"You ever been over on track number six?" Beau asked as they were walking to their trains, their MARTA train operator caps tucked under their arms.

"Track number six? What the hell? There ain't no track number six. Track number five. Track number five-A, yeah. There ain't no track number six," Simone said.

"Oh yes, there is. Track number six is where Mr. Hewitt got himself killed," Beau said, grinning.

"What you talkin' about, fool?" Simone said, making sure his hair was perfect in the mirror as they descended onto the platform in the elevator.

"They was building the Five Points Station, see, and they ran into some trouble gettin' some

bedrock outta the way. Well, Mr. Hewitt, he was a determined ol' cuss. He got himself some plastic explosives, even killt himself a lamb and smeared blood all over the place. He was gonna break that rock, by God," Beau said as they stood on the platform waiting for the subway trains to pull up.

"What happened?" Simone said, standing there with his hands on his hips.

"What happened? Crazy white man killt himself, he did. Blew the charges the wrong way. The whole tunnel collapsed on him. That's why they have track five and track five-A. And I wouldn't do my inspection over near track six. They say you can sometimes see ol' Hewitt, still stuck in the rock. Those deep parts where the old maintenance area was—those parts are downright scary. You ain't gonna see me goin' over there," Beau said. He was grinning, but he was serious.

Simone shook his head. "Beau, you is crazy, man. Believe all that shit. Damn."

Kirk and the doctor materialized on the bottom-most train platform of the central MARTA subway station in Atlanta: Five Points Station. Trains have always been important to Atlanta: Five Points Station used to be the roundhouse where trains would come in and get placed on different tracks, the commercial center of the city, if not the geographic one.

Kirk held on to Rick as he waited for the doctor to show him where to go. The doctor turned to him. "Oh! My name's Shaw. What do you call yourself?"

Kirk thought for a second. "Firebird," he said.

Shaw nodded. "All you freelance Reapers have cool names. I wish I could carry that off, but I'm just a doctor. Always have been. Well, so, ah, let's go on down, shall we?"

Kirk nodded, waiting for the doctor to move. Shaw moved past Kirk and starting walking across the platform, toward a door marked MAINTENANCE PERSONNEL ONLY.

Shaw stopped as a MARTA train pulled into the station and a wash of people streamed out of its doors. He turned back to Kirk. "You've never done this before, have you?" Shaw said, smiling.

Kirk nodded. "Yeah, well, I'm new in town."

"Oh, so you've Reaped other places?" Shaw said, watching the people move back and forth, standing as still as possible so that someone wouldn't walk through him. Several people walked up to him and, mysteriously enough, moved aside and went on their way.

Kirk nodded. He was glad for the mask: it protected his face and kept people from knowing when he was lying. He liked that. Kirk wasn't sure what the doctor could see in his eyes, which were visible through the mask, but he was willing to take the chance. All he could think about was being there for Rick, making sure that no one treated him badly.

Shaw nodded. "Well, for a better cut, I'll make sure you don't get taken advantage of in there."

Kirk grinned behind his mask. "Is there a reward for finding a dead person?"

Shaw looked puzzled. "No, there's a reward for turning him over to the Hierarchy for processing."

Kirk cursed under his breath. Sylvie had told him about this, the other night, and he had forgotten. He remembered now and felt a cold chill run through him as he realized what the doctor thought they were there to do.

"He . . . he was my friend. Can't I keep him with me?" Kirk asked.

Shaw shook his head slowly. "No. You can't. You wouldn't be able to keep him from going to Oblivion. He's not a wraith like you or me. He's just a soul. No Fetters. Nothing. He would fall into Oblivion right this minute if you let him out of those chains," Shaw said.

Kirk nodded. He looked over at Rick. Kirk knew that the doctor was one of these Hierarchy guys, and that if he refused to let the doctor take Rick to the Hierarchy, it might just cause a problem. A stink. A fight. Kirk didn't want to get into a fight here, where, supposedly, there were a bunch of Hierarchy types, maybe even the soldiers or the cops that he saw earlier. Kirk suddenly realized that he was in a lot of trouble. What was worse, he realized, he had brought Rick into death just to have him potentially end up in chains for the rest of his existence. What was he thinking?

Kirk turned back to Shaw, who was obviously beginning to suspect his identity. "Yeah, well, okay. I tell you what. You help me out and you can have all the money I get. Okay?"

Shaw nodded. "Great! Sounds great. Let's go. This way."

They walked up to the door and through it, Kirk shivering as he passed through. Walking down the stairs, they stepped into a series of maintenance corridors, catwalks, crawlways, and rail access doors. It was a maze of accessways, and Kirk immediately knew he'd get lost without help. Kirk followed the doctor into the darkness. He turned down a corridor and there, in the corridor, was a man in full army fatigues carrying a rifle with a bright white crystal attached to the butt.

"Hold," the soldier said.

"Hello, Legionnaire. It's okay. I'm a citizen—a Monitor, actually. This is a Reaper. We've got a Thrall for—" Shaw began.

"I can see that, sir. But Acquisitions is down the hall that way. This area's restricted." The soldier pointed back down the hall the other direction.

"Oh! Oh! Well, that's fine. Thank you, Officer!" Shaw said, turning around and walking back down the corridor. "Must've moved things around since I was last here," Shaw muttered to Kirk.

They turned and walked down a set of stairs into a large open room. Inside were many ghosts like Rick: people encased in slimy-looking body bags, standing or lying on the floor listlessly, enchained.

The smell was almost worse than the sight: there was the chemical smell of some foul waste here. Men dressed much like the soldier in the hallway moved among those who stood next to their enchained charges, men and women who carried their own weapons, wore armor, and acted like loners. An officer approached Shaw and Kirk with a clipboard of his own.

"Who's the Reaper?" the officer asked.

"He is." Shaw pointed at Kirk. The officer nodded. He indicated Rick. "He have any Fetters?"

Shaw shook his head. "Nope. I'm his Monitor, actually."

The officer looked tired. "Why did you come with the Reaper? We don't need that many personnel hanging out down here." Rick and Shaw stood quietly by, not answering the officer, who didn't seem to really want an answer.

"Okay, I'll give you two oboli for him. He looks like he's got a bit of Pathos to him. Let me get him linked to a line," the officer said, gesturing to some chainmongers who carried large reels of dark chains over to where they were.

"Wait a second—what if I don't want him to be taken?" Kirk said.

The officer waved off the chain men. "You gonna sell him to someone else? Look, Reaper, this is the only game in town. Unless you're with the Renegades?"

Kirk shook his head. "No."

The officer sighed. "Then, are you gonna give him up?"

Kirk looked down at Rick, who still slept inside his body bag. He hugged him, standing up. "Yeah. I guess so," Kirk said, looking out at the entire room. Everywhere he looked he saw people in chains. He saw a line of chained ghosts resting against one of the walls. Kirk felt only disgust, at himself and at the Hierarchy and their practices.

The officer pulled two large black coins out of a pouch and gave them to Kirk. "All right. Thanks. See ya later," the officer said, moving on to the next Reaper.

Kirk looked down at Rick in his bag, whispering, "Stay cool, dude."

Turning, Kirk then strode out of the room, Shaw following rapidly behind him. "Hey! Hey! What the hell? You gonna give me my coins?"

Kirk turned around in a rage. He punched Shaw in the face, kneed him in the gut, and threw him against the wall. He discorporated, looking at Kirk, shocked.

"You fuckin' bastard. That was my best friend back there. Fuck you." He threw the two coins down on the ground. "There you go. There's your god-damn money."

Shaw looked confused as he slowly reformed. He crawled across the floor to pick up the coins, his body turning black. Shaw cringed, his hands becoming claws. "S-s-s-sorry . . ." he hissed. "I'm so s-s-s-sorry," Shaw said, now a twisted, foul-looking creature.

Kirk took a step back. "Look, I'm just going to leave. You stay here, and I won't hit you again."

He turned around and ran down the corridor, following the path he remembered—the path back to the surface, leaving Shaw far behind him. Shaw didn't seem to follow him, but Kirk was sure that he'd go to the guards to report the incident.

Turning the corner, he found a stairwell and began climbing stairs. Stepping through another door, Kirk stood stock-still as he heard a voice. He was in some kind of maintenance corridor, just off a storage room that apparently was being used as an office by the wraiths there.

Standing quietly in the hallway, he listened to the wraith's conversation.

"So, you want me to search for someone, Jebediah?" a female voice asked.

"Yes. His name be Kirk. Kirk Rourke. He is supposed to be one of the Restless. I'd ask that you keep this quiet, Sophia. I would like this to be conducted with great subtlety. I would like it to be conducted before the next shipment of soulfire arrives," a male voice, soft and very Southern, replied.

Kirk peered around the corner and into the room, where he saw a man with a full white beard, long white hair and a black mask of some kind.

"Certainly, sir. I'll get right to work on it. Although, I must warn you, a search of this kind—might take a while. It depends on how close he is, and how stationary . . ." came the female voice.

Kirk didn't wait to hear any more. He ran down the hall, and, closing his eyes, dived into the wall. He flew through it, sliding through walls of cinder blocks, electrical wires, and brick, until he finally broke free in darkness, landing on his feet and slowly becoming substantial again. His guitar had fallen free from where he'd tied it to his back; he resecured the bonds quickly. Then, looking up, he saw the train tracks with the third rail humming nearby. He climbed a set of access stairs to the bottom floor platform, just as the southbound train pulled into the station. Kirk had learned from years of life on the street to not look back, to move nonchalantly. He quietly moved onto the train, standing in one corner, trying not to be squashed by the people there.

As the train pulled out of the station, Kirk thought he saw Shaw flicker into existence on the train platform, looking around for him. He stood stock-still, sure that Shaw couldn't see him. Shaw was still turned in the other direction when the train moved into the darkness of the tunnel. But he did see, out of the corner of his eye, a flash of light illuminating a sign which said TRACK 6, CLOSED. Then there was nothing but darkness, and more train stops.

As the passenger load thinned out on the train, Kirk began to notice an old lady sitting with a lot of bags on one of the seats. She was obviously a bag lady, a homeless person. For a long time, Kirk thought she was just like the other homeless people who hung out on the train—then he realized (looking through her at the afternoon sun) she was one of the dead. He switched seats to sit with her, and she grudgingly made room for him.

"How is you, young man?" she asked him.

"Just fine, ma'am. Just fine. For bein' dead," Kirk said, smiling.

"Bein' dead ain't so bad. Not so bad as Jessie thought it would be," the woman said, smiling.

"Who's Jessie?" Kirk asked.

"Jessie? She's me," Jessie said, smiling a graveyard smile.

Kirk nodded. "Ma'am, can I ask you somethin'?"

"You can ask me somethin' and somethin' else again. Cause you already asked me somethin' when you asked if you could ask somethin'. If ya follow me," Jessie said, grinning again.

"Ma'am, do you know a Jebediah, an old-lookin' ghost with white hair?" Kirk said.

The woman thought for a moment, nodding to herself. "Yes, I do believe. I do believe that sound like Magistrate Jebediah. He runs a court over in Decatur. Why do you want to know, son? You ain't in trouble are ya?"

"No, ma'am. Not that I know of. Thank you, ma'am," Kirk said, moving away from her.

"Now, shug, don't you go on and run off. Jessie wants a friend. You come on back over here and let's us talk together for awhile. Where you from, boy?" Jessie asked.

"Atlanta, ma'am. Lived here all my life," Kirk said.

"You sound like a South Georgia boy to me," Jessie said.

"My momma's parents are from South Georgia. St. Mary's," Kirk said.

Jessie nodded. "I rode the rails down there once. Very nice place. Pretty beaches. Do you like pretty beaches, son?" Jessie asked.

Kirk shrugged. "I guess. I didn't visit too many beaches when I was alive. Now that I'm dead, I figure I won't have to learn to swim."

Jessie shook her head, grinning her ragged-teeth smile again. "No, now, son, learnin' to swim is a good idea even when you're dead. That's what movin' through the Tempest is, anyway—swimmin'. Or like enough to it. You look real young. You ain't a baby-ghost are ya?" she said quietly.

Kirk considered what to tell Jessie. He hadn't wanted to blow his cover, but if he ignored her, she'd clearly get annoyed with him, and that would be just as bad.

"Yes, I am," Kirk said.

She laughed. "You seem to want to think about that a bit. Like you weren't sure what you should say. Well, you can just not worry about ol' Jessie. She's a good lady."

Jessie bent down to Kirk's ear. "Good Christian lady, Jessie is. That's right. I don't think God's gone and turned His back on me, no suh. If'n His eye's on the sparrow, you can be sure His eye's on me," Jessie whispered to Kirk.

Kirk had heard of the so-called "churchy" types from Sylvie. He remembered what she had said earlier, about how they believed in God and that angels talked to them.

Kirk looked at Jessie, sizing her up. He wondered if she believed in angels, too, but she didn't look like someone who was bad, or harmful.

Jessie looked at him and smiled, putting something in his hand as she did. Kirk looked down at what she had placed in his palm and saw a tiny, rusty steel cross—real enough.

"God wants you to know he cares, my boy. God cares about you, even if you are dead and lost to him right now."

Kirk nodded, looking at the cross.

"You got any kin among the dead here in town?" Jessie said.

Kirk shook his head absently, then thought about Greymaster for a minute and wondered if he counted.

Kirk began to think, not answering Jessie. Was Greymaster his father? It sure seemed like it. Somehow it had to be true. It was so strange, Kirk thought, about how it seemed that Greymaster knew him so well, about how his dreams were so realistic and how his father was so true to what he was now. His mother had always described his father as being a very gentle, sweet man: who was this monster who wore the grey mask?

Jessie smiled. "I'm prayin' for you, son. You got a lot on your mind, don't you?"

Kirk nodded. His mind jumped around: his new

friends, his old friend Rick, his new son, Sylvie.
Greymaster. Jebediah. Jeb . . .

"How is it that they got the same name?" Kirk
asked himself, aloud.

"What's that, sugar?" Jessie said as the train car
pulled into the next stop.

"Oh, nothin'. Just thinkin', like you said, Jessie,"
Kirk said.

Jessie stood up with all her packages. "Well, now,
boy, Jessie gonna have to take off now."

"Where are you goin', if I can ask?" Kirk said.

"Susie's Bar. It's a Haunting place. You're welcome to come along, although you gonna have to listen to more of Jessie's talkin' about God and all."

Kirk smiled. "Sounds okay by me, Jessie. I was
raised Southern Baptist, but I ain't been to church in
forever, not since my grandma and grandpa died."

Jessie nodded. "That's all right. God looks out for
ya, even if you don't come to church."

At that, the train pulled into the station, and Jessie
and Kirk got off the train. Kirk watched as she wad-
dled up the stairs, and then followed the rather large
ghost up to the street level. She smiled at Kirk as
they walked down the afternoon street, keeping to
the shadows of the buildings, until she turned down
an alleyway and led him into near total darkness.
She sighed as she did, saying, "Ah, that sun's just too
bright for the likes o' me, Lord," to herself.

Susie's Bar was an old, boarded-up pool room and
bar that had been shut down years ago. In the perpet-
ual darkness of the alleyway, off the beaten track of the
street, it was apparently one of the most favorite "public Hauntings" of the ghosts of Atlanta who didn't con-
gregate around the Necropolis or with the Hierarchy.
Kirk wondered if the Hierarchy even knew about it.

He heard music inside: Dixieland jazz playing
sweet and clear. He followed Jessie through the door,

stood behind her as the rest of the wraiths in the bar greeted her. These were the ghosts who lived in the shadows of the city: Kirk saw they weren't as polished or solid-looking as the Grey Wolves or the Hierarchy wraiths he had seen. Most of them were dim, transparent. Hungry-looking, they scrabbled back and forth in the room whispering to each other, trading slivers of coins and tiny Relics with one another. Jessie led Kirk over to the corner table, where she sat him down.

"This ain't a drinking bar anymore. It's just a cool place on a hot day," Jessie said, sitting down with all her packages.

Kirk looked at the band, who were playing old, battered instruments. They ended their song and started playing the blues, deep and throaty, and some of the other wraiths in the bar looked up and nodded their heads in time with the music.

Kirk looked all around him. "Why do these people look so bad? Missing fingers, hands, parts of their faces?"

Jessie shook her head. "When the Maelstrom came, Kirk, these people were shut out. Unwanted. The Hierarchy wouldn't let them into the Citadel 'cause they won't sign up with them, and the Renegades had their own requirements. There weren't no place for them to go. So they got caught by it, out in it. Many of 'em got gone, right quick. Most of 'em didn't, though. Hung on, in pain, in need, floatin' listlessly. Until Susie found this place, an' she told 'em to come on here. That's why she run this place. To protect those who ain't gettin protected by nobody," Jessie said.

"Which one is Susie?" Kirk asked, looking around the bar.

Jessie pointed to a massive woman, a huge, naked woman with immense breasts, seated on a low cushion and holding a "court" of sorts: wraiths approached her now and then, spoke with her, and then departed back into the shadows of the bar.

Susie turned her gaze to Jessie's corner of the bar and nodded at her. "Best go and say hello, boy. It's good manners. Don't worry, she won't ask you your name. She don't bite."

Kirk nodded. Shakily, he got up and crossed the room, brushing past the tattered wraiths who scrabbled around at his feet.

Susie looked up at him, grinning. "Well, hello there, handsome. What can I do for a cutie like yourself?" she said, looking him up and down. "And I hope it's somethin' dirty."

Kirk would have blushed if he could have. He looked down at Susie, not able to keep his gaze from wandering to her breasts and back up to her face. Even though she was physically repulsive to him—her body immense and bulbous with welts and strange creases and tattoos—there was something going on in her voice, in the way she spoke, that made him vaguely (and even more disgustingly, to him) attracted to her.

"Just sayin' hello. My friend Jessie asked me to come over here and say hello," Kirk said quietly.

Susie nodded. "I'll have to thank her sometime. She's a dear. But we've met before, I think. Haven't we?" Susie said, smiling.

Kirk shook his head. "Nah. I ain't never seen you before, ma'am. No disrespect intended . . . "

Susie grinned. "None taken, certainly. But I do think that you have been here before, son, you just don' remember it. Cause you were under a Caul then, and didn't remember much a' anythin'. Good thing your Reaper took care of ya."

"Reaper? I don't remember any Reaper, ma'am. I just died and woke up one day on a roof someplace," Kirk said, puzzled.

Susie grinned. "That's okay, boy. It ain't always easy to remember time under the Caul. You can wander around for awhile, have dreams and enter them, and never know what's goin' on for real around you. But I want to tell you that you did come through here. And I do know who you are, so there." Susie grinned again, shaking out her long, stringy hair. "What's the matter, boy? Don't like naked ladies?"

Kirk shrugged. "Whatever floats your boat, ma'am. I guess you don't have to wear anythin'— you are dead and all. I guess things just aren't like they were."

"Ain't that the truth," Susie said.

Kirk looked in her eyes. "Is what you said the truth? I was here before? You weren't shittin' me?"

"No shit. Just truth. You were here, boy—oh, about six months ago."

"Six months, eh? And who was I with?" Kirk said.

"Yo' Reaper. You don't remember any of this, boy?" Susie said, shaking her head slowly, starting to look concerned.

"No, ma'am. I don't remember nothin'. Honestly," Kirk said.

Susie nodded. "Hum. Well, then, boy, I gots information for you, but I don't give info away for free."

"Well, what do you want me to do?" Kirk said, sighing. "I don't got any coins."

Susie shook her head. "Nah, I don't need no Charon-head coins. What I want is a song, boy. You a musician, or do you just carry a guitar around for pretty looks?"

Kirk grinned. "I know a few songs, ma'am."

"Well, why don't you go on over there to the band and see if they know any of the songs you do?" Susie said, and waved him on. "Then, I'll tell you all about your Reaper and everythin'. Deal?"

Kirk smiled. "Deal."

Kirk walked over to the band and said hello. The three ghosts, whose names were Blind Louie, Willie Whistle, and Bangup Benjamin grinned and welcomed Kirk. They whispered among themselves, and finally Kirk admitted that he knew the riff from "Mannish Boy."

He turned toward the dark bar, smiling to himself, and began to play the bluesy riff, backed up by Bangup's drums and Willie's horn. Kirk's guitar glowed bright blue-green with the light that was shining inside of it, and as he played, he felt the sound envelop him, shoot out in all directions, filling the patrons of the bar with passion—energy of a palpable kind. The wraiths nodded their heads as he played, a few of them changed shape in their seats, moving like flowers that stretch to catch the sun: they bent to catch his music. He felt the energy of his comrades, felt the blossoming of energy within him as he played for the sheer love of playing. Blind Louis sang, "Ain't that a man? Way past twenty-one . . . "

The entire crowd moved with them as they played. The gloom of the bar became lit with blossomings here and there of energy within: people remembering their past lives, experiencing the light of life, the fire of emotion deep in the bar.

Kirk played past the point where his fingers were cut and abraded by his guitar strings. He moved his fingers in an easy manner, one that he realized Blind Louis was matching as he played. Was Louis somehow orchestrating it all? Kirk didn't care. It felt right, and for that moment, there in the darkness of the bar, every wraith within earshot could hear the sound of hope in the darkness.

Willie hugged Kirk when the song was over, and there was a smattering of wraithly applause and a tinkling of metal in the bucket that hung on the wall for the purpose of collecting tips for the band.

"You gots to stay, boy, stay and play. Don' worry 'bout all that other crap. You ain't needin' to go off fightin', are you?" Blind Louis said, his sightless eyes seeing more than Kirk could know.

Kirk shook his head. He wished he could stay here all the time, just playing music, learning from these three incredibly talented musicians, learning about the roots of the music he loved. But he couldn't make himself forget all the things that had already happened to him: his death, the death of his friends, the birth of his son, the treatment his friend Rick got, his sister Anna. He couldn't leave them all behind, although he seriously considered it. He just smiled and shook Blind Willie's hand.

Kirk strode back across the bar to Susie as if he owned the place, many wraiths reaching up to touch him in appreciation.

"Havin' that git-fiddle helped wake those boys up, Kirk. You should stay and play with us," Susie said, grinning with her tombstone teeth.

" 'M sorry, Susie, but there ain't no way—hey how'd you know my name?" he asked, grinning.

From around Susie's other side came Sylvie, grinning and looking cute. "Hi, Kirk! Nice playin'," Sylvie said.

Kirk hugged Sylvie when he saw her. "Damn, girl, I missed you. I've been out and about. Gettin' into trouble."

Sylvie nodded. "I figured as much, Kirk. You ain't ever not gettin' into trouble."

Kirk turned to Susie. "Hey. What's the story? You were gonna tell me about my Reaper . . . "

Susie nodded and looked at Sylvie. "She don't think it's a good idea. Afraid you'll get the big head."

Sylvie looked down at the floor, then looked up coyly at Kirk. "Well, I was just worried that . . . well, I guess you need to know. I just don't want it to change nothin'."

"Why the hell would it change anythin'?" Kirk demanded.

"Well, boy, come on into Susie's office and we'll talk about it. I owe you that after that song. Geez, you made half the bar light up," Susie said, ambling through a door that had half-fallen off its hinges, on into the backroom where, away from the prying ears of those who would normally listen in on such things, they could talk in private.

Kirk sat cross-legged on the floor, idling toying with his guitar (which seemed to lose its tune faster now than ever before) and listening to Susie.

"Well, you see now, boy, I was just sittin' here in my bar, mindin' my own business, when a Ferryman showed up. Now, I don't know if you know what a Ferryman is . . ." Susie said.

"Nope. What is a Ferryman? Besides a fairy-man, which I know about already, and don't need to know anythin' more about," Kirk said, grinning.

"You hush and listen to Susie, Kirk," Sylvie chided.

"Well, you see, Charon was the first Ferryman, many, many years ago. The Lady of Fate—" at this, Susie paused, smiling at Sylvie "—came out of darkness and decreed that Charon was the man who'd be put in charge of helpin' souls get wherever they's supposed to go. He came upon a few more like himself and asked them to help out. Each one of these wraiths, back then, was given a reed boat and a pole and a scythe, and took to wearing hoods over their faces so that no one could tell who they really were. They served humanity by getting them down the river to where the Sunless Sea was and telling them how to build their own boats to get across the sea. Later on, on that same spot where the river meets the sea, that's where Charon built his city, Stygia.

"Now these Ferrymen, you see, they were important in that they helped people get right in their heads where it was they wanted to be goin' and helped 'em get that way. And after Stygia was founded and all this other stuff started happenin', well you know what? The original Ferrymen, they didn't even know what it was, but they didn't want to hang around Stygia when Charon was takin' over and makin' demands outta everyone. They weren't gonna be a party to the mass gatherin' of souls. Instead, they used their power, wisdom, and lore, and were able to continue to help individuals here and there that could use their help.

"But legends, they run deep, Kirk. And even though the Ferrymen aren't a part of the Hierarchy anymore, they are respected by all the wraiths—respected, feared, and revered. Ferrymen can do just about anythin' they want, really. And this one, her name was Sharon, I think, took you under her wing and Reaped you. She showed you a lot about the world, that I know, because she was carrying you along with her. Taught you how to use puppetry pretty well, showed you some Outrage, a little Keening such as you used here. That's how I knew you could Keen. She said you had the mark of the Firebird on you, and there ain't nobody here that ain't heard the prophecy about the 'son of the Firebird' bringing great change to Atlanta. Atlanta's the city of the Firebird, dontcha know. We've been burnin', rebuildin', and burnin' again for the longest time. And we'll keep on, keepin' on. I've seen it once, twice, three times, and it'll keep goin' on."

Kirk just sat there. "So this woman Sharon—she was a Ferryman? She's been alive that long?"

Sylvie shook her head. "She was probably one of the younger ones, actually, Kirk. What they do is train up those they think can do what it is a ferry-man does, and lead them into an initiation at the secret Ferryman places all throughout the

Underworld. Secret places where no one else can go, secret waystations that let them vanish into nothingness if people chase after them."

Susie nodded. "That's right. Them Ferrymen are powerful folks. They gots Arcanos that nobody else got: things that let them know the rightness of things, that let them keep track of people no matter where they are in the Death-lands."

Kirk sighed, holding his head. "This is too much, Sylvie. What does it all mean?"

Sylvie smiled and pinched Kirk on the arm. "Stupid. Haven't you been listenin'? What it means, Kirk, is that you're special, dammit. Not just any Ferryman chooses someone to be Reaped. There's somethin' special about you, Kirk. And I see it even if you don't."

"Special? Heh. What's special 'bout a fuckup who got himself killed just because he couldn't keep his nose out of other people's drug business? Who left behind a baby sister who's gonna get turned into a prostitute and a baby son who's gonna grow up without a father. Pretty darn special, yeah," Kirk said, anger tingeing his voice. He was feeling sorry for himself.

"That's up to you, Kirk. You can forget him and never see him, and not ever be a father. Or you can do like you been doin' and watch over him. That's the key. Watchin', protectin'. But you're right: you're gonna have to face up to what you did. You're gonna have to understand what it is to be a dad, gonna have to know that demon inside you before you can do anyone else any good," Susie said harshly, but then she smiled again.

Kirk smiled, too, shaking his head. "You mean I gotta bring Demon out and talk to him or somethin'?"

Susie put a soft, gentle hand on his shoulder. "You gotta know him. You gotta talk back at him. If he tries to make you do somethin', you turn it right back on him. Know him. Know what makes your

Shadow tick, what it is he wants. Kirk, that's the only way you can get anyplace," Susie said quietly.

Kirk nodded, listening to it all, feeling a growing fear inside of him. Could he take that? Could he see all the anger, and hatred, and what-have-you that was inside of him? Could he deal with it? Wouldn't it be easier just to keep quiet, to fight him off when he got out of hand? Still, there was tremendous truth to Susie's words.

Sylvie hugged Kirk from behind. "Kirk, you're very special, very special to this city. And you can either help destroy it, or help change it for the better. Now, I heard tell you went on over to the Hierarchy this mornin'. It's gotten out. The Circle— Freda, Duke, and Jojo—ain't happy with you, Kirk. They think you've sold out. I told them you didn't, that you just had to get somethin' done, but I need to know what it is you did."

Kirk looked shocked. "Sold out? Fuck no. Rick died. My friend, you know, the one who was burned in the raid?"

Sylvie nodded. "Yes. Where did you find him?"

"He was in his hospital room. He was in a lot of pain and, well, it seemed like the right idea at the time, so, well . . . I turned off the machine that was keepin' him alive."

Susie chuckled, shaking her head. "Oh my, my."

Sylvie looked very concerned. "You killed him, Kirk? Why?"

Kirk shrugged. "It . . . seemed like . . . well, he was in a lot of pain. I just wanted to give him peace."

Sylvie shook her head. "Kirk, did Mr. Demon put you up to this?"

Kirk thought back. He remembered Mr. Demon asking him to do it, taunting him. "I reckon you're right, Sylvie. He did. Does that mean it was bad?" Kirk felt a pall of guilt fall around his shoulders.

Susie spoke softly. "It's always best to leave the living to living, as long as they can, Kirk. If his soul was still in his body, then there was a chance for him. You never know what a person's Fate is until you actually see it happen. You joggled Fate's arm, Kirk. Made him die early, maybe."

Kirk looked down. "Yeah, well, the Hierarchy has him. I wish it had never happened, but there's nothing I can do about it now."

"There's a few things you can do about it. But Kirk, you shouldn't have done that. Specially since Mr. Demon was suggestin' it—that shoulda tipped you off right there."

Kirk heard Demon chuckling to himself and shook his head, hanging it in shame.

"Don't give me that puppy-dog look, lookin' like you're all sorry you did what you did. I know you're sorry. It doesn't change what you did. Still, I might have done it myself if I were in your shoes, Kirk. I understand what you did, I just don't agree with it," Sylvie said.

Kirk nodded slowly. He looked up at Sylvie. "I hate the Hierarchy. They suck. Do you see how they treat people? Puttin' them in chains, shippin' them around like cattle. I can't believe that shit."

Sylvie nodded, looking around nervously despite the fact that no one but she, Susie, and Kirk were present. "Yeah, I know, Kirk. I ain't too happy with them myself. But it seems to me that some of the Renegades are just as bad. I can't trust any of them."

Kirk nodded. "I know what you mean. I don't think I'm with any of them. I'll stand next to my friends—you, Sylvie, and maybe the rest of the Circle if they'll get their panties unwadded, but dammit, I'm just not a big joiner. Still, if I have to, to find out what I am, and to rescue Rick, I'll join the Wolves."

Sylvie smiled. "I can understand that, Kirk. I wouldn't ask you to turn down a chance to learn about what you are. You need to. It's important."

Kirk nodded. He stared off into the darkness of the back room, his eyes glazing over as he thought. He turned back to Sylvie. "Is Greymaster my father?" he asked, quietly.

Sylvie didn't answer. She looked at Susie quietly, smiling.

Susie smiled, waving her hands, getting up slowly. "That's my cue. I'm outta here. Y'all have a good talk," she said, trundling into the front of the bar.

Sylvie waited until Susie was gone, then whispered so that she couldn't be heard from the other room, "Kirk, that's for you to find out. I can't help you with everything. I will tell you that I think if you want to join the Wolves to find out about your life, and your destiny, then I say go for it. You have to understand, though, that it's getting close to the end of the time that I can be with you and tell you what all to do. You've come very far, very far in the past day or so, ever since you went from bein' a layabout on that roof of yours to bein' a free spirit. Now you know a lot more than you did. You gotta do somethin' with that knowledge, Kirk. You can't just stay the way you are. You have to go on. I'll help you whatever way I can, but I can't do it for you," Sylvie said, smiling.

Kirk nodded, thinking. Questions were boiling up inside him, and he asked them whenever he could get ahold of one long enough to understand it. "Am I gonna hurt that little baby if I keep hanging around it? Is it a good idea for a ghost like me to hang around a baby?"

Sylvie shook her head. "Not unless you decide not to work on knowing your Shadow, knowing what it'll do, and knowing what it won't do. You won't help that boy if you're not able to protect him from your demon. But Kirk, you were right about one thing: that boy needs a father. Needs a real father, not the kind of father that abuses or ignores his kid. A father that loves him, really loves him. Can you do that, do you think?" Sylvie said, looking into Kirk's eyes.

Kirk nodded. "I . . . it's scary, Sylvie. But I can do it. I . . . feel something about him. It's very strange. It's not like anything I've ever felt before. I guess I feel . . . responsible for him. Like I need to protect him."

Sylvie nodded. "Those are good feelings. They do you credit. Now, you wanted to go and see Anna, make sure she was okay? I can take you there if you want, but I have a feelin' that you're not gonna like what you see."

Kirk nodded. "I want to go. I have to go. I want to see my sister."

Sylvie nodded. "All right, then. Let's go." She offered her hand to Kirk.

"Sylvie? I just wanted to say thanks. I realize that you do a lot for me. A lot of work. I've seen what the Hierarchy is like: everything is all cut and dried, pay for this and pay for that. You ain't never asked to be paid. I want you to know I appreciate all that you've done for me, and for my—for my family."

Sylvie smiled. "Kirk, would it hurt your feelin's if I told you it was my job?"

Kirk shook his head. "Nah, but isn't it a shitty job? Helpin' out dopeheads who fuck up things?"

Sylvie smiled again. "Nope. I wouldn't trade this job for anythin'."

Kirk shook his head again, looking down. "Thanks again, Sylvie."

"You're welcome," Sylvie whispered. "Now, can we get goin'?"

Kirk nodded, and they vanished.

———

There were always two or three cars in the Rourke's driveway inside Royal Pines Trailer Park, next to the double-wide that Mama Rourke had bought on the money from her widow's military benefit. The cars were of various different makes and manufactures, some luxury cars in good condition next to trashed-out Toyotas and Buicks. The neighbors had gotten used to the comings and goings that always seemed to be going on around that trailer: people arriving and leaving in cars all night long on the weekend. And one of the windows on the trailer always had light coming from it and the music of some blues CD of one kind or another. The smell of incense wafted out into the night— that and heavier smokes. The Rourke family didn't own a drier: their clothesline on Monday afternoons looked like a what's what of trashy lingerie: tiger-print teddies, black leather bras, nylon panties from Wal-Mart with holes cut out of the crotch. Red candles burned in the window, and everyone knew what went on there. As long as they didn't do what they did out in the open, people in Royal Pines were willing to let them keep doing it. It was their way of makin' a living, and who wanted to be responsible for ruinin' someone else's livelihood? Most of the men who drove up to the trailer on the weekends were nice enough, quietly entering the trailer and just as quietly leaving.

J.T., the landlord of Royal Pines and biggest cheese around there, took a cut of the business that Kirk's sister generated and fielded any complaints the neighbors had. Usually all it took was offering the complaining woman's husband an hour with Kristy and the problem was solved—after all, they were proper ladies who always "obeyed" their husbands, weren't they?

Kristy was sixteen going on thirty. She'd gone to work part-time for J.T. last year, making money on the side while still going to high school. But this year things were so tight for their family, with Momma being on AFDC and smokin' crack, that she dropped out of school when she turned sixteen and went to work full-time. She would sleep until noon or one o'clock, wake up, eat a double Whopper with cheese for breakfast (which J.T. brought every afternoon) and service J.T. (he always demanded one free fuck a day as part of his fee—luckily he was pretty easy to please). Then she'd take a scalding-hot bath, shave her legs, and get ready for her first customer. She'd sit and watch MTV and read trashy novels that J.T. brought her until her first john showed up. When Anna came home from school, she'd stick Anna in the back room (it did have a bathroom, after all) and tell her to watch TV. Anna had learned a long time ago to take the frozen dinners out of the freezer and nuke them in the microwave, so she only had to worry about some strange man lookin' at her funny when she did it. Anna had gotten good at being really hard to see and really hard to hear. She knew somehow that the way J.T. looked at her was unhealthy. Luckily, she never had to speak to anyone, never wanted to speak to anyone, didn't think she could remember how to talk, not since Kirk had left.

Anna would nuke her dinner, then walk to the back room, lock herself in, and watch the same videotape over and over on the VCR: a collection of *Barney and Friends* videos turned up loud enough so that she didn't hear the sounds from her sister's business. She loved Barney, a purple dinosaur who loved everyone. She couldn't wait for the song that told her she was loved everyday. She wanted to believe Barney, but when her mother would come home from work (either at the paper factory or at the "lingerie model studio" that J.T. ran over on Cheshire Bridge Road), she'd usually come home in a bad mood. That meant a beating for Anna if she interrupted Mommy's smoking, or her shootin' up, which she usually did in the kitchen.

When Kirk and Sylvie materialized outside the trailer, Kirk shook his head at the three cars that were in the small driveway. He looked over at Sylvie, who looked concerned.

"Kirk. There's something you gotta know. I know you know how to do stuff—powers and all. I want you to know that everytime you mess with mortals with your powers, where you touch them, you give your Shadow a chance to screw with them. You need to watch how you use your powers around the living. Especially out here where people believe in ghosts and they're lookin' for any reason to get into the *Weekly World News* or something. Do you understand?"

Kirk nodded. "No fancy stuff. No showy stuff."

Sylvie nodded. "That, and no skinridin'. What you see, you have to accept, Kirk. You can't change it quickly, and you can't change it using your power. You have to fix things a different way."

Kirk nodded. "All right, then. Let's go see what's what. Looks like Mom's not home yet."

Kirk stepped through the closed door of the trailer, feeling a pang of familiarity at the place. He saw his Elvis collector's plate on the wall, saw his Atlanta Falcons pennant that he had gotten the first time he saw them play at the stadium. But his attention was distracted as he heard the door to his sister's room open up and she came walkin' out, a cigarette tucked daintily between two fingers. She was wearing a purple nylon teddy with a black garter belt, and stockings that had runs in them. Her face looked like an Avon lady's nightmare, although Kirk could see where her customers might see it as being "exotic." Two guys were flanking her, wearing nothing but their white T-shirts, boxer shorts, and boots.

Kirk shook his head, not wanting to see what she was going to do with them. She unfolded a futon in the living room, grinning wickedly as she said, "Now, y'all know there's an extra charge for two guys at once. I don't do anythin' kinky without chargin' for it. Why don't y'all just put your money down first, before we get started? That way, we don't have to worry about it later."

The two big country-lookin' guys went for their wallets (they kept them tucked in their boots) and counted out a hundred dollars each. "Is this enough?" one of them asked, grinning.

Kristy nodded, brushing one of her peroxide-blond strands out of her face. She walked back down the hallway and threw the bills into her money jar. Kirk turned his face from what happened next, walking down the hallway. He peered into his sister's bedroom and saw that she had taken his TV and had bought a brand-new VCR (the box was still next to it) that she was using to show porn videos. Kirk walked past his door, which was padlocked like he had left it. He remembered the drugs he had stored in there, wondered for a second if he could somehow get in there and get those drugs. He realized Mr. Demon was chuckling to himself.

"I'll help you get that door open," Mr. Demon said, laughing.

Kirk shook his head. That time was past: how was he gonna be able to deal dope from beyond the grave, anyway? What was he thinking? He did worry in the back of his mind about someone finding the drugs and busting his family, but then realized that it was probably only a matter of time before they were busted; either that, or J.T. was also payin' off the cops to keep them out of trouble. That would be his style.

Kirk walked to the rear of the trailer. He saw Anna, her knees tucked up underneath her, clutching her Barney doll and singing quietly along with the video. The TV screen was the only source of light in the room, and Kirk felt a pang of fear for his little sister. She was so small, so delicate. He smiled as he saw the teddy bear he'd given her so many years ago (now old and battered, with an eye missing) enjoying a place of honor next to her pillow.

Sylvie whispered to Kirk, "The innocent can see us sometimes, Kirk. Be careful."

Kirk took off his mask, and looked at Anna closely. He didn't want to scare her, but he desperately wanted to talk to her.

Anna looked up from her video and glanced around the room as if to see where the sound had come from. She looked right at Kirk.

"K-Kirk?" Anna said, looking at him wide-eyed.

Kirk nodded. "You can see me?"

Anna nodded quietly.

Kirk smiled. "How are ya, pooh?" He sat down on the bed next to her.

"Not so good, I ah, I've been sick. Had the flu or somethin'. J.T. won't take me to the doctor, keeps makin' me drink Nyquil until I go to sleep. I hate him. I thought you were dead. That's what Mama said," Anna said in a nearly monotone voice, one that belied the intensity of the emotions underneath.

"I am dead, Anna. I'm just here for you to see me," Kirk said. "I'm wantin' to help you get out of here. Do you want to go?"

Anna nodded slowly. "Yeah. I don't like Kristy's job. J.T. looks at me funny. And Mama been takin' too much medicine lately. Kirk, are you gonna take me away?"

Kirk shook his head. "No, sugar. I'm not. But . . . but I'm going to get you out of here somehow. You might have to be here a little longer."

"What are you gonna do, Kirk?" Anna asked, her brown eyes wide with wonder.

"Somethin'. I don't know what, not yet. I'm gonna find someone who'll take you out of this place," Kirk said.

"Oh, I don' wanna go to no foster home where they make you go to bed early and don't let you watch Barney! I heard about that from a kid at school," Anna said.

Kirk grinned. "Well, we'll see what I can do, Anna. I just want you to hang tight here, okay?"

Anna nodded. "Have you seen Daddy?"

Kirk looked over at Sylvie, then back at Anna. "Why do you ask, Anna?" Kirk said, trying to hide concern from his voice.

"Oh. Because I figured you'd see him, since he's dead, too. Is he helpin' you?" Anna asked.

Kirk shook his head. "Nope. I . . . I don't know if Daddy is here or not, Anna. Not for sure."

Anna nodded. "You remember when you used to tell me stories about him being brave and strong and good? I used to believe that he watched over me, even though he was dead. Like you. Now that I see you, I guess I was right. He did watch over me. Right?" Anna asked.

A cold shot of fear ran though Kirk. "I—I guess so, Anna. Have you ever seen Daddy, like you've seen me?"

"Daddy? Oh, no. I've only seen the Wolfman, like you. He comes and watches Kristy work sometimes. He likes to watch her. Then he watches Mommy take her medicine and sometimes yells at her. But Daddy's never been here," Anna said.

Kirk nodded, a dark chill rushing through him. "Does this Wolfman sometimes wear a mirror-mask?" Kirk asked.

"He has a mirror-mask that he puts on when he leaves. I saw him leave one night when I was outside playing," Anna said quietly.

Kirk felt the cold of Oblivion stealing through his entire body. He clenched his teeth, trying to force it out of him. He turned around to Sylvie. "Does Greymaster have a Fetter here?" Kirk asked.

Sylvie wasn't surprised at the question, but it was clear that she wanted Kirk to come by the information he was seeking through his own efforts. Sylvie nodded slowly, in the direction of the hallway.

Kirk turned back to Anna. "I have to take a walk now, Anna. I'll be back in a little bit."

Anna nodded and went back to watching her video.

Kirk walked back into the hall, followed by Sylvie. He could hear the grunts and cries coming from the living room and shuddered. He felt Demon inside him waking up at that sound: heard him whispering something foul about going and watching it, but he wouldn't do that. He stood at the door of his room, looking at the LEGALIZE POT NOW! sticker on the door, and looked at Sylvie, who nodded. "It's in there," she said.

Kirk stepped through his door and suddenly was in his old room. Looking around the room, he realized that nothing in it was really that important to him. His bed was still unmade, his clothes were lying around. No one had come in to clean the place up, or clear out his stuff. It was as if he had just left it and was going to be right back.

Sylvie held her hand out, slowly moving around the room. "I'm looking for the Fetter. It's around here someplace."

Kirk nodded. He felt the demon churning in his stomach, whispering to him, "Listen, listen." Kirk could barely stand, feeling the feelings he felt. His eyes blinked; he cleared his vision. What was that? What was it that memory denied him?

A hand, holding his. He looked down, down at the bed, sitting there quietly, his sixteen-year-old blood pumping, roaring through his veins. Kristy was there, she was moaning, she was moving hard against the man in her bed, her body covered in sweat.

A hand, holding his—a gloved hand. "How long would he watch?" his demon asked. He shuddered. He felt Demon making him watch, chittering as he watched, laughing at Kirk's reaction, watching his sister.

Kirk wanted to scream, he wanted to jab hot pokers in his eyes. He didn't want to be here anymore. He wavered, staring at Sylvie as she looked around the room. "Are you okay?" Sylvie said. "Oh damn, Kirk. You're not okay."

Now Kirk wasn't even seeing Sylvie. Kirk was looking down at his bed, watching as his sister changed positions and started moving again. His aura was dark, fiery motes dancing within him.

Sylvie sighed. "You've got to resist him, Kirk. That's the only thing I can tell you to do. Resist! Don't let him take you. Don't!"

Kirk felt the turning, the worms eating his guts. He sank to his knees, trying desperately to turn his face away. Demon laughed, keeping his eyes open. "You want to watch, don't you, Kirkie boy? Go ahead, boy. Watch. You'll love it," Demon spat into his ear.

Kirk shuddered again. Sylvie stood back away from him, afraid of what his Shadow might do to her if she got in its way. Kirk stood up and walked to the closet. His hand glowed with fire, and Sylvie saw it open. From out of the closet a sword floated—a military sword: a Marine sword. Even though it was tarnished and old, it was still clean. The sword floated to Kirk's hand. He stood there, fire in his eyes, holding the sword, watching as fire danced down the blade.

Sylvie realized that the sword was a physical object, something in the living world. Looking at it with her lifesight, she suddenly realized that the sword was the Fetter that Kirk was looking for. Greymaster's Fetter.

As Kirk made contact with the sword, flames danced down the blade. Suddenly, in the darkness of the room, he erupted into fire, burning bright. Wings spread from his back, and Sylvie's eyes got bright and large as she looked on the power of the Firebird.

Then, suddenly, the sword fell to the bed below it, and the fire burned off like fog on a summer morning.

Kirk looked hard at Sylvie, having shaken off Mr. Demon once again. "That's the Fetter, isn't it?" Kirk asked.

Sylvie nodded.

"My father's sword. I got that sword from the guys at his funeral. He had said he wanted me to have it. Hmm. Wonder why," Kirk said cynically.

Sylvie nodded. "Let's go, Kirk. It's not good to talk around someone's Fetter. They can sense it. I'm not sure if he can sense what just happened, but I think you shouldn't touch it again."

Kirk nodded. "I'm done here. I want to go to the Grey Wolves' place. I know what I have to do."

Sylvie nodded, unwilling and unable to change Kirk's mind.

"So, Firebird, you decided to return to us, did you?" came his father's voice from behind the grey mask.

"Yes, sir. I've seen enough of the Hierarchy to know that it's full of shit. I'd like to join contingent on guaranteeing some aid from you," Kirk said, Sylvie standing beside him. They had traveled through the Tempest easily and had been admitted to the Greymaster's presence almost immediately.

"What aid would that be?" Greymaster asked.

Kirk pushed a hank of his hair out of his face. "I

want to go in and rescue Rick, my buddy. He was taken by them."

Greymaster nodded his agreement. "Sounds fair enough. Gentlemen, if you will, get this soldier a kit and a gun. Will you be staying with your charge, Miss Sylvie, or do you trust my tender mercies?"

Sylvie looked at Kirk, who nodded at Sylvie. "I think he'll be all right on his own, Captain. I don't expect he'll be needin' my help no more."

Greymaster nodded. "We'll whip him into shape. Give him basic training in five days. That should teach him all he needs to know."

Sylvie nodded quietly, trying not to get emotional in front of the Greymaster. She looked worriedly at Kirk, but realized that this was the path of his destiny. He must walk his own road. Sylvie stood on her tiptoes and hugged Kirk, holding him briefly before releasing him.

"You know what to do," Kirk whispered in Sylvie's ear. They had discussed a few things during their travel, and Sylvie had agreed to every one of them.

Kirk stood staring at the Greymaster, wondering how much the man knew about him. Wondering if he knew that Kirk was fully aware of who he was. Whatever the case, Greymaster was playing his game very well, treating Kirk as any other Lemure he might take under his wing. But Kirk could feel Greymaster's eyes on him wherever he was in the room, and knew that something must be apparent to the wraith who was his father.

He could only wait for him to reveal his hand. Until then, Kirk would be the best damn little soldier that his father could ever want. Kirk was sure that he could do anything the man asked of him, and desperately wanted more training in the secrets of the magical arts that allowed wraiths to do special things.

Kirk was given a bedroll, a rifle, and a pale white cloak. He waved good-bye to Sylvie as they marched him off to his barracks. He couldn't help but wonder if this was, in some strange way, helping the demon inside him.

In the darkness of his barracks, he thought he could hear his sister, Anna, crying. He also wondered when he'd see his son again.

5

FATE AND
THE FATEFUL

One two three four
Every night we pray for war
Five six seven eight
Rape. Kill. Mutilate.
  —U.S. Marine Corps training chant,
    Camp Pendleton, quoted in
    the *San Francisco Chronicle*,
      January 6, 1989

Ghost Story:
The Swamps of Parris Island

You there, recruit. Do you want me to tell you that
your mother loves you? That you are her bestest
boy? Well, I won't. I won't, and you can hate me
for that. I give you permission to hate me, recruit.
In fact, if you can stop whimpering and sucking
wind long enough to find the energy to hate me, I
will be duly impressed with you for the first time
in your miserable life. But you should take heart,

recruit. Do you know why? Because I am not the DI in the swamp. I am not that man out there who rides boys like you until they are nothing but bloody flesh hanging off bones. I am not that man, because if I were, they'd lock me in the brig. But, son, let me tell you, if you ever decide that this is too much, that my tender mercies are too harsh, just tell me. I'll be glad to let that DI in the swamp take a crack at your hide.

Now why don't you get down there in that mud and give me fifty just for puttin' your filthy eyeballs on me. Let's go!

Kirk had become the subject of one man's torment. Something that was supposedly called "training." During the day, Kirk was forced to run the interior of the warehouse repeatedly, until he nearly discorporated from fatigue. At night, Kirk was given over to the tender mercies of Dr. Teeth and his unique teaching techniques.

Somehow, Dr. Teeth had managed to capture the bare essence of every power known to ghosts in the Shadowlands and store the essentials of them in his skulls: head bones he found floating in the Tempest, and some others that he collected himself. The skulls' eyes were the portal through which the uninitiated learned the secrets of power. But each time Kirk looked into the eyes of the skulls, Mr. Demon would come out of the black pit in the center of his skull and begin screaming in Kirk's ear. He would pass out, unconscious, and awaken the next morning with a severe headache. At first he didn't think it was having an effect. Then, one morning, Kirk was late for muster. He missed the morning call because he had to polish his boots and his mask. He was terrified to be late, not knowing what the DI (a terrible man from the swamps of Paris Island named "Gunter") would do to him if he was late for muster, but knowing that it was something he'd rather not do. However, being late entailed more than just not being there. AWOL was not being at the right place, at the right time, in the right uniform. So even if he skipped shining his mask, he would be AWOL.

Still, as he finished the last buffs of the mask, he put it on carefully and then began to run toward the parade ground out in front of the warehouse, in the old parking lot. Instead of running, however, Kirk suddenly found himself flickering through the Tempest and materialized just as the call to muster ended.

Gunter didn't let him off easily for that almost failure, however: sensing Kirk's lateness and his tension, Gunter rode the recruit the rest of the morning. He forced Kirk to stare at the bright sun until he was blind, then made him find a way through a rope maze. He hobbled Kirk's legs together by thrusting a Relic iron pin through them and then forced him to fight off two other armed soldiers. They beat him to a pulp, although Kirk learned that Gunter was even more sadistic than he thought: Gunter had Usury, the power to give back Corpus when it had been taken away. Gunter was able to essentially "heal" Kirk's wounds, thus enabling him to further torture the boy.

Several times Kirk felt like just giving up. But a feeling deep within him wanted to get through this, knew that his father would, somehow, respect him more if he did. And there were other things: his promise to Cindi, the hope that his son would still live. He knew he couldn't let them down.

Greymaster remained aloof, watching Kirk from afar, speaking with his instructors privately, treating him like every other new recruit. Kirk watched him out of the corner of his mask every time he was nearby, simultaneously attracted to and repelled by the man's presence. He knew that everything he was, and everything he could be, counted on him surviving this training.

Gunter gave him hell for his Firebird mask. He called him "birdie-birdie" most of the time, making him tweet and "flap his wings." Once, he threw Kirk from the roof of the warehouse to see if he could really fly. Gunter told him that he wasn't worthy to wear the wolf mask, that he would never be a Grey Wolf. Kirk took the curses in stride: inwardly he knew that the Firebird was his symbol, that he was the Firebird no matter what anyone else thought. It was not Mr. Demon's symbol: it represented something greater and more powerful than him.

The demon within him loved Gunter. Loved the torture that Kirk was going through. It grew strong; Kirk could feel it like a lead weight inside of him, a burning weight that curled up in his bowels like a fiery enema. Demon began to whisper taunts, curses, taking its cue from Gunter. They worked together: one hammered him from without, the other from within.

Still, Kirk never lost the feeling that something else was at stake here. He dreamed about his baby boy, dreamed about a new life for little Jeb and for Cindi and for Anna. The short minutes of slumber he got every day were filled with moments of pure peace, as if something was reaching out from Heaven to touch him. He wasn't sure what to think about that, but he did come to associate sleep with an almost reverential sense of worship. Sleep and dreams became the food and drink of his soul as his ghostly body was pounded, worked, tortured, trained, thrown, and burnt.

But, he learned much. He learned how to charge a gun with Pathos, the energy within him, "juice" his DI called it. He learned how to use a gun with soul-fire attached. He learned about darksteel, what it was, how it felt (he carried around a wound made by a darksteel dagger for three of the five days). He learned the proper names for all the powers of the dead, called Arcanos by the Domem (the older wraiths). He was told the complete history of Stygia, the Hierarchy, the Heretics (those churchy types that Sylvie had told him about), and the Renegades— from the first Renegades who escaped the tyranny of Stygia after the fall of Rome to the brave hordes that attacked the Onyx Tower just before the Third Great Maelstrom. He learned about Maelstroms, about the Nihils, which were gateways to the Tempest. He learned what the Tempest was: a place of chaos bordering on the "nothing," the Oblivion deep at the pit of everything. He was told that no matter what or in whom he believed, he'd better keep his beliefs to himself—the Grey Wolves weren't interested in any Heretic warriors among them. They were a mercenary company, pure and simple, working for themselves for the greatest part, except when Greymaster dictated otherwise. Greymaster had no serious political agenda—he simply wished to overthrow the local Hierarchy and take all the souls gathered there for himself, letting the bureaucracy of the soul trade handle the system just as it did now.

Kirk was forced to listen to long indoctrinations that several Wolfguards (the wraiths closest to Greymaster) gave to him and some of the other, lesser-ranked Grey Wolves. He became convinced that, even if they were not the Hierarchy, they would be just as bad or worse. He became hardened within himself as he entered the fifth day of training, realizing that, in order to continue, he would have to bury his true feelings deeply. The Ceremony of Initiation was nigh, something that the DI and Dr. Teeth had mentioned in passing several times: it was the ceremony which would make or break him as a Grey

Wolf. He would either be accepted into the group, the Cohort (which was what they called themselves) or he would be denied and destroyed. Kirk quaked with fear when he thought about the latter prospect.

Kirk had been assigned cleaning duty in the weapons locker, and he was cleaning the weapons with a dirty rag to keep the Oblivion crud off of them so that they didn't jam when they were fired. There was a large steamer trunk there, one that Kirk had never looked in, because it was always locked. On the fifth day, however, it was not locked like it usually was; he opened it up with a gasp. There in the steamer trunk was the backpack of plastic explosives that had been in the bunker: enough to make the entire warehouse jump in the living world. No telling what would happen if it was detonated in the Shadowlands: Kirk had learned that Maelstroms often resulted from terrible explosions in the Shadowlands. He had also learned that Pathos would be required to fuel the chemical reaction for the explosives. Kirk wondered what use Greymaster had for the bomb backpack, but didn't linger long looking at it, as his DI was soon back on his case, demanding that Kirk clean all the guns again.

As night fell on the fifth day, the call went out to summon all the Grey Wolves for a meeting. The moon was new: no light shone in the sky. One by one, the Grey Wolves flickered into being around the warehouse, adjourning within. The Greymaster sat resplendent on his throne, looking out at his crack assortment of troops, relishing the moment of them all being gathered together. Their grey cloaks, each of them a special artifact made by Dr. Teeth, shone mirror-bright in salute as Greymaster stood and called the meeting of the Cohort to order.

"Tonight we invite one of the Restless to enter our number, as once we all were invited. This is a special privilege at this time, just before our greatest triumph. Tonight, the operation we have been conducting for the past six months will come to fruition. Thanks to the diligence of our intelligence corps, we stand ready to proceed. We have but to initiate our own, and then send our teams out into the night, to secure the most precious objective we have ever sought—the power we will need to dominate this city and deny the Hierarchy their advantage. So, now, without further words, I give you Dr. Teeth for the initiation ceremony."

A low howling noise issued forth from the Wolves' masks, an eerie sound that made Kirk tremble within. Dr. Teeth emerged from behind a curtain, carrying a cup of strange liquid. The liquid burned from within: a kind of plasm mixed with "juice," was what Kirk made it out to be.

The cup was brought to the Greymaster's hand. "Thus we seal the training of this Wolf with the drink of fire. Let his true nature be revealed."

Greymaster handed Kirk the cup, which felt warm in his hand and steamed. Kirk looked at the drink and smelled the noxious fumes, and he tried in vain to hide the disgust he had for it. Then he realized what the cup meant: he would have to unmask for everyone to see while he drank.

Kirk slowly, carefully slid his Firebird mask up on his forehead. Looking warily at the rest of the Grey Wolves, but turning away from the face of the Greymaster, he tilted the cup and downed the whole drink.

Fire burned through him. He wanted to scream in pain, but he held it in. He felt the fire inside of him, burning, eating, desperately wanting to break free. He put his hands down by his sides, but the pain wracked through him and he went to his knees. The fire inside of him was vicious, angry, almost like drinking barrow-fire: a sentient kind of flame, it ate at him.

The scream that was building in him became too

much to contain, and he screamed aloud, an ejacula-
tion of raw pain. As he screamed, he realized that
fire was shooting up and out of his mouth. That he
was spreading his arms, which were becoming fiery
wings. The rest of the Grey Wolves stood back, moving away with great respect as his scream went off
the high end of the human scale and became a
screech. Fire boiled through the room.

Then, as quickly as it happened, it was over.

Kirk stood in the center of a ring of wraiths, who,
swords drawn, had already committed to destroying
him should he attack Greymaster. And in the silence
that followed the great fire, there came a low chuckling sound. For a second, Kirk couldn't tell whether it
was Greymaster or Mr. Demon chuckling. But soon
Greymaster began to laugh even louder, and he
stepped forward, through the ring of warriors, striding into the center of the circle and grasping Kirk by
the arms.

"Kirk! Kirk! My son! You!" the Greymaster said.
"Look at them! You scared the fuck out of every single
one of them. They'd have shit their pants if they still
did that sort of thing. Look at them. Well, my great
Grey brothers, this here is my son—my son! Come
to join our grand and glorious organization! Well, boy, I
had no fuckin' idea. I had no idea who you were. You've
changed quite a bit, you have. Where's that half-assed
drug addict I used to know, eh? Eh? I know where he
went. He got ate up, chewed up and spit out, didn't he?
Didn't he? Gunter took right care of you, didn't he?"

Kirk was grinning, but it was a false grin, one that
he sincerely hoped his father couldn't read. As his
father unmasked himself, Kirk suddenly felt a wave
of hatred and fear boil up from within him. "Hello,
Father," he said quietly.

"My Wolves! Welcome my son into our ranks!
He's survived the initiation, and it's time to link his

lifeweb to the Wolf," James Rourke said, his grey mask now cast aside.

A curtain was pulled in the living world, and a terrible sculpture was revealed above the Greymaster's throne. It was a large, ravening, slavering, enraged wolf's head, a mask made of pure iron and steel that had been forged in the living world and hung there.

Kirk looked at the monstrous thing and thought, *Geez. How stupid . . .* for a moment. Then the thing looked at him. Looked into him. It seemed to move in the shadowy light, beckoning him forward.

Kirk walked toward the great wolf-head. Dr. Teeth motioned to two Wolfguards, who came to stand between him and it. They touched Kirk, pulling as they did a single strand of light from him, a strand which stretched thinner as they pulled. They placed the two strands in the wolf's mouth, and it closed shut.

Suddenly, Kirk felt drawn toward the wolf, as if it were pulling him closer and closer. The rest of the wolves howled as he was pulled up and into the wolf, vanishing from sight.

Kirk felt, for a moment, completely subsumed by the intensity of the energy flowing through him. He looked down at his body, at the center of forty separate strands of light, all of them radiating out from the center of the wolf mask. Kirk felt himself being connected to the mask in some tangible way, felt his consciousness extend to it and its vicinity just as the forging was complete.

Kirk knew, without a doubt, that the wolf mask was now a Fetter for him; a weak one, true, but one nonetheless.

So, Kirk thought to himself, *this is how they achieve such complete unity and operate so closely together.* A central Fetter would allow them to do many things, including defend their headquarters even when they were away. Kirk had learned much from Dr. Teeth's teaching skulls: much information that came unbidden to him when he chose to concentrate.

Feeling the connection complete, Kirk emerged from the mouth of the mask and stepped down to the floor below. "You are now one of us, a Grey Wolf," Greymaster called out. "We salute you!"

The Wolves howled, their voices carrying out into the night. Kirk howled back at them in response and was admitted into their midst, one of them, belonging but not belonging. Kirk donned his mask again, shaking hands and being welcomed by all those around him.

He couldn't help but think of the day, soon, when he would get to the truth of it all.

The Midnight Express is one of the mysteries that the dead live with on a nightly basis. When one is dead, the strange and bizarre seem commonplace: it's not hard to accept that a ghost train boils up out of darkness each night at midnight, as it occurs all over the world. The train follows midnight as it strikes on clocks all over the planet.

The express has cars from virtually every decade since the locomotive engine revolutionized travel in the early 1800s: boxcars from the infamous Holocaust trains to Auschwitz, cars from the Simplon-Orient Express, Pullman cars, cars from the Old West, cars from circus trains. No one in Atlanta knew how Engine #13 was assembled, only that a Ferryman ran it, and it was always, *always* on time.

Because it was run by one of the Ferrymen, Kirk knew that very few wraiths were willing to risk the power of a Ferryman and attack the train. It was something usually reserved for fools and crazy wraiths to try. And yet, tonight, because of the shipment of soulfire that the Grey Wolves had discovered would be on the train, they were willing to take the risk.

Greymaster briefed his troops in the shadow of the great wolf mask. One of his Wolfguards wove his own energy into the essence of dreams to show a diagram of the attack site, painstakingly memorized and carefully recreated. The diagram was three-dimensional: it was of the Avondale MARTA station—several stops before the Five Points Station on the east line.

"At twenty-three-thirty hours this evening, we will ride the MARTA to the attack site, all cloaked. Utter silence should be in effect. The train will appear here—" Greymaster indicated the spot with his finger on the three-dimensional image, which flickered and grew in size as he spoke. "It will slow to a stop inside the Avondale Station, at which time Team Alpha will cause a diversion for the skinlanders on the bridge, here." Greymaster pointed to the bridge which spanned a highway, connecting the station with the parking area.

"Then, Maslow, your team will be responsible for skinriding any cops in the zone and clearing the platform. This is important, as we don't want any Hierarchy types who might show up interfering with the activity. It is imperative that the platform get clear, and get clear quickly, before the train arrives. The train will pull into the station at roughly twenty-three-fifty hours, as it will still be scheduled to make its stop at twenty-four hundred hours in the Five Points Station. I know J.W., the conductor, and he's a stickler for the train being on time. And, of course, unless he and his Ferryman put up a fight, we shouldn't be a factor in delaying the train. Let me make this absolutely and positively clear: in anyone's dealing with the train, you're going to have to keep in mind two things. First, do not under any circumstances threaten or attack the train itself unless you get word from me. Now you know why some of you who've got particularly gung-ho Shadows have been assigned to Team Alpha: we can't have you Shadowing out and attacking the train. I have heard tales of the power of the Ferryman who runs the express: he's got Arcanos that we've never seen, and his scythe has been known to shatter wraiths into a thousand shards, making ghost hamburger before reforming. This guy's a major player, and I don't want to tick him off in the least. Well, not any more than we're already going to just by doing this. Second of all, and this is important, too: don't delay the train. Don't get in its way, don't stop it. Don't try to get someone else to stop it. This will also piss the Ferryman off. In my experience, he doesn't mind fighting going on inside the train and on the platform: he takes offense when someone attacks the train or makes it late. So let's not offend him, gentlemen. Now. We have reason to believe that a special Hierarchy freight car will be attached to the express this time. The freight car will hold not only the soulfire but roughly ten to thirteen Hierarchy Legionnaires guarding it. It's important that Team Beta be on deck and ready to move against this car as soon as possible. If all goes well, our operative aboard the express will have secured final plans and all will run well.

"Beta: you folks are in charge of engaging the Hierarchy people inside the freight car and keeping them busy for the two minutes that the train will be paused at the station. That is all. There's nothing else for you to do. We'll take care of the rest. Now, who's not taken care of by this?"

Kirk raised his hand. "What team am I in, sir?" Kirk asked quietly.

"Kirk, you're with me. Command and control. We'll be monitoring things from the other side of the tracks, encloaked."

Kirk nodded. He couldn't help but feel the sudden wave of jealousy that swept through some of the Wolves.

"Anyone have a problem with that?" Greymaster asked, looking around. "Truth be told, I can't trust a green recruit to anything complicated. This mission is too important. So, if you folks think I'm playing favorites, you've got another thing comin'," Greymaster said sternly.

The Wolves stood quietly. Greymaster nodded. "Good. Good. I'm glad we're all in agreement. It's important for this job. Now, Team Delta, you folks are the rear guard, support, and in charge of moving HQ. I imagine the Hierarchy already knows about this place, and besides, we've been here too long anyway. You folks have been assigned some skinpuppets to drive the mask and the rest of the Relics to the new HQ. I want you to be in touch by Harbinger as soon as you're in position, and I want it to be by twenty-two hundred hours, at the very latest. Make sure you're not followed. Folks, I believe we all know our jobs here, so let's get cracking, and we'll close the operation down by oh-two hundred hours. Vanish well, my Grey Wolves. Don't disappoint me," Greymaster said, and there was a roar of men running to various positions, forgetting for a moment that they were soldiers who had died once already—like all good commanders, Greymaster had convinced them that they would not die this time.

A light rain was falling. Inside her hospital room, Cindi held on to her baby, rocking him quietly. She pulled the covers up around him. He was sleeping, a blessed event. He had screamed all day long. She thought back to the night she'd given birth, the vision of Kirk she'd seen and the promise he'd given, to always be there.

"Well, Kirk," Cindi said quietly. "Well. If you are keeping your promises, which I doubt, you're around here someplace. Someplace. You better be, damn it. Can't you do something to help keep Jeb alive? They tell me he has an even chance to live, but Kirk, that's not good enough. An even chance to live is an even chance to die, Kirk. You have to know, you have to know how to help him," Cindi said, looking out the window, tears mirroring the raindrops on the glass.

Then, somehow, Cindi knew he was there. Somehow, he was there, listening to her. She felt something—a presence—in the room.

"Kirk?" She spoke quietly.

Kirk had felt the pull all the way from the warehouse, and knowing what he knew about Argos, he didn't need Sylvie this time to visit Cindi. He simply wished himself there, and he was flying through the cold of the Tempest. Standing in the hospital room, looking at his little boy, at his girlfriend, he took a step toward the tiny light with the dark streaks running through it. He looked at Jeb, lying there, asleep on his mother's tummy, and felt a pure twinge of love as he looked at his gentle, delicate face and little hands. He wanted to hold the boy, to caress him, but couldn't. Somehow, he knew that's what the boy needed the most.

Cindi relaxed as she felt his presence, although Kirk felt her will flagging and realized she could not hold the child in her arms forever.

Stepping out of the room, Kirk walked down to the nurse's station. The only person there was a hospital volunteer, a woman dressed in a peach blouse and slacks, her grey hair up in a bun—someone's grandmother.

Kirk sat down next to the woman, who was knitting something. He could feel the loneliness dripping off her like rain off of an old tenement building.

Looking at her, he could tell that she had raised many children, loved them all, and watched them leave the house, one by one, forgetting about her.

How many times had she sat, lonely, like this? Kirk didn't know. But he knew that she needed something Kirk could offer her.

Kirk took off his Firebird mask and set it on the file cabinet. He clasped his hands together and quietly began to talk to her, humming phrases of music as he did, whispering in her ear. He felt the fullness of his idea, of his need, begin to cause his own energy to be released: he saw it as streaming blue and green light out of his hands and his throat as he hummed. As he spoke, his words became her ideas.

"You need a new person to look after, ma'am. You were always looking after children, and now your children are all gone. They're too busy to have children of their own. You need to hold a baby, listen to its heartbeat, listen to him breathing. Now, ma'am, there's a baby just down the way, just down the way. Do you remember the new baby just down the way? The baby which was born hurt. He needs so much attention. Do you remember?" Kirk whispered into her ear, hoping that at least her heart would hear. For a moment, she did nothing.

Then she looked up, put down her knitting needles, and walked over to the floor registry. Looking at the list, her finger slid down it until she reached Cindi's room. Kirk nodded, walked up behind her. "Yes. That's it. Go for it," he whispered into her ear.

Whether or not she heard him, she glanced at her watch. Shaking her head, she started to walk back toward her seat. Just at that moment, Jeb woke up and down the hall came the sound of an infant screaming. Kirk could feel the anguish and the need in that cry. The woman shook her head again and started to pack up her knitting for the night.

"No! You can't! You can't just turn your back on him. He needs you," Kirk yelled at the woman.

She looked up, as if she had heard, but then turned back to her bag again.

Kirk cursed under his breath. Jeb let out another long wail. "Please. I need you," Kirk said quietly.

"You can't force her to love someone, Kirk," came a voice behind him. He whirled, his grey cloak flowing behind him. "Who said that?" Kirk said.

"It's me, Kirk. Doncha remember Sylvie?" she said, stepping out of the shadows. "My, my. Don't you look nice? All dressed up," Sylvie said. Her voice and manner did not match her congratulatory words.

Kirk turned around. "Something has to be done. I can't keep leaving you as a baby-sitter for them both."

Sylvie shook her head. "That Cindi girl's on her last legs, Kirk. I don't know if she's gonna make it. She's been playin' with fire in her head, thinking death thoughts. The power to change is still hers, but . . . Fate doesn't smile on that child. Not unless somethin' changes soon, Kirk."

Kirk nodded at the woman, now waiting for the elevator. "That's what I'm trying to do."

Sylvie shook her head. "It has to be her choice to get involved, Kirk. You can't make her. You can't force people to do what you want. Do you want your son to start down the path you're on?"

Kirk turned to look at the woman, then whirled on Sylvie. "What do you mean? What path?"

Sylvie shook her head slowly. "I—I—can't say, Kirk. I've made a promise. You have to understand that."

Kirk nodded slowly. "All right. So you know I'm doing something wrong, but you can't tell me what?"

Sylvie gritted her teeth. "No! I can tell you. I told you. Don't force it. The living must go their own way. You can suggest. You can ask. You can plead.

But you can't force them to do what they should. That is the way of things."

"Who says?" Kirk spat.

"I say," Sylvie said quietly.

"That ain't good enough," Kirk growled.

"It has to be. It used to be." Sylvie stood quietly in front of Kirk, watching as the storms of his Shadow started to move, like an advancing front, across his countenance.

Sylvie held up her hand, watching as the elevator door opened and the woman stepped inside. Kirk was almost growling as he watched the elevator door close. He turned on Sylvie, who stood with her arms folded.

"Look how you've changed, Kirk. How much have you been changed in the past five days? What about the plans you and I made? Have you forgotten?" Sylvie said accusingly. The door to the elevator bank next to them opened, and the night nurse came on duty, cursing quietly that the volunteer had left her post early.

Kirk watched her and turned back to Sylvie, standing well out of the way of the mortal. "No, I haven't forgotten. I—I just want to know how he's going to stay alive. I don't want him to die." They continued standing in the hall, looking down it and listening to the cries of the baby in the background.

"Jeb? Kirk, Jeb's got a fightin' spirit, somethin' fierce. He's got a fire in him. Just like his pa. He's gonna do fine, if we can find him some help. If we can get someone to watch over him. And I want you to do that. But you got things to do right now. Things you know you should do. Things you can't turn away from. It's your Fate," Sylvie said again, this time more firmly.

Kirk's eyes squinted. "I don't believe in Fate. Ain't no such thing."

Sylvie nodded. "Perhaps you're right Kirk. Fate's not a strong argument anymore. But look inside yourself. You told me to do these things, to look for your friend, to look out for Anna and Jeb. To get you information. And your Circle is waiting. Just like you asked for. Just like you needed."

Kirk nodded slowly. "Yes. Just like I needed. And they came through for me?"

"Yes. They're waiting for my word. I came here to see if you still wanted to go through with it. You know you're throwin' away all the training you've gone through. You know they'll try to destroy you after this, no matter what the cost. You can never go back," Sylvie said seriously.

Kirk nodded. "I know. It—it doesn't matter." Kirk thought for a moment about his father, about how proud he was of Kirk's achievement, and felt a shiver of sadness run through them. "Not much, anyway," Kirk said.

"I always knew you were a traitor, a rat's ass fuckin' traitor'," Mr. Demon said inside his head. "If only I could I'd scream it out to every fuckin' wraith in hearin' distance. You slip up once, and I'll spill the whole can of beans, buddy-boy. I'll blow the whistle so loud they'll nail you seconds afterward. You better watch your step, you whining mama's boy. One slip, and you're mine."

Kirk's frown turned to a slow grin. "I must be doin' somethin' right, Miss Sylvie. Mr. Demon's got a firecracker up his butt."

Sylvie laughed. "It's not always reliable, doin' the exact opposite of what Mr. Demon wants. But it's a good indicator you're goin' in the right direction."

Kirk nodded. He flung open his grey cloak and took a step forward to wrap his arms around Sylvie and hug her.

She smiled. "I don't get too many of those. It's good to know you're still on the team, Kirk."

Kirk nodded. "Do you think we have a chance in hell?"

Sylvie shook her head. "Nah. But we do have a chance here. Now, here. Take this."

She gave Kirk what looked to be a little toy compass and a silver figure-eight pendant. They glowed from within, just a little.

"That compass will find Rick's soul. It's keyed to him," Sylvie said quietly. "Just give it a little juice if it starts to get dim."

Kirk nodded. "Lifeweb?" he asked quietly.

Sylvie shook her head. "A family secret, sort of. A different sort of magic."

Kirk nodded. "And the figure eight?"

Sylvie grinned. "That's not a figure eight. It's an infinity symbol. Don't give it to anyone but Rick: it won't work on anyone but him. Give it the juice, put it around Rick's neck, and get the heck out of there. Rick will be safe after that."

"What the hell? What will happen?" Kirk asked.

"He'll be taken out of there. Taken to where the Hierarchy can't get him," Sylvie said.

"Where will he go? Heaven?" Kirk whispered.

"Never you mind, Kirk Rourke. You just do what you're supposed to do," Sylvie said quietly.

Kirk nodded. His face changed as he remembered something. "Wait! Sylvie! I just remembered something. The Wolves: they're looking to get a big source of power. Some kind of massive energy source."

Sylvie nodded. "The ration of soulfire from Stygia. It's due on the next Midnight Express. It will be guarded, and—wait a second. They plan on attacking the express?"

Kirk nodded.

"They're crazier than I thought. Kirk, don't you get in the way of the Ferryman who runs that train. He will hurt you, and badly," Sylvie warned.

Kirk grinned. "You folks are really scared of those Ferrymen aren't you? They must be tough shit."

"Something like that," Sylvie agreed.

Kirk thought for a moment. "How am I going to get to Rick during all this?" he asked.

Sylvie smiled. "You know how to ride a train, don't ya?"

Kirk nodded. "What will happen if the Greymaster gets that power, Sylvie?"

Sylvie shrugged. "Who knows? I can't imagine he'll be any better a ruler than the Hierarchy."

"No, he won't. He's a bastard through and through. And his men are very highly trained. I think he'll rule the city like it was a military base," Kirk said quietly.

"You know I'm with you, Kirk. We all are," Sylvie said.

Kirk nodded slowly. "All the way?"

Sylvie smiled. "Yes. All the way."

Freda and Duke were encloaked with darkness, crouched at the outer edge of the Grey Wolves' security perimeter. Duke ticked off their current operation in his head: he had been in the 'Nam too, just like some of these guys. He knew what they were doing—looked like a standard convoy setup: a mortal moving truck and a pickup. Three skinpuppets (their aural glow black and grey with their possessors' own auras) hustled something covered in canvas into the waiting truck, and with a minimum of time wasted, they slammed the rear door down and moved out.

Duke turned and nodded to Jojo on the roof of a nearby building, who then vanished. He turned to Freda. "Let's catch the next train to Avondale, shall we?"

Freda nodded.

———

Jojo materialized next to Sylvie, smiling, his long fingers draped over her shoulder. She jumped. "Don't do that!" she said. "You scared me."

Jojo grinned behind his monkey mask. "They got movement. We ready to go. Hey, Kirk."

Kirk grinned. "Hey, Jojo. Thanks buddy. I—gotta go say good-bye."

Jojo nodded. "Give the little tot some of this—" he said, smiling, reaching out with his finger to give Kirk some Pathos.

Kirk nodded, accepting the energy. "Thanks."

Jojo nodded. "He's a good boy."

Kirk grinned and walked down the hall. He turned the corner and saw Cindi rocking the boy in her rocking chair, her arms shaking. He walked up to Cindi quietly.

Touching her, he gave her some of the energy he had for Jeb, and she immediately calmed down. He turned and touched Jeb, as well, crooning as he did so, and Jeb slowly began to wind down, like a steaming tea kettle being lifted off the stove, his cries less piercing, until finally the little boy grew quiet and snuggled close in between his mother's breasts.

"You be good, now, you hear? I'll be back," Kirk whispered. Jeb turned his head around to look at Kirk for a second and actually smiled at him.

Sylvie touched Kirk on the arm. "Come on, Kirk—it's getting close to time to move out. You'll be missed back at the warehouse."

Kirk pointed at Jeb, smiling. "Look! He smiled at me!"

Sylvie shook her head. "Kirk, you don't know nothin' about babies. He probably just got gas or somethin'. Come on," she said, pulling him into the hallway.

Kirk stopped at the door and waved good-bye to Jeb, who giggled at him. Grinning, feeling somehow recharged, he walked back down the hall to Jojo.

"See ya later, dude. Thanks for everything," Kirk said as he grasped the edges of his cloak and pulled it up around him. A cloud of black Tempest-energy whirled around him, and he was gone.

Kirk almost didn't make muster. He stood next to the Wolfguards as they waited for Greymaster to emerge from his quarters. Team Alpha had already left for the site. Team Beta was going through a final weapons check before moving out. Kirk felt the tug of the now-hidden mask as it was being moved. No wonder Greymaster wanted it in position before they moved out: it would distract the entire troop if it was constantly popping up in their thoughts. Kirk realized that sharing a common Fetter was a great strength and a great weakness at the same time.

Then the Greymaster emerged and all snapped to attention, even Beta Team, who were splayed out across the floor inspecting their weapons.

"As you were, men," Greymaster rumbled under his mirror mask. "Kirk. I looked for you earlier. Where were you?" Greymaster said quietly.

"I had to go get some juice, sir. Sorry for my absence," Kirk said quietly.

Kirk felt his father's eyes sweep across him even though he couldn't see them behind the mask. He felt the tingle of some Arcanos being used on him. "You didn't go runnin' to the Hierarchy, did ya, boy? Or back to that Sylvie bitch?" he asked quietly.

Kirk felt Mr. Demon well up inside of him and clenched his teeth as he forced the foul thing back down. "No, sir. Just around the corner."

Greymaster nodded. "Very well, then. You ready to kick some ass?" he asked quietly.

"Sir?" Kirk said softly.

"You heard me. You ready?" Greymaster demanded.

"Sir, yes, sir. I'm ready," Kirk said.

Greymaster nodded. Kirk wondered if his father had more in mind for him than just "command and control" like he had said earlier. "Very well,. then, troops. Let's move out to the site. Let's go! Midnight approaches!"

The packs of Grey Wolves moved out, vanishing into the night as they did.

Kirk felt the compass and the eternity necklace in his pocket grow cold as they entered the Tempest, and realized that he felt ghost vibrations in his chest as he remembered what it was like, long ago, when his heart used to pound. He felt that way again, just like he used to feel before a big fight or before his main connection would happen. His heart beating quickly, adrenaline running through his veins—this was what it felt like. As he stepped out of the Tempest on the other side of the jump (one of the Wolfguards leading the way), he realized that some of the other wraiths there were also lit from within by the passion of the moment.

Kirk shook his head, looking at the railway with its third rail on the other side of the track and at the train station as normal, mortal trains arrived and departed on about a ten-minute cycle. Kirk was willing to bet that, somehow, tonight the mortal train wouldn't coincide with the Midnight Express.

"Kirk, I want to speak with you a moment," the Greymaster said, pulling Kirk off to one side. "You've got a special mission in this," he said quietly.

Kirk felt a cold chill go through him. "Sir. I'm ready, sir."

"Don't give me that drill instructor crap. I want you to listen to me. You're going to have to do something

to impress the heck out of these guys, or they will
never follow you," Greymaster said, quietly.

"Like what?" Kirk said.

"Like, you're going to have to save the day here.
Now, listen to me, boy, and listen good. If you fuck
this up, I'll have your ass in a sling so fast it'll make
your head spin. I want you attach yourself to the
Crystal Sphere that's going to be waiting on you on
the other side of that train door and encloak it. Make
it vanish, along with you. Then I want you to Flicker
it one car down, either way. I don't care which. You
decide. Pick a good car, though, boy. There's some
foul cars on the express, places you don't want to go
into at all. Then, just hold it until the backup gets
there and off-loads the sphere. You might be
attacked by some passengers, but I think you can
handle that, can't you?"

"Sir. Yes, sir," Kirk said.

Greymaster nodded. "Tonight will be glorious, my
son. We will rule this city, after this. And you will
become recognized among my Wolves as the Firebird
of prophecy: the bringer of the winds of change! Heh.
I hate that prophecy crap. But it works—I've seen it
too many times not to believe in it."

Kirk nodded. He watched as Team Beta boiled up
out of the Tempest, then perched on the pylons
which held up the south side of the station, across
the way from the main platform.

Kirk looked at a bank clock just down the street: it
read 11:48. He felt the rush of anticipation and, off
in the distance, heard a lone whistle—a train call in
the darkness.

6

GHOST TRAIN

Ghost Story:
The Midnight Express

When you've worked the railyards as long as I have, boy, you learn not to look down the track so many times. You deal with the train in front of you, not the one comin' down the track. Why's that, you ask? Well, because of the ghost trains that'll come down the track if you're lookin' for them. You don't believe me? They'll rush up out of the darkness on a full head of steam and nearly run you over. Used to be, when I was a boy, I'd see one pass by my window every night, just about midnight: the whole thing growlin', huffin', and puffin', rushin' by full of old cars that got themselves wrecked at some point. If you see one of those trains, boy, don't you dare look into the conductor's eyes: he's been known to scare a man completely to death before. Just you watch. Heh. Or don't watch . . .

The Midnight Express was on time, as always. It boiled up out of a Nihil and rushed onto the tracks near Avondale Station, heading for its first stop. The Grey Wolf agent on board was named Brenner, and she had asked to depart at the Avondale stop for "security reasons" when she boarded the train the night before. It had been a rough twenty-four hours for Brenner, who had to share the compartment with just about every freak of death she had ever seen. She was glad this was nearly over, even though she still had some work to do and the truly stressful part of this mission wasn't exactly over.

She had already managed to do what she had come to do: a small chip of the giant wolf mask, magically imbued by Dr. Teeth months before, had been placed under the sphere of soulfire in the Hierarchy freight car attached to the train. She had used her grey cloak to enhance her ability to Enshroud and move unseen through the Hierarchy's watchful security. She had even positioned herself so she would be able to run out and throw open one of the freight doors at the appropriate moment.

She felt the curious motion of the train change as they moved closer to the station. Any moment now, and all hell would break loose. Behind her wolf mask, she smiled. This was going to be *fun.*

"You sure you've got your orders straight, boy?" Greymaster said, looking down at Kirk.

"Yes, sir. I'm sure. You want me to nab the soulfire, cloak it, and move it to another car. I think I can do that. One problem, though. How do I find the soulfire in the train?" Kirk said, trying not to let his nervous voice or the demon inside him betray his true feelings.

"A fragment of the wolf mask should be in place near or on the thing. Just Argos in there to it. Even a green recruit like yourself should be able to do that."

Kirk nodded slowly.

Greymaster put a large hand on his shoulder. Kirk felt the man's terrible sword scrape against his side. "You ain't havin' second thoughts, are you, boy?"

Kirk shook his head. "I—I—just want to do good for you, sir." He realized it was only partially a lie. He actually did want to make his father proud of him, in some sick way. He couldn't forget the fact that here was the man who used to comfort him in dreams, who was always watching out for him, or so he thought. But then there was the Fetter, and what Anna had said about the Wolfman. What was that all about?

Greymaster grinned behind his mask. "Yeah, I know, boy. That's good. That's real good. When you're done here, I want to show you the good side of this life. You have to know that there are some sweet, really sweet, things you can do when you're a spook. Things you couldn't ever even think about when you were alive." He laughed. "You'll probably get a kick out of it."

Kirk looked up at his father, for a second wondering if the man's Shadow had taken control of him from the way his voice sounded. But there was no dark aura, no tangible sign that it held sway. Kirk had never seen the Greymaster's Shadow come out before and wondered morbidly what it looked like, what it did.

Kirk was amazed at all the thoughts running through his head as he waited for the train to arrive at the station. Time seemed to stand still. He was suddenly seized with a deep, gripping fear, a fear like he'd never felt before. As if cold hands were clutching around his heart. He had no idea where this feeling had come from (although some reasonable part of him had already begun to suspect Mr. Demon), but he suddenly realized that he would rather be anything else, do anything else than what he was doing. It was all he could do not to Flicker out of there and leave.

He wrapped his hand around the infinity pendant, holding on to it for strength. It gave him cold comfort, but somehow its certainty, and his promise to Rick, kept him in place.

Then he saw it: the train. Chugging down the line, a curl of black sulfur smoke boiling up out of its stack, the number thirteen illuminated by the glow of its single headlight. He thought he could even see the red glow of twin eyes in the engineer's compartment, the black robe of the Ferryman glowing from the fires that ran the engine.

Kirk felt the chill of his final decision wash over him. It was time to do what he was meant to do. It was as if the light of the train galvanized him into action.

"Prepare, boy. Don't fuck this one up," Greymaster said quietly, drawing his blade and vanishing from sight.

The train loomed closer.

"Train sighted. Get ready," Duke said.

Freda nodded, wordlessly arming herself. "I just hope the kid makes his move. Otherwise this is going to be a real short trip."

"Give the wolfies my love," Duke said, grinning.

Freda managed a wolfish smile from behind her mask. "Oh, I'm sure they'll be delighted to see me," Freda said. Jojo moved his hands over the mask she wore, crooning to it, feeling it changing. "What was that?" she asked.

"Just a little surprise for the wolfies, yes? Yes. Surprise!" Jojo cackled.

Freda shrugged her shoulders, but she knew better than to ask the trickster Jojo about his business. She posed like a striking cobra, waiting for the train to enter the station.

The light rain was still falling in the parking lot of the MARTA station when felony theft took place.

"Hey, man, what you doin' with my car, man?" Huey, a black man with an Atlanta Falcons T-shirt demanded.

"I'm takin' it, that's what," said the Grey Wolf possessing a hapless businessman who had obviously been working late and on his way home.

Huey grabbed the skinpuppet and slammed him up against his car. "Hey!" the skinpuppet yelled. A few MARTA police down the way moved closer to the scene, drawing their weapons.

"All right . . . break it up."

The skinpuppet turned toward the cops and began to mindlessly utter a stream of obscenities. Inwardly, his skinrider grinned: this should be enough of a diversion. He watched as a flood of mortals came walking across the bridge that spanned the main road and connected the parking lot to the station: the other team must've done their work clearing out the platform already. Clockwork. Everything was going as planned.

The train began to slow. Brenner stood silently next to the door of the train, watching carefully, her hand on the hidden souled revolver she carried with her always. She heard the Hierarchy guardians taking up position as the train came into the station: they had good training, she knew. She wondered if even a squad of Wolves could take them down. As she waited for the train to come to a stop, she wondered idly how they were going to move the soulfire off the train, but decided that was outside her ken. She was through here.

There was only one kink in the mission. A grey-hatted Hierarchy type had gotten on the train with her last night. She had watched him almost the entire time, but he had done nothing. She felt that he must be some kind of powerful wraith: his aura didn't show, and he was quietly ignored by all the wraiths on the train, even the crazier ones. He never moved from his place, seeming to sleep but not ever Slumbering. He read from a Relic book constantly: a book with no title on the cover.

Brenner had used every trick she knew to try and figure out who this guy was, but he was either too oblivious or too good at remaining incognito. This one loose strand worried her, but soon he passed into the realm of things she could do nothing about. She would remember to include him in her report to the Greymaster, however.

The train slowed and pulled into the station, perfectly aligning itself with the platform, which had suddenly emptied of skinlanders as waves of fear swept the frightened masses up the stairs and out of sight. The team of Grey Wolves was ready as Brenner leapt out and pulled open the freight car doors.

"Danger! Critical warning!" barked out one of the Hierarchy guards as the Wolves fired and advanced on the guards surrounding the tarp-covered sphere of soulfire.

––––––––––

"Go," Greymaster hissed, hitting Kirk on the back. Kirk nodded and surrendered to the power of his Argos, flickering across the Tempest in a matter of seconds and materializing in the freight car, which was filled with Grey Wolves and Hierarchy guards.

Throwing himself at the sphere, he threw his cloak around it. Only one Hierarchy guard, a green-coated soldier from World War I by his dress, turned and caught sight of Kirk as he embraced the sphere. The doughboy raised his rifle to fire—at nothing, as Kirk vanished into the Tempest.

Seconds passed.

"Disengage!" the Wolf leader yelled as the train began to move again. All of the Grey Wolves fighting in the train moved back, performing defensive maneuvers as they retreated.

Three Hierarchy guards jumped onto the plat-form, dark smoke surrounding them as their Shadows leapt into control. The Wolves kept fight-ing, knowing that these Centurions had been driven over the edge with rage and would not stop until they were discorporated.

Kirk materialized in a dark freight car. It smelled sickly-sweet here. The shadows moved indepen-dently of his motion. The only light was the burning green of the soulfire within the sphere, cloaked in a tarpaulin and his own grey cloak. He shook from the effort of moving the object. Suddenly, in the darkness, a Grey Wolf materialized as the train began to move. He froze, not knowing what exactly to do. Freda was supposed to be here, to make the connection, to take this thing off his hands. Where was she?

The Wolf shook its head. "You sure picked a spooky fuckin' car," came a familiar voice, but he couldn't quite place it. The Wolf walked toward Kirk, holding out his hands. "Great. You got it. Let me have it. Come on, boy, I don't have a lot of time."

Kirk shook his head slowly. "I . . . can't let you take it."

The Wolf pulled off its mask. "You don't recognize me?" Freda said, moving closer.

Kirk felt the tension leave him as he saw his friend. "You scared the shit out of me."

No room. There's no room here for you. . . . came a spectral voice from the shadows.

Kirk shuddered, as did Freda. "S-s-sorry. I had no idea. Just what is this place?"

Freda looked down, remasking herself. "Freight car from an Auschwitz train. Part of the Holocaust. Look, we can't do anything to change the Hell that these souls are going through. Just give me the sphere and let's go."

Water. Give us water. Please. Just a little water.

Kirk saw tendrils of shadow reaching out to caress the sphere, to seek a hole in the tarp and start draining the soulfire from it. Tearing the fragment of the wolf mask from it, he shakingly handed Freda the sphere. She nodded at him. "Get out of this car, Kirk. Go two cars up, that's the passenger compartment," she said, and vanished.

Kirk felt an icy chill grip him as he saw the sphere vanish with her. Now his Fate was sealed. He turned the mask fragment over and let it drop soundlessly to the shadowy floor.

Feed us. We're so hungry. Just a little food.

Kirk shuddered again as he vanished.

———

The train rumbled on, moving swiftly toward its destination with midnight. Kirk materialized in the passenger compartment. He sat down in an unoccupied seat next to someone who was sitting on the floor, clouded in his own Slumber. He held on to the compass and watched it, watched as the needle changed direction as they got closer to Rick.

He didn't look up as a figure dressed in grey sat down next to him and tried not to turn his masked head to see. He didn't want to know who it was; the fear in him still wanted to escape this place, and he was doing the best he could to stay calm.

"Hello, my boy," the grey-clad man said, easing back his flannel hat and pulling at his long white beard. Kirk involuntarily turned: the man's voice was familiar.

The voice, the face, the grey robes, the sickle symbol keeping his cloak pinned—these could only mean one thing: Hierarchy.

Kirk shook. "Are you Jebediah?" He whispered the name that had haunted him since he had fled the Citadel.

"Glad to see you know me, son," Jebediah said. It was definitely the soft, Southern voice that had asked about him in the Citadel, so long ago. The man wasn't wearing a mask now, and he smiled at Kirk. "I have come here to talk to you. It's important that you listen to what I have to say."

Kirk narrowed his eyes, not knowing what to think. "Look, uh, I'm just riding this train and I don't . . ." Kirk said.

"Don't lie to me, boy. I can smell a lie coming a mile away. That's my job. Now you just shut up and listen to me. I don't know how, just exactly, but you, my boy are a grand mistake. You shouldn't be here. The O'Rourke family Curse should have died with me," Jebediah said.

Kirk shook his head, confused. "What the hell are you talking about?"

"You heard me. You're an O'Rourke boy. Ain't ye?" Jebediah said quietly.

"Rourke, yeah. My dad said his dad dropped the O' part a long time ago," Kirk said.

"That's right—ashamed of his true heritage he was. Silly fool. Still, he had a right to be, perhaps, more so than his kin. His heritage was a curse as well as a blessing. The Curse that followed our line, grandfather to grandson, throughout history. I died so that there would be an end to it, killed by some of my Irish friends who did it in a ceremony from the ancient times. I swore not to carry on the Curse. And yet, somehow, my boy, somehow your father was affected. My grandson."

"My—my father?" Kirk said, shock running through him like a douse of cold water. The train shifted as it entered a tunnel, and the entire train shuddered as it ran through a moving MARTA train, insubstantial and unnoticed.

"You're my great-grandfather?" Kirk said quietly.

"Aye. You're quick enough when you want to be. Now, listen to me, for when the train arrives at the station I be no longer your kin and be then Hierarchy, and I must act as Hierarchy do. I know not where your father is: I've been unable to locate him, no matter how long and hard I search. But you must decide, as I did, to not further the Curse. I don't know how to end it, boy. I thought that everything I did would end it. It is a foul thing, and has cursed our family for many generations. But you must do all you can to forswear the Curse that makes us wraiths!" Jebediah said, his voice quaking with emotion.

Kirk looked hard at Jebediah from behind his mask. "And what am I supposed to do about that? Go to Oblivion?"

Jebediah shook his head. "I cannot advise you. I don't think that jumping into Oblivion will fix the Curse. I don't even know what originally caused it. But hush and listen again. You wear the mark of the Firebird. And yet the Firebird will bring you only great pain, great destruction. You must not use its power. It is the spirit of the curse, made manifest in you, the youngest male of the clan once known as Riorche."

Kirk squinted his eyes. "I don't understand what you mean. It's just a mask."

Jebediah shook his head as the train began to slow. "No, son. No it's not just a mask. It's also a sign, a sign that a prophecy is being fulfilled. You are the Firebird. You bring death, destruction, utter change. Behold the mark of the Firebird as it tormented me." Jebediah drew back the cuff of his jacket to show Kirk a bird-shaped scar raised as if it had been made by the touch of a white-hot brand on his wrist.

"See, there. And it will so claim you, if you do not put it aside," Jeremiah said.

Kirk felt the tug of his infinity pendant. He looked first at Jebediah, then at the slowing train platform outside his window, then back to Jebediah.

"Thank you, Great-grandfather, but I have to follow my Fate," Kirk said quietly.

Jebediah shook his head. "No, boy. You can change your Fate. Or, if you can't change yours, you can change your son's. Don't let the Firebird go free."

"How do you know about my boy?" Kirk said.

Jebediah smiled. "That's what Monitors are for, boy. To tell you things. I was the one who visited him. Tiny thing. Half-dead already. Do you really want Oblivion to claim that tiny soul?"

A flash of anger burned through Kirk. He stood as the train slowly came to a stop. For a moment Jebediah looked as though he would lunge for him, and Kirk remembered the man's promise about resuming his duty to the Hierarchy once the train stopped. Outside, on the platform, it was completely empty of people (cleared no doubt by the Hierarchy people upstairs), but filled with Centurions. Kirk wondered how he was going to escape this whole thing.

"Good-bye, Great-grandfather. Unfortunately, I can't stay and chat. I've got to start turning things around," Kirk said, adopting some of the man's Southern formality.

Jebediah just shook his head and hung it in shame. "Boy, you're not listening to me. If you would let me help you, come with me, I could—"

Kirk turned and, without looking back, leapt out of the train as it finally stopped, suddenly vanishing into the Tempest. This time, however, Harbinger Centurions were awaiting him in the Tempest. They swarmed around him, trying to grab his legs and arms, hoping against hope that he would have the desired soulfire that had gone missing. He held up his compass and fueled it with Pathos, following the bright shining light pointing to his destination. The light lanced through the darkness, burning arms and legs that got in the way. Suddenly he felt a connection at the other end, and he felt his entire body fold from the sudden acceleration toward his target.

Rick was hanging in darkness from his chains, completely unaware of his lot. Having materialized unexpectedly fast, Kirk had to take a moment to adjust to his surroundings. Clearing his head, Kirk touched the lock on the chains and tried to open them, shaping his fingers into picks like Dr. Teeth had taught him. He struggled with the padlock, feeling it start to click open. The chains fell to the ground with a clatter, the padlock went flying, and Rick collapsed to the cold cement floor. At the far end of the room a steel door opened, and a few Centurions came into the room as they prepared to move the shipment of new souls out to be placed on the Midnight Express: they hadn't noticed Kirk in the forest of chained souls.

"Clear this whole place out. We have to make up for the lost soulfire somehow. No holding back this time," came a Centurion's voice, and several wraiths began hefting the bodies in a fireman's brigade out the door and on down the line.

Kirk unmasked and peeled the thick Caul off of Rick's head, feeling his friend begin to stir. Rick shook his head once, then twice, then opened his eyes.

"Kirk?" he asked sleepily. "Kirk, is that you? Damn, man I had this shitty dream. You were dead, and I died in an explosion, and shit, it really sucked."

"Sorry to tell ya, dude, but you ain't dreamin'. This is reality," Kirk said quietly, holding up a length of chain. He hoped he wouldn't be heard, but the worker wraiths were making enough noise rattling chains and moving souls around that he didn't think there would be a problem.

"Oh, shit. I'm dead. Oh, well," Rick said. Kirk grinned. Rick had never been one to dwell on shit that happened. Rick looked up at Kirk. "What are you, some kind of soldier now?"

"Something like that. Look, Rick, I'm going to help you out. You're not like me. You don't have anything keeping you here. Look at you now: you're starting to get thin and see-through. That means Oblivion's pulling you down now that the chains aren't around you. What you need to do, Rick, is get the fuck out of here, someplace safe. I've got something for you, and I want you to take it and get the hell out of here. I got you into this mess, and—" Kirk said.

"I remember! You pulled the plug. Oh, damn! That was the worst, Kirk. I hated it. I hated you. Why didn't you let me live? I had a fuckin' chance," Rick said.

Kirk shook off his friend's vehemence. "Look, will you shut up and listen? I'm sorry you're dead. I can't help that now. All I can do is make sure you don't end up like these poor bastards. I can make sure you get out of here and get someplace where you'll be safe."

Someplace safe. That sounded so good to Kirk right now. His head was filled with images of his father, of his great-grandfather, of the battle. Of the Centurions and probably Grey Wolves who were now searching for him. All because he thought he was doing the right thing. He looked at the infinity pendant, and it glowed blue in the half-light of the room. The workers were almost done with the front half of the room, loading the souls onto dollies and pushing them off to the train. Kirk heard the train whistle blow once, like a warning. Kirk wondered for a second what the pendant would do if he willed it to function.

A voice boiled up from within him. "Try it."

Kirk felt his hand move to the pendant, alight with Pathos. Kirk watched helplessly as his hand closed around the pendant and it was set afire with blue flame. Suddenly it shot up into the air, held down only by the necklace it was on. It bobbed at the end of the necklace like a tiny steel balloon. Blue arcs traveled down it.

Kirk turned to Rick. "You have to take it. Pull your arms out of the Caul and take it. I can't . . ." Kirk tried to wrest control of his hand away from the beast inside him, to no avail.

Rick began to struggle. Now the light of the fire was illuminating half of the room, and workers began to point and call for the Centurions. Kirk wanted to curse, but even now, the Shadow within him had tightened its power and would not release its hold.

Rick broke his arm free from the slimy plasmic Caul and reached out for the necklace. He fell, face forward, onto the concrete, his fingers dancing within inches of the loop of blue-fire. Kirk growled wordlessly as he struggled to wrest self-control from the Shadow. He couldn't do anything to save his friend now: it was up to him.

"Fucking wonderful," Rick said, struggling, trying to break his other arm free and somehow right himself.

"Freeze!" called a Centurion from the door, and Kirk almost laughed. As if he was going anywhere.

Rick moved himself across the floor to Kirk and grabbed his leg. Pulling himself up with the one arm, he teetered in his ovoid Caul and turned around to grab at the necklace one final time before the Centurions could intervene.

Fingers danced through the darkness.

Blue fire illuminated Rick completely, burning through his entire Caul, as his fingers grabbed the necklace. For a second Rick rose into the air, burning off blue flame as he did. An infinity symbol burned itself into Rick's forehead, and even the Centurions in the room couldn't look directly at the fiery blue-white light. Looking down at Kirk, Rick smiled for the first time in a very long time. "I can see it now. It's all very simple," Rick said.

Kirk looked up at him. The blue-white light was like the summer sun melting an ice-encrusted lake; slowly he felt control returning to his limbs.

Rick looked down at Kirk. "Man, I never thought I'd say this, but hell. I forgive you. I forgive you . . . everything. If I had known—"

With that, the blue-white light surrounded Rick and he rose up through the roof, burning through the Shadowlands, rising up faster and faster. Even those who perched atop the Citadel reported later that the burning light didn't stop at the roof: it flew straight upward and into the black, stormy skies of the Shadowlands, until it couldn't be seen any longer.

Kirk backed up against the wall as he saw the Centurions advance on him, their hands on souled weapons that gleamed like stars in the shadowed storage room.

The blue-white flare of light that shot up from the Hierarchy was misinterpreted by many. The Grey Wolves thought it some sort of signal flare made of pure Pathos to warn patrols of the raid. Other wraiths thought it some sort of demon, or avenging angel rising up out of the Citadel, as if the Heretics had somehow managed to recruit one of the Unending to their service.

Far away, on the roof of the old Sears Building, Sylvie, Jojo, and Duke all knew what it meant: that Kirk had accomplished what he had set out to do. Sylvie smiled as she watched the light of Fate carry Rick away. She had no way of knowing where Rick was going, exactly. She just knew that it was someplace safe, which in the Shadowlands could be a kind of heaven.

Sylvie smiled. "Okay, let's go. Spread out and see if you can help Kirk," she said to the other two wraiths on the roof, and they vanished one after the other. Sylvie was proud to see that they had properly learned the Argos she'd taught them.

Sylvie was suddenly alone, but filled with warm energy as she realized that she had helped Kirk set Rick free. It was part of who she was: helping people was second nature to her. Even though it always gave her a large rush of passionate energy—triumph—she did not do it for the Pathos alone. She knew her place in the great Web, realized that what she did now affected all that she had done, all that she would ever do. She shuddered at the enormity of the pattern of all Fate-twines.

There was a coughing sound behind Sylvie as a figure flickered into view. The figure was wearing a black gown with a black veil. Turning around, Sylvie gasped as she recognized the symbol of the Lady of Fate on a ring on the woman's hand. "Greetings to thee, Lightbringer," the woman said quietly to Sylvie.

Sylvie curtseyed as best she could, shaking as she was. This woman was a Matron of Fate, a prophetess of great power. Her simple glimmerings were nothing next to the light that the older woman was able to see by.

"And also to you, ma'am. Did I . . . do something wrong?" Sylvie asked quietly, looking up, unconsciously using her little-girl eyes.

The Matron shook her head slowly. "No, my child. You did remarkably well. I am very pleased with you. Surely you can see your place in all of this?"

Sylvie shook her pigtails slowly. "No, ma'am. I've not got the sight to do that."

The Matron *tsked*. "We shall have to see to thine own education. Still, now I am come to bring a thing which has been left into my care up until now."

Sylvie watched as the Matron flung aside her cloak, revealing a tall scythe: the blade made of darksteel, the handle exquisitely carved with a battle-guard. This was no reaping tool, no farm instrument, but a weapon of battle.

"Beyond the darkness lies the fire. Beyond death lies the truth. Look ye to stop what must be stopped.

A circle has no beginning, but make this an ending, else the spiral will ever curve downward," the Matron whispered in her heavy Irish brogue.

The Matron gave the large scythe over to the keeping of the girl, who could barely keep it upright. "That is the weapon of the Firebird. I cannot shelter it any longer. It longs to be with its master. It will have its own way."

Sylvie nodded slowly. "What shall I do about the baby, Matron?"

She smiled. "Ah, yes, the child." Her face grew cold. "Kill it quickly, mercifully. Unless it has a proper home and family by the half-moon, it will die a terrible death." Only when she had pronounced sentence on the babe was she able to show her true feelings: a plasmic tear welled at the corner of her spectral eye. She dabbed at her eyes with a black handkerchief.

"What next, Matron?" Sylvie asked quietly.

"Ahhh, yes. Now, my dear bairn, you will know the true meaning of the word 'patience.' For you must wait. Wait, watch, and see. Keep your own counsel. The skein of Fate is so twisted now that none can properly unravel it. Where the Firebird is concerned, keep silent. Kirk must find his own way, now. There can be no turning back for him," the Matron said quietly, her voice chill.

"Yes, ma'am. I understand." Sylvie leaned forward to kiss the Matron's ring.

The Matron smiled at the young girl and placed her hand on the girl's head. "Now may the Laird bless ye and keep ye, and lead ye home should ye be lost," she said quietly.

Sylvie felt the blessing of Fate wash over her as the Matron did this, felt the woman's Pathos burn through her for a moment. Then all was well. She felt inordinately calm, even though a troop of Grey

Wolves could materialize all around her at any moment.

When Sylvie looked up, the Matron was gone, and only a cool wind carrying night smells reminded her where she was. Sylvie turned toward the east and waited. She felt the Fate-twines slowly turning, slowly unraveling, and knew that she must wait here for her destiny.

Kirk stood with his back against the wall, the Centurions advancing. He wished for a moment that he had been armed with one of the souled weapons, but had no such luck. He looked at his possible escapes: one door. The walls, floor, and ceiling were hard cement, painful to jump through.

One of the Centurions opened fire on Kirk, and Kirk saw time slow as the bullet raced toward him. Looking down, he saw the ammunition enter his plasm and penetrate it, burning a hole, moving through him. It seemed to be on fire. The bullet opened a conical exit wound behind him as he felt it leave his body. Another bullet ripped through his chest. Suddenly, the fiery pain from the first bullet hit him, followed quickly by the blazing inferno of torment the second wound caused.

Kirk bellowed out his pain, throwing back his head and nearly dislocating his jaws. He felt open, terribly vulnerable, totally out of control. His rage boiled out of the deepest parts of him, and somehow in all that pain he was able to reach up, out of himself, out to something far away.

Blazing light surrounded him. Fiery red-orange glow. Fire burned through the room, swathing him in licking flames, burning all around him. He raised his arms and saw them fan out into wings with fiery feathers. He turned to face the troops head-on, undaunted by their weapons. A puff of breath brought burning flames issuing forth from his mouth, melting souled guns and singeing wraiths with a consuming fire that only Oblivion could conjure.

Kirk lifted up one of the guards with his arm/wing and threw the hapless Centurion into, and through, a wall. The other two Centurions retreated, moving back as he walked toward the door. Somewhere in all the fiery destruction, he heard his Shadow laughing at him, but somehow it did not matter now. Kirk turned to view the entire room full of chained and bound wraiths. His vision blurred in rage: how could they do this to simple souls, souls who had died with visions of Heaven dancing in their heads? Why did they enchain all they touched?

With a gesture, Kirk felt fire pour forth from his claw/hand, watched as the flames engulfed the room, seeking after the chains themselves, moving like sinuous snakes of brilliant glowing orange, until they wrapped around the chains, setting the dead free.

Kirk heard his Shadow laugh with glee as, one by one, the will-less ghosts sank into the floor, falling into the Tempest. One by one they were lost to Oblivion, as the barrow-fires grew higher and surrounded the room. Kirk could barely think human thoughts: the fire in his brain was such that all he could feel was utter, overwhelming anger and rage.

Kirk took a step back and unfurled his great wings. They snapped smartly outward and he suddenly realized that he was flying, dizzily moving through yards and yards of cement, then pure rock as he rocketed upward.

"Now you're sure it will be safe?" Freda asked Meany, standing next to the Gypsy Wagon inside the World of Krafft.

Meany was juggling glowing skulls, end over end. "Sure. No problem. It'll be as safe as coffee. Safe as a dog's nose in a sledstorm. Safe as a pig in a blanket. Real safe."

Freda looked down, shaking her head. Why had Duke chosen this moron for guard duty? "Look, it's very, very incredibly important that you protect the sphere. If anyone's going to get any soulfire at all, we're going to need you to protect it."

Meany nodded. "Not to let anyone near the sphere unless he has a note from you."

Freda shook her head. "No, nobody's supposed to see the sphere. Nobody. Understand?"

Meany nodded. "Not to let anyone see the sphere except Nobody."

"No, no, not Nobody. Not anyone," Freda said.

"That's what I said. Not anyone except Nobody," Meany said, looking falsely puzzled. He enjoyed messing with Freda's head.

"Who is Nobody?" Freda asked, beginning to get exasperated.

"I don't know, I thought you were speaking hypothetically," Meany said quietly.

"I *was* speaking hypothetically! I said 'nobody.' As in not a single one." Freda could barely contain her annoyance.

"Right. But several can see it at once, right?" Meany asked.

"No! Nobody—oh, I mean . . . Well, dammit, you know what I mean," Freda said frustratedly.

Meany nodded. "Right. I know exactly what you mean. No problem, boss. You leave it to me, I'll take right care of it. Forget it even happened."

"Meany. You can damn well bet that I won't forget it. If you give this sphere away, I'm going to have to hurt you. Hurt you big."

Meany smiled. "You promise?" But he took the

sphere, and it vanished, and Freda got a sense that, just by looking into the clown's eyes, there would be no way in hell anyone would touch it. She worried a little that she'd have to beat the clown up to get it back, but that was something she'd deal with when she needed to.

It was dark within the truck as it trundled along the back streets of Atlanta, moving carefully so that no police car would accidentally stop it. So dark, in fact, that no one noticed the two figures materializing out of the shadows, grinning quietly behind their masks. One, hunched over, ran over to a steamer trunk and, just as quietly as he had arrived, motioned to the taller one to come and help him carry it. Only a sliver of light from the top of the truck shone down on the lion-head mask of the taller figure as he walked over to the steamer trunk and helped the smaller one heft it. It was very heavy and felt warm from the heat of the concentrated Oblivion that was contained within it. The taller one counted quietly in the darkness. "One . . . two . . . three . . ." and there was a brief flare of reddish light as the two vanished with the box.

Boiling up through the concrete and rock of Five Points Station came the Firebird. Passing by the living, who even in life felt a wave of heat from its fiery wings, it flew up into the dark sky of the Shadowlands, beating its wings and shouting aloud its birth cry.

There had been a night like this before, long ago, on August seventh, when the sky turned red in both the real world and in the Shadowlands—red from the burning flares of the guns besieging Atlanta.

Now the red tinge to the sky would be written off as a result of air and light pollution, nothing strange, but those who knew, those who were aware of more than just the everyday, would know that something was afoot in the lands of the dead.

Kirk exalted as the Firebird completely consumed him. He had never felt so full of power and energy, completely united as he was with the fiery being within him. He turned and flew—flew across the rooftops of the city toward a feeling, an instinct. Something that he needed, that he would need on his journey, was waiting for him.

The black-streaked fiery wings dipped on the downbeats, caressing the rooftops and searing through the night sky. No Legionnaire or Centurion gave chase, but as if in answer a great gonging sound echoed throughout the Necropolis, bringing with it a chill of fear. The gong was only sounded when something of great and terrible danger to wraiths everywhere was afoot. The Firebird had come: was the rest of the prophecy far behind?

Sylvie saw the gleam of the fire burning over the rooftops of the city. She held the basalt black scythe next to her side, barely able to handle its weight. She moved back, creating a space for the Firebird to land, for it was flying this way, its tail trailing a line of red light behind it. The Firebird backwashed with its immense wings as it neared the rooftop on which Sylvie was precariously perched and slowly, slowly descended with its claws to clutch at the rooftop. The fire immediately began to die down, a black streak at the center of the bird's body slowly taking on a man's shape and form.

Kirk stepped out of the burning flames, his face set and his eyes intent on Sylvie. His Firebird mask was gone, burned off his face by the power of the fire.

When Kirk spoke it was the Firebird, not Kirk's voice. "You hold the sacred weapon. Do you wish to give it up? To give it to me?" The Firebird's voice came hollowly out of Kirk's throat.

Kirk could feel the righteous rage, the thirst for pure destruction that welled up within him when the Firebird exerted itself. And he could also feel its strange humanity, as if the Firebird was some kind of conglomeration of a thousand different souls, all of them united in a single purpose.

Sylvie nodded. "I don't got the means to prevent you from taking this, Kirk. But I gotta tell you something. You're walkin' a dangerous path now. Your Fate is uncertain."

Kirk nodded. "That's as it should be. It's good to know that it's not tied up, not destined for a boring existence followed quickly by total nothingness."

"I warn you, Kirk. The path you choose will take you to the final death," Sylvie said quietly.

"Final death? You don't know how good that sounds right now. Did . . . did the others do as I asked?"

Sylvie nodded. "By now everything is as you asked. You must understand, Kirk, that we do not do this for the good of the Firebird. We do it because you are one of us."

"What is the Firebird? I—I don't understand," Kirk said quietly. "It's not Mr. Demon, is it?"

Sylvie shook her head quietly. "No, Kirk. No, it's something else. Something more powerful than the Shadow within you. It is your instrument of Fate, your higher self. Your Eidolon, made real in this world. That is why it burns so brightly. Still, it is a creature of destruction and fire, a creature that ultimately serves Oblivion."

Kirk nodded. "I—I—didn't ask for it to come. It just came to me—I was trapped. Completely. There was nothing I could do."

Sylvie smiled. "Kirk, one thing I've learned from Fate is that there are always choices. There are always pathways that are chosen and not chosen. People have tendencies that make them biased to a specific path, but they can decide to go against those tendencies. Only people who have stopped thinking, stopped making choices, are truly doomed," Sylvie said quietly, the wise words sounding very strange from her little-girl mouth.

Kirk felt the fiery being within him burning to be set free, and yet somehow he realized the truth of what Sylvie said. Looking out over the city, there was a hushed moment when all was at peace. He looked at the city he had grown up in, the city he had grown to both love and hate. He thought about his father, and his great-grandfather. For a bare moment, he thought about his little son and his sister. Turning back to Sylvie, he reached for the scythe she held. "I can't see another path. Not right now. I hope—I hope you can forgive me," Kirk said quietly.

"It's not my place to forgive you. I'm just here representing Fate. To tell you that there is a choice and not make you choose one way or another," Sylvie answered.

Kirk nodded absently, for the scythe was thrumming in his hands, almost moving and twisting like a living thing. He squinted at it. He looked up at Sylvie. "It wants something," he whispered.

Sylvie nodded. "Each weapon is a shard of the Firebird's egg, Kirk. Your father's weapon. Jebediah's blade. The scythe you hold. They long to be reunited. Each reunion will see the Firebird grow stronger."

"The Greymaster will be looking for me now," Kirk said.

Sylvie nodded. "You have sealed that part of your Fate. You must face him, Kirk. But you don't have to do it alone. You can summon your Circle and go to meet him with them."

Kirk shook his head. "Nah. This is my fight. I'll take care of it myself."

Sylvie tried to think of words she could say. It was hard for her: she saw the Fate-twines straightening down to two or three potential paths, but was forbidden to further help Kirk.

Kirk felt the fires within him start to burn again and he looked out across the city. Turning back to Sylvie, he tried to console her with a look, but she wouldn't return his gaze. As Kirk felt the fiery wings unfurl, he turned away from her and, with a single leap into the air, was gone, burning across the night sky.

Sylvie watched him go, holding on to her doll, suddenly feeling very small, very young, and alone.

It was dark inside the trailer. Mama Rourke was still out working. Anna was asleep in the back bedroom, clutching her purple dinosaur, the TV making snowy shadows on her face from the static. Kristy was asleep on the futon in the living room, still wearing the zebra-pattern teddy that she'd put on for her last client, who had been thankfully brief. She'd locked up her money in a strongbox and took a few pills to be able to get to sleep without the nightmares she was accustomed to having.

But there was one man who had the keys to the trailer who would not be denied. Not ever. J.T. loved to show Kristy how much he owned her, how much he could use and abuse her. Without a knock, J.T. slammed his key in the trailer door and opened it. A rush of cold night air came in, but that wasn't enough to wake up Kristy in her drugged sleep. He laughed to himself as he closed to door and slid the bolts closed. J.T. flicked on the TV in the living room, popped a porno video into the VCR, and rewound it. He went to the refrigerator and pulled out a cold beer, popping the top as he licked his lips, looking at Kristy's young/old body lying there, half-exposed under a blanket on the futon.

He sipped his beer for a moment, watching the video, fumbling for the belt on his trousers. He laid his dirty and stiff pants across one of the kitchen table chairs and kneeled down on the floor, moving one of his large and overly callused hands over Kristy's leg and up to her face, shaking her. "Hey, hey. Hey, baby. Wake up."

Kristy shuddered and awoke sleepily, looking up into J.T.'s eyes. She tried to smile at J.T.: he liked it that way, but she couldn't. She saw the light behind his eyes, the strange light that told her that he wasn't going to be easily gotten rid of tonight. "Hey, J.T.," she said, trying to sound friendly, but not being able to hide the irritation in her voice.

"Hey, baby, who loves ya?" J.T. said, smiling.

Kristy tried to shake herself awake. Her heart started to beat harder: whenever J.T. didn't ask her about her money right away, she got worried. That meant he was thinking about something else, and Kristy didn't want to think about what he was thinking about.

She started to sit up, and he pressed her back onto the futon. "Hey, where ya goin'?" J.T. said, grinning. "Don't you know I love ya?"

Kristy nodded, lying back, getting more and more afraid. Now he was getting pushy. J.T.'s breath smelled horrible. Looking past him, she saw nothing but the porn video he'd been watching. "Where's Mama?" she asked quietly.

J.T. smiled. "I don't know shuga. I guess she's out workin'. But I came to see my darlin' baby. Are you ready for your big daddy?"

J.T. wasn't able to see the red orange glow outside the window; the light was in the Shadowlands only. He wasn't able to see the black-robed figure carrying a huge battle-scythe walk into the trailer through the door. Kirk stood there quietly, the fiery light from his heart insulating him briefly from the evil words his demon would be saying about the scene that was going on on the futon.

Kirk felt the hate that he held for J.T. boil up out of the deepest parts of his soul. He wished that the scythe was real, that he could take J.T.'s head off with it. He saw the large, bulbous man's body roll on top of his sister, saw his fingers moving over her, ripping at her lingerie.

"Get the fuck off of her," Kirk said under his breath. J.T. stopped, froze. He looked around the room for a second. Somehow, Kirk was getting through to the real world. "That's right, you bastard. Get off of her, leave her the hell alone," Kirk said.

J.T. stood up slowly, looking around some more. He looked down at Kristy. "You just stay there, baby," he drawled, putting his pants on. She nodded, thankful beyond belief to get even this small amount of respite. She pulled the blankets up around her, looking at J.T. as he opened the trailer door and walked out.

Kirk looked at Kristy, hoping that he could get through to her, too. "You should leave this place, Kristy. You should get the hell out of here, go up to Aunt Sara's or somethin'. Go someplace else. Anywhere is better than this place," Kirk said quietly.

She shook her head like something had stung her, but didn't respond. She just pulled her legs up to her body, holding on to them, trying to control her shaking.

Kirk moved down the hallway, past Kristy's room, and phased through his old door. He looked down at his father's Marine sword on the floor, burning with his father's power. He lit up his hand with power and lowered it to the hilt of the blade, knowing that the energy would get his father's attention.

"I wouldn't waste your juice like that, son." A voice came from behind him. Kirk whirled just in time to block a heavy black machete that came down onto his scythe like a load of bricks. Kirk leapt up onto his bed, whirling the heavy scythe around to make a counterstrike.

"Good, good. Not good enough, however," Greymaster said, his ebony machete whirling in his palm like a sawblade and coming down on Kirk's arm. The heavy blade caught his arm and ripped into it, biting deep. Kirk yelped in pain. He jumped back, through the window, falling backward and landing in the gravel outside the trailer. The Greymaster flew through the window, diving after him like a predator-bird aiming at prey.

Seizing the handles on his scythe, Kirk pulled himself up quickly and felt the fire from within him burn up around his arms as he took a slice at his father, aiming the blade to reap his father's spectral head from his shoulders. The machete came up and blocked the strike, hooking in and pulling Kirk off balance, moving like a cobra to sneak past Kirk's guard and hit him once again, this time firmly in the chest.

Kirk felt the bite of the blade and wondered if this was darksteel. He worried that the Greymaster might be destroying him bit by bit as they fought. The unfamiliar scythe was more of a hindrance to him than a help, but he knew that this was a fight for his existence, plain and simple. Kirk realized that the eyes behind his father's mask were dark, full, with no pupils: completely controlled by his Shadow.

Kirk felt the scythe moving of its own accord, twisting and twirling in his hands as he defended himself against the terrible dark machete. His whole body shook as he took the force of a single blow on the basket-guard handle of the scythe, and he felt every muscle on his body strain as he lunged to slice at the Greymaster.

The edge of the blade ran along the Greymaster's outstretched arm and bit deep, but not deep enough. Kirk followed through, and the Greymaster saw a hole in his defense. A lunge by the captain was enough to drive the blade firmly into Kirk's Corpus, pinning him against a tree next to the trailer and holding him fast. With his mailed fist, his father bashed the scythe from Kirk's hands and it clattered to the ground, so much wood and metal now that it had left his hands. The Greymaster came down on the scythe with a single step and it shattered.

"So, my little Ferryman," James Rourke said under his breath, mocking his son. "I believe you have something of mine. And I intend to get it."

Kirk felt the fear within him, the fear of the man who was his father, and felt that fear freeze him like an icy vein running through his whole body. "I—I don't know. I can't tell you. It's gone," Kirk said.

"Gone. Far from it. Your Circle has it, don't they, boy?" James said, moving the edge of his blade to Kirk's throat.

"I don't know," Kirk said again. With a single thunderous slap, Kirk felt the man's mailed fist rake across his face. Although he couldn't feel the pain, the tremendous weight of the hand and the fact that the blade in him tore at his body even more was enough to make him whimper.

"I trusted you, Kirk. And you dicked me over. And I don't take kindly to being dicked over. Now, you are my son, and you appear to be some kind of

Firebird as well, but if you don't tell me where you put the soulfire, and help me get it, I'm going to destroy you and start working on your Circle."

Kirk looked at his father, looked at the man who held the face of his own personal demon, and shook his head once, slowly, but very definitely.

James Rourke laughed. He laughed wickedly, laughed with pleasure. He moved back from the tree, watching Kirk as he tried to squirm off the black machete's blade, to no avail. "You see, my boy, I know the Destroyer well. And I am sure that you know what his power's like. The Firebird's not just yours, you see. He's mine, too. See, that's what this pistol's all about."

James Rourke drew his Relic gun, the pistol that Kirk himself had recovered. "And that's why I'm going to blow you away with it. Sayonara, little boy. I guess the Firebird's going to have a new master now."

One bullet. Kirk shook with the impact. He felt the fire burn into him.

Two bullets. Waves of shock roared through him, a firestorm in his belly, in his shoulder.

Three bullets. Pain, white-hot heat. Burning death.

Four bullets. Now Kirk wanted to leave this world, leave everything. Oblivion beckoned to him like a chilling drink of pure poison, a tempting drink.

Five bullets. Chamber nearly empty. Kirk felt the Firebird leave him, felt the fiery heart that had been his flee. Instead, the bullets that were lodged in his body started burning anew, like tiny fires in his flesh.

Six bullets. Nothing. Darkness.

7

THROUGH THE TEMPEST

Jesus lover of my soul
Hide me, oh my Savior
Hide me till the storm of life is past
While the stormy waters roll
While the tempest still is high.
—Song from "sassafras, cypress & indigo,"
Ntozake Shange

Kirk fell. All that he was, all that he carried, fell from him. He lost all cohesion, falling through the ground, down into the Tempest. Instead of its traditional purple-blue tinge, the Tempest now held the color of Hell, the color of lambent flame. Bloodred and fiery blackened orange streaked out to surround him. A tunnel of fiery light engulfed him as he fell, and he heard laughing, singing, chanting all around him as he fell past the fires of Hell itself.

The feeling of falling was excruciating. It felt as though he would never touch bottom, that he would never be allowed the peace of unconsciousness or

the finality of impact. Just falling, turning end over
end, moving downward, feeling for the first time the
true weight of Oblivion that tugged at his every pore,
at every part of him. He could no longer feel the
holes in his body, for he had none: he just felt the
raw nakedness of his psyche exposed to the tender
mercies of the sea of shadows.

The tunnel he was falling through seemed inter-
minable. It was, however, no relief to Kirk when suddenly the falling slowed, and then slowly stopped,
and he was instead standing in a dark hole, a dark
cave somewhere in a world he had only had nightmares about.

Kirk sensed his Shadow around him everywhere,
as if he had somehow fallen into the foul demon
himself and was in the belly of that beast. Was this
going to be his Fate for eternity?

He took a step forward, found black gravel and a
path leading through scrub. Looking down at himself, he saw the blue uniform of a U.S. soldier from
around the time of the Civil War: a Yankee. Kirk
shook his head. He was sure that his hold on his own
sanity was completely gone, that somehow the nothing had swallowed him up and that he would forever
be in its terrible grasp.

Still, in Hell you do what you can to keep your
mind occupied. He followed the path of gravel up a
small hill and over the top, looking down into a valley and a scene that nearly turned his stomach.

Everywhere he looked he saw men dressed as he
was, smiling and grinning and shooting guns into the
air. He saw other men, and women, and children:
they were dressed in buckskins and furs: Indians. U.S.
soldiers rushed into the huts of the people living here
and rushed them out, setting fire to the huts. A marshal stood up in his stirrups in the center of the clearing, reading aloud the dictates of his superiors, telling

the assembled Indians that they were to depart the area for a specially prepared reservation out West.

Men, women, and children were forced from their homes as Kirk watched. Suddenly he looked up to see a tall man on a white horse carrying a service revolver. "Come on, boy, get on with them. You gotta get outta here, too. Let's move it! This ain't your land no more."

Kirk looked down at himself, saw the buckskins on his own body, the red war paint on his arms and hands, the feathers that were wound into his long black hair. He was now one of the Indians they were removing from this place.

One of the soldiers laughed as he taunted an older woman who was having trouble making it up the hill. "Come on, Granny! Come on! You gotta get movin', don't want to keep everyone else back. Come on, Granny! Let's move it! Hey, you—hey boy! Come on over here and get Granny to move her fat lazy ass," called the soldier, gesturing at Kirk.

Kirk moved over to help the woman up the hill. Her pitted face was ancient: she wore many necklaces and seemed important, dignity evident in her walk. She spoke a language Kirk had never heard before, and yet he understood her perfectly clearly.

"I am old, I have lived. You do not need to help me. I don't mind if they kill me. What will I do but live on? I know that I have won against them already. The bodies of the fallen will return. The fires of their hatred will always be returning to them."

Then there were gunshots; the soldier had grown impatient and no longer wished to wait for the old woman. She fell to the earth, a strange smile on her face, as fire rushed up out of her eyes and covered Kirk's senses, blacking him out for a moment.

———

Looking up, he saw a completely different scene. He saw the darkness of a night sky. A jungle was around him, thick with thousands of different kinds of plants and trees. The jungle itself seemed to breathe, and the breath that it was spitting out was thick and heavy and surrounded Kirk like a foul wet wool blanket, covered in the slime and sweat of a great festering beast. He moved through the jungle, clutching his M–16, trying to keep low, trying not to get shot at. Things were changing around him, and he knew that he had no control over his world, over his actions, that he could only move through this nightmare world and look for the way out.

His gun was cold in his hands and he knew that somewhere out there were quite a few men and boys who wanted him dead. They knew the jungle much better than he did, knew the darkness like an old friend, and were much better at crafting the indigenous weapons of war that the jungle offered.

All Kirk knew was that somewhere around here was a checkpoint and that he had to check in after his patrol. He had no idea how he knew this: the logic of the nightmare was clear to him, however.

He moved through the trees and into a clearing filled with GI's. A few of them saluted him. "Captain Rourke. Good to see you back," one of the men said. "Lose another patrol?" one of the men said from behind him.

Kirk turned around. "What did you say?"

No one was willing to own up to the comment. Kirk turned again, and out of the corner of his eye saw a man standing just out of sight: a man clad all in black.

Whispers came to him as he moved through the clearing, among the men, whispers of the thing in the trees, in the jungle. It was waiting for him.

"Everytime that old boy slept, his shadow would

come to pay court to me. Yeah, boy," came the whisper, in his father's voice.

"Captain!" the radioman called. "I got orders. Move up to new map coordinates and maintain position on that hill."

Great, came a thought unbidden to his mind. *More target practice. And we're the targets.*

"Let's move out!" Kirk called to his men as he strode into the trees. "I'll take the point."

They moved carefully over the intervening terrain, working together like the seasoned patrol they were. Kirk kept glancing to his left and to his right, expecting sniper fire at any moment.

As they were working their way up the hill, Kirk felt a twinge of uncertainty and saw the shadowy figure out of the corner of his eye again. Then, quietly, he looked up and saw a shorter brown man, maybe a boy, in his perch high above the jungle floor. He was clutching a sniper rifle and keeping quiet, taking aim at one of his wing men.

"HEY!" Kirk yelled, but it was too late. Gunshots erupted all around him. The man to the left of him fell with blood gushing from his eye. The man to the right of him took three shots at nothing before he, too, died. Gunfire ricocheted all around Kirk, but he was unharmed. More death, all around him: men falling like reaped wheat, and nothing, nothing at all that he could do about it.

Kirk looked at the gunman in the tree, unable to see his many brothers in the bushes, and screamed at him, felt the gunsight line up on his forehead, felt the bullet enter his head . . .

Looking up, he saw that he was young again. Sitting in his room, listening to his Metallica records, smoking some pot, talking to his girlfriends on the telephone. It was a typical Friday night for him: his mom out working at the factory, his sister Kristy asleep. This was before Anna, Kirk guessed, in a moment of clarity realizing that this was still a nightmare, still some terrible home movie that his demon had dreamed up.

Kirk kept listening to the record, and it kept skipping. Something about the skipping unnerved him, because it stirred up a very unpleasant memory, one that he had thankfully forgotten.

Something picked at the scab of that memory, threatening to reopen the old wound. Kirk felt cold fear wash through him as he shut off the record player and picked up his electric guitar, keeping the amp off so as not to wake Kristy. He played through some riffs, just fooling around, trying to calm himself. It was strangely pleasant to be back in his old body, back as he was before he died, before he had gotten into dealing, before . . . before tonight.

There was a sound in the front room, announcing his mother's arrival home. Kirk stubbed out his pot pipe and threw it into the cigar box he hid under his bed. He listened for her weary footsteps coming down the hall, but none came. Instead, he heard talking, laughing. *Oh, great,* Kirk thought, shaking his head. *She's gone and got another guy at some cheap bar someplace. Now I get to listen to the bedsprings creak all night.* But the thoughts were like the echoes of a far-off dream to him, because he was reliving it this time, just as it had happened many years ago.

Kirk heard the talking grow more intense. A chill of fear ran through him. He moved to the door, hearing the voices clearly for the first time.

"Come on, baby, you know you want it. How long has it been?"

"Not too long, but you just gotta give me a little time, I ain't no motor scooter you can just jump on. . . . "

"Come on baby, what do I got to do, send you an engraved invitation? I thought this is what you wanted, huh? Come on, baby, I'm real hot for you."

Then he heard his mother's voice muffled, as if someone's hand was clapped over her mouth. He stumbled down the hallway, looking at the shadows that danced from the light in the kitchen. He turned the corner into the living room and saw a man, some coworker of his mother's, tying her hands together with the scarf she always wore. The scarf that Kirk had given her for Christmas, last year. Her work uniform had been ripped open, her bra askew. She was struggling underneath him, fighting, kicking, but to no avail. Kirk could do nothing in his young body, nothing but scream at the man to stop. The words came from somewhere else, muffled to his ears.

The man turned to look at Kirk, and suddenly Kirk saw his father's face. His father who had been dead for several years. Somehow, he saw his father raping his mother. His mother, who would never speak of this night, who would carry the man's seed inside her and give birth to Anna nine months later.

Kirk screamed, and all was darkness.

This was a secret meeting, Kirk knew. No one from the tribe would've come to this meeting. It was forbidden to discuss what would be done here, but the elders had agreed that it must be done. The wise men and women had gathered around this fire and had described what must be done. The white men might carry the fire, they might carry the guns and the horses and all the power of their armies and their government, but they would not know the secret ways, the magic ways.

This was not a good path, and all those who were here knew it. They knew it was not proper medicine, that it was some foul, black sorcery that would doom them all. And yet, they knew that it was always best to curse quietly, to curse well, and to curse subtly.

The men had spent most of the day slaughtering trees around the campsite and cutting them into logs, just as the white men had taught them.

They took the logs and piled them high, piled them as high as they could reach. It was no longer necessary to worry about the fire burning out of control; this was not their land any longer, this was the war-ground. The wise ones moved among the warriors who had agreed to be here, to sacrifice themselves for the good of the people. They painted the Firebird on them, the symbol of their vengeance, the bringer of their curse.

Kirk stood and watched as they lit the pyre, as they danced around it, whirling and yelling out their anger, their hatred, their sadness. In their madness they leapt over the flames, finally catching afire and throwing themselves into the heart of the living flame, dying as they did. The air hung thick with sickly-sweet smoke as one by one they placed themselves on the bier of fiery death.

The Firebird grew up out of these flames, and Kirk watched as it reached toward the sky, toward the middle distance, and toward the earth. It was a creature of death, a creature of destruction, summoned to carry out a curse forever.

When the dance was over, all the wise men except one quietly departed. They knew that this curse would not drive the white men from the land. They knew that in many ways there wouldn't be any way they'd reclaim what they had lost, or if they ever did, it would not be worth anything to them: what good is a bunch of stone buildings and no living trees?

Still, Kirk needed to know something. He moved to the wise man, who bowed to him briefly and seemed to want to speak with him.

"Why are you letting me see this?" Kirk asked quietly. "Aren't I descended from those who drove you from your land?"

"Our enemy has become our ally. The circle has come around again. This is what happens with curses. They are hoops, circular. They keep coming around and around, until justice is served," the wise man answered.

"How can justice ever be served? This is futile," Kirk said.

The wise man looked at him sternly. "Justice is served when the right thing is done. Justice is served when one single man can change because of our curse. If one man walks a better road because we have cursed his kind and his city, then that is the object of the curse, and that is justice. But not one man has ever apologized for our destruction. Not one man has ever asked us for forgiveness and brought us gifts to appease us. Not one man has offered us restitution for the dead men, women, and children who have been lost to the Hungry Snake. So, the curse will continue, and our fire will spread again, to cleanse and start everything anew," the wise man said.

Kirk nodded as darkness overcame him again.

"Too easy. You've gotten off too easy. Now let's see a true test," a voice whispered behind him. Kirk turned, but no one was there.

It was still dark, then he was floating and in an old tenement somewhere in Atlanta. He saw Cindi sprawled out on the couch, her heroin works still on the coffee table in the living room where she had just used them. She was sleeping, while a caterwauling child screamed in the background. Kirk moved through the house to where little Jeb was screaming, and Kirk saw him not as a little boy but as the monster he had become: a thing with blackened skin, razor-sharp pointed teeth, a forked tongue. The boy was screaming, his diapers black with some combination of baby shit, blood, and some other goo. The howl was demanding, and Kirk didn't know what to do, how to quiet him. "Feed him," came a voice. Kirk shook his head, not seeing a bottle. "Feed him, Kirk."

Kirk shook his head again, then he realized the boy had quieted down when he brought his hand near. Kirk held up his hand and the boy watched his fingers move past, moving his head in time with his father's hand. The boy wanted something. Kirk moved his hand closer and the boy grabbed ahold with an unearthly strength. Kirk felt a pain like a beartrap closing on his hand as the boy bit down and began gulping the blood that poured from his fingers. Kirk watched as his own son drained the blood from his body, chewing on his finger bones and hand, biting them off and continuing to eat.

"Still want to let the brat live, Kirkie boy?" the demon said. "You could kill him, you know. Put him out of our misery."

"N-n-no! I won't!" Kirk said.

Demon whispered, "Now you can see why I didn't put an end to your skinny ass. Ain't fatherly love wonderful?"

Kirk jerked his hand back, and the boy started screaming again, straining against his baby bed to try and get at Kirk's fingers some more. A knife materialized in Kirk's hand. "Just do it, Kirk baby. Just do it. Do us both a favor."

The boy screamed and spat and hissed and tried desperately to climb out of the bed to get to Kirk. He shuddered as his own son licked up the blood that was spattered on his face and on the bed's rail.

"Ain't he a beaut, Kirkie boy? That's what he is

going to look like when we get through with him. Pretty boy. But you can put him down now if you want. Go ahead. Thrust the knife in," Demon said.

Kirk took the dagger and plunged it into the boy's heart, and a second later he was tiny, little Jeb, who could barely hold on to life. Kirk was suddenly standing in a hospital room with Cindi standing next to him in shock as he plunged the knife into his own son's chest. She screamed at him to stop, but it was too late: a little black blood was already flowing from the tiny corpse's lips. Kirk turned away, but the scene was still imprinted on his inner sight.

Then darkness, thankfully, took him.

"Is this all there is? Nothing but torture? Nothing but doom, death? Is this all there is for me?" Kirk asked quietly, in the middle of his own Hell.

He was sorry to see the darkness go: as frightening as it was, it was better than anything he had seen here yet. An altar and two fat black candles came into view. This place was once a beautiful cathedral, tall, perfect. And Kirk knew immediately where he was and what was going on. He saw the black streaks on the walls, smelled the vague scent of kerosene mixed with smoke mixed with holy incense.

He stood and watched the dark, smudged service, heard the burnt organ playing in a surreal mockery of its former glory. The Church had long ago abandoned the cathedral because it was just too expensive to pay property taxes on it, so it had gone unused for the longest time. The Dragons had made their home in it. They were a neo-Nazi group out of Forsyth County who had been making money by selling cheap drugs to the folks in Cabbagetown and Sweet Auburn. They hated Africans, Koreans, and everyone else, and Kirk hated them because they liked to bash motorcycles. He didn't like them getting close to what he considered his turf: the Five Points area and all around there. Yet they had moved in, with a lot of swagger and fuss, making their presence well-known and, some said, conducting strange religious services in the old cathedral.

Kirk saw himself pull up on his old motorcycle and saw his gang fan out around him, grinning as they each carried a can of gasoline or kerosene. The Dragons were off watching a movie at the I–80 Drive-In, so they had no idea that someone was about to put their favorite hangout to the torch.

Kirk watched as he ran up the steps, spreading kerosene as he went. He took a crowbar to the front doors and broke through them, moving into the vestibule and dousing the thick carpet liberally with the sickly-sweet smelling liquid.

He laughed with his buddies as he moved through the pews, turning them over, getting a thrill out of setting fire to the House of the Lord.

They grinned at each other as they moved on up to the front of the building, where they took a trash can (the altar having been removed long ago) and filled it with newspapers to make a new altar of flame.

Kirk watched as the two altar boys stood by silently, watching his younger self and his gang work over the cathedral. Kirk didn't have to strain to see out the front door as he and his gang ran outside. Mounted on his cycle, Kirk took a homemade Molotov cocktail and lit the rag on the end. "See ya, suckers!" the young Kirk yelled, and threw the bottle at the steps of the old cathedral. The fire caught quickly, and then raged up the steps and into the building. Kirk watched as the fire licked its way through the whole nave, burning up the walls.

Suddenly the fire was everywhere at once, and there was no place for Kirk to go. The fire burned him, just as it burned everything. He looked for the altar boys but could not find them anywhere: instead he saw a woman dressed in an ancient black gown, moving through the flames as if they weren't there. Kirk had never seen the woman before, but she seemed to give off an air of pure power and calm as she floated through the flames.

"This is what damned your soul to Hell, boy," the woman said quietly.

Kirk nodded slowly.

"Before this, you were able to be saved. But you burned a House of God to the ground, and for that you will suffer in the eternal lake of fire," the woman said to him.

Kirk could say nothing to his accuser, feeling the flames around him, but noting that her presence dimmed the fires just a little.

"So, that's why I'm here?" Kirk said quietly.

"No, this is just the waiting place. You wait for judgment, wait to be judged. Wait for the final days when God will return to claim thee," the woman said.

"Who are you?" Kirk asked.

"In life, I was Mary Riorche, your great-great-grandmother. I lived a simple life, a life of piety, and I was slain by the Curse that haunts our family," Mary replied.

"I keep hearing about curses here. The old wise man said that curses have a purpose. What's the purpose of the curse on our family?" Kirk asked.

"There is none that I can tell. Its purpose is lost to us. It is a sin that our family must carry forever, it seems. None can break the pattern. From grandfather to grandson, or now, in these times, from father to son. And ye, now dead, will be no father to that

boy of yours. Ye surely must know that," Mary said
warningly.

"How do you know so much about me?" Kirk
asked. He felt a tremendous respect for her, despite
what she said.

"I have been watching thee, Kirk Riorche. God has
given me the knowledge of what ye are, of where ye
are. He has shown me your path, and I watch ye. He
protects me even now, even in this Hell of your
demon's creation."

"You mean . . . you are not like the other things
here?" Kirk asked.

"Nae. I am just as real—at the moment, more
real—as you. I have come to see how you have fared
in your Harrowing," Mary said.

"I don't know. I can't escape this place," Kirk
said.

"That's because you've yet to find the thread that
will lead you out. You must find the thread of Light
to lead you out of darkness—you must reject the
Shadow, deny him success. But, if you keep reveling
in your darkness, you will never find that thread,"
Mary said as the fires burned up, making sparks, and
burning his eyes as darkness fell on him.

Kirk was alone on a dark street. What could harm
him here? He walked down the street, past shops
that he did not recognize. The cars on the street
were blurry, muddy, as if someone had put a filter
on his vision. Each car that rolled by sounded like it
was muffled, as if his ears were wrapped in cotton.

As he moved down the street he realized he was
in a very bad part of town, one of the worst. Women
hung out here, looking for tricks. This was where
some of his dealers used to work the streets, usually
getting busted, but always getting out in a few days

or a week and getting back into pushing. He moved past them, one by one, remembering what Mary had said about turning away from his darkness. Still, he couldn't find any light here: there was no thread to pick up.

One of the girls called out to him. "Hey, hey, mister. Want a date? Want a cheap date?"

She came up to him, dressed in a black leather jacket with a skimpy camisole underneath, and a black leather skirt. Her face was smudged and badly done up. "Come on, mister, it's only twenty-five bucks. You got that, don't you?"

Kirk turned back toward her. It had been a long time since he'd been close to a woman, any woman, like this. She was pretty in her own tainted way. Despite her hardened exterior and tough-girl attitude, the way she smiled at him seemed strangely intimate and familiar. The way she clutched a silk rose in her hand was kind of innocent and sweet. Kirk couldn't help but wonder what she would be like, what it would be like to touch her.

Still, Mary's advice came back to him and he turned away. "Look, ahh, no offense, but, ahh, I'm sorry, I just . . . I just can't."

"Oh. Okay." Kirk looked at her again, in a different light this time. She looked much different: Kirk saw the lines under her eyes, the color of her eyes, the true color of her roots, the shape of her face.

Kirk felt a cold chill of ice run through him as he realized who he was looking at.

"Is . . . is your name Anna?" Kirk asked quietly.

She looked startled. "Yes . . . No. No, my name's Debbie."

"Which is it?" Kirk asked quietly.

"I'm not supposed to give my real name," she said. "Are you some sort of cop?"

"No. I'm just . . . I'm just a friend," Kirk said.

"Not any kind of friend I want to spend time with. Unless you've got twenty-five bucks," she said.

Kirk couldn't help but look in his "wallet"—he took out the leather billfold his nightmare had supplied him and ran his fingers through the cash there. There was three hundred dollars in the wallet. He reached in and pulled out all three hundred. Somewhere he could hear the demon laughing at him, encouraging him to buy her for the whole night, saying "Yeah, that's your little sister Annababy . . . ain't she sweet?" but Kirk wasn't listening.

"Look. This is all the money I have." Kirk said.

Anna looked at him. "I . . . I don't do strange stuff."

Kirk shook his head. "No. I am giving you this. Get off the street. Find someplace to go. I don't care where. Stop doing this. Your brother wouldn't want you to do this. Your mother wouldn't."

"My brother's dead. My mother is a whore, too," Anna said quietly.

"Well, you've got . . . you've got a little nephew. His name is Jeb. You need to go and live with him. Go and see Cindi."

Anna looked amazed. "How did you know? I used to go over and play with Jeb everyday—after I knew about him. Cindi didn't show him to Mom until he was three."

"Just do what I ask, okay? You need to go see Cindi. Give her the three hundred if you have to. Just get off the street. Okay?"

Anna nodded. Kirk waved at a taxi passing by and it pulled up to the curb. "Get in," Kirk said quietly.

"Why should I do what you say?" Anna asked.

"Because. Because, dammit, if you don't . . . I don't know what I'll do. You've got to, Anna. If not for yourself, for little Jeb. He needs his aunt," Kirk said.

She got into the cab. "You know, you remind me a lot of my brother, what I remember of him. You're all right. Here . . . take this to remember me by." She handed Kirk the silk rose, smiling at him as the taxi drove off.

Kirk looked down at the rose, felt the gentleness inherent in such a gift.

Suddenly the rose blossomed in an aura of silver light. The light grew and spilled over Kirk's hand, streaming down his body. Kirk could hear his demon screaming in the darkness as slowly, carefully, he rose up off the street, past the nameless buildings, rising up into the darkness of the night sky.

Suddenly, all was darkness, but this time there was peace.

8

THE RETURN OF
THE FIREBIRD

*Easy is the descent to the Lower World; but, to retrace
yours steps and to escape to the upper air—this is the
task, this the toil.*

— The Sibyl to Aeneas in *The Aeneid*

Kirk never thought he would be happy to see daylight
again. Even though it burned his ghostly eyes and
made him shiver with its intensity, he stood out in the
bright sunshine atop his school. He soaked up the
energy of the sun as he lay back on the roof, breathing
from the effort of raising himself up out of the darkness of the Tempest, of the Harrowing he'd just barely
survived. His body still bore the scars of his fight with
his father, but he was now in control. His scythe was
missing, but he was sane. He was soon able to crawl to
the shadows, where he felt a little more comfortable,
and waited as the sun slowly moved and ducked down
under the skyline. He had no idea how many days had
passed, if any, and had no idea where his friends
were, but at least he was there and in one piece.

Kirk felt a curious peace, something that he hadn't felt since his death. Something his Hell had given him was a kind of knowledge about himself, answers to many questions that he had asked of himself or of others.

He shuddered as he remembered the scenes that had played out in his own private Hell, but they had also given him valuable wisdom. Looking out into the fading sunlight, he realized that what he was experiencing wasn't something personal to him: the Curse of his family was circular, a cycle, from grandfather to grandson, from father to son. Kirk's father had given it to his son just as his grandfather had given it to his grandson. The way of Kirk's Shadow was powerful, as was the way of his higher self, but neither one was what Kirk wanted.

Kirk looked out over his city, the city where he was born, and realized that he stood between many great powers, all of them vying for his attention, all of them asking him to be a certain way, to do a certain thing. The Hierarchy wanted him to go to Oblivion. The Renegades wanted him to join them. The Heretics wanted him to do the right thing. And yet he knew that he could not please any of them and still be true to himself. He knew that nothing he did would satisfy any one group, and that he was tired of living for these massive powers. He would take the middle ground. He would follow his own Fate, make his own decisions. He also knew in his heart that there were a few things he must do, that had been prescribed for him to do, and if he ignored them he would suffer, as would the entire city.

For a moment he felt as though the entire Necropolis was his single vast Fetter, sick with the corruption and pain of a hundred years. He felt the weight of his duty on him, but also the light-headed feeling of being sure of his course now. Mary had shown him the way to pass through the fire of his higher passions. Anna, an Anna he hoped he would never know, had taught him how to turn away from the Shadow that threatened him. The only way he would succeed at all would be to follow his heart, to do what he felt was right, and nothing more.

As the last light fell behind the buildings, Kirk found himself wishing for his guitar, sighing as he remembered he'd left it back at the Wolves' warehouse. As the shadows grew long over the city, Kirk began jumping through the Tempest, moving from point to point, getting his bearings, and then making one last leap.

Kirk hadn't noticed the incredibly quiet, very patient Monitor who had been left behind several days before to watch the school building Fetter. The Monitor got down from his perch on a building across the street and made his way, through the Tempest, to the far-off Citadel.

The Grey Wolves' new hideout was in a now empty building which used to house a print shop. It was called the Ryco Building. It was particularly useful because it was right next to a train trestle (always a plus) and right down the way from the Jimmy Carter Library, so it was not exactly the kind of place you'd picture a bunch of Renegades setting up shop. No one had dared to go near the Greymaster since he learned about the disappearance of the soulfire. He was incensed; his Shadow seemed to be continually in control. There was talk among the Wolves, quiet talk but talk nonetheless, that the boss's Shadow had taken over completely, forever, and that they were now being led by a Doppelganger. But no one, not even Gunter, was willing to confront the old man to his mask. No one was willing to risk the wrath of that darksteel machete of his.

Word was that the Firebird had made off with the soulfire and that Greymaster had killed him before he had been able to obtain knowledge of where the stuff was being kept. The Grey Wolves were maintaining an extremely low profile in light of their recent failure. Even though the Hierarchy was freaking out (banging their silly gong and sending troops all over the place), there was not a single Wolf to be found in the whole city. That was because they were all hiding in the basement of the Ryco Building at Greymaster's command.

Meanwhile, squads of Hierarchy legionnaires fanned out through the Necropolis, bringing word to gather all the citizenry into the Citadel in preparation for a Maelstrom. The Anacreon of War had been in council for most of the night deciding what to do about the sighting of the Firebird, and they eventually agreed unanimously to sound full alert and open the doors of the Citadel to all Hierarchy wraiths in the city. This ruined social events that some of the more well-to-do wraiths were planning, but everyone had either heard of the Firebird prophecy, or had seen the outline of the fiery bird blazing across the sky an evening before.

The Heretics took to their secret catacombs, moving their people deeper underground and into the more powerful Haunts in preparation. The only exception to this were the Children of the Grand Dragon, who had been called up by the Greyboys to join together and meet in the basement of the Fox Theatre. They formed a rowdy Renegade faction that threatened to spill over into the living world with their shouts and demands for action.

Even the restless in the Oakland Cemetery were quieter than normal, seeming to prepare for a terrible battle that evening.

All was strangely quiet as Kirk materialized in the vast, empty warehouse where the Grey Wolves used to dwell. He stepped through the open bay doors and walked into the quiet concrete Haunt, feeling the comforting chill of the lessening of the Shroud here. He walked across the floor to the storage area and immediately wished for a light. Then he remembered his new-found powers and held up his hand. A blue-grey light burned from within his palm and illuminated the entire chamber. Looking over in the corner, he saw his ancient guitar still sitting there, untouched. He carefully examined it. He had learned enough from the Wolves to know that you never just gave anything to the enemy, and he figured the guitar was booby-trapped somehow.

But it wasn't, and he took the guitar up in his hands and felt the comforting weight as he slung it around his neck and plucked at the strings, tuning them briefly (and very roughly). He launched into a few practice riffs, moving his fingers up and down the frets, thrumming the strings without making a sound. He wished he had some soulfire for the guitar. It'd be nice to play it without having to feed it his own juice.

Kirk heard something go crunch out in the warehouse and stopped playing immediately. He ducked back against the wall and even went so far as to shape his left hand into a tight, sharp spike should anyone come through the door. The spike glowed for a moment from the small amount of juice he spent on it.

Step. Step step. Step. Footsteps coming his way.

He couldn't help but worry that the Wolves had somehow followed him back to the warehouse, had somehow known that he was here. He knew that, handspike or no, he wouldn't last long in a fight with a fully armed Wolf: the darksteel machete of his father's had left him with more lasting wounds than he wanted to admit to himself.

Kirk held his breath as he waited, and finally a figure stepped into the storage room. A green light bathed the room.

"Kirk?" came a small voice. It was Sylvie.

He released his breath and stepped out of hiding. "Sylvie!"

"Kirk! You're not gone!" Sylvie said. Her grin was very wide, her pigtails flying.

Kirk embraced his friend. "I made it through, Sylvie. And now I know what you were talking about. I had to go through Hell before I figured it out, but I did."

Sylvie smiled at him. "I'm glad, Kirk. I really am."

"How's Jeb?" Kirk asked quietly, not really wanting to hear bad news.

"He's— He's okay. There's some problems, but . . ." Sylvie said.

"What kind of problems?" Kirk asked worriedly.

"Kirk, they can't stay in the hospital forever. In fact, their Medicaid runs out in a day. Department of Family and Children Services is going to do an evaluation on Cindi tomorrow to see if she's fit to take Jeb home. He's stabilized, but he needs a lot of special attention. Frankly, Kirk, I don't think he has much chance if he doesn't get a nice place to live. I don't think Cindi can hack it."

Kirk shivered, remembering the hellish vision of his son. "I agree. We gotta do something, Sylv. And there's one person in the whole world that I'd trust to do anything like that. I am going to need your help to talk to her."

Sylvie smiled. "Oh, Kirk. You've—you've really changed. I don't know what happened to you, but you're very different. It's scary, in a way, but it's very good. I see the future getting brighter for you all the time!"

Kirk shook his head. "I ain't no different. I'm

just—I think I got my priorities straight, if you understand what I mean."

Sylvie smiled. "I think that's exactly what's going
on."

"Let's go, Sylv," Kirk said.

"Where to?" Sylvie asked.

"Would you believe the Probation Office?" Kirk
said, grinning.

Deep in the Citadel, an entire floor of the MARTA
station had been cordoned off during the day by
skinridden MARTA workers, and the area was being
used as a staging ground for the legionnaires who
were being assembled for the massive operation that
had been ordered by the Anacreon of War earlier in
the day.

Fearing a Renegade assault with the surety of the
coming Maelstrom (so reasoned the Hierarchy), the
Lord of War had decided to do a little preemptive
cleanup of the "known Renegade Haunts" in the
area of the Necropolis. All members of the Hierarchy
had been ordered to report for war duty at the
Citadel.

This included Jebediah, who reported wearing his
Mask of Honor and took the honorary title of
Centurion, in charge of a small group of Legionnaire
squads.

Sir Alisdair, a Knight of the Sickle, was clearly
upset that the Anacreon of War did not feel his
forces could handle the threat themselves and had
had to resort to calling up the levies. He charged
back and forth in the staging area, huffing while
seated on his horse and barking orders at the con-
scripts, most of whom were consigned to garrison
duty anyway. All except Magistrate Jebediah, of
course. His Mask of Honor was enough to gain him

an invitation to the knight's war camp, a pavilion that was set up to one side of the staging zone. It was here that Jebediah rested until his patrol was supposed to go out, and it was here that he noticed a very old and honorable Monitor named Gregor move into the tent and speak to Sir Alisdair in a whisper about a wraith rematerializing at the school where he had been positioned by one of Sir Alisdair's own patrols several days before.

Jebediah couldn't help but pick up on this: his own particular Fatalism was developed enough for him to pick out the "golden threads" of Fate that wound their way past him. He was discreet enough not to show Alisdair a flash of recognition when the information was imparted, but Jebediah knew that this could only mean that Kirk had been through a Harrowing and survived. He was half relieved and half annoyed: how simple this all would have been if he had been lost. And yet, the thread of Fate that Jebediah followed with his meager powers was definite, clear, and strong. Perhaps it was good that he did not lose to the Tempest.

Jebediah knew the first place he'd look when his patrol was set loose, however, for there was a last chance that the boy might be turned to some good purpose.

It was getting close to midnight again: almost a full day since the Wolves' failure. Greymaster emerged from his brooding loft and begin to quietly growl orders—orders that were memorized and followed to the letter.

A pack of Wolves were set on the trail of Kirk's Circle, particularly the Gaunt called Sylvie. Another pack was set on the trail of Kirk himself, in case he had survived the severe damage that Greymaster had given him. A third pack was sent to all the corners of the city in order to discover what was up. Greymaster needed information if he was to turn this terrific defeat into a victory. He knew that the soulfire and the stolen explosives were still somewhere in the city. Kirk's Circle didn't strike Greymaster as intelligent enough to get rid of the stolen goods. Besides, the fact that they had stolen both of those items and none of the other weaponry meant a lot: obviously Kirk had been planning something very close to what the Greymaster had been thinking of himself—to use the soulfire to fuel a huge explosion.

Still, as reports began to filter back to the Greymaster, he realized that this was a particularly unique time in the city's history: two powerful groups of anti-Hierarchy wraiths were openly allying, and the entire Citadel was on alert. It was a perfect time to unleash all of his former plans. He'd just have to find another way to get them all to follow him.

The Greymaster's mind was cunning, sly, and incredibly sneaky. It took only a few moments to put the pieces together, and soon Greymaster was calling to Dr. Teeth, his Masquer, with very specific instructions.

Kirk almost smiled as he entered the old Floyd Veteran's Building, walking up the steps and riding the elevator with Sylvie to the fourth floor, to the Probation Office. Although he both loathed and despised the office and all that it had meant to him as a teenager, he felt like it was almost familiar, like an old wound: annoying, but familiar.

Still, there was one person in the corridors and labyrinths of the office complex inside the Probation wing that he did want to see. Her name was Jo, a fairly heavyset African-American woman who had made a career out of being a probation officer. She always made Kirk stop and say "African-American" everytime he said "black," just to annoy him. She had also insisted that Kirk call her "ma'am," the only woman who had successfully managed that in any kind of consistent fashion. For Kirk, she had been something of a rainbow at the end of a long period of utter hell in his life. Sure, she could throw him right back in jail, but it seemed like she actually gave a damn about him. She actually cared whether he made it or not, which was something his mom had never really voiced an opinion about. Jo had a sign in her office which was very appropriate for her. It read: "I'm 51% Sweetheart and 49% Bitch. Don't push it!" She was very good to Kirk until he showed signs of selling drugs again, at which point she would come down on him like a load of bricks and he'd stop again. For a while. He almost wished he'd listened to her in the first place: he might be alive today if he had.

Still, although he didn't know why he knew this, he had a strong feeling that Jo wouldn't refuse him help, even from beyond the grave.

Sylvie smiled at Jo when she entered the office, but Jo didn't show any signs of noticing her, so Kirk made his way into the office where she was filling out reports and forms on the various convicts under her loving care. The other really impressive thing about Jo was that she had never lost a probationer: she'd never lost track of any one of her charges. For some reason, she had this uncanny sense of when someone was even thinking about breaking their probation. And she'd get up in the middle of the night, in the middle of church, in the middle of a doctor's appointment, and demand to make a telephone call, whereupon she'd proceed to give the probationer a serious tongue-lashing and thoroughly spook them. She called it her "psychic beeper service," and it only took one use of the "psychic beeper" before Kirk believed completely in it. He tried to not even think hard about breaking probation, although he'd never actually tested to see if she'd call if he was just fooling around. Somehow, either her own brain or her "psychic beeper" knew when someone was about to skip out for real.

So, Kirk wasn't entirely surprised that she was able to pick up on his presence: after all, she'd watched him for nearly five years.

At first she only looked up and around the room, as if there was a fly buzzing around her beautiful Nubian features. But after a while, she was convinced that it was something different. Kirk didn't say anything to her directly, because he didn't want her to get scared like the volunteer in the hospital.

He waited until she settled down again and started doing paperwork, then he sat down in the chair across from her desk—the chair he'd always sat in and described (the boring version) of what he'd done the previous weekend.

"Kirk, I think she's some kind of natural medium," Sylvie whispered, and suddenly Jo looked up, looking around the room, still unsure of their presence.

Kirk nodded, grinning. "I think you're right," he whispered as softly as he could, and Jo stopped again.

Jo got up, looked around her office, and then wandered briskly out into the hallway to see if there was anyone there. When there wasn't, she shrugged her immense shoulders and stepped back toward her desk. Kirk had to have some fun with her.

"Psst," he said quietly.

She stopped, put her hands on her hips, and swiveled 360 degrees, looking in every nook and cranny for the source of the noise. At one point she looked right at Kirk, but kept on searching the room.

"Psst . . . Ms. Jo. Over here," he whispered again.

Jo got a huffy look on her face and put her hands on her hips. "All right. I don't know where you gots the microphone, but I ain't buyin' it no more. I want you to come out in the open where's I can see you, or just stop messin' with me. Is that you Clarice?" she called out to the open office.

Sylvie covered her mouth and tried not to laugh at the woman's expression. Sylvie couldn't remember the last time she'd had as much fun as this.

Kirk smiled. "No, Ms. Jo. It's me. You remember Kirk, don't you?"

Jo put her hands on her hips again and huffed. Then she closed the door to her office, walked over to her desk, and sat down behind it. She started going through her paperwork again, as if nothing had ever happened.

Kirk whispered again, "Jo?"

"That's Ms. Jo to you," she came back, clear and loud.

"Ms. Jo," Kirk whispered.

"That's me. What do you want Mr. Spook?" she whispered, so that no one in the hall would hear her talking to the air.

"It's me, Kirk. Kirk Rourke. You remember, don't you, Ms. Jo?"

"I—I think I do. Kirk Rourke. Oh, yeah! Narcotics. Possession with intent to distribute. First-time offender. I heard you were dead. Dealing drugs again. Heh. Serves you right," Jo said, looking at a book that she carried with her always.

"Not on your shift, though, Ms. Jo. I was straight and narrow then," Kirk said quietly.

"Bull pucky, Kirk. You were funnin' yourself, and funnin' Ms. Jo. You were just waitin' to go right back to dealin'. See you got messed up by a punk with an autofire gun. That's as it should be," Jo said, talking louder this time. She seemed to be handling the fact that she was talking to a dead person rather easily.

"So, do you always talk to your deceased probationers?" Kirk said, a little annoyed that she wasn't particularly frightened, but glad as well that she was able to speak to him.

"Kirk, honey, when you've been in the business as long as I have, you gotta learn to expect just about anything. I tell you what, this job ain't nothin' if not intrestin'. Not that I need a whole hell of a lot of intrestin'."

Kirk smiled at Jo. Sylvie waved him on, obviously excited that he had made contact with her.

Jo said, "So, what can I do ya for? You get in trouble with Hell and you ain't got a decent probation officer down there?"

Kirk smiled. "Nah, I ain't in Hell yet. Well, I visited, but it ain't my style, Ms. Jo. No, I got me a little black—"

"African-American," Jo interrupted.

"—African-American girl who's my guide and friend. Her name's Miss Sylvie. She's here, too."

"Oh, my. Well, I s'pose you don't take up much room, so I guess it's okay she don't have a chair," Jo said, throwing up her hands. "Okay, so I am going crazy. This is good, I've been waiting for an excuse for a vacation for a while."

"Wait, Ms. Jo—you can't go just yet. I need to talk to you about somethin' important," Kirk said hurriedly.

"Important, eh? Okay. If'n it's important enough to talk 'bout from beyond the grave, I guess that's what I'd call important. Here, let me put my phone on hold so I can talk to you without interference." Jo pushed a button on the phone, picked up the receiver, and put it back down again.

"So, how can I help you, Kirk?" Jo asked calmly.

"You can help my girlfriend. And my new baby son," he said.

Jo shook her head and looked up at the ceiling. "Oh, Lordy! A baby boy and yo ol' girlfriend. Oh, Lordy!" she said, shaking her head again. "Kirk, I just don't know. Didn't I tell you to keep that thing in your pants? Who was it? That Kirsten girl you was seein'?" Jo asked accusingly.

"No, ma'am. Her name is Cindi." Kirk felt about sixteen years old again, and suddenly felt ashamed that he was having to talk to Ms. Jo at all. Still, he needed her, and she hadn't said no yet.

"Cindi, eh? She an addict, too?" Jo asked.

"Yes, ma'am," Kirk said quietly.

"Figures. Figures. What's her last name?" Jo said, going over to her computer screen.

"Staples, ma'am," Kirk said.

Jo punched a few buttons, then waited for a moment. "Lordy, I don't know what You is doin' to me, but show me the right way ta go!" she whispered under her breath.

Sylvie smiled. "She's a good woman. She'll do what's right," she whispered.

"Shush ya whisperin'! I gots to think here!" Jo said, waving an arm behind her.

The screen paused, then filled with a lot of information. "Let's see here, Cindi Staples, pregnant eight months, convicted of driving under the influence of narcotics, in possession of a felony amount of crack cocaine. Oh, boy. First-time offender. I think that's Clarice's department. Looks like the judge hit her with one of those new child abuse statutes when you takes drugs while you're pregnant. Yeah, here it is, a court order that she undergo natural childbirth and not get any painkillers after the delivery. Ooh, boy! Talk about your cruel and unusual punishment! I've been a momma twice now, and you couldn't pay me not to get a shot of Demerol and a spinal block. I tell ya, that child's had it hard already. Well, what else do you want to know?" she asked.

"What's going to happen to her?" Kirk asked quietly.

"What's going to happen? Let's see. DFACS is scheduled to take possession of the child. Social worker's report shows she's not a fit mother. The little boy's got a fifty-fifty chance to live, by the DFACS report here. That poor boy. He didn't ask to be born a drug addict, now did he?"

"No ma'am. Ma'am, can you help me with him?" Kirk asked.

"What do you want me to do with him? He's a baby. I's done my baby time. I done raised two babies and I ain't about to start raisin' a third," Jo said, crossing her arms.

"But, Jo, you gotta know, the kid is gonna die unless he gets some serious lovin' care. And Cindi, well, she needs someone to look after her, too. Also, you 'member my little sister, Anna? She's in terrible trouble, too."

Jo crossed her arms. "What do I look like, Kirk? Super Woman? I don't think so! I see this kind of hard-luck case come across my desk every single day. Do you think that if I went out and got involved with every single one of them I'd have any time for myself or my plants or my boyfriends? I don't think so."

Kirk sighed. "How many dead people ask you for help?"

Jo thought about that. "Not many. Maybe you're the first."

Kirk spoke up. "Then, you've got to believe me. This is important to me. Very important. And . . . it's important to Atlanta, to everything. I'm sure of it."

Jo sighed. "How is a scrawny little kid and his scrawny druggie mom important to the city of Atlanta?"

"Trust me, Ms. Jo. Have I ever lied to you?" Kirk asked.

"Don't make me answer that question, Mr. Rourke. I'm sure that you would not appreciate the answer."

Kirk grinned and shook his head. He was losing; he felt there was nothing more he could do. He hated to see his little boy die, but he knew that there wasn't anyone else who would stick up for the little guy.

"Well, I want to thank you Ms. Jo," Kirk said, the sadness evident in his voice.

"Wait a minute now, hold on there, hold on just a second there, Mr. Rourke. Is that a tear I heard just now? Are you cryin' for this kid?" she asked.

Kirk nodded, but Sylvie motioned to him: clearly Jo couldn't see him, only hear him.

"Yes, Ms. Jo. I'm crying right now. I don't want to see the little guy go. I really . . . I really love him. I've never even touched him for real, and I still love him more than I can tell you. I just don't know what I'm gonna do when he's gone."

"You love this little crack baby?" Jo said quietly, shaking her head. There was a tear in the corner of her own eye.

Kirk sighed. "Yes, ma'am. I love him with all my heart."

Jo shook her head, looked up at the ceiling again. She started cursing under her breath, snapping off her computer monitor, getting her stuff together, filing her paperwork.

"Oh, great, Kirk, you've gone and made her mad," Sylvie said.

"No, Miss Sylvie, no, he ain't got me mad—well, not at him anyway. At myself. I just can't believe I heard what I just heard. Kirk Rourke, a hardened drug addict and pusher with a history of beating up gangsters, smokin' crack, and burnin' down churches, and he's standing here sayin' that he loves a little baby more than anything. Well, if that ain't why I'm a probation officer, I just don't know what is. I got to give that little boy a chance, and I got to give Kirk a chance to know what it means to be a real human being, even if he is dead already. So, dammit, you've convinced me. I guess I'm going to have to make the guest room into a nursery. And we'll look into this thing about Anna, too," Jo said, sliding on her immense black trenchcoat and grabbing her umbrella. "Now, how's about tellin' me where I have to go, and let's keep it quiet so that I don't get locked up myself for being crazy. Hear?"

"Yes ma'am. Thank you ma'am."

"Humph. You can thank me when you figure out how to change diapers from beyond the grave," Jo said, muttering under her breath as she walked down the hall.

Dr. Teeth had just barely been able to reassemble his laboratory when the Greymaster was suddenly standing outside his door, waiting for the good doctor's services. Dr. Teeth had erected the giant wolf mask in the back room and had set up his teaching skulls and his other equipment, and he walked among the instruments charging them with his Pathos, listening to the Greymaster's instructions as he went.

"I can tell you, sir, that your good son is indeed still in existence. I cannot seem to get a lock on his current location, but I do definitely feel that his life-thread has not been cut," Dr. Teeth said, grinning wickedly. "Furthermore, I have developed a few handy items in the interim which should be very useful in locating Kirk's Fetters from a distance. It was quite easy, actually, since we own one of his Fetters already. Frighteningly simple, actually. I have a few locators ready for your men," Dr. Teeth said. He was always careful to say "your men" or "the men," never "his men." Although the men feared him, he had no delusions of being able to rule this wild bunch of mercenaries.

"Excellent, Dr. Teeth! I have need of some of your Masquing skill, as well. I want you to make me a Firebird mask, just like the one Kirk wore."

"But of course, sir. That was my second priority," Dr. Teeth said, pulling off a black burlap cloth from a stand which held just such a mask, and bowing gracefully from the hip.

Greymaster smiled as he fitted the mask to his face. "Excellent."

Jebediah had accompanied Sir Alisdair's patrol. Their first stop was a little-known place of refuge for the Renegades that Alisdair had been watching for weeks, waiting for just such a moment. Jebediah shuddered at the absolute relish he heard in the voice of the knight as he listened outside the bar.

"Well, Miss Susie. They call you Proud Susie, is that not true?" You don't seem to be too proud now. I wonder why that is?" Sir Alisdair said, striding forward to fix the last chain in place. She was nearly clothed in chains, the foul black Stygian kind. The chains that would prevent her from leaving, prevent her from protecting herself with her Arcanos. The knight smiled behind his helm, enjoying her helplessness.

"You're supposed to be a loyal citizen of Stygia, a member of the Hierarchy. I'm afraid you'll have a hard time convincing the Magistrate of that—it's known you harbor Renegades, Heretics, and your Circle is famous for keeping souls out of the hands of the Hierarchy. You are a little conductor on the Railroad, are you not?"

"I don't know what the hell you're talking about. I can tell you this, mister. I run a clean joint. My wraiths are all citizens. I check their seals, I make 'em pay their tithes. What more can you ask of a citizen?"

"What more can I ask? Quite a bit more. How about, oh, loyalty to the Empire? Surely loyalty is within your capabilities. I realize that you're a lesser wraith, hardly more than a wastrel. Still, if one of the Renegades comes to your very door, I would think you'd report it to the nearest Warder. Why did you not do this?"

"I don't know what you're talking about."

"Fetch the wraith who was witness to this crime," the knight said to an underling.

Soon a hooded figure was brought before Susie. It was drooping and nearly transparent: they hadn't provided any juice in a while and the Corpus was in tatters.

Still, Susie knew the wraith before they even lifted the hood off. "Jessie." She cursed under her breath. Jessie, whose last Fetter was itself in danger of being destroyed. "Damn, Jessie. I would've helped you. You didn't have to go to them."

Jessie looked down at her feet. "I'm sorry, ma'am. I'm sorry, Miss Susie. . . ."

The knight nodded and a Centurion unlocked Jessie from her chains.

The knight spoke up, indicating his stool pigeon. "This loyal citizen says that she saw you harbor one of the outlaw Ferrymen here, just three days ago.

You also promised to help an Enfant, a new wraith who is an outlaw from the Empire already. The wraith called Kirk."

They had released Jessie, who stood, rubbing her wrists and her thick legs where the manacles had bitten into them. Susie looked as indignant as she could, chained as she was to the wall.

"I don't know what you're talking about. I'm not a mind reader, if that's what you mean. If a Ferryman comes into my place, how am I gonna know? It's not like I can do anything about it, anyway. Your Warders are never around when you need them," Susie spat out, and tugged against her chains. The immense amount of darksteel that was required to hold her great bulk against the wall jingled strongly as she moved.

The knight shook his head slowly. "Oh, my, Susie. You are quite the raconteur. I do so love your stories. Unfortunately, you must understand that I know your heart. Indeed, I know where your last Fetter is. If you don't help me located the outlaw called Kirk, I'll be sure that a certain stained-glass window is destroyed, and rather quickly. It would be a pity to see such a beautiful work of art destroyed. Such a pity."

"You bastard! I don't know anything about where he is. I—my tale-teller, Sylvie, has got him. I don't know where they are, or where they're living. I only see her once a month, anyway, on Story Night."

"And where, then, is the tale-teller to be found?" the knight's tone was polite and as comforting as a bed of shattered glass.

Susie looked to the knight, to the Centurion, and back to the knight. Her head lolled to one side where they'd slapped her: she could feel her body slowly starting to slip away, into the Tempest, losing cohesion. Still, she couldn't betray Sylvie to them. "I—I don't know—" she whispered.

A Centurion stepped forward. In his glowing glove was an ancient corn-husk doll: a living-world object that, to any humans standing in the pool hall at the time (not that there were any) would be seen floating across the bar top. "Sir, I make this to be one of the girl's Fetters. Shall I assign a Monitor to secure it so we can wait for her return?"

"No, that won't be necessary, Centurion. We'll find her using the doll, wherever she is." The knight smiled behind his helm. He drew his Stygian dagger, the darksteel blade seeming to suck in light from around it. He stepped closer to Susie. "Ah, my dear. It is, how shall we say? Unfortunate. Very unfortunate that you decided to lie to us. You see, if you had admitted to knowing where she was, I would've let you continue to exist a little while longer. Only now, well, I'm going to have to utilize my executive privilege. Do say hello to your Renegade friends once they join you in Oblivion, won't you?"

Susie screamed, as did many of the other wraiths in the bar.

The knight took the blade in his hands, kissed it once, and plunged it into Susie's belly. He watched as the darksteel sucked up Susie's life force, and then twisted the blade, drawing it up and across her neck. With no effort her head parted from the rest of her spectral body, and suddenly the chains fell limp as her form dissolved and flowed down through a crack in the floor. Susie had only screamed once, and after that had not uttered a single sound: she had just watched the carnage and wasn't even able to struggle when the blade finished her.

Behind his helm, the knight smiled again. He strode out of the bar and into the street, where his midnight black horse waited. "Do what you have to. Get me the girl called Sylvie," he commanded his Centurion. He turned to Jebediah, who was still waiting with his own honor guard. "Let us continue our patrol, my dear Magistrate. I'm sorry that you had to be near such an occurrence. I assure you it is not my normal way of dealing with the foul scum. This place is to be shut down!" he called out, and with that, his dark steed was off, riding through the storming swirls of the Tempest like a nightmare.

In the darkness, the Hierarchs left didn't notice a single thick-legged figure slipping away from them, vanishing into the shadows.

Proud Susie's bar was desolate as the Greymaster's squad moved through it. Jacko and Fritz were up front, on point, and Harlan, Dean, Kribbs and Rogers were backing them up in a V formation. Kribbs shook his head. "Fuckin' 'archs. Proud Susie din' never hurt no one," he cursed under his breath.

Harlan looked up at Fritz. "Any ideas, Fritzie?"

Fritz grinned and picked up a flinder of wood from the floor where the tables had been shattered. He shrugged, closing his eyes. Harlan saw juice burning within him and waited: he knew that reading Fate-twines wasn't something you rushed. He also knew that Greymaster would not be pleased if they found absolutely nothing from this raid—and, lately, his displeasure was starting to take a turn for the nasty. Harlan waited, shifting his eyes from the sentinels posted at either side of the doors and Fritz. When Fritz spoke again, it was in a voice different than his normal one: Harlan had been told it was the voice of Fate. It rang true.

"Hierarchy Centurions—and a knight of Stygia— were here. Here, Proud Susie was tortured. Here, Susie was lost to us, lost to Oblivion at the point of a darksteel blade. They are hounds, who hunt as barghests for another one—the son of the Firebird.

They hunt for a small black girl who carries the powers of dreams in her hand. They hope to find Firebird's son through her. They have her Fetter, a doll, with them. After that, the twines get too tangled to see." Fritz's Fate-voice tapered off, and he sagged a little as the power left him.

Harlan nodded. "That'd be Kirk and his friends. Great, they're looking for him, too. Let's secure the area and get back to base," he said, looking out the front window of the ruined pool hall and nodding to himself slowly. Kribbs looked up at Harlan.

"You think this will be enough for Greymaster to get the other Renegades together? To move on the Citadel? I'd like to see those fuckin' 'archs blown to Oblivion because of this," Kribbs said, looking Harlan in the eye.

"You forget, Kribbs. Susie was a black woman. Do you think the old boy Renegades, the Klansmen, are gonna give a damn about Susie?" Harlan laughed bitterly. "I loved this place, too. Hell, I did my first skin-ride right over in that corner. It was sweet. Still, Greymaster ain't going to order any attack until he's damn good and ready."

Kribbs shook his head. "I have this feelin' that ol' Greymaster and the 'archs have got an understandin'. It just seems to me that there's many times either side could'a attacked, and they just sit there waitin'."

Harlan shook his head slowly. "You don' know what you're talkin' about, Kribbs. Now, secure the area. This place could be valuable to us, and if the 'archs come back, I want to know about it. I'm going to call the report in."

Kribbs saluted smartly, almost facetiously. "Yes, *sir*, Lieutenant, sir!" he barked, growling under his breath, and stalked off to do his duty.

———

In a secret ceremonial chamber beneath the Fox Theatre, a large group of wraiths had gathered, bickering, yelling at one another, with no faction accepting a clear leader. For the Heretics here, the Sons of the Dragon who were at one time involved with the Ku Klux Klan; the Firebird, seen burning over the Citadel in downtown Atlanta, was the sign for which they had waited a long time. Greymaster's old Circle, called the Greyboys, had a loose affiliation with the Dragon-Sons because of their particular anti-Yankee, pro-White bent. The Dragon-Sons had a version of the Firebird prophecy that had the Firebird ruling them as the son of the Dragon himself, whatever that was. The Greyboys were loosely controlled (in the absence of the Greymaster, who all Greyboys still respected despite his departure from the group) by Aleck Heck, a Confederate lieutenant and hero of the Battle of Leggett's Hell (even though the Confederates lost that battle).

Aleck was up on the podium talking to the assembled. "I tell you my friends, it's August! And what does August mean to yew? I'll tell you what it means! The Naht of Fah! The Night of Fire!" Aleck yelled at the top of his wraithly lungs.

A chant went up, "Night of Fire," over and over again, until Aleck calmed them down.

"And that's tomorrow night! The sky will turn red as blood and already those Archy boys have predicted a Maelstrom. Got all their pantywaists in their big ol' Citadel, safe and sound. Now what about we go on over to the Capitol building during this supposed Tempest (sheyeah, right) and get ourselves some soulfire! Eh?"

The chant went back up, especially among the Greyboys who were fond of their rifles, "Soulfire! Soulfire!"

"I say that's what we do! And another thing—I—" Aleck started to speak, but his voice caught in his throat as he noticed the Greymaster at the far end of the room, flanked by three of his famous Wolfguards. Quiet fell on the room like a quilt across a bed on a winter night.

"What's this I hear about soulfire? You boys want soulfire, we got it. We're the folks," Greymaster said, continuing to walk down the aisle.

"That's na' what I heard," Aleck said, his voice going nasal.

Some of the Greyboys laughed, but most of them just looked uncomfortable.

"Oh, is that right? And what did you hear, Aleck Heck? That I had the soulfire but lost it from right in front of my nose? Heh. And you know me." Greymaster shook his head. "It's pathetic. Pitiful, really, how much you slobs will suck right up and spit back out."

"What are you tahkin' about, Greymaster?" came a voice out of the crowd, echoed by a few from all sides.

"What I'm sayin' is . . . well, you figure it out. Let's say you come into a great deal of soulfire. Are you gonna go yellin' and scah-reamin' about it to everyone? Why, no. You're gonna keep it real quiet. Why you might even tell a fib around so that not everybody an' his brother'll come lookin' for ya. Particularly those Hierarchy types!"

A roar went up among the crowd: they hated the Hierarchy almost as much as the Greymaster did.

"So! If'n you've heard tell that I lost all my soul-fire, well you can just go right on spreadin' that rumor, and it'll be good for you an' me. But for now, I wanna show you just exactly what kind of juice I got to burn."

And with that, Greymaster changed. He grew. Not starting in any specific place, but growing to almost a head-and-a-half taller than Aleck Heck. His body was like a bodybuilder's: strong, tenacious, tough. He grinned widely. "Ain't never seen nothin' like that, have you? Well, it's a little trick I picked up from Dr. Teeth, and you better believe it feels good."

A general laugh went up through the crowd, with a few hoots and jeers. The Greyboys loved it: they had missed a strong leader like Greymaster and had started to hate Aleck's smart-ass ways.

"So, my friends, just what are y'all gonna do about this Hierarchy business? I tell you, it seems like you can't turn around without the Hierarchy pokin' their nose in your business. Everyone knows they're working with the Sweet Auburn folks to cut our power in half and keep us from ruling this fair city. What do you propose to do about that, Aleck Heck?" Greymaster said, using his huge form to good effect by bellowing louder than the smaller Aleck.

"He ain't nothin' but a whiner, Captain!" came a call from the crowd.

"Throw the bum out!" called an older wraith.

Greymaster took the podium next to Aleck and held up his hand so he could be heard. "I'm here to tell you that poor Aleck don't mean to be weak, but he just ain't got the force of prophecy on his side," Greymaster said, pulling back his hood and revealing his new black-and-silver Firebird mask. It was more of a helm, really, with the phoenix's wings erupting out of the sides and the long sinuous neck coiled around the top, red fangs gleaming, and the fiery tail tucked around his neck. It was beautiful work, and it had its intended effect.

All through the meeting hall, wraiths knelt on one knee in the traditional gesture of loyalty and fealty to one's lord. Even the normally rowdy, proud Dragon-Sons knelt on the floor, one by one.

Behind his mask, Greymaster felt the rush of power as he realized the combined strength that was gathered before him. Now, he thought happily, he had but to harness that strength and get it fighting as a single unit.

"Hurry up and wait! Hurry up and wait. I tell you, these county boys, that's all they want to do to you," Jo said under her breath, listening to the traffic that passed by the admissions station in the hospital.

Impatient, Jo got up and walked over to the nurse's station. "I don't suppose you've got that paperwork on Ms. Staple yet, have you?" Jo asked quietly, although the annoyance in her voice was clear.

"No ma'am. Not yet. Please just wait. Our DFACS person will be with you soon." Jo nodded and shrugged and went back over to her seat.

Sylvie and Kirk stood out of the way near her, so she could whisper to them from time to time. Kirk looked at Sylvie, who nodded. "Look, Ms. Jo, I gotta go do some things. Are you gonna be okay here with just Ms. Sylvie?"

Jo nodded to herself. "I believe we girls can get along just fine, by ourselves. Just you make sure you get back here soon. I ain't taken care of no baby by myself."

Kirk grinned and hugged Sylvie once before vanishing.

It was all quiet in Oakland Cemetery, which was a strange event by itself. Usually, each night, the ghostly drones, those ghosts without will or thought, would emerge from their crypts and march across the intervening spaces between their graves and attack each other, sometimes brutally. Alliances would form, falter, and fall, only to be reformed again another night. Only the Hebrew section was off-limits and peaceful: the rest of the cemetery was a battleground. Except for tonight. No horns were blown, no troops made movements from grave to grave. No brilliant colonel made a beginning cavalry charge with the dying of the day's sun. It was a kind of peace that was uneasy, a sickly quiet that forebode something much deeper.

Sir Alisdair, Knight of the Sickle, had been given the Horn of the Legions by the Anacreon of War. This treasured ebony horn was an artifact straight from the vaults of Stygia itself. The governor of the city wished to make it known to the Renegades of Atlanta that there was a reason why the Hierarchy ruled the lands of the dead, and that it was not just the soulfire that continually trickled from the city of the dead. It was the sheer force of numbers, organized troops, special reserves, and highly trained legions that worked together as closely and as perfectly as clockwork, with precision timing and accuracy.

His death-horse prancing at the gates to Oakland, the Death Knight blew the Horn of the Legions not just once, not twice, but three times, each note sounding louder, clearer, and stronger than the last. As the song of the horn reverberated across the marble tombstones and among the granite crypts, as if in answer there came a ghoulish humming, a howling, a kind of wordless song that built slowly, mounted from the lips of hundreds of restless dead. This was a moment of glory for them: once again they were being summoned up out of their homes and shelter and called into the service of their country. It mattered not that their country was of the dead, and that their service was a grisly, spectral one. They knew only the rush of the march, the call of the line, the tempo of the drumbeat. What they wanted was the thrill of the charge, the anguish of the skirmish, the triumph of victory. Somehow the horn reached out with its one-note song and convinced them all that the way to glory was to follow.

Jebediah almost felt moved to cross himself as he saw the legions of the restless dead move across the graveyard and, regardless of their former affiliations of Grey or Blue, black or white, watched the drones form up in perfect marching units. This was War's finest hour, and the Anacreon must have something invested in this, something beyond the mere pomp and ceremony of this large band of ghostly warriors.

Jebediah knew that the Necropolis would not know peace for many a day. A single ebony gem on his ring finger lit up, and he motioned to a Legionnaire to take his place as he went to attend to some business. Stepping into the shadows, Jebediah vanished.

The night air was uneasy and full of strangeness in Atlanta. Even in the living world there was a kind of crazy scent to the air. The gangs noticed it: the Red Dogs and the Black Falcons, the Hellbringers and the Kaz Society. The Triplezees and the Muck-lucks. The Fine Gentlemen and the Dragons: they all sensed it. Turf was turf, and the gangs of Atlanta had begun the evening by staking their new claims on new turf. Spray paint had put colors on walls, slogans on streets, marking new territory as the secret map of violence suddenly changed its boundaries. Quiet plans were made, whispered promises, silent curses, huddles, deadly plans. Cars were commandeered or stolen. A sporting goods store near Emory was broken into and emptied of its rifles and its baseball bats. Although the special gang task force unit had some hint of what was going down, they had heard rumors of a turf war for weeks, without any move-ment. How could this be the night?—a relatively cool, only slightly humid night in August. Hell, the moon wasn't even full. How were they gonna see to fight, even if they were only going to bash each other's heads in?

The watch commander ordered a couple of extra patrols, a few more beat cops posted in key areas. The Underground precinct remained open for an extra hour, but it looked like nothing was going to happen on this Friday night. Not at 9:00 P.M. Not at 10:00 P.M. Nothing. The streets were quiet; the little hooligans had obviously decided to watch the World Series instead of fuck around on the street.

Hooray for baseball.

Renegades are naturally superstitious: that's because, if they're gonna survive, they gotta be. There's always a reason behind the prophecies, the special rules of the Shadowlands. There's always some wisdom locked away. That's why the World of Krafft was full up on this Friday night, full up with wastrels, fence-sitters, a few Heretics, and some other freelance Renegades who weren't into the big rally going on downtown. The place was packed for two reasons. The first was that the Maelstrom gong had gone off the night before: the gong that the Hierarchy beat to signal the coming of a Maelstrom. Even though a Maelstrom had yet to show, most of the wastrel wraiths who had survived La Tempest Madrino, the Great Mother of Storms, were still alive because they had been near a particularly strong Haunt at the time, not because they were off lolly-gagging or skinriding. They recognized the imminent need for shelter at a time like this. All over the city, wastrels and those who had nowhere else to go were coming to the World, and Meany was cleaning up: he had hired two bruisers to help him with security and he was raking in the soulfire, Relics, and oboli. He had even made enough soulfire to start up the merry-go-round for a little bit, as long as wraiths were willing to chip in now and then to keep the thing going. The Hearse Riders were all here, a bunch of kids who loved the merry-go-round, who would play on it for hours if they could afford the juice. The other wastrels just liked the Haunt: a strange place, a quiet place, a safe place, and not one that was strategically important.

The other fairly terrifying superstitious omen that the wastrels of Meany's World kept repeating to one another as they filed up the huge, very long escalator was that the Scarletts had abandoned their post.

Down below, in CNN Center, there was a movie theater that showed *Gone With the Wind* on a continual basis, and the famous Three Scarletts of Atlanta (three lady ghosts who each believed they were Scarlett) never missed a show. That is, they never missed a show unless there was some bad business afoot.

Several Grey Wolves had arrived early in the evening and hung out around the World, apparently hoping to catch sight of someone from Kirk's Circle, but to no avail. They stayed as long as they could stand Meany's questions, annoying songs, and singing. He harassed them until they nearly broke out weapons on him, but no one broke out weapons on Meany, not on his own turf. There were parts to that amusement park that he and he alone knew about, and you didn't want to cross him.

So, the Grey Wolves had left in the early evening.

Just as Meany had planned.

Freda and Duke had been hanging out in the Gypsy Wagon in the World for most of the day, playing card games of many differing types: Duke had been a soldier for most of his life and had learned that a good card game can help pass the time without making the senses dull. And you didn't feel too bad about leaving behind a pack of cards if you got jumped. Still, Duke was pretty darn proud of the deck of cards he had assembled: a complete poker deck. The only problem was that the backs were different because he had had a devil of a time finding a complete run. Even when he had tried to bring over a complete pack of cards by destroying one in the living world, he never quite got them all: some perversity of chance or ill luck always meant that an Ace, a Jack, or a Queen was left out.

Freda was beating Duke in a third round of draw poker when there was gentle knock on the door and Kirk stepped into the wagon. "Are we ready folks?" he asked, grinning.

Duke shook out his mane of hair and looked at Kirk. "Welly, wellly. Look at you. Been through hell and back. Well, my boy, I want you to know that we've gone through our own version of hell for you. Do you know what ol' Meany does to you when you're just hanging out with him? Geez, I never thought I'd see a whoopee cushion and a joy buzzer again."

Kirk grinned. "It's good to see you, too, Duke. Guys . . . Freda . . . Duke. Thank you. You've done an excellent job, and I owe you one."

"That's right, m'boy you certainly do, and you can start by lighting this here cigar!" Duke said, grinning, holding up a Stygian cigar and puffing on it as Kirk put a burning fingertip to the end.

Freda shook her head slowly. "I hope you know what you're doing, Kirk. I don't like the idea of the Hierarchy benefiting from what you plan to do."

Kirk nodded. He sat down next to Duke, across from Freda, and looked her in the eyes. "Freda, how did you die?" he asked quietly, never having had the time to ask her such a thing.

She shrugged. "It don't matter."

"Matters to me," Kirk said.

Freda gave Kirk a pained look, shot an angry look at Duke. "Why? It don't matter. It's over."

"It matters to me, Freda. I want to know," Kirk said.

"I was raped," Freda said. "The guy cut me up pretty bad."

Kirk nodded. "Yeah, somehow I got the sense that something like that happened to you. Well, did you take care of the bastard?"

Freda looked at Kirk, puzzled at first, then she grinned slowly and nodded. "Yeah. I took care of him. One night he decided to take a flying leap out a fourth-story window. Too bad he was better at falling than he was at flying."

Kirk grinned and nodded. "Got what he deserved. Well, you see, my dear Freda, this bastard—this Greymaster—he needs to get what's coming to him. He's got a lot to answer for."

Freda nodded. "You put it that way, and it makes sense."

Kirk nodded. "Makes sense to me, too. I used to be angry about it. Now I'm just decided. I'm going to take care of him like he took care of me. Like he took care of Mom. Like he took care of Kristy, my sister. I'm going to make sure that the buck stops with me. Stops now."

Duke looked at Kirk and nodded. "If you came in here screamin' for vengeance, I would'a told you to 'go screw yourself. But I know the kind of feeling you have. I've felt it before myself. It's like . . . Fate."

Kirk shook his head. "Nope. Not Fate. My choice. But I think that, for now at least, my choice's what Fate would have happen. I hope."

Freda put down her hand of cards. "Let's go, then."

Duke swore quietly under his breath. "And here I was about to win my first hand."

If it weren't for the sentries that Greymaster had posted up on the street, none of the Renegades would've known about the troops of Hierarchy soldiers moving through the city, "securing it" against "Renegade activity." The fact of the matter was there was barely a wraith at large in the city. The Maelstrom gong had seen to that. Greymaster had just finished revealing himself as the Firebird when a messenger stepped up out of the Tempest next to him on the podium. Whispering in his ear, in that closed-hand way that all Grey Wolves whisper so that not even other wraiths can hear, he told Greymaster about the legions of the dead marching down Peachtree. Smiling down at the gathered throng, impassioned by his words and the promise of free soulfire, and caught up in the power of the Night of Fire and the mythic Firebird, Greymaster was like an archer who, having notched and drawn a great and terrible arrow, had no other choice but to let it fly.

"My fellow grand and glorious Renegades! I have just been informed by my Harbinger that a force of Hierarchy dead has been sighted marching down Peachtree. The streets are quiet, the mortal world sleeps. Let us bring destruction to the enemy, and glory to ourselves! Remember Leggett's Hell! TAKE BACK ATLANTA!" Greymaster yelled, and with a single growling roar the Renegades assembled moved as one.

Kirk watched as Duke carefully assembled the blast pack full of plastique. It was a fairly simple fuse, yet it took all his demolitions skill to put it together. The entire steamer trunk was packed to the gills with the stuff. He took a Relic basketball that Meany had in the Gypsy Wagon and made an indentation deep in the middle of the claylike plastique in the trunk.

"That's where you're going to want to put the soulfire for the bomb. The detonator, here, has its own soulfire just in case." Duke held up the little plunger with the radio antenna attached. There was a half-moon of soulfire crystal attached to the side: it glowed like a deadly little night-light.

"Of course, unless the soulfire ball is in there, what you're going to get is a poof and not a bang. With the soulfire ball inside the trunk, what you're going to get is a huge *kaboom*. What I'd do is plunge the detonator and then Argos out of there as far as you possibly can. Then get to a shelter ASAP, because there's probably going to be a Maelstrom of some kind or another right after the bomb goes off. Understand?" Duke said, looking into Kirk's eyes. Kirk nodded.

"I'm going to have to face him back at the trailer—my old home. That's the only place where I know for sure he has a Fetter. I don't want you guys to be any-where near that place, okay? I want you folks here, hiding out like the rest," Kirk said quietly but firmly.

His Circle-mates were never the expressive kind: they hardly knew what to say. Standing there, for a brief moment, Kirk thought Freda was going to hug him, but he thought wrong.

Kirk bent over the heavy steamer trunk, shoul-dered the backpack, and wordlessly stepped out of the back of the Gypsy Wagon.

As he walked quickly toward the shadows, ready to dive into them, he was brought up short by a figure standing amidst the detritus of the forgotten amusement park.

It was Jebediah, in his Confederate dress uniform, unmasked to face Kirk alone.

"I guess you're here to stop me," Kirk said slowly, his heart sinking.

Jebediah stroked his beard and took a step forward so that his face was out of the carnival light. "My dear boy, if I were younger, I would be taking you into the Citadel right now, taking you in and forcing you to swear allegiance to the Anacreon of War, to whom you so clearly belong. If I were just a little younger, I would've brought a squad of Centurions along with me, to clap you in chains, just for being a confirmed Renegade. But I've been living too long in this modern world, Kirk. I have seen too many things. I have had my fill of death, of killing. Did you know I've sentenced men to be sent to Oblivion? I've seen the way their eyes look as they contemplate that darkness. In my secret thoughts, my most private thoughts, I have thought that I must surely be destined for the hottest fires of Hell, should the Lord decide to make his judgment upon me. Still, looking back on my life, I have always been the one to try and do the thing which is right. Even in death, I have followed that particular dictum. And now I find myself without my favorite black-and-white rules, in a world full of only grey."

"So, you're not going to take me in?" Kirk asked hopefully.

"No, I'm not, my boy. I have come to realize, through either the curse or the blessing of knowing the secret will of Fate, that there are things which must be done, regardless of whether one man considers them good, or evil. These things are like natural storms: they come, they go, and they have a vital place. No, my son, my great-grandson whom I have never known, and now will never hope to know, I do not wish to apprehend you. What I wish to do is to ask you if you have thought about my words to you on the train. Have you marked well the Curse that follows our family?" the magistrate asked, emotion creaking his voice.

"Yes, Great-grandfather. I know what you're talking about. I think I know what this Curse is, and I mean to end it here, with me," Kirk said stridently.

"I am glad that you are thinking that way. And yet I hope that you are not struck with the same futile hubris that I was struck with . . . somehow, dear James, my dearest grandson, somehow he ended up cursed, as Restless as I am," Jebediah said.

Kirk nodded. "I believe I know why. I went down into the Hell of the Tempest, and I saw many things. One of those things was a scene of my father, moving through the jungle in Vietnam. There was a—a dark Spectre that haunted the woods all around him, that followed him and hounded him. That encouraged ambushes and skirmishes against him and the people that he led. As my own Shadow, the demon inside of me has my father's voice, could it be that this Spectre who haunted my father—would that be your Shadow, sir?" Kirk asked quietly.

"But—but I guard my Shadow well. Always. I have never let it loose without my knowledge. It is always bendable to my own will," Jebediah said, but as soon as he said that, his face changed, showing a look of sudden surprise.

"My Shadow . . . it laughs at me! As if there is some secret joke that only it can understand!" Jebediah said.

"We were told—in basic training—about how some people's Shadows can travel around by themselves sometimes, sometimes without you ever knowing. Perhaps this . . ." Kirk said.

"Impossible!" Jebediah interrupted. "That can't be. I . . . I would've known by now, surely. I would've been able to discern this terrible thing by now! After all the Pardoners I've visited!"

Kirk shook his head. "I have been in the worst of all Hells, Great-grandfather. I have seen the worst that the Shadow can be. And I know that he can do anything, or just about anything."

Jebediah just looked down, not meeting his great-grandson's gaze. Then he looked up and tipped his Confederate hat. "I do want you to take care of that little boy. I have been around to see him, and I find him to be a meager morsel at best."

Kirk nodded.

"And keep that father of yours away from him," Jebediah said, striking a terrific chill of fear in Kirk's heart.

The hospital was a madhouse. There were gang fights breaking out all over the city, and the ER was filled with gangsters, people with slices in their skin and bullets in their bones who would occasionally break out into little side fights while waiting to get sewn up from the first fight. Jo wasn't afraid of them, she just put on her probation officer's badge and look of frigid hell, but the people that she was trying to talk to, to get Cindi and Jeb out of the hospital, were too busy to see her. Her patience was near its end.

Sylvie's patience was also nearly gone. She strode across the room, carefully avoiding the gurneys moving back and forth through Admissions, and stepped into the restricted area where all the clerks were.

She stepped over to one of the clerks and, with a twinge of disgust (Sylvie never much liked to skin-ride), slowly sank into the large admissions receptionist. A moment later . . .

"Ms. Jo Evans?" the admissions receptionist said.

Jo smiled and sauntered over to the front desk. "About time."

The woman smiled. "What is it that we need, Jo?" she asked.

"What do you mean *we*? *I* need to get a girl named Cindi Staples and her rug-rat Jeb out of this hospital and take 'em home," Jo said.

The woman punched up a few keys on the computer keyboard and looked down at them.

"Oh, no, Jo. They're gone. They've been checked out already!" And for the first time Jo caught the hint of Sylvie's voice behind the receptionist's.

"Oh, really? Oh, my. Who got 'em?" Jo asked.

"Someone named J.T. Emerson. Address is 1316 Royal Pines Way. Royal Pines! That's where Kirk lived! Oh, no!" Sylvie said within the receptionist. Then the receptionist shivered as Sylvie stepped out of her.

Sylvie jumped up on the counter and slid across, jumping down to stand in front of Jo. "We gotta get out to Royal Pines. Now," Sylvie said.

The receptionist stared blankly at Jo for a second. "Did I call you up here for something?" she asked absently.

Jo smiled. "Oh, no, ma'am, I guess not. Thank you anyway."

Jo turned around and started whispering to Sylvie as she walked toward the elevators. "Okay, but this better not be any wild goose chase. I done enough chasin' wild gooses today."

Kirk wanted more than anything to Argos over to where Sylvie was picking up Cindi and Jeb and see how they were doing, but he knew that he had a job to do and that would just be putting it off. He turned to look at Jebediah in farewell.

Jebediah shook his head and offered his hand to Kirk, then pulled him into a rough embrace. "Kirk, my boy, I would wish you luck, but I have my limits. Just be sure that what you're doing is what you're supposed to do. I don't know how to tell it any plainer than that. Good night," Jebediah said, tipping his hat again, and slowly faded from view.

Kirk turned and closed his eyes, visualizing the trailer at Royal Pines, and stepped forward into a Nihil, the Tempest, and away.

The battle was raging in the streets. Renegade and Dragon-Son fighting together, side by side, against the more organized but less brutal Hierarchy forces. They climbed up and over cars, positioned themselves in the middle of the street and behind street sweepers, made flanking maneuvers through parking lots and down stairs and through parking garages. Several wraiths had sprouted wings and had begun fighting dogfight duels in the air, raking at each other with claws or slashing with swords and long spikes. Then the gunnery arrived on the scene and everyone took to trading pot-shots from behind heavy cover, choosing their ammo usage very carefully, utilizing stealth to its best advantage. Everyone was conscious of how much juice was burning up in the battle, and of causalities on both sides.

Curiously enough, the major players in the battle, the Greymaster and the knight, were both missing from the main fray, although none of the combatants had any time to wonder where they were.

Kirk had wanted to arrive before his father, had wanted to be there and set up his battlefield appropriately. But apparently someone—or rather something—had already been to Kirk's old home and left.

The trailer door stood hanging open. Inside was a shambles: the signs of a struggle and a hurried search were evident even from outside.

Kirk had been taught how to use his hands as entrenching tools, and the soft shadow-earth under the shadow-gravel wasn't hard to dig in. He dug down just enough with his shovel-hands to plant the steamer trunk after firmly attaching the soulfire sphere inside it and locking the trunk shut. He quickly covered up the hole and kicked gravel back over it.

It was at this point that Kirk heard a scream coming from another trailer—a scream that sounded curiously like his mother.

Kirk went around the back of the trailer and opened up his senses to the noises.

"Oh . . . oh, please stop. Please, we'll do anything."

"I've heard that before. I don't believe you. Besides, I like this. This is fun. I wonder how Anna will do."

"No! Not my baby! You promised!"

"I didn't promise anything. . . . "

Kirk clenched his fist. Somehow J.T., whose voice he now recognized, had dragged his mom into his trailer and was beating her.

Kirk snuck around the front of the trailer and phased through the door, stalking his way back through the tiny corridor to the rear bedroom, from which he had heard the noises.

He felt his demon clawing inside of him, laughing and jeering as he saw his mother chained to the wall with a crude set of hardware store chains and J.T. standing over her doing unspeakable things.

Kirk's anger flared. He watched his hands go from normal to flame-red and, in his outrage, slammed J.T. in the back.

He jumped, looking around. "What the fuck?" J.T. said.

He looked around, then he focused his eyes right on Kirk. What was he? Another natural medium? Or something different?

J.T. turned around and threw a heavy black wool blanket over his mother, then stalked past Kirk and went into another room. Kirk followed the man in: watching J.T. lie down on a foul-smelling bed (really more of a collection of rags), he nearly screamed as he saw a terrible black radiance surround J.T.

Suddenly, the Greymaster slid out of the fat bulbous body and, grinning, bowed slowly in front of Kirk, who was backing away from his father.

"Well, there you are, Kirkie boy. Nice to see you again. I wondered how long it would take before you showed up. We've been having a good ol' time. Unfortunately, everyone's all tied up right now. Why don't you look next door? I'm sure you're gonna see someone you know."

Kirk took the bait: he couldn't afford not to. He stepped through the wall of the trailer and gasped as he saw Cindi manacled to a heavy recliner and little Jebediah on his back in a large drawer.

"Gee, I guess you didn't realize that I had really good Monitors working for me, Kirkie boy. Yeah, boy, we were able to hunt down all your silly little Fetters. See here?" the Greymaster said, pointing to an ancient teddy bear sitting on the shelf.

Kirk whirled around to the Greymaster. "You bastard. I'm going to send you straight to Hell!" he yelled, growing claws from his fingers.

"Unh-uhn-unnh. Tsk, tsk. I wouldn't do that if I were you, Kirkie boy. See this grenade? It's real. One flick of my wrist and blammo—there goes your little boy, your widdle teddy bear, and your bitch. I'm sure you wouldn't like that."

Kirk looked down at a string tied to the firing pin of a grenade, and the other end to a steel ring that was within Greymaster's reach.

"Gee, I thought you'd be more amenable once you saw my little prize setup there. Come on outside, let's talk man to fuckup," Greymaster said, grinning, and stepped back down the hallway and out of the trailer.

Kirk phased through a window, burning some juice to recharge his body a little. He glared at Greymaster.

"What do you want from me?" Kirk said, fingering the trigger of his detonator, wishing he could blow the Greymaster to smithereens right then and there.

"What I want from you, Kirkie boy, is your pretty little light show. Your Firebird imitation. I want you to go help rally the troops downtown, so I can lead them in an attack on the Citadel," Greymaster said.

"You're fucked if you think I'm going to do that," Kirk answered.

"Oh, no, my boy . . ." Greymaster said, but paused as a passing car's lights pierced through him. "Oh, no, my boy, you're the one who's fucked. You see, if you lose all your Fetters, you're gone. Completely. I've got a team of skinpuppets set up at your widdle high school ready to blow it sky high as well. And I can break your bond with the Wolves at will. So all I gotta do is give the word and you're Fetterless."

Suddenly a floodlight came on and filled the yard of the trailer with blinding luminescence. A large woman wearing something which looked like a police uniform, and carrying a gun, moved across the front lawn and down toward Kirk's trailer.

"Oh, shit. You stay here, Kirkie boy. If you don't, it's kerblam on your Fetters. Got me?" Greymaster said as he passed through the wall of J.T.'s trailer, presumably to skinride the pimp again.

Kirk had a secret thrill when the woman returned, her face now glowing in the light. It was Jo! Jo was on the case. All he had to do now was get her attention.

"Hello there, officer," came J.T.'s drawl from the trailer. The Greymaster had his J.T. act down pat. "What's the problem?"

Jo turned and faced the huge man. "I've had reports of a break-in and some trouble in this neighborhood."

"Trouble? What kind of trouble?" J.T. asked.

Kirk made his way slowly over to Jo, then cursed under his breath as his foot knocked up against something hard and sharp on the ground.

Bending down, Kirk ran his hand along a shattered piece of wood and a smooth curve of metal. A slow smile crept across his face.

Jo stood with her hands on her hips, holding her gun down at the floor—but at the ready. "You're gonna tell me there ain't no trouble around here, when I can clearly see there is?"

"Shoot him, Jo!" came Kirk's cry, as J.T. moved faster than any man his size should have been able to move and made a grab for Jo's gun.

J.T. grabbed the pistol and trained it on Jo, who started to raise her arms.

Kirk took the smooth curve of steel and held it over his head. Bringing the steel down and releasing it, he threw the head of his old, broken scythe at J.T.

The scythe flew, end over end, and landed, point first, thrusting its way into J.T.'s forehead, which suddenly became Greymaster's forehead. J.T., devoid of his driving force, slumped quickly to the ground, and Jo was able to get the gun away from him. Greymaster screamed as the darksteel of the scythe blade sank into his Corpus, through his head, and screamed again as his motion caused it to move even deeper. Greymaster writhed on the ground, screaming in pain.

"Jo! Listen to me. You have to get Anna, and Cindi, and Jeb out of here now. Sylvie! Show Jo where my teddy bear Fetter is. I need her to take that, too."

Jo shook her head. "Teddy bear? Kirk, you too old to play with dolls."

Jo went into the trailer. She found Anna hiding in a kitchen cabinet, still shaking, and then Cindi and Jeb (luckily the keys to the shackles were hanging on a peg on the wall) and Anna's teddybear, as well.

Kirk watched with one eye on the Greymaster, who was starting to lose cohesion and trying to flow off of the burning darksteel, and with the other eye on Jo as she herded all her charges out to her Ford LTD.

Kirk could barely wait a second longer when he saw his father work his way free of the darksteel and reform quickly, sprouting several weapons from all over his body.

"Oh, so we're going to play smart-ass soldier now, are we? Well, let's do that. I'm going to kick your ass, just like I kicked it before," Greymaster said, advancing on Kirk.

Kirk smiled. "No, father you're not. Not this time."

Greymaster shook his head. "You just don't ever learn, do you boy?"

Kirk smiled as the Greymaster stood one step closer.

"No, Father. It's you who never learns. Surprise!" Kirk said as he thumbed the trigger on his detonator.

———

From far off to the west of the city there rose a giant ball of red-orange fire in the Shadowlands, a strange lighting effect that, just for a moment, entered the living world's view. Scientists would explain it as a strange effect of air pollution and city lights, but if any of them had been alive on August seventh during the Siege of Atlanta they would have recognized it instantly. The night the whole sky turned bloodred and the doom of Atlanta was foretold was one that the old-timers would remember forever.

Atop the boiling cloud of red-orange flame rode the Firebird, streaking across the sky like a rocket. Underneath its fiery contrail there seemed to be a welling up of flaming red clouds that suddenly began to boil up out of the ground.

A Maelstrom had begun.

Kirk watched as, far below, the great firestorm swept over Atlanta and burned across the city. Like a huge, rushing, virulent plague, the fire crept across the city, engulfing it completely. Kirk saw from within the veil of flames that surrounded him as the entire Underworld was doused with fires of purple, red, gold, and yellow.

It was a magnificent sight. Caught in the flood of fiery clouds, the huge Maelstrom cleansed all traces of the Dragon-sons, the Hierarchy troops, and the Greyboys from the streets of Atlanta.

Kirk watched as the great storm mounted, built to a crescendo, and slowly began to die down, banking its embers as, one by one, the buildings became visible again.

That night, all over Atlanta, fires broke out spontaneously.

But then again, Atlanta is always burning.

Afterword

Congratulations is due to Jeb M. Rourke, summa cum laude graduate of the Class of '16 from the University of Georgia. Mr. Rourke received his B.A. in Celtic Studies and Confederate History, and is pursuing a Masters in Emory's Theology department. We wish him all the luck in the world.

Excerpt from Jeb's summa cum laude speech at graduation:

> And in conclusion, I would like to quote from one of my father's diaries. "At the heart of the Fire there is always Truth. Below the darkness, there is also Truth. But the truth we live is the truth we walk with day by day." I want everyone to know that I do not think I could've made it to the place I am today without the help of my father, who, even though he died before I was born, has always been a source of inspiration for me. Thank you very much.

ENTER
THE WORLD OF
DARKNESS™

SUCH PAIN

◆

NETHERWORLD

◆

WYRM WOLF

◆

DARK PRINCE

◆

CONSPICUOUS
CONSUMPTION*

◆

SINS OF THE
FATHERS*

*coming soon

The World of Darkness™ is a trademark of the White Wolf Game Studio. *From* **HarperPrism**

HarperPrism

and Tomorrow

WRATH OF GOD by Robert Gleason. An apocalyptic novel of a future America about to fall under the rule of a murderous savage. Only a small group of survivors are left to fight — but they are joined by powerful forces from history when they learn how to open a hole in time. Three legendary heroes answer the call to the ultimate battle: George S. Patton, Amelia Earhart, and Stonewall Jackson. Add to that lineup a killer dinosaur and you have the most sweeping battle since *THE STAND*.
Trade paperback, 0-06-105311-2 — $14.99

THE X-FILES™ by Charles L. Grant. America's hottest new TV series launches as a book series with FBI agents Mulder and Scully investigating the cases no one else will touch — the cases in the file marked X. There is one thing they know: The truth is out there.
0-06-105414-3 — $4.99

THE WORLD OF DARKNESS™: VAMPIRE— DARK PRINCE by Keith Herber. The ground-breaking White Wolf role-playing game Vampire: The Masquerade is now featured in a chilling dark fantasy novel of a man trying to control the Beast within.
0-06-105422-4 — $4.99

THE UNAUTHORIZED TREKKERS' GUIDE TO *THE NEXT GENERATION* AND *DEEP SPACE NINE* by James Van Hise. This two-in-one guidebook contains all the information on the shows, the characters, the creators, the stories behind the episodes, and the voyages that landed on the cutting room floor.
0-06-105417-8 — $5.99

HarperPrism
An Imprint of HarperPaperbacks

PR-001